Physical Education

Physical Education

Maggie Barbieri

Minotaur Books 📖 New York

PHYSICAL EDUCATION. Copyright © 2011 by Maggie Barbieri. All rights reserved. Printed in the United States of America. For information, address St. Martin's Press, 175 Fifth Avenue. New York. N. Y. 10010

www.minotaurbooks.com

Library of Congress Cataloging-in-Publication Data

Barbieri, Maggie.
    Physical education / Maggie Barbieri.—1st ed.
        p. cm.
    ISBN 978-0-312-59329-2
    1. Bergeron, Alison (Fictitious character)—Fiction.   2. Crawford, Bobby
(Fictitious character)—Fiction.   3. Women college teachers—Fiction.
4. Police—New York (State)—New York—Fiction.   5. Bronx (New York,
N.Y.)—Fiction.   I. Title.
    PS3602.A767P48 2011
    813'.6—dc23

                                                                2011026756

First Edition: December 2011

10 9 8 7 6 5 4 3 2 1

With love to Jim, Dea, and Patrick

Acknowledgments

I sometimes say that writing saved my life. In a way it did, keeping me focused in a positive way while going through a trying time. But without the support, care, and clinical expertise of the staff at the NYU Clinical Cancer Center—Anna, Kathy, Rajni, Crystal, Caroline, Norma, Nelson, Rosie, Queen, and Nurse Joanne—I wouldn't have had a fighting chance. I thank them every time I see them and every time I write a book, and it never seems to be enough.

Thank you to my wonderful agent, Deborah Schneider, who guided me through this process with good humor and grace.

Thanks also to Cathy Gleason, whose gently worded emails to me should be published in a book called "How to Handle a Needy Author Who Can't Do Math."

Kelley Ragland, Matt Martz, Andy Martin, and Sarah Melnyk at Minotaur Books are a dream team. That's really all I can say.

Marian Edelman Borden, Alison Hendrie, Ted Hindenlang, and Susan McBride are always there with a kind word or an astute critique during the writing process. Thank you.

And to my family—Jim, Dea, Patrick, Bonnie, and Diego—thank you for listening to my half-baked ideas, my hare-brained schemes, and my imagined capers and hijinks. Much love to you.

Physical Education

Prologue

I had already learned that he knew how to lie.

After all, our entire relationship had almost not started because of one, little lie.

And, yes, it's still a lie if it's a lie of omission, no matter what he tells himself.

One

Every women's magazine I had ever read, every married friend I had ever had, and every romantic comedy I had ever seen had led me to conclude that married sex was a big, giant snore.

Fortunately for me, I have a pretty boring job and unlimited access to the Internet.

Problem solved.

I knew from experience that things settle down after a few months—or in the case of my first marriage, a few *days*—so I thought I was prepared for anything. What I didn't realize was marrying the right man helped, as did being in love with the man you had married, neither of which had been the case the first go-round. Oh, and did I mention that husband number one was an inveterate liar, cheat, and general all-around scoundrel?

As a result of all of this past unpleasantness, I was pleasantly surprised by my betrothal to one Robert Edward Crawford, also known as Detective Hot Pants—or so he was dubbed by my best friend, Max Rayfield, who knows from her hot pants. That guy, a retired altar boy, was true-blue, and I was lucky to have found him, even if the circumstances of our first meeting, during a murder investigation no less, weren't exactly a "meet cute."

Crawford and I have been married for a few months, and while I thought he might tire of my pillow talk and limited sexual repertoire, the opposite has been true. Guy can't get enough of me. Maybe it's because he spends most of his time around dead people and the people who lie about killing them, but he continues to find me endlessly fascinating, both in and out of our Sealy Posturepedic. This is a good thing because I am a terrible cook, and as Max always likes to say, "You're either good in bed or good in the kitchen. I, myself, happen to make a fantastic chicken *français*." In that regard, she's really not doing herself justice because if there is one thing that woman is good at, it's getting men to do what she wants. And that has nothing to do with breaded chicken cutlets fried in vegetable oil.

I think she might be selling herself short.

I am a professor at a small Catholic university located at the northernmost tip of New York City. I was in my office and in the midst of one of my many bouts of illicit daydreaming when I was interrupted by a knock at the door. Paul, the new mail guy on my floor, was a pleasant, middle-aged man who had lost his job, bad economy and all, and joined us the week before. That's what I had gotten from the thriving St. Thomas rumor mill anyway. I enjoyed him much more as a delivery person than our previous mail guy, who had no inner censor when it came to his comments on my sartorial choices and who often left me shaking my head in disbelief. If he had been anywhere but at St. Thomas, he would have been fired. Here, though, he had gotten promoted and was overseeing many of the men and women who delivered mail around campus. That's the way we roll around here at our Catholic university. Paul poked his head in and asked if he was disturbing me.

"Not at all, Paul," I said, taking in his perfectly pressed blue slacks and white polo shirt with the Blue Jays logo on the left breast. It took a secure man to wear a shirt with an angry-looking Blue Jay on the front of it. He only delivered mail directly to my office if the mail slot by the floor receptionist's desk was too small to hold the bulk, so I wasn't surprised when he produced a large, flat envelope and a box of books that I had requested from a publisher. Along with my full-time teaching load, I had been charged by my boss, the venerable Sister Mary McLaughlin, with picking a new literature textbook, a task in which I was not remotely interested. I did find that the college textbooks reps were more than happy to take me to lunch every week to secure the three-hundred-copy adoption of the book, and that was a nice side effect. But analyzing how many Renaissance poets there were to, say, medieval ones was just not in my bailiwick. Deciding whether two or three olives made the perfect martini was more in my bailiwick. As to the other stuff, I just didn't care.

Paul came in and handed me the flat, rigid envelope, which looked as if it contained contents that were not to be bent, as well as the box of books. I groaned. The box was heavy and contained another four or five books for review, I suspected. He put the box of books on the floor, and I flung the envelope onto the top of my filing cabinet. "Thanks, Paul. Did you have a good Christmas?"

He seemed surprised that someone had taken the time to ask. "Why, yes, I did. Thank you for asking."

"Did you cook?" I asked, settling back in behind my desk.

"Yes, I did," he said, leaning against the doorjamb. "It's just me and my mother, so not too much cooking to do."

I don't know if his intent was to make me feel sorry for him, but he did. The thought of him cooking for his presumably elderly mother and sharing the holiday meal with her alone made me a little sad. The thought crossed my mind that if he stayed on at St. Thomas, and by his amazing work ethic and the speed at which the mail got delivered, it seemed that he would, I would invite him and his mother to Easter dinner.

He hooked a thumb in the direction of the main office area. "I'd better go," he said, and moved his cart along to the next doorway.

I figured Paul for single. No ring, probably lived with the aforementioned mother. This would be good news to one of my colleagues, a newly divorced, forty-year-old physics professor named Liz Jenkins, who sat in one of the other offices on the floor. To say that she was on the prowl was not doing the prowl, or those who prowled, justice. I was sure that she had already checked out Paul's unadorned ring finger and was wondering what it would take to wrangle a date from the fit, swarthy, and not-that-bad-looking mail carrier. Okay, so he was a *Meet the Fockers* Robert De Niro and not a *Raging Bull* De Niro, but she was desperate and, I had found, not very discriminating. She had once dated one of the cafeteria workers for three months before she discovered that the man who visited him weekly to have lunch with him wasn't his brother, as he claimed, but his parole officer. That didn't stop her from having one more "breakup" date with him.

She was in my office before Paul had even vacated the floor. Her expertly highlighted blond tresses fell below her shoulders in a messy, yet assembled, kind of hairdo that would have looked like a rat's nest on my head. "He's cute," she whispered, loud enough for me and everybody else on the floor to hear.

"I think he's single," I said, but not really paying attention. In my more than a decade of teaching at this school, I think I had uttered that sentence at least twenty times to Liz, even when it was clear that her intended paramours were playing for the other team. After her relationship with Parole Pete, as he was known around these parts, I figured that her dating a possible homosexual was a step up on the dating ladder.

"He's kind of cute." She swiveled around, something that couldn't have been easy given the way her pants hugged her heart-shaped butt.

I'm not one to judge. My husband is the cream of the crop; everyone else pales by comparison.

She fluttered about in my office for a few more minutes, the color rising in her cheeks, the plan to ambush Paul, the mail carrier, growing in drama with every passing moment. Should she bring him coffee? Write him a note? Just ask him out directly? She talked herself into, and then out of, going out with him. Then she talked herself back into it again. She even went so far as to get mad at him for not calling her back after their first imaginary date. I took the opportunity to clear out my e-mail in-box, pack up my books and papers, and turn off my desk lamp. It was only when I exited my office that she got the hint and retreated to the safety of her lavender-scented office.

My phone rang right as I was locking up my office door, bleating out Crawford's special ring: Hall and Oates's "Private Eyes." There aren't too many songs written about cops, so this was as close as it was going to get. He hates it, and sometimes, just to annoy him, I'll call my phone from his, just so the song will play and make him crazy. I'm special that way.

"Hey, Crawford."

"Are you on your way home?" he asked.

I had to admit, I was a little tired. I wasn't sure that a night of sexual gymnastics was on the docket and told him so.

"I just wanted to tell you that I'll get the Chinese food," he said. "But thanks for letting me know your plans for the next several hours. I was just thinking about dinner and wanted to save you a trip to Happy Garden."

He sounded uncharacteristically sour; is that what twenty-four hours without sex will do to a guy? Me, I'm kind of like a camel that way; I'd been in the desert for so long before I met him that I could live without it for long periods. "I'm just leaving now so I'll see you in twenty-three minutes, no traffic." I hoped that his mood would improve in the time allotted for the trip.

In the time between my exiting the office and his phone call, several e-mails had filled my box, a few with those little red exclamation points in front of their subject lines. Two were from my boss, Sister Mary, who never met an exclamation point she didn't like, and one was from a student who was submitting an essay to a literary magazine and wanted my feedback. By the next morning. I hastily texted Crawford to let him know that I would be later than I thought and opened the essay, which at first glance looked fine. Not what I would have written, but fine nonetheless. I corrected a few grammatical errors and sent it back to the student. I decided, foolishly, that Mary could wait. It was after five, the sun had just about set, and I had some Chinese food to eat. I left before anyone else could get their claws into me.

The beauty of the St. Thomas campus never gets old. Look due west for the most incredible views of the majestic Hudson River, at almost its widest point here at the northern edge of New York City. Winter was here, and even though the giant oaks on my college campus were bare, they were still spectacular. The air on campus was fraught with a charged energy that I chalked up to sexual frustration, or maybe it was just my imagination. You see, this is a Catholic university and the administration does its best to make sure that the students are focused on studying, Jesus, and athletics, in that order. No sex allowed. The administration's focus on all things nonsexual had thus far proven to be spectacularly unsuccessful. These days, though, St. Thomas University was boasting of a pretty good women's basketball team—Crawford's daughter being an extremely talented center on the St. Thomas Blue Jays, who had yet to win a game despite being favorably ranked—and a good men's swim team, so the athletics take up a bit of the coeds' time.

When I was a student at the school, there were no men, and the women's basketball team had been coached by a septuagenarian nun named Sister Peregrine, who decided that I was "too short" at five-ten to be a center, a position that I had played since third grade on my CYO basketball team, and cut me from the team after one year of playing time. Fortunately, that same year, the school saw a rise in recently emigrated women from the Eastern Bloc who filled out the team in terms of size and, fortunately, skills. That landed Sister Peregrine in the consolation match of the East Coast Catholic Schools' Basketball Conference, or ECCSBC as it is affectionately known, and she became something of a legend at school until her untimely demise three years ago under the wheels of a New York express bus, an event that made her legendary in a completely different way.

Meaghan Crawford had had her heart set on Stanford University, but unfortunately, her dad's New York City cop's salary couldn't handle the tuition and the frequent cross-country flights. That, coupled with the fact that Meaghan is a twin and her sister needed an education, too, had tilted the scales in St. Thomas's favor when they offered Meaghan a full academic ride to the school. This decision had the added bonus of allowing her to play Division III basketball, because if there was one thing that Meaghan did well, besides school, it was play basketball. Her playing on the team was a slam dunk, so to speak. Although Crawford would have preferred I had access to his other daughter, the ill-behaved Erin, I had the opportunity to spend time with Meaghan, who rarely, if ever, did anything wrong.

I was looking forward to getting back into Blue Jay basketball.

Under the tutelage of a rumored maniac named Coach Kovaks, the St. Thomas Blue Jays were expected to have an excellent season, even if they hadn't done much at all to date.

I made my way to my car and looked forward to a quiet night at home with me, my husband, two orders of General Tso's chicken with extra MSG, and my dog, of whom Crawford had become co-owner upon our marriage. Trixie Bergeron-Crawford, as she is known, is a one-hundred-pound golden retriever of dubious retrieving skills, but with such a never-ending store of unconditional love that we forgive her for her spotty memory and inability to bring back a stick thrown for her pleasure. She's beautiful and loving and far more forgiving than I, but does have a taste for black suede, which has resulted in more than one missing pair of shoes or boots.

How did I get so lucky? I had no idea. I put the key in the ignition and started for home. A great husband, wonderful friends, a job I could do in my sleep; did it get any better than this? I didn't think so, I thought smugly as I wended my way off campus, pulling past the guard booth at the entrance to the school and rolling down my window to bid the night guard a good shift.

The guard was a recently retired police officer named John Dugan, who had put in his twenty and then gotten the hell out of Dodge. According to Crawford, who had worked with him, Dugan had ridden the desk at the Fiftieth for many years and hadn't seen a lot of action, so he was perfect for a stint as a St. Thomas security guard. Crawford was never sure as to why he wanted off the force so bad; the gig he had afforded a steady shift, full benefits, and not a lot of danger. I wondered why myself, but because I'm married to a homicide junkie, or so it seemed, I didn't think I'd ever find out.

"Have a good night, John," I said.

"You, too." As I started to pull away, he put his hand on the window frame. "Hold up. Your trunk isn't latched."

"It isn't?" I looked in the rearview. From that vantage point, it appeared closed. I wondered why the car hadn't alerted me to this issue; it practically lets me know when I have to change the lint filter in my dryer, but this? Nary a beep nor a warning.

He trotted around to the back of the car. "Nope!" he called.

"Huh." I put the car in park. Dugan attempted to close it, pushing down with the palms of both hands. I watched as the trunk flew up, obscuring his face.

I got out to inspect. "Never had a problem with it before," I said as I took in his expression. His face, usually ruddy and healthy looking, was paler than a fish belly. He stepped away from the car and attempted to say something to me, but all that came out of his mouth was some kind of sound that was a cross between a moan and a retch.

This wasn't going to end well. I knew that before I saw the pissed-off-looking St. Thomas Blue Jay embroidered on the front of the white polo shirt glaring up at me, blood spattered across its beak. Paul, late of the St. Thomas mail room and life in general, didn't look so happy either, consternation etched on his lifeless face.

Two

Carmen Montoya had a backside that defied gravity.

Her partner, Champy Moran, had none at all.

Together, they made an interesting pair.

They work alongside Crawford in the detective squad, so I was offered a few considerations as a result of their professional relationship with my husband. First, I didn't have to go down to the precinct for them to take my statement, and second, they sent a uniformed out to get coffee for both me and John Dugan, maybe thinking that by getting us full of caffeine, we would have a clearer recollection of what preceded our discovery of the late Paul, the mail carrier. We were sitting in one of the conference rooms in the library, not far from where my car had been left and where yellow police tape was strewn about, looking far more cheerful in the drab winter landscape than it should have.

I wrapped my hands around my cup of coffee, dully answering any question that Carmen or Champy could come up with. No, I hadn't seen Paul before the previous week. No, he hadn't done anything to make me suspicious. No, he hadn't said anything to make me think that he was in danger. Yes, he was a wonderful mail carrier. I wasn't entirely sure but I thought he was single.

Carmen stood up and stretched, her tight turtleneck rising up and revealing a stomach much tauter than it should have been, given that she had birthed four children. "What a mess," she said, shaking her head. "You're out another car. You know that, right?"

I did. I had been down this road before and knew that my car would be taken away and stripped down to its basic nuts and bolts, the detectives looking for any sign of what had happened to Paul or why he may have ended up in my trunk.

Crawford was outside, having arrived a lot quicker than I thought was humanly possible, though he was without his partner, Fred. He wasn't going to "catch" the case because of my involvement, but he was going to stay around and get as much information as possible before taking me home.

Champy looked at me. "Smells a lot like Miceli."

The thought had crossed my mind, but I hadn't wanted to verbalize it, particularly so indelicately. Peter Miceli had been— and maybe still was, for all I knew—the puppet head of a New York crime syndicate, and with my luck, someone I had known long ago when I was a student at St. Thomas. Long story short? His daughter was killed a few years back, the trunk of my car used as her final resting place, and although that case had brought Crawford into my life, it had also reintroduced Peter into it as well. Peter was now residing in a maximum-security facility in Indiana, thanks to my testimony at his racketeering trial, and wasn't expected to get out anytime soon. Suffice it to say that he cannot contact me using any mode of communication, and so far, he hadn't. But a body in my trunk? It resembled the initial case a little too closely.

Oh, and did I mention that his wife had ended up dead in the midst of this as well? And that Miceli carried a bit of a torch for me, as odd as that sounds? All of these details were ones I was trying to forget and had almost successfully put to rest—up until this very moment.

I saw Crawford's face in the little, round window of the conference-room door. "Are we done here?" I asked, my hands still shaking.

Carmen pursed her lips and studied me for a minute. "Yes. We're done." When I got up from the table, she gave me a hug, which was almost enough to send me over the emotional edge. "Listen, *chica,* hang in there. You know you're probably not a suspect, right?" she said, smiling.

"Honestly, the thought never crossed my mind," I said.

Champy hitched up his sans-a-belt pants and rested his hands on his hips. "You really need to think about getting a car without a trunk."

"I think you may have mentioned that before," I said, pointing to the door. "Crawford's out there."

Carmen put her notebook in her pocketbook and motioned toward the door. "I may need to talk to you again."

"Understood."

"Right. You're a pro at this," she responded, opening the door and letting me out.

Crawford and I were in his car when I asked him how he had gotten to the scene so quickly.

"I was in the area."

"I thought you were on your way home when I called," I said.

"I had to run an errand before I left."

"Where was Fred?" I asked, wondering about the partner who spent more time with my husband than I did.

"Back at the squad."

We left it at that. We were home faster than I anticipated, thanks to the lack of traffic and Crawford's lead foot. Although he had been quiet during the car ride, he started talking as soon as we were in the house. I held up a hand. "I don't want to talk about it." I had already talked about it, and talked about it, and then talked about it some more. That's the thing about being a witness to the aftermath of a homicide: you have to answer a lot of questions multiple times. And then when you think you're done, you start all over again. The story this time was simple. Paul delivered my mail, I was rushing home to eat Chinese takeout, and, no, I had no idea how he had found himself into my trunk in the middle of a bustling campus. The only thing I could figure is that he had been placed there during the hours when dinner was served, when the majority of students could be found in the one dining hall on campus and the paths and byways of the campus were virtually devoid of life. "I was going to invite him and his mother to Easter dinner!" I blurted out.

"Huh?"

"Paul," I said, sitting down at the table to cry. "He and his mother. I think they lived together and they only had each other for company over the holidays."

Crawford seemed confused and I couldn't blame him. He asked me if I wanted something to drink.

"Yes. Pour me a stein full of chardonnay."

He looked at me quizzically. "We don't have any steins."

He's always been kind of literal. "Then just hand me the bottle."

A few minutes later, I was slugging back cheap white wine from a giant goblet decorated with the St. Thomas insignia and digging into a plate of leftover chicken that he had found in the refrigerator and heated up for the both of us. We had never gotten to get our Chinese takeout. I was starving, which wasn't surprising. It takes more than a still-warm dead body to put me off my dinner. He waited until I had eaten most of the food before peppering me with questions.

"How long has he been in the mail room? Did he look familiar to you? Where did he come from? What kind of job did he have prior to the mail job at St. Thomas?" Crawford took a breath and I took that as an opportunity to break in. I noticed that although he had watched me eat, he hadn't touched the plate of food that he had put together for himself.

"It's all in the report, but in order of your questions: one week; no; I don't know; supposedly stocks and bonds." I held my glass out for a refill on my wine. "I know what you're thinking."

He refilled my tumbler and then sat down heavily in the chair next to mine at our tiny kitchen table. "What am I thinking?"

"It's reminiscent of when Kathy Miceli was found in the trunk of my car."

"You're right. That's what I was thinking. That's what everyone is thinking. They'd be stupid not to think that."

"You were also thinking that I was showing tremendous restraint by not fainting, puking, or bursting into tears."

He wasn't thinking that but he allowed that it might have crossed his mind at some point.

"But he's just Paul from the mail room, right? Who would want him dead?"

"I guess that's what we'll find out," Crawford said, his face sad. "Maybe he's not just 'Paul, from the mail room.'"

I took another swallow of wine. With each subsequent taste, it was getting better. That's the thing with cheap wine. The more you drink, the better it tastes. "Everyone in the tristate area and beyond knows about my connection to the Micelis, I'm sure. Maybe someone is messing with me."

Crawford traced a whorl in the wood of the table with his finger. "Maybe. But who'd want to mess with you?"

"I don't know." I chugged back some more wine. "I know what you're *not* thinking."

He raised his eyebrows, moving chicken around his plate with his knife.

"You're not thinking, 'Oh, God, why did I marry her?' or even 'Why the hell does she keep finding dead bodies?'" I looked over at him, but his face remained unchanged. "You're also not thinking that this could be the reappearance of Peter Miceli in our lives." The last one was a stab in the dark, and even I didn't believe it, but I hoped that I had maybe missed something and this was all just a weird coincidence.

He looked up. "Two out of three ain't bad."

He was right. One body found in the trunk of your car is one thing. Two? Those kinds of coincidences just don't exist.

"God, I hate him. Why can't he just leave me alone?" I asked.

Crawford finally stopped pushing his food around and took a bite, grimacing; it was now cold. "Let's not jump to conclusions. "When I go in tomorrow, I'll check it out. I'll get all the info when I get in from Champy and Carmen." He spied a hunk of chicken cutlet on my plate. "Want that?"

I pushed my plate toward him, and he speared the hunk with his fork. He had gotten his appetite back. All it had taken was a good murder.

Three

Crawford was sitting disconsolately at the kitchen table when I walked through the door the next night, an open bottle of Beck's in front of him, Trixie's head in his lap. He was still dressed for work in black pants, a white shirt, and a striped tie, his holster running across his back and ending at his hip. His gold detective's shield was clipped to his shirt pocket. I stopped right inside the back door and put my messenger bag on the counter. "You don't look good. Bad day?" I had had a rotten day myself. The president of our college, a tiny little bureaucrat named Mark Etheridge, had chewed me out, for what, I don't know. It's not as if I had killed the guy and loaded him into the trunk of my car. The school was all over the news again, as were some unflattering pictures of me taken from my faculty website, something that I should not have been concerned with, but was. I had spent the better part of the morning trying to figure out how to upload a picture from my honeymoon onto the site and had only succeeded in changing the picture to a standard gray silhouette.

I had been told by Etheridge to "lay low." I resisted the urge to tell him it was "lie low," which I suspect was the proper urge on which to act in that case. I put myself in his shoes, a place in which I could understand his exasperation with me; after all, this wasn't the first time I had attracted unflattering press for the school. I also guess I was lucky that he didn't fire my ass, but then again, who would teach a bunch of bored teenagers and young adults for the whopping salary that I was paid? Not too many people, I suspected.

Crawford hadn't answered me so I repeated my question. "Bad day?"

He wiped a hand over his eyes. "I think it might be."

I leaned against the counter, jingling my keys in my hand. "You don't know yet?" This didn't bode well.

He shook his head. "But I have an idea."

"Spit it out, Crawford."

He took a deep breath. "His name is Vito Passella and he's a Lucarelli."

I shook my head to clear the cobwebs. I must have misunderstood him because none of that information made sense. "What? Who?"

"Paul. His real name is Vito Passella. He's a soldier in the Lucarelli crime family."

According to Crawford, who seemed to know an awful lot about these things, the Lucarellis were one of the five crime families in the New York area and mortal enemies of the Micelis, something going all the way back to Sicily. I didn't know when the rift occurred and I didn't care. All I knew is that someone connected to the Mob had been masquerading as a mail carrier at St. Thomas, and that didn't sit well with me at all.

"There's more," Crawford said. "There's information to suggest that Passella's death had something to do with the Micelis."

"What kind of information?"

He didn't answer. "There's also concern about the reasons he was working at St. Thomas."

"Maybe he wanted to get out of the life?" I offered.

The look on Crawford's face told me that I was grasping at straws.

I worked that new development over in my brain for a few minutes, coming to one conclusion. "He wanted to get close to me?" Oh, boy. Liz Jenkins would really be pissed off when she found out that part.

"We don't know. There's evidence to suggest that maybe Vito didn't need the St. Thomas job as badly as you thought he did."

Obviously. I felt sick to my stomach. I knew we were both thinking the same thing, but neither of us said it. Meaghan. I was at the school, but so was she. Whom exactly did Paul want to get close to and why?

The next morning, a chilly Saturday that felt more like Antarctica than the New York metropolitan area, I felt as if my sinuses were stuffed with cotton and my throat was raw from all the crying I had done during the night. I didn't know what was worse, having Peter Miceli possibly worming himself back into my life or having to deal with the constant worry about Meaghan. Before we went to bed, we went over a variety of different scenarios that had Meaghan transferring and me resigning, but agreed that we wouldn't do anything until Carmen got more information about Vito Passella, his connection to the Lucarellis, what he had done to piss off the Micelis—if anything—and what this all meant to our family. When I got up, my head hurt and my eyes were dry. Crawford was gone and I had no idea where he might be. A quick search around the bedroom revealed no note, but his dress shoes were right where he had left them the night before. I looked out the window and saw that his car was still in the driveway. He couldn't have gone far.

I went downstairs and, after walking Trixie, wrote a note explaining where I was going and what time I would be back. Before I left, the phone rang and I wasn't surprised to hear Carmen Montoya's gentle alto on the other end.

"Hiya, girl. What's happening?"

"Oh, not too much," I said, pouring myself a glass of orange juice. I shook the container and heard enough sloshing around for Crawford to have enough when he reappeared. That man without orange juice is not a man you want to spend any time with. "It's day two and I haven't found another dead body."

She chuckled. "That's good." She noisily slurped from whatever she was drinking. "Listen."

I've found that whenever a conversation starts with "listen," the information to come won't make you happy. "Yes?"

"You haven't had any contact with Peter Miceli since he left town, have you?" I heard the squawk of the police radio in the background and could picture her sitting in the passenger seat, Champy driving them to some unpleasant situation.

"Not at all." I took a sip of the orange juice, but it had lost its taste. I put the glass down on the counter, noticing that since we had installed granite, food detritus resided there undetected. I whisked a cluster of Italian-bread crumbs into my free hand. "Why do you ask?"

"What about Crawford?"

Now why would she ask that? "Not that I know of. Again, why do you ask?"

There was a fair amount of dead air before she responded, "Oh, no reason."

Which meant, of course, there was a reason. I barely had the words out of my mouth when she begged off, citing a radio call that she and Champy needed to respond to. Convenient.

Had Crawford been in touch with Peter Miceli? I sure hoped not. Would he have told me if he had been? I sure hoped so. Any contact with Peter Miceli is something that I wanted to know about, even if the truth was uncomfortable to know. I thought the likelihood of Crawford's having anything to do with my former nemesis, now in jail for the better part of his life, was slim to none, but it was still strange that Carmen had asked. Covering all of her bases? Or her sizable backside?

I'd hash it out with Kevin. I grabbed my purse, checking to see if I had my phone, and went out the back door, avoiding a pile of leaves that had collected at the edge of the patio and that had been there since Halloween. Crawford's a great husband but a terrible caretaker. He's also cheap, so that figures into his decision not to hire a group of guys to come and do the lawn cleanup between seasons. This was it, though; the place looked like hell. I decided that I was going to hire someone and have the person come when I knew Crawford wasn't going to be around. He'd never notice that things looked as they should, and he would never miss the hundred bucks that it would take to get the house looking shipshape.

I approached my car, parked right in front of the door of the detached garage, the one that had never had a car parked in it. I had brought a lot of crap to the marriage, but Crawford? He could open a Crap "R" Us store and still have enough crap to keep him surrounded in crap until the day he died. The door to my car was open—I never lock it, much to his chagrin—but just as I reached it, I heard his voice in the garage. He was talking, obviously never having heard me coming. Although my first instinct was to barge in and let him know I was leaving, something about his tone—hushed—made me stop.

And listen.

"She won't be happy. She doesn't like change."

If he was talking about me, he was right on that account.

"Guns?" he asked. "Enough to make it work."

A buzzing started in my ears. He was a cop. Guns are part of the job. Should have been innocuous enough. So why was he whispering into his cell in the garage?

After listening for a few minutes, he continued, "If it gets me closer to getting out of here? I'm in."

My purse fell to the ground. Unzipped, everything that was inside came out, things rolling to and fro on the pavement. I heard Crawford say, "Gotta go," and end the call. I went to the ground and began cleaning up the mess; a perfume bottle had shattered, the smell of lilacs and bergamot wafting up to my nose and giving me an instant headache. It was a few seconds before I realized that Crawford was kneeling beside me and asking me what I was doing.

I kept my eyes on the change that had spilled forth from my wallet. "I'm going to see Kevin. Have breakfast. Shoot the breeze."

"I'll come with you."

"No!" I said a little too loudly. "No," I said, dropping my voice to what I thought approximated a normal timbre. Inside my head, it sounded fake and forced and a little shaky. "I need to talk to him about a few things. I want to go alone."

He rocked back on his heels. "Hey." He took my face in his hands. "Hey, look at me."

I met his eyes.

"What's going on?" he asked.

"You want to get out of here?" Although I had thought that I had left the sad, betrayed Alison behind, she had reappeared on the driveway, insecure, paranoid, and off-kilter. You don't get cheated on in a marriage as much as I had by my first husband and get out without some battle scars. I thought mine had healed. I was wrong.

He got that confused look on his face that looked suspiciously like Trixie did when she smelled something of unknown origin. "What are you talking about?"

"Why are you talking on your cell phone in the garage?" I asked, shoving nickels and dimes back into my wallet. "Guns? Getting out of here? What were you talking about?"

"What are *you* talking about?"

"We have no secrets. You don't go into the garage to talk." I didn't go into detail about Ray and his secret garage cell phone, the one next to the hedge clippers, the one with the numbers of everyone he had cheated with behind my back.

Crawford held up his hands. "Okay. Okay." He sighed, running his hands over his face. "Okay." He helped me put the rest of the items back into my pocketbook, then pulled me up, his hands gripping mine. "It was work. That's all."

I took a few deep breaths. "Where do you want to get out of? Not here, I hope." The tears were making their way from behind my eyes, but I refused to let them out.

He hugged me. "Not here."

But he never did give me a direct answer and I let it go because I wasn't really sure I wanted to know.

Four

Still rattled, I headed off to see Kevin. I was angrier at myself for allowing hysteria to get the better of me, but as Crawford had reminded me, seeing Vito Passella laid out in my trunk would unnerve even the steeliest of personalities. Implicit in that was that I didn't have a steely personality, but that didn't offend me. The acknowledgment of how upsetting that discovery was, coupled with the idea that my old nemesis, Peter Miceli, might have had something to do with it, made Crawford give me a pass on my meltdown.

He said he had been in the garage so that he didn't wake me, but this was new behavior for him and I wasn't entirely sure I believed him. The call was work-related, that much had been clear, but why the cloak-and-dagger?

I was looking forward to seeing Kevin, who had a soothing influence on even the most agitated person. I hoped this whole venture to see him—and traveling in the greater New York area is definitely a "venture"—wouldn't take more than a couple of hours, but I am a native and know that anything and everything can happen on the roads. Just watch the news—it does, regularly. I wasn't surprised to find myself, just thirty minutes later, sitting on the Cross Bronx Expressway in snarled traffic that had been caused by an overturned tractor trailer, the most common cause of traffic congestion in New York City. I don't know where all these tractor trailers are going but they sure seem to overturn an awful lot. The cars on the highway crept along until I got to my exit, and I exited onto Randall Avenue, making my way over to the main thoroughfare of Throgs Neck, New York.

If I had to rely solely on Max for a shoulder to cry on, I'd be lost; she can be unsympathetic, to put it kindly. Actually, if it didn't have to do with her, it wasn't much of her concern, and since this didn't affect her at all, I was certain I wouldn't get anything approaching sound advice or even good listening. Thankfully, my other best friend in the world is an almost-defrocked priest named Kevin McManus, who up until several months before had been the chaplain at St. Thomas. Circumstances—in the form of a student who had accused him of "inappropriate conduct"— had conspired against him to have him removed from school and from the priesthood until the whole matter could be properly investigated and hopefully resolved. Let's put it this way— the Catholic Church in conjunction with St. Thomas University investigated at a snail's pace. It was unlikely that Kevin would be back anytime soon, if at all. I was entirely convinced of Kevin's innocence and had spent much of the previous months defending his honor to the gossipmongers at St. Thomas, but I was fighting a losing battle.

His replacement, a mealymouthed guy named Father Dwyer, who looked as if he had never met a bottle of altar wine he didn't like, did nothing to discourage the disparaging remarks made about Kevin at the same time he was undoing the advancements made by Vatican II. We now had fewer female altar servers, the goal being to get rid of all of them eventually; mandatory attendance at Holy Days of Obligation for faculty with the punishment being one lost personal day for every missed Mass; and repeated attempts to disband the Gay and Lesbian Student Union. I still wasn't sure how they could enforce the lost–personal day rule, but since I don't have a friend on the Supreme Court or the inclination to look this up from a legal perspective, I've registered a silent protest only and never attend Mass on campus. A host of other things were insulting enough to the practicing Catholics among the teachers, not to mention the lapsed Catholics, and, yes, non-Catholics. My friend Dr. Fareed Muhammad in the Business Department really wasn't pleased by the memos he received imploring him to attend Mass on the Feast of the Immaculate Conception. But it had bridged the gap between him and Rabbi Schneckstein of the Religious Studies Department, so I guess that was one good thing to come out of the whole mess. And I also got to spend a little more time in the vicinity of Fareed's total hotness, which was also a nice by-product of all of this religious unpleasantness.

After all these months, I still didn't know anything about what did or did not happen with Kevin and the student, a person whose identity was unknown to me. Kevin wasn't telling, and the powers-that-be on campus certainly weren't either. I had tried to find out, but it was a well-guarded secret. Due to a slip of Kevin's tongue after a chardonnay or three, I did know that the student was female and still a student at St. Thomas.

Kevin had moved back to the two-family house that he had grown up in on the curiously named Hollywood Avenue, a street that wasn't quite as glamorous as its name would imply. It was lovely, dotted with two-family homes, but Hollywood it was not. More like Burbank, maybe. Throgs Neck is located at the ass-end of the Bronx, right on the Long Island Sound, and while many homes are fortunate enough to have a water view, Kevin's did not. I had been to visit him a few times, in between his shifts as the events manager at Vista del Sol, a catering hall at the end of his street with a splendid view of the Sound, and while his apartment was quite nice, it was not the place that Kevin would choose to live in if he had his druthers. Kevin is more of a West Village kind of guy, not wanting to go too far to get his fill of overpriced food and cheap white wine. The apartment was located in the house in which Kevin had grown up with his five brothers, and his mother still lived in the larger unit on the top floor of the two-family. Something told me that Mrs. McManus wasn't entirely unhappy about having Kevin around. Kevin was a lot of things, and one them was a mama's boy of the highest order. He licked his wounds under the watchful gaze of his mother, who plied him with pot roast and chardonnay, so I wasn't completely surprised by the chubby man who answered the door to his abode.

He held up a hand before I could get a word out. "I know. The double chin. I'm working on it."

I leaned in and gave him a kiss on the cheek; I felt better just seeing him. "You've got to lay off the pot roast, son."

"And you, my friend, need to lay off the dead bodies in the trunks of your cars," he said, stating the obvious.

I put my hand over his mouth. "This is a 'no dead body talk' zone."

"Let me just ask one question," he said, as he ushered me into his living room. "Does this have anything to do with the Micelis?"

"That's the sixty-four-thousand-dollar question. My guess is yes."

"What does Crawford think?"

"I thought we weren't going to talk about it," I said, a little testy. "If you want any information, read the papers. They know more than I do."

He eyed me warily. "Enough said." Kevin knew that if he pushed any harder, I'd crack, and if history was any judge, I wasn't a lot of fun to be around once the hard outer shell was compromised. But that didn't stop him from asking one more question. "Was it bloody?"

"Enough!" I shouted, loud enough, I expect, for his mother to hear us.

He grabbed me in another hug, then let go and held me at arm's length. "You okay?" he asked, studying my face.

"I'm okay." I kissed his cheek. "Just so happy to see you."

It had been several months since we had last seen each other, but the apartment hadn't changed much. It looked pretty much like his residence at St. Thomas because his furniture had gone from there to here. I noticed a few touches that hadn't been in evidence at his school residence, namely a couple of new black-and-white photographs that captured the beauty of the Sound at different times of the day and not religious in nature at all. I remarked at how beautiful they were.

"Thanks." He motioned to the couch for me to sit.

"Where did you get them?"

"I took them."

"I didn't know you were into photography."

"I didn't either," he said. "My therapist thought that some kind of art therapy might be a good way for me to get rid of some of my stress, and I started taking photos."

I was shocked. They were good. "Wow, Kevin. Who knew?"

He made his way to the kitchen, calling back to me. "Yeah,

the archdiocese really doesn't foster creativity. Or did you not know that?"

I chuckled. "Oh, I knew that all right." I settled back into the chintz-covered sofa and looked around the living room, noticing that Kevin's antiques fit in, but not quite as well as they had in the prewar six-room apartment with the river view that was his home at St. Thomas. Although he had made this apartment cozy, I couldn't help wondering if the unpacked boxes in the adjacent dining room signaled that he wasn't getting too comfortable here. I noticed a New Testament, its cover worn and its spine cracked, sitting on the end table alongside a small notebook marked JOURNAL on the outside. Kevin's rosary beads, a gift from one of the nuns at St. Thomas and purchased at Pope John Paul II's funeral in Vatican City, sat atop the notebook. All of a sudden, I felt sad for him, sadder than I had felt the entire time he had been dodging accusations and lying low with the press since the story had gotten in the local city papers. His spiritual life was obviously still important to him, but he had been cast out both by the school where had had spent the past several years and the organization that he had devoted himself to for the better part of twenty years. My eyes stayed on the New Testament with its tattered cover, his name printed neatly on its spine, and decided that this wasn't the time to be dumping on him. This was the time for him to be dumping on me, but I knew the chances of that happening were slim.

Kevin came back in with a carafe of coffee and some scones that his mother had baked. A crock of butter, much more than a condiment in the McManus home if Kevin's double chin was any indication, was also present. Kevin poured me a cup of coffee and settled into a wing chair across from the couch. "What's going on?"

"Not much," I lied. "What about you? What's going on?"

"Busy time at the catering hall," Kevin said ruefully. "I'm working like crazy."

"They're lucky to have you," I said, attempting to focus on the positive: Kevin had a job in a lousy economy, it suited his skill set, so to speak, and he wasn't living on the kindness of strangers.

"So how's it working out with the new guy?" he asked.

"Father Dwyer? Not so great. He's kind of a putz."

"I had heard that. Ultraconservative is what I heard."

"That's an understatement."

"What's he doing?"

I outlined a few of Dwyer's edicts as Kevin's eyes grew wide. "Seriously? The dismissal of female altar servers is one thing, but getting rid of the Gay and Lesbian Student Union? Where will those kids go for community?" He looked up at the ceiling as if the answer were there. "And don't even get me started on the whole Holy Day of Obligation thing."

"I know, Kev."

He ran his finger over the edge of the end table where his personal things lay, his fingers grazing the worn Bible; a slip of paper jutted out from between its worn pages. "How are you going to function there?"

"Me? Well, as long as they leave me alone, I should be fine."

He raised an eyebrow. We both knew that my being left alone was unlikely.

"I'm sure they'll find something to serve as my penance. Last year it was becoming the resident director at the coed dorm, so who knows what Etheridge has in mind for me now?" I dropped my head into my hands. "I try to stay out of trouble, Kevin, I really do."

"I know," he said softly.

"So why does this keep happening? Why can't I just live my life and be happy?"

"I guess that's another sixty-four-thousand-dollar question."

I got up. "You know what's another question?"

He raised his eyebrows in question, while surreptitiously pushing the paper back between the folds of the Bible.

"Why Carmen asked me if Crawford was in touch with Peter Miceli."

Kevin's poker face is just about as good as anyone's I know. He has to be good at keeping secrets; his vows require that. But something behind his eyes as he took a sip of his coffee made me think that he knew more than he was letting on. Why was I surprised? Kevin always knew more than he was letting on. That was almost a job requirement for being a priest: interacting with those about whom you knew far more than you wanted or needed to. "Why would she ask that?"

"I guess because she wants to know," I said, stating the obvious. "Do you think there's any reason for Crawford to be in touch with him?"

Kevin set his cup back onto the saucer, rattling both slightly. "I can't think of any."

I wanted to ask him what he knew or what he really thought, but knew that I wouldn't get an answer. Kevin was no longer a practicing member of the clergy but still held himself to the strict code set forth in the vows he took at his ordination. I also knew that Kevin was Crawford's go-to guy when it came to letting off a little steam. Crawford sees a lot of bad stuff in his line of work, and although he doesn't let on how much it gets to him, I know that it does. I've always encouraged him to use Kevin as a sounding board, and thankfully, he'd taken the advice over the years. I waited a minute but Kevin had nothing to add. I stood. "I guess I should be going."

Kevin jumped up from the couch. "Wait. I have something for you. I want to give you one of my photos." He headed back through the middle room and into his bedroom. I knew I didn't have long, but I couldn't resist trying to get a glimpse of the return address on what appeared to be a letter, the paper he had fingered during much of our conversation. I wondered if it was from the chancery and held some news about his fate. Or if it was from someone at St. Thomas. I didn't feel good about snooping—I never do—but I couldn't help myself.

I wished I had. Sometimes I would be better off living by the code of ethics set forth in my early school years, in which someone's property is their own and not for you to touch, but the temptation was just too great. Kevin was hiding something from me, and that just didn't sit well with me. I reached over and pulled the letter out just far enough to see who had written it. I couldn't determine the author, but I could see from whence it came.

And since I only knew one person in Indiana—and was pretty confident that Kevin did, too—I knew immediately that the letter was from Peter Miceli.

Five

Crawford and I had a quick dinner at one of our favorite neighborhood restaurants near St. Thomas before the first home game of the season. He didn't ask too much about my visit. He knows that my friendship with Kevin is strong and that his dismissal from St. Thomas continues to upset me. He's not quite sure what to do when it comes to Kevin, now that he's virtually a layperson. It's as if Crawford doesn't know who Kevin is anymore now that he isn't a "real" priest. Although Crawford is a half-assed Catholic at best, he still has some old-school thoughts about the faith and priests in general. For instance, when Kevin was at

St. Thomas, Crawford rarely called him by his first name, opting for "Father McManus" instead. Crawford also went to confession if he thought that there was even the most remote possibility that he would be receiving Communion in the coming days or hours, even though his Communion-receiving opportunities were few and far between. And he carried a rosary in his pocket, which to my mind was a good thing. The Catholic in me prayed that it would keep him safe from harm, even though the intellectual in me knew that it was merely a talisman.

We didn't talk about what had happened that morning. I also didn't mention the letter from Peter Miceli, as that was Kevin's business, but I did show him the beautiful photograph of the Throgs Neck Bridge at nighttime that Kevin had blown up and framed for us. I left it on the dining room table so that we could decide where to hang it. I was still troubled by Kevin's continued contact with Peter, but not surprised; I knew that Peter held a special place in his rotten little heart for Kevin. First, there was the whole Mob-respect-for-clergy thing, and the fact that Kevin had buried Kathy. I had suspected, but never confirmed, that Kevin had stayed in touch with the Miceli family through the years, and Peter in particular. I'm sure that Peter took full advantage of Kevin's good nature and stayed in touch. You never knew when a good word from a priest, even one on his last clerical legs, could come in handy with the parole board. I'm sure Peter would work the whole "changed man" routine at some point to get out of prison, back to New York, and into all of his special hobbies: racketeering, prostitution, drug running, and general mayhem.

Crawford had returned to bed after I left and slept most of the day, which wasn't unusual when he had a Saturday off. I remarked on the rosy glow in his cheeks and the absence of the ubiquitous circles that usually anchored his eyes. He rubbed his hands over his freshly shaved face. "I feel much better."

I took a sip of the martini in front of me and studied his face.

"Carmen asked me today if you've had any contact with Peter Miceli." I kept my eyes on his face, looking for a sign that he was about to lie, even though I knew that catching Crawford in a lie was practically impossible. Part of his job is knowing when and how to lie. Although I was sure he was always completely honest with me, it bugged me that even if he decided at some point not to be, I would never know.

"Why would she ask that?" he asked.

"Good question." I waited, not saying anything else, hoping my silence would help him formulate an answer that was at least plausible.

"They're working all angles."

" 'They'?"

"Yeah, Carmen and Champ. I am trying to stay out of it," he said. "For obvious reasons."

"That makes sense." I plucked an olive from my drink and ate it. "Back to my question."

"Which was?" He was stalling.

"Why would Carmen ask me if you had any contact with Peter Miceli?"

"Oh, right," he said, smiling. He knew I was onto him. "She's covering another angle."

"Is that it?"

"That's it." I consulted my menu and was ready to order when the waitress, a former student of mine, returned with my second martini and Crawford's beer. I handed her the menu, waiting until she was back at the bar before asking him what Carmen, or anybody else working the case, had in terms of information or clues.

His face lit up; although he doesn't do it often, he loves talking about cases. "Interestingly enough, it seems like Paul's, er, Vito's, story checks out." He looked behind him to see who was in the vicinity of our table and, confident that there was no one of interest, continued, "Carmen seems to think that maybe he was trying to get out of the life"—Crawford smiled and pointed his finger at me—"just like *you* suspected, and he really was just a mailman."

I was pretty gullible, but that explanation strained the limits of my gullibility, even if I was flattered that one of my theories had sort of panned out. "Which leaves the question of why he was killed?"

"Here's the thing with the Mob. It doesn't matter what you did or to whom, if you piss someone off, you're going to get whacked."

A shudder ran up my spine. I wondered if that extended to college professors who testified against Mob bosses.

"I know what you're thinking," he said, "but you don't have to worry. There was a coup underfoot in the Miceli organization long before you got involved. Let's just say that certain Miceli capos are happy that Peter's away. It's like before: They let him think he's in charge, but really, he wields very little power."

I started to take a dainty sip of my drink but ended up down-ing half of it. "Oh, that's a relief. And you know this how?"

He smiled the smile that had made me fall in love with him all those many months ago, but it wasn't enough to assuage my uneasiness. "I know lots of things. You know that." He leaned back in his chair while the waitress placed a horribly wilted salad, covered in ranch dressing, in front of him. He dug in, impervious to the sight of the saddest-looking salad known to salad prep in front of him. "Within the organization, the people who cared were happy that Peter was going away. It gave them the opportu-nity to right the ship, so to speak."

"So he doesn't have a lot of power?" I asked as I watched Crawford eat a particularly rotten-looking tomato. I pulled the plate away from him. "It's for your own good," I said to his pro-testations.

"Not that we are aware of." He pulled the plate back in front of him. "A little salmonella never hurt anyone."

"Eat at your own risk."

He cleaned his plate and pushed it to the side. "He can't hurt you anymore," Crawford said softly.

I crossed my arms on the table and looked out the window of the restaurant. I hoped he was as sure as he sounded.

I didn't want to be a victim of "famous last words."

Six

After dinner, we headed over to the St. Thomas gymnasium, which had not changed a bit since I had been a student there playing dodgeball as part of the "physical education program." And I use that term loosely. I had needed one more semester of phys ed before graduation and had spent the last months of my undergraduate career at St. Thomas dodging the ball-throwing skills of Patty "the Hammer" McIntyre, who had been my archenemy and a woman determined to make my life a living hell for some unknown reason. I heard that Patty had gone on to a career as a corrections officer in the New York City prison system, which didn't surprise me one bit. I entered the gym and shuddered slightly, reminding myself that I was no longer a sweat suit–wearing seventeen-year-old freshman with a bad perm. I was here to see my stepdaughter play, and save some really bad ballhandling by the girls on the court, I was not likely to sustain a black eye from the game, as I had in senior-year phys ed.

Crawford and I navigated the bleachers and ended up a few rows behind the St. Thomas team, with a great view of the court. I only heard a few muffled remarks about my recent brush with death; most people wouldn't think twice when overhearing the words *trunk* and *Mob* in the same sentence, but I wasn't most people. I tried to hold my head high, pretending that I was just an ordinary spectator and not the vehicular version of the Angel of Death. Crawford and I sat and watched the team as they took their warm-up shots, Meaghan looking confident and sinking every shot she took.

"She's so good," I said to Crawford, who looked tickled to see his daughter in a St. Thomas uniform, a blue jay embroidered across her chest. At nearly six feet, Meaghan wasn't the shortest girl on the court, but she wasn't the tallest either. The College of New Rochelle team boasted a six-foot-three-inch center who seemed to have at least fifty pounds on the skinny Meaghan, who was built exactly like her father, down to the unusually large hands. I said a silent prayer that she wouldn't start in the game because the opposing center looked as if she ate skinny freshmen for breakfast. Images of Patty "the Hammer" McIntyre flooded my brain and I shook them off.

A couple were making their way up through the bleachers with the young woman barely masking her anger that the people at the end of our row were taking their time to make room for them. I closed my eyes. It could only be one person, and that was Crawford's other daughter, Erin, Meaghan's twin and a supreme pain in the ass. Trailing behind her was her boyfriend, a young man inexplicably named Fez, whom she had met at SUNY–New Paltz during orientation before the semester started. We had only met Fez once, and he hadn't left much of an impression from our conversation; his appearance was another story. They made their way along the bleachers, Erin giving someone a hostile "Sorry!" that sounded more like blame than repentance for stepping on his toes. As she got closer, I heard her muttering that he should have moved his feet faster, and my suspicions were confirmed.

I plastered on the smile that I always had on my face around Erin. She and Meaghan couldn't be more different both physically and emotionally. Meaghan had the build and temperament of her father, whereas Erin . . . did not. She was one hundred pounds of piss and vinegar, and being around her was like being in the presence of a hostage-taker: you didn't make a false move for fear of getting stabbed with the verbal equivalent of a dinner fork through the hand. Come to think of it, she might stab me with a dinner fork if I didn't pass the salt fast enough, but I was quick with the sodium handoff when I had to be. Although she had the appearance an angel, her face a heart-shaped, blue-eyed study in a blending of her mother's Polish and her father's Irish heritages, she was someone to be feared. *Anger* was her middle name.

Erin had never really cottoned to me, and her disdain only became more pronounced after Crawford and I married. Unlike her sister, who was practical and realistic, Erin thought that given the right circumstances—me dying, for instance—her parents might get back together. Christine and Crawford had been separated for a long time, though, and Christine had moved on just as Crawford had. I had only met Christine's new husband a few times, but by his veiled comments, I surmised that he was persona non grata in Erin's world as well, and that made me feel marginally better about our tenuous relationship.

I do my best around Erin, not trying too hard, not trying to win her affections by doing things I wouldn't normally do, such as giving in to her request to buy her ridiculously priced boots that she claims would make her "so happy." For Crawford's and Meaghan's sakes, at least, I hoped Erin could find a way to stop seeing me as the enemy. She doesn't have to love me, but if she liked me, I'd be happy.

Fez, the boyfriend, was an enigma to me. We had met once, and that was during a visiting day at New Paltz. A tall, thin, heavily tattooed kid with dreamy brown eyes and pouty lips, he could probably have financed his college education with a modeling career if only he tamed the curls that topped his head and shaved the scraggly beard and mustache that covered up the kind of skin that could only be found on kids who had access to some excellent dermatology. Behind the beard was a set of teeth that had obviously been attended to by a good orthodontist. He had one of those earrings that went through his eyebrow and made me feel weak every time I looked at it because I could only imagine what it had felt like going in. I deliberately avoided looking at his eyes and always focused on his mouth, until I realized he had a stud through his tongue as well. I didn't even want to think about where else he might be pierced and how much that might have hurt, because if I have learned one thing from working on a college campus, it's that if you saw someone with a visible piercing, chances were that there were more elsewhere. Downtown, so to speak. Don't ask me how I know that. Although Erin claimed that Fez was an "artist" and didn't "play by the rules," he had *trust fund kid* written all over him, right on down to his $500, deliberately ripped jeans, expensive sneakers, and extremely well-cared-for skin. Plus, he drove a BMW 7 Series, and those babies don't come cheap. I didn't know the trust-fund part for sure, but I was pretty confident. I made my theory known to Crawford repeatedly because if Fez was anything other than a poseur, Crawford might either

(a) die from worry or (b) shoot the kid on the spot. I wasn't going to be party to either scenario, so I continually assured Crawford that we could have worse problems than Fez with his shiny teeth and clear skin.

Erin finally found herself a seat beside us and flung herself onto the bleacher as if she had crossed the Donner Pass to get there. "You remember Fez," she said, nodding in his direction.

Fez responded with a head nod and held his fist out to me, for what purpose I wasn't sure. I touched his knuckles tentatively with the tip of my index finger and, by his reaction, gleaned that that wasn't the right response. When he saw Crawford beside me, though, he stood. "Sir." He extended a hand and shook Crawford's hand. It didn't escape my notice that he shook his hand out beside his thigh after releasing Crawford's death grip.

"What are you doing here?" I asked, then amended that greeting to "What a nice surprise."

"It's one of my sister's first games. Did you actually think we wouldn't come?" she asked.

"It's just a lovely surprise," I said, sounding like someone I didn't know.

Crawford leaned over me. "It's really great that you're here, Erin," he said, his tone warm. He iced up a bit as he added, "And you, too, Fez." I could see Crawford's jaw working on something and it wasn't a big smile. I worried that he would develop TMJ if he kept clenching.

"Do you want to switch seats?" I asked, hoping that Crawford would want to sit next to his daughter and relieve me of having to bask in her hostile glow.

"Nope," Crawford said quickly. "All set." I suspected he was just as afraid of her as I was, but he would never admit it.

I thought of another tactic to get away from her. I looked at the clock and saw that the game wouldn't start for five minutes.

"Want some candy?" I asked Crawford. I looked at Erin and Fez. "Candy?" They declined and set about making out, the alternative to candy, I gathered.

"We just ate," Crawford said.

"I know. Do you want some candy?" I asked again. He was infuriating like that. Ask a question, get a ridiculous answer.

"What's your point?"

"My point is that we just ate. And you had dessert."

"Doesn't make me a bad person. I repeat: do you want candy?"

"Yeah. I'll take a bag of M&M's."

I made my way down the bleacher steps, saying hello to a few students whom I recognized. I saw a couple of professors and waved to Rabbi Schneckstein, who was seated on the opposite side of the gym and who seemed to have his entire family in tow, including the youngest of his seven children, a toddler no more than two. Who brings a two-year-old to a college basketball game? Rabbi Schneckstein, that's who. Abe is hardly ever seen after school hours without one or two little Schnecksteins in tow. I pointed to Meaghan as she took a practice three-pointer and nailed it. He responded by giving me two thumbs up, taking his hands off the toddler and immediately losing sight of her as she made a beeline for the bleacher steps. He caught her just before she tumbled between the slats of the seats, grabbing the back of her overalls. The rest of the children, who ranged in age from about nine to three, were sitting quietly, pulling items out of a bag that I suspected held kosher snacks. There was no sign of Mrs. Rabbi Schneckstein, so I guessed it must have been "Mommy's night out" in the Schneckstein household.

"Hey, sister! Either move or sit down!" someone behind me called out. I moved along, not sure if the "sister" allusion meant that he thought that I was a St. Thomas nun or if it was just one of those catchall names for someone people don't know.

I passed by the home bench and nodded at our coach, a recently hired addition to the phys ed department named Michael Kovaks. Kovaks was tall with a pockmarked face. He had played at Princeton back in the early eighties and had a decent record as a player. According to the head of the phys ed department, Kovaks was a real find, having decided to get out of corporate America and return to what he loved: basketball. He had only coached one other small college team, another D-III school, and the team had done well under his tutelage. This made St. Thomas ready to take a chance on a coach with little experience. I did know that he ran tough practices, and Meaghan was put through her paces six days a week with only Sundays off to catch up on her sleep and her homework. I had tutored her through a few Freshman Comp papers to get her up to speed on her academics, basketball being her main focus. Crawford was happy she played basketball but not at the expense of her schoolwork. He was already wary of Coach Kovaks and his intensity.

Kovaks nodded back at me, going back to the clipboard in his hand. As the girls warmed up, he shouted directions at them, sprinkled with a few words of encouragement. Truly, he didn't sound like a bad guy, and he seemed to know his basketball, even if he ran the girls ragged week in and week out.

I headed out to the hall, which served as the de facto refreshment area, and greeted the young woman sitting behind the table that held the snacks. "Hi, Mary Catherine," I said. I took in her silky camisole and skintight jeans and was happy that the more things changed, the more they stayed the same. Mary Catherine and I had a history together, and that involved my keeping her out of the mostly male dorm where I had lived the previous year while subbing for an AWOL resident director. Mary Catherine's deal was that she wore most of her lingerie on the outside of her clothing and spent most of her time developing a killer tan, whereas my deal was that I thought she should focus more on developing her mind and avoid a future of skin-cancer diagnoses. See our dilemma? She regarded me smugly, knowing that she had lied for me once, pretending to be my niece during an ill-advised caper, and that I probably owed her one at some point down the academic road. "Hi, Dr. Bergeron."

I picked up Crawford's M&M's and grabbed a bag of Reese's Pieces. "Mary Catherine"—I held the bags aloft—"how much do I owe you?"

"How are you?" she asked, the concern on her face letting me know that she had seen at least one of the countless television and print reports on the murder. She took the five I proffered and leaned over her change box, her breasts spilling out over the top of her camisole. The guy behind me nearly choked on a piece of popcorn. "I haven't seen you since last semester. And now . . . this."

Yep, she'd seen the news. "I know," I said.

"Why do you think they picked your car?"

Why, indeed? "I have no idea."

Mary Catherine, it would seem, did. "I bet it's those Miceli people again." She put a hand on her hip. "I remember when their daughter was found," she said, shuddering. "Do you think they're trying to tell you something? You know how the Mob is. They wait until you get really comfortable, and then *whack*!" She banged the candy table for effect. "They take you out. Or they take away the one thing you love." She smiled, as if she had just recounted the details of her latest vacation. "I have every season of *The Sopranos* on DVD."

I decided to change the subject. "Don't you need another three credits in English? You really should get that out of the way before soon." I tore open the Reese's and poured several into my mouth.

"As a matter of fact, I'm thinking of taking your Beat Poets course next semester." She leaned in conspiratorially. "I heard it's an easy A."

"You did?" I leaned toward her so that we were close enough to kiss. "I don't give easy A's."

A group of students approached and began rummaging through the candy. "That's what I heard," she said, and winked.

I winked back. "Take the course. Especially if you're feeling lucky." I had turned into the professorial version of Dirty Harry.

I walked away, taking in her confused expression. Mary Catherine might think she's slick, but she doesn't get irony, and sarcasm is way above her. I was deep in thought about Mary Catherine's revealing clothing when I bumped into a man by the gym door. He was wearing all black and looked vaguely familiar to me but I couldn't place him or even determine if I had ever met him. I figured he was the father of one of my students; I come across hundreds of parents every year and run into them in sundry places, such as the Food Emporium, only to draw a complete blank on their names. I find a loud and overly friendly "Hi!" goes a long way to making them think I know exactly who they are. I murmured an apology and kept walking, my mind now off Mary Catherine's décolletage and on the guy in black.

I went back into the steamy gym just as the clock buzzed, signaling that the game was going to start. The stands had filled up since I'd left and I scanned the crowd, looking for Crawford, who was deep in conversation with someone who appeared to be another St. Thomas Blue Jay parent, a man about our age in one of the school's purple-and-yellow sweatshirts. I raced up the stairs so I would be in my seat by the time the game started and threw a hip into Crawford, who had moved no closer to Erin. "Move over."

He motioned to the guy sitting next to him. "Alison Bergeron, Lou Bianco."

"You teach here, right?" he said without the requisite greeting.

"Yep," I said, training my eyes on the court. The name didn't sound familiar, but that didn't mean I hadn't had a Bianco kid at some point in my career. And the way he was looking at me indicated that my reputation preceded me in the Bianco household. That's what a couple of murder investigations will do for your reputation. "Do you have a daughter on the team or are you just a Blue Jay fan?"

That broke the ice. He pointed to number 16, a girl who unfortunately shared her father's heavy eyebrows and low hairline on an otherwise pretty face. She was powerfully built with muscled legs and toned arms. By the way the team set up on the first play, she appeared to be a point guard as well as a defensive specialist whom the other team couldn't get around under the boards. Finally, St. Thomas had a rebounding powerhouse in young number 16. Hallelujah.

"Kristy," Lou said, his eyes not leaving the court. "She's a sophomore." He pointed to another girl on the bench. "And number twenty. Elaina. She's my other daughter. They're twins."

I didn't know either of the Bianco girls, but that wasn't surprising once Lou told me that they were both in the nursing program, and since I hadn't followed Blue Jay basketball up until recently. Unless they had passed through my section of Freshman Comp, which neither had, I would have no reason to know them. I made some chitchat with Bianco about Kristy's obvious talent, not mentioning that it didn't look as if Elaina would leave the bench anytime soon; she hadn't even taken off her warm-up pants, which was usually a good indication of a second- or even third-stringer. The girls weren't identical twins; Elaina had long, dirty-blond hair that she had captured, messily, in an elastic band.

I hadn't taken much interest in the team prior to this year, but Meaghan's participation had made me a Blue Jay fan. After a few minutes, she was subbed in for the starting center, who was holding her own against the redwood tree who was the College of New Rochelle center, but was wearing down. Meaghan bounded onto the court and took her place in the center of the key as the College of New Rochelle point guard made her way down the court. "She's very talented," I said to Lou, watching his daughter steal the ball from the opposing forward, who was powerless to do anything but watch as Kristy Bianco sprinted down the court and executed a perfect layup. Clearly, this was going to be the Kristy Bianco show from beginning to end. Meaghan was left a little flat-footed in the backcourt, and I heard Crawford sigh beside me.

I put a hand on his knee. "It's early. Patience."

He tore open his M&M's and poured the contents of the bag into his hand. Through a mouthful of multicolored candy, he attempted to tell me what he thought Meaghan should have done in that situation. I didn't know why it mattered; we had scored. So what if she hadn't trailed her guard providing coverage? It was all the same to me.

Erin stood and screamed something at Meaghan, obviously knowledgeable about the game. God knows she had sat through enough games throughout Meaghan's high school career. She turned to me and her father. "Who's the Blue Jay chick who can't go left?"

I pulled her down to her seat and leaned into her. "You can't say stuff like that. Her parents are probably sitting near us."

"Who cares? It's number sixteen. Man, she sucks."

I gave her a hard stare. "Cool it. Right now," I said as I realized that she had just impugned the ability of Lou Bianco's daughter. He sat like a stone next to Crawford, fortunately having the good sense to keep his mouth shut when confronted with a mouthy teenager. I looked deep into her eyes. "Do not embarrass your father. Or your sister."

She looked away and turned to Fez. Before she turned completely toward him, I heard her mutter, "Bitch," and it wasn't under her breath, either. I made an effort to block her out completely. Crawford seemed not to hear what had been said, or chose not to, I wasn't sure which.

Thanks to some good blocking by Meaghan—who finally realized she was playing in the big leagues and stepped up her game—and some fancy footwork by Kristy, we were well ahead as the first half came to a close. Kovaks was running back and forth along the sidelines, screaming at the girls to put on a full-court press, even though they were ahead by sixteen points. I took in Meaghan's red face and the sweat stains on her uniform that had appeared as she doggedly covered her opposing player.

"Meaghan! Cover her!" Kovaks screamed as Meaghan lost her man in the scrum for the ball.

"Yeah, Meaghan! Cover her!" Erin called from beside me.

Meaghan looked helpless as the opposing center popped up with the ball and headed toward the basket.

"Crawford! Defense!" Kovaks called out.

The center headed toward the basket, Meaghan trailing her slightly. As she went in for the layup, Meaghan threw up an arm, the center threw an elbow, and the entire group of spectators gasped as the elbow connected with Meaghan's nose, the sound audible in the sound-drenched gym. The center made the shot, Meaghan crumpled to the ground, blood flowing from her broken nose and onto her jersey, the floor, and the referee, who raced to her side after calling a time-out. Crawford turned to stone beside me.

"Intentional foul! Intentional foul!" Kovaks hollered, his face getting redder by the minute.

"You've got to be kidding me!" Erin said, throwing her hands up. "That was intentional!" she cried. She turned and looked at me, and then at Fez. "Right?"

Fez looked up at her. "Probably," he said, for fear of disagreeing.

Crawford rose and put his hands in his pockets. He rocked back and forth, not sure what to do. Finally, parental concern got the better of him and he pushed his way past the other spectators in our row and headed down the bleacher steps and onto the court, where Meaghan was still supine on the gym floor.

Kovaks threw his clipboard down and picked up a chair. He seemed to be less concerned with Meaghan's well-being than the fact that an intentional foul had still not been called. He threw the chair toward the far end of the court to the amazement of everyone watching the spectacle. The Schneckstein toddler began clapping, gleeful at the commotion.

It's times like this I'm glad that I teach in a school known for its nursing program. Three of my colleagues had raced out of the stands and were beside Meaghan before Crawford actually reached her, and while one was examining her nose, the other was taking her blood pressure with a cuff that had seemingly appeared out of nowhere. I looked across the gym and saw the rabbi shepherding his kids out of the stands; an irate coach and a bloodbath were apparently more than the brood could handle on a Saturday night.

The girls on the team had wisely taken their places on the sidelines, fretting as Meaghan stayed on the ground. I could tell from the body language of the nursing professors that they wanted her to remain on the ground until they could get the bleeding under control; it looked as if Crawford and I would be spending the night in the emergency room. Meaghan is as tough as nails, even if she seemed a little small and young out on the court that night. I was more worried about Crawford, who stood against the wall under the basket, his face pale and drawn. All of the good health that he had exhibited earlier had drained from him and he looked as if he were going to vomit.

Kovaks continued his performance until the ref, a short, swarthy-looking guy I wouldn't mess with, approached him and put his hands on Kovaks' chest to stop his theatrics. My attention was divided between watching the ministrations to

Meaghan and Kovaks's histrionics. After several minutes, he finally sat down, his hands on either side of his head. The referee called the foul and reprimanded the opposing center. Meaghan got up and the people in the gym erupted in thunderous applause; she asked for the ball and went to the foul line, sinking two foul shots before walking off the court and falling heavily into a chair on the sidelines, her jersey pulled up to her nose to stanch the flow of blood.

Kovaks never moved from the sidelines, his head still in his hands. When he finally did get up, he stumbled slightly as he moved toward center court and the refs, who were conferring about what kind of punishments, beyond the technical, to mete out. A few more stumbles toward the activity and then Kovaks was down, too, falling with a thud that reverberated throughout the hall. Rabbi Schneckstein and his little ducklings froze at the exit, one of his daughters dropping her bag of kosher snacks to the floor. The toddler, however, was rapt. Clearly, this was no episode of *Dora the Explorer.*

The people in the stands were in shock, letting loose with an audible gasp. We all fell silent as one of the nurses rushed to Kovaks's side, taking his pulse. Meaghan was back on her feet, toeing the sideline, watching anxiously as her coach lay motionless in the same circle where the girls had taken the initial jump ball to start the game.

I had forgotten about Lou Bianco beside me, chomping on a bag of popcorn as he watched the dramatic events unfold. "Who coaches the team if he dies?" he asked with not the least bit of irony.

I looked over at him in disgust. "You're kidding, right?"

"Not really," he said, popcorn spilling from his mouth and onto his St. Thomas sweatshirt. "If this blows the season, I'll be pissed." He swept some popcorn from his shirt onto the floor. "And he had better get my other kid in the game."

I moved away from him as quickly as I could, but didn't get far. The other spectators were packed into the row, people who had only cared about Meaghan's technical foul shots just moments earlier now murmuring excitedly about this turn of events.

The gym was remarkably quiet and controlled, given the bizarre circumstances, just a low hum of conversation breaking the complete silence. I frantically waved toward Crawford, but he was on the outskirts of the scene with Kovaks, keeping a safe but available distance.

My colleague Diane McGovern hovered anxiously over Kovaks' body, looking up finally and finding Crawford. She beckoned him over and he knelt beside the coach, looking at her intently, nodding after a few minutes. He made another call on his cell, then found the director of security, a retired cop who happened to be at the game and who spoke the same language as Crawford. Jay Pinto listened to Crawford and then made an announcement, instructing the spectators to stay in the bleachers so that the EMTs could find their way in and take care of business.

Erin looked at me, her eyes big. "This is a freaking amazing basketball game." She turned and looked at Fez. "Amazing, right?"

Fez nodded, his black curls springing back and forth in agreement. "Amazing."

What was even more amazing was when Kovaks suddenly sat up. Diane rocked back on her heels, staring at Kovaks as he protested to her that he was fine. The spectators let out a collective sigh of relief as he struggled to his feet and made his way to the sideline, assuring the players and all of the people who were on the floor that he was fine. I looked at Fez.

"That was weird."

"Weird," he repeated, a nervous tic I attributed to his dating the stick of dynamite that was my stepdaughter.

Weird didn't begin to describe it. *Surreal* was more like it. Particularly when I got the news via text the next morning that Coach Kovaks—much to Lou Bianco's dismay, I'm guessing—had passed away in the wee hours of the morning, a victim of a massive coronary.

Seven

Crawford stole off in the early-morning hours on Monday after our eventful weekend without saying good-bye or giving me a kiss. The news of Kovaks' death had spread quickly. Abe Schneckstein had found out first and sent me a text knowing that I would be interested, given my personal connection to the team.

The college grapevine was in full bloom shortly thereafter, and I received not one, but six, phone calls detailing what my friends on campus knew about Kovaks's death. For me, it was great. Now, no one was talking about me and the death knell that the appearance of my car seemed to hasten. Although I was sorry that the coach had met his Maker, I was delighted that there was something else to keep everyone occupied, for at least a little while. The autopsy report would be a few days off, at best, but evidence was pointing to the coronary that everyone suspected at first. Seems our basketball coach indulged in some not-so-healthy pursuits, such as closet smoking, and out-of-the-closet drinking. The theory remained that he was pretty much a goner before he had gotten the key in the ignition of his car. The mountain of fast-food debris that had been found in the backseat of his luxury SUV also gave the impression that this man was not one for healthy living; apparently Coach Kovaks was a fan of the Big Mac. His wife had told someone in the Nursing Department who told someone in the Business Department who told me that his blood pressure had been through the roof and his record of taking medication was spotty at best. It came as no surprise to anyone who knew him that he had expired at the ripe old age of fifty. He had been a candidate for a coronary or stroke for years and had lived longer than his lifestyle should have allowed.

Lou Bianco had also sent an e-mail to the parents of all of the girls on the team demanding that we get together with Etheridge and the athletic director to find out what they were doing to make sure a new coach was put in place immediately. According to the e-mail and Bianco's information, Etheridge already had a "plan in place," but that wasn't good enough for the father of the twins. He wanted to vet the new candidate, someone who must have appeared out of thin air, as far as I could tell. Did Etheridge have someone waiting in the wings? Kovaks's body was barely cold and they had a replacement? I couldn't get a ream of paper delivered to my office from the supply room in less than two weeks, but they already had someone qualified to coach a D-III team? Now that was some serious focus on the Athletic Department's part, if you asked me.

Meaghan had spent the night with us, so I went to her room and tapped lightly on the door to wake her up. "Meaghan? Honey? Time to get up." We had agreed that after sustaining a broken nose, she needed a little TLC. Since her mother had moved to London recently with her new husband for the next two years and maybe more, the best place for her to be was with us. Her nose was swollen, but besides that, she was no worse for wear, taking the whole thing in stride. I preferred not to think about it because every time I let my mind go to the place where her nose had been snapped in two, I got a little weak. I had even gagged once when the doctor had described the packing that he had shoved way up into her sinuses. He said she could keep playing basketball if she got a protective face mask; our goal that week was to get one as soon as we could so that she could resume practice with the coachless team.

While in the waiting room at the hospital Saturday night, she let us know two things: first, there was no assistant coach, as we had gleaned from Kovaks's solitary performance. Seems that Marcy Pearson had quit the week before, finding Kovaks completely insufferable. Second, no one on the team would be all that distraught that he was gone. Sure, they were unhappy that he had died during the season, but his death was as dramatic as his life had been, and they were apparently inured to both. He ran hard practices, denigrated some of the larger girls for their lack of "willpower" when it came to food, and barely had a nice word for those girls he did like. Such as Kristy Bianco. He tried to put a good face on at games, Meaghan said, but the real Coach Kovaks had been a "dick."

God rest his soul.

"Your father wouldn't approve of language like that," I said, half-kidding, pouring her a big glass of milk and placing it beside the plate of pancakes I had made her. Trixie sat expectantly at her side, waiting for a piece of pancake to make it off Meaghan's plate and into her smiling retriever mouth.

Meaghan dug in, her appetite or ability to chew not impacted by the giant watermelon of a nose in the middle of her face. Her voice was more nasal than usual on account of the packing in there. "Well, he was." She drank half the milk in one gulp. "Just don't tell my dad."

"That he *was* a dick or that you *called* him a dick?" I like to be entirely clear on what Crawford gets told.

"Both."

Sounded like a reasonable request; Crawford's sexy but a complete square. "What time is your first class?" I asked. I was showered and dressed but she was still in her pajamas, tattered flannel pants with the New York Ranger logo on them and an oversize NYPD sweatshirt.

"Nine ten."

It was eight thirty. "We'd better get going," I said. School, with no traffic, was a good twenty-five minutes away. Traffic was another story, and since this is the New York metropolitan area, there's always traffic. All the time. It's one of life's sure bets. "Hop in the shower."

"I don't need to shower." She handed Trixie a piece of pancake, even though I had told her a million times that the dog shouldn't be fed from the table. Trixie is a wonderful dog, but give her a piece of pancake, and next thing you know, she's wresting a T-bone steak from your clutches while you valiantly try to avoid upending the propane tank attached to the barbecue grill.

"Get dressed?" I asked.

"Nope. I'm good to go." She stood and stretched, her fingertips nearly grazing the ceiling in the kitchen. I'm tall, but she's gigantic.

I resisted the urge to roll my eyes, but you'd think I'd know better after all these years that going to class unshowered and in one's pajamas was perfectly acceptable at St. Thomas.

"I'll just go like this," she said, forking another pancake into her mouth.

Of course you will, I thought, as I grabbed my messenger bag from the counter and looked for my keys, which spent time in a variety of places in the house, none of them being the key hook by the back door. I told Meaghan to go out to the car and wait for me; I would find my keys and be there in a minute. I "tossed" the kitchen, as Crawford would say, not finding them, getting stressed by the minute thinking about the start time of Meaghan's first class. Once I was done in the kitchen, I raced upstairs and looked around the bedroom, pulling open drawers with wild abandon and flinging clothes to and fro. My last spot to check was Crawford's nightstand drawer. I didn't think they were in there, but you never knew. Maybe he had my extra set tucked away for situations just like this one. I pushed aside a paper-back thriller, an old copy of *Time* magazine that had the second George Bush on the cover, and a variety of odds and ends. Man, the guy had a lot of paper clips. I slipped my hand under the book and the magazine, my fingers grazing something cold and hard.

His badge.

Crawford didn't go anywhere without his badge. I had found that out early on. I traced the badge number—4499—with my finger, wondering why he would have left it here. And why he would have stuffed it into the back of a rarely used drawer. I didn't have much time to think about it, though, because all of a sudden Meaghan had become the most punctual student in the world and was pressing the car horn relentlessly in my driveway. I spied the spare keys on the floor next to Crawford's dresser and beside a pair of his discarded pants and grabbed them, heading back downstairs.

I stopped and kissed Trixie on the head and started out for the car.

A few minutes later, I was pulling onto the highway that would take us to school. "What did you do with your bloody jersey?" I asked, my heart rate finally returning to normal when it was clear that we would get to school on time.

"I threw it in the hamper in your closet. But you can just throw it out. I have an extra."

"Really?"

"Yep. They gave us two home jerseys and two away jerseys. I'm okay as long as I don't get injured again."

Now I knew why the faculty didn't get raises; the money was going to multiple jerseys for the student athletes. "So the girls really aren't going to be upset that he died?" I don't know why I couldn't wrap my brain around that concept, but I couldn't. I hated my ex-husband, but even I had been a little upset that he had been murdered.

Meaghan shrugged. "We mostly hated him."

"I know, but he *died*."

She shrugged again. "And we *hated* him," she repeated, as if I hadn't heard her the first time. As mature as I find Meaghan with regard to most things, I had to remember she was eighteen. A kid. No different from the other eighteen-year-olds I came across daily. When I thought about it like that, it didn't surprise me that she didn't have any allegiance to the coach and had moved on, without another thought, to the next thing in her life, which was her pursuit of the face mask. "When can we go shopping for the face mask?" she asked, as we pulled into the front entrance of the school. I flashed my ID at the guard at the gate and pulled through, slowing while going over the numerous speed bumps that lined the path to the building where I parked my car.

"How about after my last class? I can pick you up at three forty."

She shook her head. "I have a class."

"After that?"

"Can't we go at lunchtime?"

"My lunchtime isn't the same as your lunchtime." I taught straight through until three thirty, and by that time I was ready to gnaw off my own arm I was so hungry. But I was willing to forsake eating in the quest for the face mask, which I didn't tell her, not wanting to sound like a martyr. "Three forty. That's all I've got. The dog walker's off today so I have to get home to Trixie by five or things at home will get extremely . . . untidy. How about tomorrow?"

She thought about that for a moment. "Maybe." Her response was unconvincing, and I could tell that the only thing that would work for her was my driving back to St. Thomas to get her after her class, and she wasn't resting until she got me to agree to that. We sat in silence, our face-mask standoff. "When's my dad done with work?"

I hesitated. In about five years? I thought. "Not sure. He seems to be working a bunch of really complicated cases, and I think he's going to be putting in a lot of overtime." That was a massive understatement and I wasn't entirely sure it was true; would Crawford be assigned or having anything to do with the Passella case? Unlikely, given his final resting place, but you just never knew. The police department, like most businesses in the United States, was working with fewer employees and fewer resources overall. Maybe Crawford would end up working the case as if I had nothing to do with it. If so, we'd probably see less of him than we already were.

She sighed, exasperated. My teaching and her father's work as a homicide detective didn't seem to fit in with her schedule, and this didn't make her happy. "So when am I supposed to get the face mask?" she asked, her voice rising. "We have another game on Wednesday!"

I reminded her, as gently as I could, that the team didn't have a coach, which was going to impact the team's ability to play their regular schedule.

"We'll play," she said, as if what I had suggested was completely preposterous. "They'll find another coach."

I shook my head before resting it on the steering wheel. I didn't have the energy to explain the process of hiring a Division III basketball coach in the competitive New York metro area, so I just let her believe that having a coach by the next game—in two days—was a completely reasonable assumption. We parted company in the parking lot, not having reached consensus on when we would buy the face mask or when, even, we would see each other again. I let it go. I have found that the stepmother/stepdaughter dance is less a waltz than a tango—everyone locked in a graceful give-and-take that sometimes ended up with someone's toes getting stepped on.

I went into the office area off of which all of the Department of Humanities instructors had offices, mine included. Dottie Cruz, the laziest secretary ever to grace the main Humanities desk, was reading a paperback, the cover of which was half torn off. The word *desire* remained as the only part of the title that could be read, so it gave me an inkling that she wasn't reading the latest Philip Roth. I bid her good morning and scampered over to my office door before she could engage me in conversation about her world, which included her impending marriage to one of Crawford's colleagues, a rotund beat cop named Charlie Moriarty, who found Dottie endlessly fascinating and apparently—if the conversations I overheard that took place at Dottie's desk were any indication—sexy. I didn't see it. Dottie favored black hair dye and Day-Glo matching legging/tunic outfits. But who am I to judge, having made a few fashion missteps myself over the years. To each her own.

I was almost to my office when Dottie called my name. "Dr. Bergeron? Sister Mary wants you upstairs. Stat."

Stat? I thought. That was an interesting choice. But then again,

Dottie is the kind of person who says "ay-sap" instead of "A-S-A-P," so I wasn't entirely surprised. I turned around.

"Like now," she said.

"I get it." I opened my office door and flung my messenger bag onto the guest chair in front of my desk and hightailed it up to Sister Mary McLaughlin—also known as the head of the English Department—and her immaculate office situated right across from that of the president of the college.

I tapped lightly on the glass on Mary's shut door and heard her clipped Irish brogue as she answered me. The sound of that voice never failed to give me chills, and not the good kind. I stuck my head in and hesitated. "Should I come in?"

She regarded me with impatience. "Of course. Didn't I ask you to come up here?" She sat ramrod straight behind her tidy desk, her hands folded in front of her.

I sat down and ignored the bead of sweat running down my spine. I regretted wearing a cashmere turtleneck, an expensive item that would be ruined if I continued to leak sweat like a marathon runner on mile twenty-five.

"I don't know why I'm doing this, but I am," she said, more to herself than to me. She shook her head violently as if trying to forget something that she had just remembered. "Anyway . . . I don't really like you."

That wasn't a surprise to me, but I had never heard her verbalize it and was taken aback. I'm sure her dislike had something to do with our long history together, which predated my employment at St. Thomas and began when I was a freshman here. My huge ego, bestowed upon me when I had graduated at the top of the class of my small, Catholic, all-girls high school, had gotten me into more than a few scrapes with Sister Mary, who didn't find my witty insouciance in research papers to be either witty or insouciant. Also, my incredible sleuthing skills had caused her drug-dealing nephew, formerly employed at our respected institution, to currently reside at a halfway house in upstate New York for first-time offenders. Or should I say first-time offenders with big-time lawyers? "Is that why you called me up here?" I asked.

"I don't like you, but I respect you. Lesser women would have been felled by your circumstances but you remain resolute. I respect that. And believe it or not, I find you to be an incredibly insightful teacher."

Hmmm. That was something, I guess. I still didn't have tenure, so how insightful could I be?

"So, although I would never have thought myself to be in the role of your protector, I find myself uncomfortably ensconced there."

Whatever that meant. I waited. I used my better judgment and didn't blurt out, "Cut to the chase, Sister," although that was my first, and burning, inclination.

"In a few hours, you will be called to President Etheridge's office."

I moved to the edge of my seat. Was I finally getting tenure? Or was this another ruse to get me to do something that I had no desire to do? Rumor had it that Etheridge and Dwyer, that weasel they called Kevin's replacement, were looking for someone to run the God Squad, and it sounded like just the kind of torture they loved to inflict on someone like me, particularly after the events of the previous week. The God Squad was a group of conservatively minded Catholic students who, while doing good works, implored President Etheridge and Father Weasel to reinstate a daily Latin Mass, which was under consideration. Another of their main causes was to see the campus Gay and Lesbian Student Union disbanded, a cause we knew Dwyer was all over. "I refuse to be the head of the God Squad," I said with the same resoluteness that Mary so admired.

She looked at me sadly, as if I were more stupid than even she had imagined. "No, Alison. It's not the God Squad."

"Whew!" I said, wiping a hand across my brow. I looked at her face, remembering at that moment that Mary doesn't like slapstick and she abhors sarcasm. I dropped my hand into my lap.

"It's the basketball team."

"What?"

"You heard me."

"I thought you said 'the basketball team.'"

"I did."

"What about them?"

Mary crossed herself. "God rest his soul, but Coach Kovaks has died."

"I know. I heard." She might live under a rock, but I don't. Word gets around. I think I may have been the third person to know after the Widow Kovaks and Abe Schneckstein.

"And the assistant coach resigned last week."

I stood. "I don't know what you're getting at," I said, even though I suddenly kind of did, "but I have work to do. Real work. That doesn't involve basketballs."

Mary busied herself rearranging the religious iconography that adorned her desk: a statue of Jesus praying at the Mount, a framed photo of the Blessed Virgin, a miniature sculpture of the pietà, a small vial of holy water from Lourdes. Her eyes rested on the framed photo of the Blessed Virgin, whose care I suspected I needed. "Don't say you weren't warned."

Warned about what? I turned toward the door and put my hand on the doorknob, stopping when she called my name. "How is Father McManus?" she asked, her voice barely a whisper. We rarely speak of Kevin on campus, and if we do, it is in the hushed tones of those who gossip about sordid situations.

"Well, he's almost not a Father anymore," I said, turning to face her. "But you know that."

"You may not know this, Alison, or even want to believe it, but I am one of Father McManus's staunchest supporters." Her eyes met mine. "And believe me, it does not behoove me in any way to put myself in that position."

I've been behooved into a few positions myself, and it's not a comfortable feeling. I threw down the gauntlet. "So if you support him so staunchly, help me find out the truth. Help me find out who is framing him and why." Because that's what I truly believed—he was being framed and it was my job to find out why. I had floated through the previous months in a haze, not really caring about why he was being framed, only hoping and praying that through some miracle he would be exonerated and back at the school. But it seemed that all of the hopes and prayers in the world weren't going to make that so. In Mary's office, I had an epiphany. I had to find out myself. My promise to Kevin had been halfhearted at best, with my being preoccupied with my own situation. But here, in Mary's office, it was clear what I had to do. I took her silence as acquiescence.

She changed the subject. "As for President Etheridge? I suggest you capitulate."

As if I had a choice. Because if I had learned one thing at this institution of higher learning and torture, it was if they wanted me to do something, they usually had me by the short hairs. Capitulate? Sure. That's how I ended up leaving the president's office an hour later laden with a file box of the accoutrements the interim head coach of a Division III women's basketball team would need: playbooks, schedules, rosters, strategy notebooks, and a whistle. I had watched my fair share of NCAA women's basketball and had studied the coaches' attire. I figured that all I needed to complete the transformation from kind of stylish college professor to dowdy college basketball coach was one severe, ill-fitting, monochromatic suit in a drab mustard color and sensible shoes. I drew the line at cutting my hair into a modified mullet. The hair stayed.

I slogged along the marble-floored hallways of the administration floor of the main building and wondered how my life—

which I had tried to carefully construct so that nothing surprised me—had become one that I barely recognized.

William, one of the other mail guys, was blocking the entrance to the stairwell with his giant cart, and when a polite request for him to move didn't work, I gave a toot on the whistle and watched him throw an entire bag of mail in the air, startled by both my rudeness and the shrill sound. I have that effect around mail guys now; they think that if they don't do what I say, they'll end up getting whacked.

I looked at the whistle in my hand and decided that if nothing else, I would enjoy having it in my possession.

Eight

Much to my surprise, Max and Fred were waiting for me at the house when I got home at four thirty. Fortunately, they didn't need to use the bathroom, weren't thirsty, and had just eaten, or else they would have let themselves in by breaking a window or ripping one of my screens. That was their modus operandi whenever they couldn't gain entry to my house, and it didn't make me happy. They were seated on the front steps looking like a normal couple, even though anyone who had spent thirty seconds in their presence would find out that they definitely weren't.

For one thing, the size differential is considerable. Max is Tinker Bell and Fred is Gigantor. Sure, Crawford's tall, but Fred's built like a redwood tree. And there are a lot of petite women in the world, but none with the lack of body fat like Max. She's a tiny-limbed, muscled pixie who eats whatever she wants, whenever she wants, and drinks like a fish. If I can be so clichéd, she has the metabolism of a hummingbird. Fred, on the other hand, is six feet five of solid, firmly packed flesh who seemingly eats small rodents for breakfast and who was once a defensive tackle for his college team, where he went on a full scholarship and majored in criminal justice. According to Crawford, he's an investigative genius, an attribute I've yet to witness. I'll just have to take his word for it. I simply can't imagine how you investigate without talking, but I'm still learning about this homicide-detective thing. He's a half-Samoan, half–African American Brooklyn guy through and through, and when I need a laugh, I think about the times I've seen him among Max's Lilliputian relatives.

I had written Max an e-mail telling her that I was now the coach of the Lady Blue Jays. Although I sounded calm in my e-mail, she had obviously sensed that I wasn't happy. My mind was racing. Wasn't it enough that I had to deal with my car's becoming a Mob graveyard? Now I had to coach the basketball team? I guess as penances go, this wasn't a terrible one, but still. The time and energy it was going to take to coach the team was exhausting to think about, let alone execute.

I approached them tentatively. Whenever they visit, I usually end up having to cook, and I knew that all I had in the refrigerator was vodka, olives, and the largest block of cheddar cheese I'd ever seen, compliments of a student from Vermont who got a B– in my Creative Writing class despite having no handle on grammar and not being really all that creative. "What are you doing here?"

"Nice greeting," Max said, leaping from the front stoop and onto me, her idea of a bear hug.

Fred grunted and I couldn't tell if that was "hello" or something that held a deeper meaning. He laid a meaty hand on my shoulder and pushed down, which I interpreted to mean that he was concerned.

"What's this about?" I asked, unlocking the front door and letting them in. At the sight of Fred, Trixie ran and hid under the dining room table, otherwise known as her "safe place." I brought them into the kitchen and pulled open the refrigerator. "Vodka? Cheddar cheese?"

Max launched herself onto the island and dragged her butt up and down the granite, trying to get comfortable or clean it; I wasn't sure which. "I'll have a shot!" she said enthusiastically.

"I was thinking more like martinis, but I'll give you a shot," I said, pulling a few glasses from the cabinet. I knew Fred rarely drank, so I handed him the only other cold beverage in the refrigerator: a small carton of chocolate milk left over from Meaghan's visit. He took it and greedily guzzled the contents, a little chocolate milk spilling onto the front of his giant dress shirt. I poured Max a shot and made myself a martini, waiting until I had taken a sip before paraphrasing my original question. "To what do I owe this honor?"

Max looked at me quizzically. Although she runs a cable television station and has been dubbed the "queen of reality TV" by the kind of people who know who their queen should be, she can be incredibly dense.

"Why are you here?" I asked. I told Max to open the back door for Trixie, who could frolic in my fenced-in backyard while we chatted.

Fred spoke. "We're worried about you."

"Because of the dead guy in the trunk?"

"That and the other thing," Fred said.

"Because of the basketball team?" I asked.

He nodded.

"You're more concerned about the basketball team than the dead guy in the trunk?" I asked, incredulous.

Fred nodded again. "We're all over the dead-guy thing, but you're all alone on the basketball thing. That concerns me."

"I'll be fine," I said before bursting into tears. That was unexpected, but not more than finding myself wrapped up in Fred's tight embrace, my head buried in his starchy white shirt. "Really," I said to his size-eighteen collar. "I'll be fine," I said, even though I knew I wouldn't be. It wasn't the basketball team, and we both knew it; it was the body, and the blood, and the pissed-off Blue Jay. It was Crawford, working day and night and making phone calls from the privacy of the garage. It was all of that plus the basketball team. I pulled away from Fred and wiped my eyes with a paper napkin, taking care to get rid of the mascara that had slid down my face. I looked at Fred. "Sorry about the shirt."

He grunted again and shrugged.

I pulled a chair up to the kitchen table and sat down. "So guess what else."

"You're pregnant," Max said without hesitation.

"No." I did some mental math in my head and concluded that I definitely wasn't. "No. Not pregnant."

"You're going to join Weight Watchers," Max tried.

I looked down at my gut. She was two for two. "Now why would you say that?" I asked, wounded. I'm no hard body, but I'm not fat either. I'm normal. On good days, I'm a size ten. When I've overindulged, out come the twelves. I'm certainly not a *Biggest Loser* candidate. I believe the term is *zaftig*. I decided that I wouldn't let Max take any more guesses. "I have decided to accept the position and become the interim head coach of the St. Thomas Blue Jays." As if I had had a choice. But I decided if I said it out loud to them, it was now a reality.

Fred pounded the table. I think he was happy; sometimes it's hard to tell. "I love the Blue Jays."

"You do?" I asked.

"Sure. I follow them in the Bronx section of the *Daily News*. You've got that amazing shooting forward this year. What's her name? Bianchi?"

"Bianco. Kristy Bianco." It didn't make sense. "Why do you root for them? They never win."

"I like an underdog."

That explains it.

He chugged the rest of his chocolate milk. "Why you?"

Indeed. Why me? "It was explained to me like this: Coach Kovaks is dead, his assistant quit, and they need a warm body until they can find an experienced warm body. The women's volleyball coach is pregnant and due any day, all of the coaches of the men's teams turned it down, and I need to do one more 'extraordinary' thing before getting tenure." I guess wearing a hair shirt was out of the question, so this was my new penance for ending up with another body in my trunk and bringing disgrace and dishonor to our venerable institution. I left that last part out and just smiled ruefully. "Funny, right?"

"What do you know about basketball?" Fred asked, gravely serious.

"I played CYO."

"Who didn't?" Fred asked. Catholic Youth Organization basketball was a staple around these parts; they took everyone, despite that it was an extremely competitive league, something that was in opposition to its "Everyone's a winner!" philosophy.

"I also spent a little time as a Blue Jay myself," I said proudly. "I was pretty good actually."

"You're tall. You'd better be." Fred rubbed at the mascara on the front of his shirt, making the stain worse. "You need help." He was pretty certain of that by the way he said it. He was right.

"No shit," I said, and took a slug of my drink. "And who's going to help me? Most of the people I teach with are nuns. And Rabbi Schneckstein doesn't strike me as being an imposing force under the boards. Oh, and he'd be the lone male on an all-female team."

"Hey, maybe you could get that hot guy in the Business Department? That Osama bin Laden guy?" Max offered helpfully.

"You mean Fareed Muhammad?" I asked.

"Right. Him! That'd get me to some games." Behind me, on the counter, she was tapping furiously on her BlackBerry, as was often the case when she lost interest in a conversation.

Fred was pensive. I think. Either that or he was pissed that Max had a crush on Fareed, as any other hot-blooded woman would, given the whole dark eyelashes, French accent, and pouty lips thing he's got going on. Not that I've noticed. Fred rubbed his hand over his shiny bald head. Finally he spoke. "I know someone who could help you."

I brightened, either from there now being hope for my situation or the grade-A Russian vodka coursing through my veins. "Really? Who?"

Max jumped from the counter and pushed her BlackBerry in front of my nose. "Him."

I took the device from her hand and stared at the dated photo on the screen. In it, a tall, robust-looking teenager with caramel-colored skin and a giant Afro was driving to the basket, having left a bunch of smaller guys in his wake. He was graceful and athletic, judging from the shot he was going to take, a reverse, one-handed dunk. I could tell the picture was from at least two decades ago because said teenager was wearing short, tight basketball shorts, a look that was popular in the eighties. He looked vaguely familiar but I couldn't place him. I scrolled down to see if there was a caption and saw the name: Charlemagne Wyatt. I looked at Fred. "You?" Crawford and I had only recently learned that Fred was a nickname for Charlemagne, of all things. We never did figure out—or even ask—if his parents were really into the founding father of both the French and the German monarchies or shared a really sick sense of humor. But once we both met Fred's younger brother, Pepin—also known as "Dave"—we were pretty sure it was a combination of both.

"He was All-City," Max exclaimed, jumping on his lap and kissing his bald pate. "And he had a rockin' Afro."

"Is there a sport you didn't play?" I asked.

"I was never a gymnast," he said, completely serious. As if gymnastics programs enlisted young men whose legs were wider than a traditional pommel horse.

"You'll really help me?" I asked.

"Sure," he said. "As long as nobody else gets murdered in the Bronx, I'll have a lot of free time."

I couldn't tell if he was serious or not. I knew for sure that he was selling his work ethic short; nobody worked harder or put in longer hours than Fred did. He didn't "do toilets," as I had learned a few months earlier when some heroin had collided with my plumbing, but he was always the guy who went in first and the one that Crawford wanted at his back when Fred didn't lead the way. Might as well have him at my back during my hopefully short tenure as coach. I extended my hand and we shook. "Deal."

"When's the next practice?" he asked.

I didn't know. "Tomorrow?" I would have to jump in sooner or later.

"You don't know?"

"No, I really don't." I'd have to text Meaghan to get an idea of when practice might take place. "Let's just say seven o'clock to-morrow night unless you hear from me."

Max got off Fred's lap. "Dinner?"

I shook my head. "I don't think so, Max. I have work to do and I'm kind of tired."

"Come on," she whined.

"I wouldn't be good company."

"Suit yourself." She started for the back door. "Good luck with the whole"—she waved her hands in the air while searching for the right words—"basketball coaching. And all the other stuff."

I didn't know what the other stuff was—perhaps the pregnancy or the Weight Watchers—but I accepted her good wishes and sent her on her way. Fred lingered for a minute in the kitchen, looking around uncomfortably. He kissed the top of my head, the first display of affection that had ever been exchanged between us, save the hug he had given me earlier. "Maybe we'll have fun," he said, shrugging.

Maybe we would. Or maybe this, like so many other things in my life so far, would turn into the train wreck it was likely to become.

Nine

Along with inheriting a basketball team that I was not remotely qualified to coach, I had also inherited another office, and a really dirty one at that. It was located at the bottom of the Athletic Center and was completely windowless. I figured that if St. Thomas was going to embrace athletics, as the administration claimed, and encourage people to see our sports' teams in action, they would at least give their coaches decent accommodations. No such luck. I entered the late Coach Kovaks's office, wondering if the cobwebs that greeted me had grown since he had died or were a leftover decorating accessory from his tenure as coach.

I walked around the small space—eight feet by eight if my estimation skills were accurate—and took my place behind a big metal desk strewn with papers. Kovaks didn't seem to be terribly organized, but my opinion changed when I opened the desk drawer that housed neatly arranged files, all labeled with each girl's name and containing all of their pertinent information. High school stats, previous St. Thomas stats, if applicable, height, weight, shooting percentage, strengths and weaknesses—they were all there in black and white, reducing each girl to a bunch of numbers. There was no editorializing, just statistics. I went through the files, counting fourteen in all, knowing that there were fifteen girls on the team. Unfortunately, I didn't know every single girl on the team so I couldn't immediately ascertain who was missing until I spied a roster pinned to an overly crowded corkboard directly across from the desk. I pulled it off the wall and compared the list to the group of files, and when I was done, I knew that the only player who didn't have a file was Elaina Bianco. I pushed aside a stack of papers on the desk and rummaged through other drawers, but my search came up empty. No Elaina.

I was ruminating on that when the phone rang, startling me. I looked at it, wondering if I should answer it; after all, I was the basketball coach, sitting in the basketball coach's office, and could answer the phone without any repercussions regarding privacy. Was there someone who actually wanted to talk to *me*? I guess I had to find out. "Hello?"

"Dr. Bergeron? Lou Bianco."

Of course. It was only a matter of time until he tracked me down. I looked around, wondering if he had a hidden camera in the office; how else would he know that I was in Kovaks's chair going through his files? I pulled myself in closer to the desk, steeling myself for the inevitable onslaught of suggestions and questions related to the team. "How can I help you, Lou?"

It started with getting Kristy more publicity in the local papers and ended with my playing Elaina, if not as a starter, then as a first sub. I hadn't seen anything thus far to suggest that Elaina was capable of even being on the court, and if her lack of a file was any indication, neither did Kovaks. How in God's name had this girl even made the team? "I will take that all under advisement, Lou."

"So we'll see more Elaina? She's really a tall guard, but she can play small forward."

Whatever that meant. I hadn't even been to one practice, let alone coached a game, so where Elaina Bianco played on the court was of no immediate concern to me. I wisely did not let him know that. "Again, I will think about everything you told me."

He pressed further. "Kristy could be the face of Blue Jay ball. You just have to make sure that that happens."

I thought that that was the purview of the college public relations department, but again, decided not to press the issue with him. "How about this, Lou?" I said as kindly as I could. "Let me get a practice or two—even a game—under my belt before we start rearranging what Coach Kovaks put into place?"

If it was possible to feel anger radiating through the phone lines, I suspected that that is what would be coming through. He was silent for a moment, seething, I imagined.

"You see, that's the thing," he said, his voice tight. "Coach Kovaks didn't know what was best for my"—he immediately corrected himself—"I mean, *those* girls. The whole team. I never approved of that hire."

As if he had a choice.

"I'm just saying," he continued, "you have more talent on that team than the current roster would lead you to believe."

"Elaina."

"Elaina."

I had to end this call and fast. We weren't getting anywhere. I was loath to let Lou Bianco know that I had this annoying habit of doing exactly the opposite when pressed, so I bid him adieu before he could say anything else.

Squeezing practice in after a day of teaching was not ideal, and I was ten minutes late due to my reconnaissance in Kovaks's office as well as my frustrating call with Lou Bianco. The girls stood around near the bleachers, watching as I trotted across the court in high heels, dragging a net bag full of balls behind me. I was so unaccustomed to the idea of coaching that it had never occurred to me to bring anything to change into, sneakers included. I dumped the basketballs onto the court and told the girls to "Go fetch" just as my phone rang. When I looked at the number, I saw that it was Crawford. I didn't know if he hadn't come home the night before or if I had been asleep and missed him altogether. Either way, the sight of his number cheered me. "Hello?" I said as I raced from the gym and went into the hallway where the sound of bouncing basketballs and squeaking sneakers wouldn't interfere with our conversation.

"Hey," he said casually, as if he were at home, waiting for me and an order of General Tso's.

"Where are you?"

"Around."

That's helpful, I thought. "I didn't see you last night."

"I know. I came in, but you were asleep so I didn't wake you. I had to leave early this morning, too."

I pondered that. "Fred and Max were over last night. You and Fred aren't working together this week?" I knew that they were together most of the time, but not all of it. Last night must have been one of those times.

"Yeah," he said, the line crackling slightly and making it difficult to hear him. "We had to go our separate ways for something."

I didn't think too much of it, anxious to get to my news. "Hey, guess who the new coach of the St. Thomas Blue Jays is."

"Sister Mary?"

"Close."

"I sure hope it's not that Fareed Muhammad guy in the Business Department or I'll have to douse you with cold water after every game."

He was right. It wasn't Fareed and he *would* have to turn the hose on me after every game if it were. "It's me. I'm the coach." I gave him the *Reader's Digest* version of how I came to be the interim head coach of the St. Thomas Blue Jays. "So there you have it."

"There are no words," he said after a short silence. After all the things that I had been through at St. Thomas, he was not entirely surprised by this turn of events. There was a lot of background noise, as if he was standing a city street. I asked him where he was. "Here and there," he said. "How's Meaghan?"

"She's good. Nose is getting better and Kristy Bianco took her to get the face guard, so there's one tragedy that's been averted."

"Tell her I love her, too."

"Have you spoken to Christine?"

"She's all up-to-date on daughter number one's injury. She was a little miffed that Meaghan didn't call her herself, but I think we'll get past it."

I heard a horn in the distance, followed by a siren, two sounds that don't inspire confidence or a sense of calm.

"Gotta go." The last voice I heard before he hung up was decidedly female and obviously in his personal space.

"Okay," I said to a dead line.

I went back into the gymnasium and saw that my absence hadn't really done anything to inspire the girls to do anything remotely related to basketball. Girls were lounging on the bench, and someone was actually French-braiding Meaghan's hair.

"Hey!" I called upon reentering. "Is this a basketball practice or a hair salon?"

Instead of instilling fear, which was my intention, the team burst into laughter. I picked up a few basketballs scattered about and started passing them to various girls on the team, but I must admit, my arm strength wasn't what it once was. Only one ball reached its intended target. "Run suicides. Shoot layups. Take foul shots. Do anything that would make me believe that your goal is to be a successful D-III basketball team," I said. I was tired already and we were only twenty seconds into my first practice.

Fortunately, the girls started to do what they were told, and a layup line, led by Kristy Bianco, formed. The girls started shooting and clapping enthusiastically, chanting something about how nobody beats the Blue Jays. I beg to differ, I thought. Up until this year, everybody had beaten the Blue Jays. I was hoping that we could have a decent season, but with me at the helm, it was unlikely.

A ball found its way to me and my reaction time was less than I would have expected, given the amount of time I had spent away from the basketball court. I instinctively threw the ball up from outside the key—a three-pointer if this were a real game and I were actually a player—and watched as it sailed through the air and into the basket. My basketball mojo was coming back with incredible alacrity, which pleased me no end. Someone called out, "Nothing but net!" and I smiled, pleased that I still had "it," whatever "it" might be. Meaghan tossed me her ball and I threw it up again with the same results. Maybe this gig wasn't so outside my skill set after all.

Behind me, I heard the sound of a basketball hitting the floor with such force it was hard to believe that it was being dribbled by a girl on the team or even a human being. I kept my attention on the layup line, noticing how, one by one, the girls stopped dribbling, shooting, and chanting. Finally, I turned around to see one Charlemagne "Fred" Wyatt, decked out in loose sweatpants and a basketball jersey, bouncing the ball on the court. The girls were mesmerized—or terrified, it was hard to tell—by his presence. Jutting from the arms of his jersey were two redwoodlike limbs, the muscles flexing every time the ball left his hands. On his feet were his usual size-sixteen, gleaming white high-topped sneakers, which glistened more than his shiny head. Only after Meaghan went over and gave him a hug around his solid midsection did the rest of the girls relax.

"Uncle Fred!" she called. "Hey! This is my uncle Fred!"

The girls were silent.

"Girls, this is our new assistant interim head coach, Coach Wyatt. Coach Wyatt, the St. Thomas Blue Jays," I said, sweeping my hand to indicate the group of slack-jawed girls who were standing, statuelike, around the backcourt. "Why don't you introduce yourselves?" I didn't know them, so I figured this was as good an opportunity as any to learn their names, which were printed on the back of their warm-up jackets, which would only be helpful if they were running away from me. Which they would probably be doing more and more once they realized my basketball knowledge stopped with "pick and roll," which up until this morning I thought was an order at a sushi restaurant.

An African American girl approached Fred and stuck her hand out. "Hi. Tiffany Mayo."

"Mayo-naise," Fred said.

"Excuse me?" she said, dropping the basketball that was under her arm.

"Mayo-naise," he said, his Brooklyn patois coming out; I rarely heard him speak, let alone speak "street," so it was a little disconcerting. "Didn't you ever see *An Officer and a Gentleman*?"

"No, sir.

"Well, now you're Mayo-naise. Rent the movie. It's a classic."

She looked at her teammates, who were assiduously avoiding her gaze and Fred's. "Next!" he called.

Elaina Bianco came forward; I looked at her a little more closely to see if I had missed any amazing athletic prowess in her. Nope. She was tall, but gangly, and not in a good way. She was about as uncoordinated as anyone I had ever seen, unlike her short, compact, and extremely athletically built sister. "Elaina Bianco."

"Lanie B," he said. She didn't look happy, but then again, I had noticed, she never did. Maybe it was the overbearing father. Or the ego-driven sister. Whatever it was, she didn't seem as if she had had a happy day in her life, and that was just a mild overstatement.

One by one, the girls came up and introduced themselves, after which they were bestowed new monikers. By the time he was done, he had crowned a Sloppy Jo (Joanne Ramirez), Spazzy McGee (Bridget McGee, who didn't seem that spazzy and looked crestfallen at her new nickname), and Cranky Spice (Kerry Harrington, who hadn't cracked a smile since I had met her as a freshman, and whom Fred had aptly named). The other names were equally appropriate and disturbing.

After he was done, he flung the ball at Kristy Bianco, or "Pasta Primavera" for some unknown reason, and it hit her in the solar plexus with such force that I thought she would be jettisoned backward into the bleachers. She caught the ball, held her ground, and glared at him in response. "Let's see what you got, Pasta," he said, and planted himself under the basket, where he waited for her to make a move. She attempted a fake move around him, failed, and her shot met with the palm of his hand, flying over her head and knocking over a garbage can for good measure. "Re-jected!" he said, and glared back at her. I thought he might go a little easier on the group considering they were female and weighed considerably less than he did. No such luck.

At that moment I became convinced that asking former Christ the King basketball star Charlemagne "Fred" Wyatt to help me coach was going to be my Waterloo, except with really tall people.

Ten

When I wasn't thinking about Crawford, basketball, or Kevin, I was thinking about Bill Bradley, the Princeton-educated, former New York Knickerbocker, and senator from the great state of New Jersey.

Don't ask me why.

Aside from the fact that he, in his younger days anyway, reminded me physically of Crawford—tall, clean-cut, and kind of preppy—the resemblance stopped there. Maybe it was because I was constantly thinking about how to keep certain girls on the team in spite of their sketchy academic records and I was wondering how one does well at Princeton while maintaining star status on its college basketball team. Or maybe I was just consumed with thoughts of tall people now that I was nearly always surrounded by lanky female basketball players and one half-Samoan brick shithouse who had renamed himself Coach Chocolate Thunder. Or maybe I was just completely exhausted by my new life, which included teaching, coaching, walking my dog, and not much else; Crawford seemed to be working 24-7. Or maybe because I had fallen asleep a couple of nights earlier after having watched a special on Bradley's career as a hoopster and it had invaded my subconscious in a way that I can only describe as creepy.

I awoke that morning from a restless slumber thinking about something that he had said to me the previous night in my dreams: "The taste of defeat has a richness of experience all its own." Was he trying to tell me that the season was going to be a total bust? If so, former senator Bradley was quite astute, considering he had never met me or any of my Blue Jays. I had tossed and turned, thinking about our next game, which would take place, away, at Manhattanville College, in the same county in which I lived. I looked in the mirror and conjured up Bradley's face. "Focus on offense or defense?"

He didn't respond, which didn't surprise me.

"Rhodes Scholar, huh?" I said, finishing brushing my teeth. I pulled the towel off my wet hair and hung it on the back of the door. "Lot of help you are."

I think Crawford had joined me in bed at some point during the night, but he wasn't there now, and his side of the bed was ice-cold. As I did every morning, I got up and pulled up the shade next to my bed, looking out onto the front yard and the street beyond it to get a sense of what the weather would be for the day. It looked to be drizzling, which was a somewhat surprising development for winter in the Northeast. What was also a surprise was the sight of my husband, in jeans and a dark

Windbreaker, walking down the street, away from the house, one hand in his pocket and the other holding a phone at his ear.

I stood with my hand on the windowsill, wondering where he was going before the sun had really risen and why he hadn't taken his car; I had a rental and didn't need his. Then I wondered if I really wanted to know.

I decided that I didn't and let the shade drop. If he wanted to tell me—if he *could* tell me—he would. That, at least, was my fervent hope.

The practice the night before had gone about as well as it could considering the girls were terrified of Fred, hated their nicknames, and were beyond exhaustion when they left because of his emphasis on running over shooting. Meaghan was particularly spent, and I told her to skip practice the next day if she still resembled the walking dead, assuring her that she would get a few minutes of playing time at the next game even if she didn't attend another punishing session under Coach Chocolate Thunder's tutelage.

I got to school and settled into my office, turning on my computer but avoiding any sites that had local news. Who needs the local news when you have your own personal police detectives either calling you or stopping by regularly? I watched as Carmen and Champy descended the stairs outside my office, knowing that they were headed toward me and feeling that my breakfast wouldn't be long for my stomach. I wondered what they wanted from me now. Shouldn't they be out investigating the murder of Paul/Vito, the unlucky mailman?

Carmen was smiling when she entered. "I hope we're not bothering you," she said, although she didn't really mean it. How could you not be bothered by two homicide detectives visiting you before you'd even had your fourth cup of coffee or seen one dissolute student?

Champy Moran hitched his pants up, as he was wont to do when he had nothing to say.

"Not at all," I said, and gestured toward my guest chairs like Vanna White. "What can I do for you?"

Carmen sat, but Moran stood. "Just a few more questions," Carmen said, obviously in the "good cop" role today even though she had never given me any reason to dislike her. She asked me a bunch of questions that she had asked me several times before. I indulged her, repeating all of my answers word for word. No wonder the mayor was constantly complaining about the overtime paid out by the police department; if even a tenth of the detectives spent their time asking people the same questions over and over, the coffers would be empty in no time. I waited while she took some unnecessary notes, after which she surprised me by standing. "Okay, that's it. Thanks."

"Anytime," I said.

Her hand was on the doorknob. "Say hi to Bobby when you see him, okay?" she said.

"Um, okay," I stammered. "You see him more than I do, though."

"Not really." She opened the door and Moran exited. "He's working another case and he's not around that much."

I tried not to let on that this was news to me. "I'll let him know that you send your regards."

"Great. And just remind me. You've had no contact with Peter Miceli since he went west, correct?"

"None. Are you still thinking that Vito Passella's death had something to do with this?"

"I'm not really thinking anything right now," she said, laughing. Her false cheer was starting to wear on me, and I liked Carmen. A lot. I wondered if I was falling into the "suspect" category and that's why she had come back. I decided I would ask her.

"You?" she said, laughing harder. "You, *chica*, are definitely not a suspect."

That calmed me slightly. "Can I ask you a question?" I went on before she could answer. "How was he killed?" I hadn't really been able to tell, based on the angle in which his body had been placed in the trunk, and while I wasn't sure why I needed to know, I realized that not reading the papers had left me without that little detail.

I could see her weighing how much to tell me. I'm sure the papers had some information, but not all of it. She was short and to the point. "Shot. Execution-style."

"Was he missing his hands and feet?" Dismemberment, particularly of the hands and feet, was a Miceli signature.

"Nope. See why I'm confused?"

I didn't actually, but I didn't tell her that. As far as I knew, execution-style killings were the purview of the Mob. So someone had gotten lazy and forgotten to leave the Miceli signature. In my mind, that didn't mean anything.

After they left, a thick blanket of exhaustion settled over me, even though it was early in the day. I wished I could skip practice that night. My day was crazy-busy with a full teaching load and a lunchtime faculty meeting on the administration floor. As I headed up there after having taught two classes in a row, I ran into Rabbi Schneckstein, coming out one of the doors off the stairwell.

"Hello, Rabbi," I said as he joined me on my ascent.

"Alison. How many times do I have to tell you it's Abe?" he said, his chubby, bearded face lit up in a warm smile. "If you persist in calling me rabbi, I will have to begin calling you doctor."

"Well, we can't have that." Although I have my doctorate in literature, I don't enjoy being referred to as doctor as much as some of my colleagues do. *Professor* suits me just fine if it's one of my students addressing me; as for the rest of them at the school, namely the faculty, I was lucky if they used my first name. I am convinced Sister Mary refers to me as "that one," but I haven't been able to get confirmation on that from anyone.

"You've had quite the . . ." He hesitated.

"Life?"

"Week, I was going to say."

"Sure have," I said.

I stopped in front of the door to the hallway that led to the conference room, and Abe grabbed the handle. He rested his hand there, not opening it; I wasn't sure if we were embarking on some kind of male-female cultural taboo that I wasn't aware of or if he wanted to tell me something. "Alison, I'd like to talk to you."

I waited. Now was as good a time as any. Anything that made me late for the faculty meeting was just fine in my book. "As long as it doesn't have anything to do with either dead guys or basketball, Abe, I'm all ears." Behind me, I heard footsteps on the steps and the very hot Fareed Muhammad brushed past the two of us, giving us a quick greeting, in a rush to get to the conference room. Abe opened the door for him before turning to me.

"You act like a schoolgirl around him," he said, chuckling slightly.

"Is that what you wanted to talk to me about?" I went with my old standby. "I know I'm married, Abe, but I'm not dead." We walked through the door and walked a short distance to the conference room, which was quickly filling up.

Abe took my arm before I went in. "No, that's not what I wanted to talk to you about. But I will call you."

We took seats around a large conference table, our numbers only representing about a quarter of the faculty. President Etheridge scheduled these faculty meetings in small groups throughout the semester, mixing us up so I was always with a different group of teachers, making it easy to find out what the faculty concerns of each department were even though I only taught with a small number of faculty. Today, no Sister Mary, but with the lovely Abe Schneckstein and the hot Fareed Muhammad in attendance, I considered it a good start to a boring meeting.

Etheridge started with the "unfortunate demise" of Coach

Kovaks; thankfully, he had chosen not to talk about the murder investigation going on right under his nose. "I have it on good authority that Coach Kovaks was a victim of a massive cardiac arrest," he said, to a collective groan of sympathy from the twenty or so faculty at the wood-veneer conference table. It seemed as if everyone was more upset at the thought of cardiac arrest than Coach Kovaks's demise. Etheridge looked at me. "Of course, we're awaiting word from the medical examiner, but it is best to consider this matter closed."

All eyes focused on me as I quickly constructed an appropriate response. "A cardiac arrest is a very tragic event. Especially if it ends in death." Obviously.

"It *was* cardiac arrest," Etheridge said, as if I needed a reminder. He nodded solemnly to make his point.

Fareed caught my eye across the table, and I might have imagined it, but I think he winked at me.

"I know," I said. "Very tragic."

"In other words, it was not a murder," Etheridge said. Again, that was directed at me.

"Cardiac arrest," I dutifully repeated so that there was no misunderstanding.

Etheridge continued to stare at me.

"My sleuthing days are over," I said.

"You say that at least once a semester," he replied.

I held up a hand. "Scout's honor. I was there. He had a heart attack. I have no doubt in my mind that the medical examiner is correct in this instance."

"And we are all very happy that you concur with the medical examiner, Dr. Bergeron," Etheridge said, his tone suggesting that he didn't give a rat's ass if I agreed with the medical examiner or not. He mumbled something under his breath that referenced dead bodies and trunks of cars, so again, a comment directed at me and my sad state of affairs. Satisfied that I wasn't going to request an exhumation of the body or bring shame to the school in some other fashion, he commenced with the agenda, which was an exercise in futility. Everyone at the table was overworked, underpaid, and had way better things to do with his or her time than listen to our fearless president drone on. I sent myself to another place where everyone liked me, I didn't have to work too hard, and Crawford could retire with a really nice pension and not have to put himself in harm's way day after blessed day.

"Father Dwyer," President Etheridge said, motioning to the chaplain who had taken Kevin's place, "would you like to lead us in prayer?"

Dwyer was a supercilious phony and I was pretty sure we would never become friends. First, there was his swooping in almost before Kevin had left campus, and then there was his extreme conservatism, which didn't sit well with me at all. In my opinion, he was doing everything in his power to make Catholicism on campus wholly unpleasant, and I wasn't even that good a Catholic, so technically, I didn't have a leg to stand on. Still, I felt I was entitled to my opinion. I had no reason to hate him as much as I did—he hadn't really done anything to me—but I did and he knew it. He avoided my eye as he led the faculty around the table in prayer, making sure to mention Coach Kovaks and his reunion with God in heaven.

I looked around the table as he prayed and saw Abe muttering under his breath at the several mentions of "Jesus" and "his saving grace"; Fareed, on the other hand, his eyes closed, head bent, looked positively reverential.

Etheridge went through his agenda quickly and then yielded the floor again to Father Dwyer, who had remained silent after his prayer. He stood and smoothed back his thick, black hair before speaking. In his hand, he held a clipboard, which he surveyed before he launched into his latest passive-aggressive diatribe centering upon the last Holy Day of Obligation, All Saints' Day, and the lack of faculty attendance at the service. The guy was a master. He maintained his holier-than-thou attitude while treating us like children; I saw the looks on several of the faculty members' faces, and he had indeed shamed them. He leveled his gaze at me. "I understand I can't influence our non-Catholic faculty, Dr. Bergeron," he said, glancing briefly at Fareed and Abe, followed by a nod to Wing Lei, a devout Buddhist, "but attendance is not only requested on holy days, it is mandatory."

I felt my face go red as all eyes around the table focused on me. "And when was All Saints' Day?" I asked, riffling through my day planner—yes, I rock it old-school when it comes to organization and planning—to look at the date.

"When it is every year, Dr. Bergeron: November first," he said, smiling a smile he didn't really mean.

Right. The day after Halloween. I made a mental note to remember that if you're going to try to stall someone with questions, make them questions that don't have an obvious answer. I stared back at Father Dwyer, who awaited my excuse and/or reason for not attending Mass. "I was otherwise engaged," I said. Who could remember? It was months earlier. I had done a lot of living since then.

He consulted the information on his clipboard. "As you were every other holy day last year." He looked up and smiled his fake-pious smile again.

"And your point is?" I resisted the urge to launch into my own diatribe about being an adult and having the right to make my own decisions, but I felt that not only wouldn't it be prudent, but I would sound like an ass, and I didn't need to add any more fuel to that fire.

"My point is that you need to begin attending Mass."
I gave him a little salute. "Got it."
"Starting with Ash Wednesday, which is upcoming."
"Roger."
He waited a moment as it became apparent that we were in a liturgical standoff. "You have no plans on attending, do you?"

"No."

He glared at me with that creepy smiled plastered on his face. It was disturbing enough to make me believe that I might actually go to hell for missing Mass.

"Oh, okay," I said, defeated. "I'll be there. Do I have to learn any new hymns or anything?" I asked, my attempt at humor not appreciated.

Fareed shifted uncomfortably in his chair while Abe passed a hand across his mouth to wipe away a smile. Dwyer, seeing that he wasn't going to gain any traction, put his clipboard down on the conference table, making a racket that woke up the one or two faculty members who were still close to dozing, a little crack developing in his composure. He looked at Etheridge for support, but interestingly, there was none forthcoming. "Well," Dwyer said, his full-blown snit reaching epic proportions, judging from his florid complexion, "I guess we'll have to discuss this later. Would you be so kind as to make an appointment with my secretary at your earliest convenience?" he asked, as if the decision were mine. He looked at his clipboard again and motioned to the two half-sleeping faculty members, singling out one of the math professors, an older guy who had just joined the staff a year ago. "I'd like to discuss this with you, too, Professor Dickman . . ."

"It's Dykeman," he said, glaring at Father Dwyer. I didn't think it was the first time he had heard that mispronunciation, nor would it be the last.

Dwyer didn't miss a beat. "And you, Professor Morales," he said to Mike Morales from the Biology Department. Neither he, nor Professor Dykeman, seemed too concerned about setting up an appointment, which made me think they weren't planning on making it happen.

I nodded dutifully, although I had no intention of seeing Dwyer voluntarily. What did I have to lose? I was already teaching a full load and coaching the basketball team; worst-case scenario would be that they'd fire me after the season, which was midway through the next semester. But I didn't see that happening. Low pay, not-ideal working conditions, and no guarantee of tenure made St. Thomas a wholly undesirable place to teach. I figured I'd use that to my advantage even if I were racking up dead bodies faster than a cut-rate mortuary.

The meeting ended after Dwyer and I faced off. I left with Abe and Fareed, the three of us promising to get together for lunch in the commuter cafeteria in the coming week. As Abe drifted off, Fareed took my arm and gently pulled me toward the rotunda that jutted out over the portico that fronted the building. Beyond us was a gorgeous view of the Hudson.

"That was quite a performance in there," Fareed said, gesturing toward the conference room, where a still-incensed Dwyer was giving Etheridge an earful. When he saw us looking at him, he kicked the door shut with his foot.

"You ain't seen nothing yet, Fareed," I said.

"How is Kevin?"

Although I wanted to say how great Kevin was doing with conviction, I wasn't entirely convinced myself. "He's moving on."

"That's good, I guess?"

"He's kind of . . . at sea," I said, finally coming up with the right word to describe my dear friend.

"At sea." Fareed cocked his head as if he didn't really understand what that meant; I chalked it up to English not being his first language. He surprised me by saying, "I imagine that that is an apt way to put it."

"That's all I can really say." I didn't know if Kevin would be cheered by the outpouring of love for him that I regularly took in for him or if he just wished everyone would forget him and his tenure at St. Thomas. I was pondering this as Fareed looked over my head and quickly bid me farewell. When I turned around, I was face-to-face with Etheridge, which explained Fareed's hasty getaway. I figured I would be getting a talking to after my throwdown with Dwyer and was surprised when I didn't. For once, I was happy to talk about basketball and the Blue Jays' schedule.

"So our next game is at Manhattanville?" Etheridge asked rhetorically. He knew the schedule by heart. Basketball was becoming a moneymaker for St. Thomas, and if he was concerned with anything on campus, it was making money. It dawned on me that Etheridge had a finance background, not unlike our old friend Kovaks.

"That's what they tell me," I said, forgetting that my sense of humor is not one shared by my boss's boss's boss. Or our chaplain.

"And we'll win, right?" he said, flashing what I could only imagine might be a smile. It happened so rarely that I had forgotten what it looked like on him. I had also forgotten that he had a mouthful of expensive implants that were so smooth and shiny that my own teeth probably looked the color of dusty chalk by comparison.

I ran my tongue over my teeth before answering, "That's my goal."

Etheridge considered that response for a moment before scuttling off. I turned and headed for the chapel, noticing a maintenance man hastily return to mopping the floor, having taken a break to eavesdrop on my conversation with both Fareed and Etheridge. I smiled as I passed him.

"Bianco can't shoot from her left," he whispered as I walked by.

"Excuse me?" Between the slapping of the mop on the highly glossed marble floor and his thick accent, I wasn't sure I had had heard him correctly.

"You heard me. She can't go left. Change her position. Keep her left of the basket." He never looked up, seemingly fixated on the back-and-forth motion of the dirty mop head slopping water around on the floor.

"Your left or my left? The left if I'm facing the basket or the left if I'm facing center court?" Footsteps behind me signaled change of classes, and one of the professors who had an office on the floor brushed past me. I looked at the janitor but he didn't return my stare.

I kept walking. As I rounded the corner toward the stairs, I thought I heard him say something else.

It sounded suspiciously like *"El padre es inocente."*

I turned around to ask him what he meant, but in an instant he was surrounded by a gaggle of nuns, each imploring him to visit her office first to fix whatever problem she had. Sister Calista was dealing with a stuck desk drawer, while Sister Louise had a broken windowpane. He caught my eye for a brief moment and then walked off with Sister Calista, who wasn't letting go of him, it seemed, until her desk was in good working order.

I called Abe Schneckstein the minute I returned to my office. "Fun meeting, huh, Abe?"

"Alison, I can't even begin to tell you how much this new chaplain concerns me."

I went through the mail on my desk while he continued to rail about Dwyer. When he was done, I chimed in, "We're stuck with him, Abe, unless we can figure out what happened with Kevin."

"So sad. It's not right, Alison. It's just not right. Kevin was a decent and wonderful man."

"He still is, Abe. It's just that now he's being decent and wonderful to brides and bar mitzvah boys and girls at a catering hall."

With nothing more to say on the subject, Abe went to his other favorite topic: Blue Jay basketball. "Tell me something, Alison. How did the other Bianco sister make the team?" I told him that I had no idea and asked for his thoughts. "I find it very odd indeed. One of my freshmen in the World Religions course was cut from the team, but according to her friends, she was far superior to Elaina."

"Really?" That was an interesting tidbit. "What's her name?"

"Amy Manning. Freshman. Probably going to declare in nursing, if I had to guess. Is still quite peeved over the entire thing. I have to go. A classroom of bored juniors await."

I didn't know Amy Manning but felt that now was as good a time as any to make her acquaintance.

Eleven

My archenemy, Dottie, was doing her best to avoid my presence when I emerged from my office.

"What did I do now?" I asked. "I'm way too tired for our usual game of *What's My Line?* today, Dottie."

"Nothing. You didn't do nothing," she said, swiveling her chair around so that her back was to me.

I leaned against the mailboxes on the wall for support. "Any messages?"

"You have voice mail, don't you?"

Good point. "Yes."

"So why are you asking me? Now that the padre is gone, who's going to stop by and see you?"

Dottie was not the brightest bulb in the chandelier, but she was hardly ever mean. Her curt tone surprised and upset me more than I wanted to admit. She was having an exceptionally bad day if her mood was any indication. I pushed myself away from the mailboxes and without another word, I went into my office, slamming the door shut before Dottie could hear me let out a little sob. She had hit on two things that cut me to the core: first, Kevin was gone and second, I had no real friends on campus now. Sure, I had acquaintances, but Kevin and I had been close, as close as two friends could be. Until I had gotten married, that is. Once Crawford and I had tied the knot, I had to admit that I had spent considerably less time with Kevin than before, and that had coincided with Kevin's ouster from St. Thomas and the priesthood. If I had to be completely honest, I hadn't given him, or our friendship, the attention they deserved, and I wasn't proud of that.

I picked up the phone and listened to it ring on the other end. I decided that I would ask him to come to dinner one night so we could catch up without talking about the messiness that had invaded his life. Admittedly, the last time I had seen him, I had gone to complain about the latest turn of events in my life, and even though I hadn't let loose as I had planned, the thought that I might have been selfish crossed my mind. We needed to spend some time together to discuss what was going on with him. I heard the phone get picked up on his end and I sat up a little straighter, expecting to hear his voice.

Instead, I got the lilting tones of a young woman who was clearly from "across the pond," as they say. "Hello?"

Momentarily stunned, I regrouped. "Um, hello, this is Alison Bergeron. Is Kevin there?" I half-expected her to say that I had dialed the wrong number, even though I was positive I had dialed correctly, but she said that he wasn't home and asked if she could take a message. "Yes. Could you ask him to call me?"

"Does he have your number?" she asked politely.

I assured her that he did, then replaced the phone on the receiver, staring at it for far too long.

I leaned back in my chair. Although the urge was strong to go home and crawl into bed with the covers over my head, my curiosity was piqued. First, there was a pissed-off kid on campus who should have made the basketball team but hadn't; and second, Kevin had a woman in his apartment, which might have shocked me more than revelation number one. Here I was feeling sorry for him and beating myself up for not spending more time with him, and there he was dating girls from Ireland. Go figure.

Instead of going with my first instinct and heading for home, I decided to do a little intradepartmental Web searching. I found Amy Manning's class schedule and saw that she was one floor above me in an Introduction to Sociology class. I waited until about ten minutes remained in the class before meandering up to the fifth floor to the classroom. Through the small window in the door, I saw my longtime colleague Rick Robeson writing on the blackboard, circling something with a flourish. I watched him teach for a few minutes before he dismissed the class. In the usual hubbub at his desk, students handed in papers and got clarification on some things he had taught before they began filing out of the room. Among the fifteen or so students, Amy Manning wasn't hard to pick out: I guessed she was the six-footer who balled up a piece of paper, pretending to take a three-point shot from across the room, which she made. Nothing but garbage can. She saw me watching her and seemed to know instinctively that I was waiting to talk to her.

She sent her other friends away and approached me. "You're coaching the Blue Jays, right?"

She already knew; the whole campus was abuzz about my inept attempts at leading the Blue Jays to the play-offs. I held out my hand. "I'm Professor Bergeron."

She accepted my hand but regarded me coolly. "Amy Manning."

The hallway had cleared out; the fifth floor had only a few classrooms, and most of those were rarely used as they weren't as technologically enabled as the ones on the lower floors. I suspected that if enrollments didn't increase in the future, this floor would be shut down completely. "Got a minute?"

"I guess." She didn't look as if she wanted to talk, so I knew I had to make it snappy.

"I hear that you tried out for the Blue Jays but didn't make it."

"It was down to me and Elaina Bianco and she got the slot." Amy shrugged. "Whatever. I'm over it." But her body language and her intonation told me that she wasn't. Far from it. She was still seething, which was apparent on her pinched face and in the way she pulled her books close to her chest.

"Why do you think that was?"

"I don't know," she snapped. "You tell me. You're the coach."

"Yes, but I didn't make the decision."

"Doesn't matter now. She's on the team, I'm not, even though I was the best in my high school. Does that make a lot of sense to you?"

That didn't make any sense at all, and I would have been happy to have this tall and coordinated girl on my team instead of Elaina, who had done nothing on the court to impress me thus far. "Did Coach Kovaks give you any idea why he might have cut you?" I asked as gently as I could.

I saw her crack when she thought back to whatever he had said. I was surprised when she told me how little it was that he conveyed about her being cut. "He said I could try out again next year. That was it." And then she started to cry.

I looked around anxiously hoping that nobody was lurking

around the hallway, particularly a faculty member who would only see a crying student and me. I didn't need anything else to make me look bad; I had a well-stocked store of bad already at my disposal. I put an arm around her shoulders and let her sob for a few seconds. This was a girl, like so many other student athletes on campus, who had found her niche and purpose through her sport, and to have it taken away—seemingly without any good reason—was a blow. She finally pulled back and wiped her nose on the edge of her long-sleeve St. Thomas T-shirt. "Sorry."

"It's fine," I said.

"My whole family expected me to play for the Blue Jays. I'm a Jew. There's no other reason for me to go to this school other than to play basketball."

"Maybe next year?" I offered hopefully.

She started to walk away. "Yeah. Maybe next year."

I watched her walk away, feeling bad that I had dredged up the whole situation for her again, but not really feeling as if I knew the whole story. One thing I knew for certain, however, was that this thing stank more than the St. Thomas gym after a particularly onerous loss.

Twelve

I was so tired that evening that I rested my head on the steering wheel of the car after I had pulled up the driveway to my house, my hands still at ten and two. Practice had been its usual athletic debacle, with Fred barking orders at girls for whom such language and candor should have been commonplace considering they had played for Coach Kovaks and they were a D-III team. Quite the contrary. Fred's constant harping unnerved and upset them more than it should have, given that he was a 260-pound bag of mush, when it came right down to it. Even Meaghan had looked close to tears at the end of the practice, and

I had gently pulled Fred to the side and had told him that if he didn't knock it off, I was going to kick him in the nuts. Granted, I didn't know what my own coaching style was like, but I knew it didn't entail running a bunch of young women ragged until at least one or two threw up from the exertion. I was hoping the next night's practice would be calmer and more productive.

I had saved two more messages from Lou Bianco, who was still wondering why I hadn't tried Elaina at either point guard or small forward. Or was it point forward and small guard? I couldn't remember. I didn't want to tell him that I still didn't know what either of those two positions were, but I did know enough that I wanted to keep her hands off the ball as much as possible, if not her feet off the court completely. The girl was a disaster when it came to basketball, even if her transcript indicated that she was a dedicated student. I don't know why she felt the need to play basketball when clearly it wasn't her thing. More to the point, I was still chewing over why Coach Kovaks had given her the coveted last spot on the team over the taller, and clearly more able, Amy Manning.

The one good thing that basketball had given me was a reason not to think about Vito Passella, his possible connection to Peter Miceli, and the fact that I hadn't seen or talked to my husband at any length since this whole thing had started. I was so bone tired at the end of every day that the last thing I wanted to do was talk about anything, choosing instead to fall into bed. But sitting there in the dark, thinking about the past several days, I let my mind wander. Who wanted Vito dead? Why did they put him in *my* car? And where the heck was my husband?

I had practically lulled myself into unconsciousness when a tap on my window scared the daylights out of me. I picked my head up suddenly, the blood rushing to my brain and clouding my vision momentarily. When the stars cleared, I turned to see my neighbor Jane, looking worriedly at me from the other side of the glass. I opened the car door and got out, explaining that

I was just really tired and that I wasn't contemplating anything drastic while resting on the steering wheel.

"Thank goodness," she said, the concern etched on her pale face. "I saw you pull up and was going to wait until you got settled inside before I came over, but you've been sitting there for close to fifteen minutes." Her blue eyes telegraphed kindness. "I got worried."

I waved a hand dismissively. "No need. I'm just a little preoccupied."

"Where's Bobby?"

I resisted my usual urge to turn on the waterworks and left it at "Working." My response was short, my tone shorter, and she wisely didn't ask any follow-up questions. The job is intense; I knew that coming in. But I hadn't seen him in a long time or even really talked to him, and I needed him. I was completely unnerved by the Paul/Vito situation, as I now called it, and I wanted Crawford around. For support. For comfort. For his gun, the one in the holster and the one I knew he carried on his ankle. To keep Carmen Montoya and Arthur Moran off my tail, even though they clearly didn't consider me a suspect. Probably.

"I heard what happened at school."

You'd had to have been living under a rock for the last several days not to have heard what had happened at school. I appreciated the concern she was showing, though. It was starting to seem that I commonly encountered dead bodies in my car, but nobody was as wigged-out as I was. Jane seemed to be, but she hadn't really known me when the first one was found.

"I figured you didn't want to talk about it."

"You figured right."

"Just tell me if you're okay."

I steeled my resolve. "I'm fine. Thank you for asking."

But even someone who didn't know me as well as Jane would know that I wasn't fine. Her shoulders tensed in a way that suggested she didn't really believe me, but she wisely let it go. "Anyway, Kathy and I have a bit of a dilemma."

No more dilemmas, I wanted to whine, but I just smiled, letting her know that I was her go-to girl when it came to such matters.

"Our hedge clippers broke and we were wondering if we could borrow yours until we get it fixed?" She pointed toward her house. "The snow did a number on our back hedge, and we really need to cut it back." She shrugged. "Good timing, huh? January?"

I exhaled loudly, relieved. That's not a dilemma. I had dilemmas and they didn't approximate the mild inconvenience of broken hedge clippers. I kept the editorializing to myself, which Jane took to be my being severely inconvenienced by the request. She began backpedaling immediately. "I understand. I know it's an imposition—"

"No. No imposition. Do you know for a fact that I have hedge clippers?" Because I didn't. I started toward the garage. "I try to limit the amount of time I do outdoor work, as evidenced by the dead mums in my window boxes," I said, gesturing toward the front of the house. A bunch of once gold and purple flowers stood erect, in full rigor, in my charming white window boxes, the smell of death emanating from them I was sure. The smell of death emanated a lot around me, it seemed.

Besides trying never to go outside unless I have to, I try to avoid the garage as well. Since Crawford had moved in, the cramped storage space had become something of a minefield. Had I known the guy had as much athletic equipment as he had, I might have reconsidered getting married. Just how many lacrosse sticks does one nonlacrosse-playing middle-aged guy need anyway? Let's not even get started on the basketballs. They came in all colors and various states of inflatedness and were strewn about the garage, serving mainly as a ground-level obstacle course for anyone trying to retrieve any item from a shelf.

I ran the gauntlet around a bunch of boxes that Crawford had stowed, tripping over a rake before finding an old gas-powered hedge clipper. I expected it would do the trick for what Jane needed to do. I yanked it from in between a refrigerator that I had stuck in the back of the garage five years before when I had remodeled my kitchen, an old dehumidifier, and the lawn mower. As I dislodged the mower and pushed it toward Jane to get at the clippers, the door to the refrigerator flew open and hit the dehumidifier, making a racket.

I handed the clippers off to Jane. "Here. I think we're done with yard work for the season, so it's not like we'll need it back anytime soon."

"Thanks. We'll be done with them soon." She started off down the driveway. "When Bobby has some time, let's all get together, okay?" she called over her shoulder.

"I'll call you," I said, making my way into the back of the garage. I went to the back of the garage to close the refrigerator door; I didn't need any varmints taking up residence in there. I had been down that road years before and didn't want to revisit it. I already had enough to handle when it came to the house without adding an exterminator to the payroll again. I pushed the dehumidifier to the side of the garage and pulled the door of the refrigerator toward me, taking a peek in to see what exactly I had left in there all those years ago.

I hadn't left anything in there, as it turned out, but someone else had. I reached in and took a large, padded envelope from the crisper drawer and held it in my hand, its weight surprising me. The envelope was banded with thick elastic and had nothing written on it to indicate what was inside or whom it was for.

I tugged at the rubber band and decided that this was my house and my refrigerator and I had every right to open the envelope. After I did and glanced inside, I was sorry.

I had seen Crawford's guns, and none of them looked like

this, a big, heavy, black weapon with a long, cylindrical mechanism sprouting from the front. A silencer. On a gun that only someone who didn't want anybody to know that they were going to be killing would use. I had watched enough detective shows to know that if you wanted to kill someone as silently as possible, you used a gun like this.

I held it in my hand for a few minutes, frozen to the spot in the garage where I was standing. I finally put it back in the envelope and into the crisper drawer, noticing now how much noise everything seemed to be making in the quiet of a suburban evening.

Everything was topsy-turvy, and nothing made sense to me anymore, but I did know one thing: I wasn't going to tell Crawford about this recent discovery. Between his clandestine visit to the garage for a secret conversation and this, I had a feeling he didn't want me to know a few things.

I flashed on the badge in the nightstand drawer, the one that he was supposed to have with him when he went to work. I thought about the woman whose voice I'd heard during our last phone call. I wondered about his cryptic answers to my questions about work, the ones that used to get me an hour-long diatribe about the bureaucracy of the police department or the stupidity of the masses.

Given all of that, I still wasn't sure why, but I didn't want him to know what I had found.

And that scared me more than the sight of the gun in my hand.

Thirteen

Crawford was drinking a cup of coffee when I came down the next morning. I had feigned sleep when he had arrived home past midnight, freezing a little bit when he pushed my hair off of my forehead and gave me a sweet kiss. He looked up when I entered, surprised to see me dressed for work.

"Isn't today your late day?"

I poured myself some coffee and leaned against the counter, trying to look nonchalant even though I was anything but. "I have a meeting."

"Really? With who?"

I attempted a joke. "That's 'with *whom*.' "

"With whom?"

"Sister Mary."

He relaxed a little bit. "How's the old battle-ax?"

"You're going to go to hell for that."

"I'm going to go to hell for a lot worse," he said, and returned his attention to *The New York Times* on the kitchen table.

My mind flashed onto the gun with the silencer in the crisper drawer in the garage. That image, coupled with his comment, made me tense up. "I'd better go."

He stood and reached out for me. "Are you sure?" he asked before he leaned in and kissed me.

"I'm sure," I said, but truthfully I wasn't. We hadn't spent a lot of time together in the past week or so and I missed him. As hard as I tried, though, I couldn't get the image of the gun out of my head. Why was it there? And who put it there? I knew who put it there, but I didn't want to give it a voice because that would make it indisputably true. So the question was "Why?" I pushed him away, pulling at the chain around his neck. "Hey, St. Michael is hanging down your back." I made sure the gold medal of the patron saint of police officers hung right between his pecs. "I was thinking. Next time you've got a few days free—"

He interrupted me with a lascivious "Yes?"

"I was thinking that we should clean out the garage. You know, get rid of that old refrigerator. The dehumidifier." I studied his face to see if it gave away anything. It didn't. He's got a great poker face. "It would be nice to be able to park a car in there. Yours, in particular. You know St. Thomas closes at the first sign of snow, so you could put your car in there and be ready for when you need to go to work."

"Not what I was thinking when you started this train of thought," he said.

"I know, but it's been bothering me what a mess it is."

He sat back down at the kitchen table. "I'm not sure when I'll have some free time to tackle that very important task, but feel free to get started without me."

So it was going to be like this: we'd see each other sporadically, and when we did, he'd expect one thing, while I would expect another. I didn't like the way things were going now that he seemed to be working around the clock and possibly on the Passella case. Or not. I thought back to Carmen sending her regards to him through me. There must have been times before when they didn't see each other; why had she felt the need to make a pointed comment like that? Things had been strained since I had discovered Passella. Now, Crawford dropped in and presumed everything would be just as he'd left it and I couldn't accommodate. I also couldn't figure out how this had happened so quickly. Oh, right, the gun where the avocados should have been and the guy in his eternal rest next to my eco-friendly grocery bags. Maybe that was it.

I'm not sure about a lot, but I was sure that having a gun with a silencer stowed in the refrigerator was not normal or usual. Oh, and that I wouldn't tell him also wasn't par for the course. I tell Crawford everything. Well, almost. I never told him that the Christmas sweater he had gotten me the year before—the one with actual jingle bells on it—had been given to Goodwill almost immediately upon my opening it. Or that I hated when he whistled.

I stood next to him, awkwardly, for another minute before heading toward the back door. "So I'll see you when I see you?"

"That's kind of how it works," he said, not looking up from the paper.

I let myself out, thinking that we were on two totally different pages and wondering how we had gotten there so quickly and without warning.

Dottie was her usual ray of sunshine when I arrived at the office. I decided not to ask her if I had any messages because we had been through the whole purpose of voice mail the day before. Her iciness was surprising to me because it indicated that something was bothering her, and if I had learned one thing, nothing ever bothered Dottie, particularly when it came to work. Therein lay the problem with our relationship. I gave her the most perfunctory of greetings and scuttled away to my office, where although I had posted office hours I remained behind closed doors.

I immediately picked up the phone and called Max.

"So what would you do if you found a big gun with a silencer in your lettuce crisper?" I asked.

"Give it to Fred. It would probably be his."

"Really?" Maybe I hadn't painted the picture correctly. "What if the lettuce crisper was in a refrigerator that you hadn't used in five years and that was in your garage?"

"Give it to Fred. It would probably be his," she said, as if this were the most obvious answer. I guess it was, when you thought about it.

"Really?"

"No, actually. We don't have a garage because we live in an apartment so it would be completely out of the realm of possibility to have a refrigerator in a garage in a house we don't live in."

I had no response to that so I started at the beginning, right where Jane knocked on the window of my car and ending with my finding the gun in the envelope. Max was silent the whole time. After a few extra seconds of silence, she spoke.

"You do know that you're married to a cop, right?"

"Of course I do."

"Then you do know that one of the items he needs for his job is a gun, yes?"

"I'm not a complete idiot, Max," I said, something that I remind her of at least once or twice a year. "His regular guns come in the house with him. When's the last time Fred put his gun in an odd place?"

"That's a little personal, don't you think?"

I wasn't being euphemistic and told her so.

"I still think it's personal."

"Forget it." I pushed back in my chair and stared out the floor-to-ceiling windows that took up one whole wall of my office. Students were arriving to the main building, where I had my office and taught, the first class of the day beginning shortly. "Do you see what I'm getting at here?"

"I guess."

"Say it."

"You're wondering if he's having an affair. The gun is a metaphor for your mistrust. You're wondering if you did the wrong thing by marrying him."

Sometimes that woman can be so obtuse. But in this case, she was half-right; I had been wondering why he was working so much but hadn't let my mind wander completely to the thought of his having an affair. "I'll talk to you later," I said, and hung up, swinging my chair around to face my desk. I put my head in my hands and took stock of my thoughts, which didn't amount to much. I had a head full of miscellaneous facts and half-truths concerning my best friend and my husband, and I didn't know where to turn. Instead I focused on what I knew, and that was school. I pulled a stack of research papers from my messenger bag and got to work on them.

No more than an hour later there was a persistent knock at the door. I didn't bother to get up, thinking that it was a student who needed help during office hours and wouldn't stand on ceremony. If it was a student, I was actually surprised that he or she had knocked; students usually just barged right in. After I beckoned the guest to come in for a third time, the door finally opened. Crawford leaned in. "I hope I'm not disturbing you."

The tension that I'd been holding in my shoulders melted away and I stood, taking his hand. It was old Crawford, the lanky altar boy whom I had fallen in love with when he first appeared in the doorway of my office to question me about a murder, admittedly not the way you want to meet your future husband. "Come on in."

He hesitated. "I know you don't teach until noon and I'm starving. Want to get something to eat?"

I pushed the thought of the gun out of my mind, but not before thinking that there had to be some kind of reasonable explanation for its existence and location, and followed him out of my office.

I came out from my behind my desk and gave him a long kiss, thinking that this might be a good time to discuss my discovery. I pushed away suddenly, my hands on his chest. "You smell like Chanel No. 5." One thing I love about Crawford, and one of the reasons I fell in love with him, is that he always smells really clean. I don't know how he does it, but his scent is nothing short of olfactory perfection for me. Today, he smelled like the perfume aisle at Bloomingdale's, his scent mixing with a powerful odor of what I consider old-lady perfume but what is really a classic in the world of French cologne. I have been known to wear it myself, but lately I had switched to a more musky scent at the suggestion of Kevin, who said I smelled as if I were a dowager on her way to confession.

"Huh?"

"The perfume. You're reeking of it."

He picked up his arm and smelled his cuff. "I don't smell it."

"You're probably desensitized to it, but trust me," I said, crossing my arms over my chest, "you smell like you took a bath in the stuff."

"I have no explanation. Maybe the car I'm using had a female detective in it the last time?" he said, his explanation not entirely convincing. How many homicide detectives, or even undercover detectives, wear French perfume?

I didn't know quite what to do with this, so like many times in the past several days I decided to ignore it. But with all the work he seemed to have inherited, coupled with his disappearances and strolls down the street at the wee hours of the morning, this gave me pause. I had hugged Carmen and she didn't smell like Chanel No. 5.

"We're not done with this," I warned.

He put his hands up. "I have no idea why I smell like women's perfume. Trust me, it's better than what I could smell like."

I didn't want to go to that place, where viscera and bodily fluids were commonplace, so I opened my office door and gestured for him to exit.

We didn't have much time, and on St. Thomas's campus, not too many choices. We decided to eat at the commuter cafeteria on the first floor of the building where I had a long-standing relationship with the kitchen staff. They know I eat a lot, and that is our secret. Marcus, the head chef, gave us both a hearty hello when we entered and instructed us to take a table by the window and allow him to whip up something special.

The best thing about St. Thomas is its location adjacent to the Hudson River, and that is also the best thing about the cafeteria. Crawford and I took a seat by the windows, as Marcus had instructed, and gazed out over the long expanse of green lawn that rolled right down, almost, to the river's edge. When Crawford had taken in all of the nature that he needed, knowing where he would spend the rest of his day, he looked at me. "I know I've been working a lot. I know this isn't easy."

"You're right. I'm doing my best." I couldn't lie and say that it was easy. It was anything but. "You know your job sucks, right?"

He nodded and smiled. "Nobody knows better than I do."

"Are you working on the Passella case?"

"A little bit. Champy and Carmen are on it," he said, reciting a line I had heard a few times before. "I've got other things going on."

"How come Fred has all this free time and you're not around at all?"

He weighed his words carefully. "I'm being pulled in a couple of different directions."

Most of which take you away from me, I thought.

"And Fred's got his own stuff going on. He's just better at time management than I am, I guess."

I went for broke. "Tell me what you're doing."

He looked down at the Formica table and traced some kind of pattern with his middle finger. "I can't."

"Anything?"

He looked up at me, his face sad. Marcus appeared with two cheese omelets and perfectly toasted wheat bread. Orange slices fanned out beside the omelet. "Enjoy!" he said, disappearing into the kitchen before we could properly thank him.

Crawford reached across and took my hand before I could grab my fork. "I wish I could tell you more but I just need you to trust me. Everything will be okay."

The food on my plate, while appearing to be delicious and satisfying, sat untouched. "I wish I could believe you." I thought I said it out loud, but when he didn't respond, I had to think that I hadn't. He dug into his food and turned the conversation to the next game, asking when it was. "Tonight. Manhattanville in Purchase."

"How's it going?"

I shrugged. "Really not my forte, truth be told."

"Fred?"

"A giant pain in the ass."

"Welcome to my world."

I filled him in on the Elaina Bianco/Amy Manning story. "Why do you think Kovaks would put her on the team when he had a better player, from all accounts, right in front of him?"

"No idea," he said. "Why don't you try out Manning, and if she is better than Elaina, give her the slot?"

I got sick at the thought. "I can't do that."

"You can do whatever you want." He poked me in the shoulder. "You're the coach."

"Don't remind me."

While he ate both his breakfast and mine, I texted Meaghan to let her know that we were in the cafeteria if she didn't have class and could get over to see her father. Just as he finished his sixth slice of toast, she appeared in the doorway and called, "Daddy!" running over and throwing her arms around him.

"Will you be at Manhattanville tonight?" she asked once she had finished covering his face in kisses.

His eyes caught mine. "I'm not sure, honey. I'm going to give it my best shot."

She looked disappointed. I saw the conflict on his face, and it was unlike any expression he had given me since he had started working day and night. Anger flickered across my consciousness momentarily, but I pushed it aside. When I thought about it logically, my guess was that he thought I could handle it and Meaghan really couldn't.

On that account, he was dead wrong.

Fourteen

The gym at Manhattanville College was packed with spectators, and I was a little overwhelmed by the charged energy for our first game with me as coach. The games at St. Thomas are low-key, with Mary Catherine selling M&M's in the hall, and the opposing team getting dressed in the biology lab that had been placed, oddly enough, next to the main gymnasium. We were relatively new to the circus that was D-III basketball and extremely unprepared. I could only imagine what D-I and D-II basketball were like and hoped never to find out. The bus ride over had taken place in complete silence, the girls having heard that the Manhattanville team was heavily stacked with big girls with amazing skills. I had planted myself right behind the bus driver, busily reviewing the playbook, while Fred grunted what he seemed to think were motivational gems to the players in the seats behind us but amounted to no more than "Don't be babies!" Or this precious gem: "Make your foul shots!" I wondered if this was the advice he had followed to become an All-City basketball player. Even my imaginary boyfriend, Bill Bradley, had better advice than that, and he was a hallucination.

Finally, I had pulled Fred down into the seat beside me and begged him to be quiet. After he had settled down, I asked him if he knew what Crawford was up to. I told him that Crawford said he was "being pulled in a few different directions." I hoped Fred knew what that meant.

"No clue," he said, staring straight ahead.

"Seriously, Fred. What could they possibly have him doing?"

"I don't know. I told you that." He sighed and the scent of garlic filled the air. "I have no idea."

"You guys are still together, right?"

"For the most part. Lots of murders. Lots of change. Lots of investigating. Sometimes we don't see each other for hours. Days even."

Same here, I thought. "There must be talk around the squad." I leaned over Fred so I could look out the window to get a bead on where we were and ascertained that we had about another ten minutes before we got to Purchase. "From what I've seen, you guys are like a bunch of old ladies at a nursing home. You talk. And when you have nothing else going on, you talk some more."

He continued to look out the windshield, ignoring me.

"Please."

"You should be concentrating on getting ready for the game." He adjusted his position in the seat, and I saw a gun on his ankle, just visible beneath the cuff of his gray dress pants. I didn't think the Manhattanville coach and staff would be entirely happy to know that the assistant coach on the opposing team was packing heat, but I wasn't going to say anything.

Once in the gym, I instructed the girls to start their warm-up. In the stands, I could see Fareed and, next to him, Max, who caught my eye and gave me a thumbs-up in addition to a wink in Fareed's direction. Fareed had let me know earlier in the day that he was coming to support us. It helped that he lived in Purchase and wouldn't be going too far out of his way to see the team fall in defeat to a squad of girls who looked as if they ate hills for breakfast and crapped mountains after lunch. Fareed looked over at Max and gave me a tentative wave, clearly nervous, as he was surrounded by Manhattanville fans and one hot-to-trot woman married to the Neanderthal assistant coach.

Lou Bianco glared down at me from high up in the stands and I looked away, not needing to be under the constant gaze of a very involved basketball parent.

The girls took their practice shots, and with five seconds left on the scoreboard, I called them over to do a pregame prayer to the Blessed Virgin Mary, who I figured wouldn't let us down unless she was otherwise occupied with working on the whole world-peace thing. Just as we had finished our devotion, the lights dimmed, and music started to play, startling all of us. The girls froze in place.

I was old enough to recognize a Temptations song playing over the loudspeaker: "Get Ready." I used to dance to it in my bedroom after my parents had gone to bed, but that didn't mean that I was happy to hear it in this context. The Manhattanville team apparently had a well-orchestrated pregame ritual that included Motown songs, dancing, clapping, and intimidation, judging from the faces of the girls standing next to me. A squad of about twenty cheerleaders, both men and women, took to the floor and began a cheer routine/dance number that brought the spectators to their feet. Bridget "Spazzy" McGee, her arms now slack, dropped the ball that she was holding under her arm and it rolled to center court. The announcer began calling out the starting lineup, who, if I hadn't heard correctly, I would have assumed were the five wives of Paul Bunyan, given the size of their thighs. Fred went into a ridiculous falsetto, attempting to sound like Eddie Kendricks, and executing some ridiculous bump and grind; he seemed to be the only person enjoying the show, forgetting that he was on the opposing team. I threw an elbow into his side, which felt about as pliable as a side of beef hanging in a meat locker, and implored him to stop.

I looked over at our starting lineup, Meaghan included, and took in their saucer eyes. Some of them had been exposed to these kinds of theatrics on their high school team, but they were a relatively young team and came from St. Thomas, a school not known for its street cred. Heck, we were the *Blue Jays*. The name alone was enough to get us a huge beatdown. Meaghan looked over at me and gave me a wan smile.

I pulled the girls back into a huddle and we linked our arms around each other's shoulders. Fred was on the outside of the circle, now dancing to the Lenny Kravitz song blasting over the loudspeaker. "Okay, listen," I said. "So they've got a lot of this kind of"—I looked for the right words, shouting to be heard over the music—"BS going on, but let's see what they've got on the court. You guys have been practicing your behinds off, and this is not the time to be intimidated." I looked at them. I regretted having to go to curse words—or curse abbreviations—but I thought the situation called for it. Elaina Bianco looked as if she was on the verge of tears, and I thanked God that she wasn't a starter, even if her father thought she was the second coming of former UConn star Rebecca Lobo. If the physique of the Manhattanville starters was any indication of their skill, and my guess that Elaina had never played basketball before was correct, she would continue to ride the bench. I started my players in the St. Thomas chant: "Saint"—clap, clap, clap—

"Thomas"—clap, clap, clap—"Blue"—clap, clap, clap—"Jays!" Yes, horribly inferior to Manhattanville's light-and-pyrotechnic show, but it's all we had. The chant was followed by an ridiculous collective squeal and a synchronized jump in the air. After that, we all stood, and I clapped a few of them on the back or backside, depending on where my hand fell. Meaghan grabbed my arm before she went in for the first jump ball and asked if I thought her father would show up.

"I don't know, Meg. Just play basketball," I said, at a loss for anything else. I looked around the now-illuminated gym and spied Lou Bianco again, who gifted me with a surly gaze, in part no doubt because I hadn't started the less-than-skilled Elaina, never returned his phone calls, and wouldn't respond to his e-mails. How many ways are there to say "She stinks"? To my surprise, the St. Thomas janitor I had encountered the day before was also there. I now considered him my "Deep Throat," given his information about Kristy Bianco's inability to go left and Kevin's innocence. I made a mental note to track him down and find out (a) how he knew this information and (b) why he was following the St. Thomas Blue Jays. I scanned the crowd for Crawford and came up empty. But I did lay eyes on the guy from the game—the one I had bumped into at the candy counter—when Kovaks had collapsed, who looked as if he was interested in anything but basketball, and that gave me pause. I knew I knew him from somewhere, but I couldn't figure out where.

Meaghan, wearing the most ridiculous-looking face guard to protect her broken nose, squared off at center court to take the jump ball, which, amazingly, she won. She batted the ball to Kristy Bianco, who headed down the right side to our basket and executed an easy layup. Max, Fareed, Lou Bianco, and the Deep Throat janitor went wild.

Unfortunately, that was the best the team looked all evening. The game disintegrated quickly, and I flipped through my rule book to see if there was a "mercy rule" whereby if the opposing team was ahead by more than fifty points, the game would be called.

Sadly, there was no mercy rule in basketball.

But apparently, there was crying. And lots of it.

We filed out of the gym, the girls in their matching St. Thomas Blue Jays warm-up suits, Fred carrying both equipment bags across his expansive back. He heaved them at the bus driver, who, after stumbling backward under the heavy load, stowed them in the cargo hold of the coach bus. The girls mounted the steps of the bus one by one, one more disconsolate than the other. Fred banged on the bus door, getting their attention.

"It's one freaking game!" he called. "Move on!"

I grabbed him by the arm and pulled him to the side. "Fred! No need to use the F-word even if it's not the real F-word. You're not at the squad. These are kids."

He looked down at me, and I got a sense of what it might be like to be guilty of a homicide and knowing that the guy gazing down at me knew, but I held his gaze. "This is D-III basketball, Alison, not CYO. There's a lot at stake here."

"Well, if there was that much at stake, they would have hired a professional coach and not thrown a literature professor into the job." A light freezing rain had started to fall and I could feel my hair blowing up to twice its size. "Get on the bus."

I followed him up the steps and counted the number of heads in the seats, discovering we were missing one. I consulted the roster and figured out it was Meaghan. I descended the bus steps again and looked around the parking lot and saw her a few feet away, her arms around Crawford, who was standing next to his car. A few feet from them were Deep Throat Janitor and Lou Bianco, an interesting duo, to say the least. Their conversation was serious, by the looks on their strained faces. Was it their mutual love of basketball that bound them or something else?

"I didn't know that you had made it," I said, approaching them.

"I only caught the last two minutes," Crawford said. He took Meaghan's arms from around his shoulders and instructed her to get on the bus. "I'll be home in an hour or two. Wait up?"

"I'll do my best," I said, thinking that exhaustion had overtaken me to the point that I would never get enough sleep to feel rested again.

When all was said and done, I was too wired to sleep. It didn't matter. He never came home.

Fifteen

Our horrific loss was splashed over every paper, local or otherwise. Fortunately, the story of St. Thomas's history-making failure to score points hadn't made it into *The New York Times,* but judging from the other papers that hit my driveway every morning around five o'clock, it was big news. I wanted to be happy to be in the paper for something other than a discovery of a dead body, but this felt worse. It wasn't as if I had gotten used to finding dead bodies and having my name tossed around so casually, but when I thought of the girls on the team and how hard they worked, the news of their horrible loss left me feeling responsible.

Apparently, we had set some kind of record for a point differential in a D-III basketball game. To my thinking, if there was any time to institute a mercy rule, it was now.

At least some good would have come out of this big, giant mess.

I had three messages from Lou Bianco, all having been placed before the sun was up. I didn't call him back. There was nothing to say.

Aside from avoiding every single person I had met in my entire life, my goal for the day was to find Deep Throat. I didn't have to look far, because Sister Perpetua, a faculty member in the nursing department, had demanded that her office be repainted while she took a group of students on a clinical rotation at a local hospital. Perpetua's office is right next to mine, and despite Deep Throat's best efforts to avoid my gaze as I walked past the office to get to mine, my lie about needing a lightbulb changed at his earliest convenience got him in there in twenty minutes' time. That gave me just enough time to come up with a line of questioning. Seeing his frightened expression, however, made me lose my train of thought.

As soon as he was in my office, I slammed the door shut. "Talk." I peered at the name embroidered on his blue work shirt. "Luis. Talk, Luis."

"*No hablo*—"

"Yes, you do *hablo*. I heard you. You said Kristy Bianco can't go left, and on that account you were totally correct. And although my knowledge of Spanish is rudimentary, I believe you said that Father McManus is innocent." I glared at Luis in the same way I glare at Fred when I want him to fall into line. It worked on Fred only sometimes. Okay, it hardly ever worked. The effect on Luis would have been comical if it hadn't been so sad; he looked as if he was about to faint.

His English was accented, but not much; my late French-Canadian parents had had thicker accents. "Listen," he said, dropping the poor-workingman routine, "you have to keep Bianco out of the backcourt. She's slow and she has a tendency to double-dribble. Let McGee take the ball in and act as point guard. She's got much better ball-handling skills. I was working in the gym during some of Coach Kovaks's practices."

"But Bianco's our star." And McGee is kind of spazzy; Fred was right. "I know we've only played a couple of games, but she's got more points this year than any other girl on the team."

"When she's got time to set up the shot, she's the star. When she gets the ball in the backcourt, she rushes and plows through the middle and always loses the ball." Luis looked down as if he had regretted being so candid.

I considered this. I hadn't been around the team that much, and as a player Kristy had a tendency to suck the oxygen out of the room with her growing ego, but Luis had a point. "I think you're right. Why do you know so much about St. Thomas basketball? Just a fan?" I asked, thinking, *Or just a perv?* What adult would be so interested in women's college basketball if he didn't have some kind of pervy agenda?

"My friend's daughter is on the team. Tiffany Mayo?"

"Mayo-naise?" Fred's nicknames had unfortunately stuck so much that at times I couldn't remember the girls' real names. Luis looked at me quizzically. "I'm sorry. That's the nickname Assistant Coach Wyatt gave her."

"She's a senior so I'm hoping that she has a good year."

Me, too, I thought, but for different reasons, most of them selfish. If the girls lost every game—particularly those playing in their last year—I would feel terrible until the end of time.

"What do you know about Elaina Bianco?" I asked.

"Nothing," he said quickly.

"How long have you been following the team?"

"I don't know . . . a season or two?"

"Did she play before this year?" I already knew she hadn't, but I wanted to see how good a fan Luis was.

I could tell that he didn't know what I was getting at, but he answered me honestly. "No."

"And you know their father?" I asked, remembering that I had seen the two talking outside the game the night before.

He shook his head. "No," he replied unconvincingly.

"I saw you talking last night."

He pointed to Sister Perpetua's office. "Can I go? I have a lot of work to do."

I moved around from behind the desk and stood close to him, my hand on the doorknob to thwart a getaway. "One more thing. What do you know about Kevin?"

At this, his anxiety kicked up a notch as evidenced by the film of sweat that broke out across his forehead. Clearly he was in his element talking St. Thomas Blue Jays' basketball, but giving it up when it came to Kevin? That was causing true physical distress. "I don't know anything. I don't know why I said anything."

"You're lying." I crossed my arms over my chest. "About a lot of things. Not smart, Luis."

"I'm not," he protested. "I just think Father McManus is a good man and I don't want anything to happen to him."

"Listen, Luis, what's going to happen to him already has. He's about this close"—I held my index finger and thumb just millimeters apart—"from getting laicized. Do you know what that means?"

Luis shook his head, avoiding my gaze.

"It means that he'll be thrown out of the priesthood, the Catholic Church, and lose everything he loves. He'll have a black mark on his record that will follow him wherever he goes for the rest of his life. He probably won't be able to be within fifty feet of a child," I said, making up the last part for effect. Kevin wasn't being accused of pedophilia—that much I knew—but I wanted to drive home just how serious the whole situation was. "And even if he is exonerated, he'll always be the priest who was fired from St. Thomas." I tapped Luis on the shoulder to force him to look at me. "You still sure you don't know anything?"

He shoved his hands into his pockets. "I'm sure." He made a move toward the door, and even though in my heels I had a good four inches on him, I couldn't prevent him from leaving.

I heard the door in the next office close and the sound of a roller hitting the ancient wall that Perpetua and I shared. I walked over to the wall and put my hand on it. "We're not done, Luis," I called, not sure if he had heard me or not.

The phone rang. Max. "You guys really stink."

"Thanks," I said, taking a seat behind my desk.

"No. You *really* stink," she said as if I had misunderstood her the first time.

"I know. Cut us some slack. We've had a tough season." I pushed back and put my feet up on my desk, crossing my legs at the ankle. I let my head loll back over the top of the chair and pinched the bridge of my nose between my fingers. "What would you like me to do exactly?"

"Coach like you mean it!" she said a little too forcefully. "Take it seriously!"

What about my demeanor led her to believe that I wasn't taking it seriously? I didn't have to answer. She told me.

"You're moping around like you've got the weight of the world on your shoulders. And you're acting like you're in a complete holding pattern." She paused to take a breath; she was on a real roll. "These girls aren't in a holding pattern, and even if Etheridge putting you in this job was the most harebrained idea anyone in the history of the universe has ever had, you have to *make it work*."

Wow. When the girl focuses, she really focuses. She was actually making a little sense.

"Now, do you want my help or what? You've got the Joliet game coming up soon, and that's a big one. You *need* my help."

"I didn't know you were offering. And, plus, don't I already have Fred?" I figured that was the most help I was going to get.

"Listen, I've got connections. Remember Jamal Sanders?"

Remember Jamal Sanders? I spent a portion of every day trying to forget him. Max had dated him when we were seniors, and he was the star of the Joliet basketball team. Joliet had been St. Thomas's brother school before the two schools went coed and merged into a fairly cooperative arrangement where students could go back and forth as classes required. The Joliet men had been D-I since the good old days and participated in late rounds during March Madness more often than not. Jamal Sanders had spent a good portion of our senior year in our dorm room, most of the time stoned on what appeared to be some potent pot. He wasn't a bad guy, just immature. But I would never forgive him for being so stoned that he thought he was using the men's room only to pee on my bed, something I only learned of after I fell into bed one night, exhausted, after working a huge party in the Sisters' dining room. I swore that I couldn't get the smell of Jamal Sanders's urine out of my nose until I was about twenty-five.

My silence was enough to convince Max that I did indeed remember Jamal Sanders.

"You know he played for the Utah Jazz? He just retired, as a matter of fact. Blew out his knee. Crying shame."

They must have loved him in Mormon country. "So what?"

"He can help you coach."

"Fred's helping me coach."

"Yeah, but we know it's all about Fred. How much help could he really be?"

That was the most sensible thing that she had said since I had picked up the phone. And a complete change of tune since she had spoken of his "rockin' Afro" in my kitchen what seemed like a hundred years ago.

"Well, you just let me know. It's one phone call."

I would have to be pretty desperate to have Max call Jamal Sanders on my behalf, but I told her that I would take her suggestion under advisement.

"You still mooning around about Crawford not being around? And that stupid gun?"

I could feel my blood pressure rising. First, Jamal Sanders, now this. "Yes, Max, that's exactly what I'm doing. 'Mooning around' about my husband not being around and stashing guns around my house."

"*Gun.*"

"Okay, gun." I'd give her that. "Fred hasn't said anything to you about Crawford not being around that much, has he?" Although I had had the discussion with Fred, he may have been holding back; he's not known for his forthrightness. I figured if he had told anyone, it was Max.

"No. Why would he?" Hard to tell over the phone, but I suspected that she was telling the truth.

"Do you think there's a possibility he's undercover?" I asked, grasping at straws. This thought had occurred to me during the middle of the night and had seemed not only realistic, but the perfect solution, at three thirty in the morning.

Max snorted, letting me know that she didn't think much of that idea. "What kind of undercover operation needs a cop who looks like a cop?"

She had a point, one that I had eventually settled on when I had a cup of coffee and was thinking clearer. Crawford would never be mistaken for a member of the general population with the way he looked. He had COP stamped all over him.

"But let's mull this over for a minute. Maybe he's investigating bad practices at a chicken-processing plant," she said. "That wouldn't be dangerous. Or maybe he's involved in some kind of undercover sting for designer knockoff pocketbooks." That would explain the perfume smell.

"I'm sure that's what it is, Max," I said wearily.

"Or maybe he's investigating—"

"Bye, Max," I said, and swung my legs off the desk.

I went back to engaging in my favorite pastime, which involved daydreaming while looking out the window that faced the cemetery. I wondered how I was going to make this basketball thing work. I wondered how I was going to keep Fred in line.

I wondered if Kevin truly was innocent or if I was committing career and personal suicide by trying to find out the truth.

I wondered if there was a reasonable explanation for the gun in my garage.

I wondered if I would ever get the answers to the questions I repeatedly asked myself.

Sixteen

Before I left for the gym, the mail came, a daily event that filled my mind with dread. The new mail guy, hopefully not a Mob-connected hit man, handed me a large box of books that I had requested from a publisher's rep who had called on me. I stowed it on top of my filing cabinet, noticing the envelope that Paul had handed me in what seemed like the last century but was really only the week before. I hadn't remembered it until just this minute and figured I should open it up in the presence of Fred since it was connected to a murder victim; all these murders had taught me something. I was late for practice, so I tucked the envelope under my arm and raced across campus on foot, the backs of my pumps digging into my heels by the time I arrived; once again, I had no suitable clothing packed for an evening of basketball. I still hadn't really accepted the fact that I was a coach, and I was so distracted that I left every day without noticing the bag that I had packed with gym clothes right by the back door. The girls, already assembled by the time I hobbled in, looked at me curiously as I called out, "Who wears a nine medium?"

My wearing inappropriate footwear was not an uncommon occurrence so I wasn't surprised when three pairs of Adidas sport sandals were tossed my way. I put on the pair that looked the cleanest and was the least likely to give me foot fungus, hoping that I was correct in my assessment. I let off some steam by throwing up a few baskets, stunning the girls by sinking a shot that I took at half-court. My arm strength, lacking at the first practice, was returning, and that cheered me.

I shared with them my latest Bill Bradley–ism: "Ambition is the path to success. Persistence is the vehicle you arrive in." They were unimpressed. "Okay, how about 'There has never been a great athlete who died not knowing what pain is'?" Still nothing. It was a relatively nice day, so I told the girls to go outside and warm up by running a two-mile loop around the campus; first one back didn't have to do the suicide drills that Fred insisted would "build character" and that I insisted would "build resentment." I didn't think it was outside the realm of possibility that the girls would return as one, thereby making it impossible to declare one winner. In case they couldn't come up with this on their own, I whispered this possibility in Meaghan's ear before I sent them on their way.

Fred made his way in through a throng of running girls, slapping hands with those who passed him. He was still dressed for work in gabardine trousers, a starched white oxford, and a blue blazer, his plainclothes uniform, as it were. He cleans up pretty well. If you can get past the scowl and the overall general poor attitude, he doesn't look as much like a serial killer as he could. As he got closer, I noticed his tie had orange basketballs stitched into the dark blue fabric. It seemed as if he was taking his responsibility to the team seriously.

"Where are they going?" he asked, looking after the bunch of extremely energetic girls.

"Outside. Hey, you're all spiffed up." I was used to seeing him in his giant sweatpants and sneakers at practice, not work clothes. I put a hand on his lapel to smooth it down.

"Have to go back to work."

"Busy night?"

"Triple/double."

That was Fred-speak for a triple homicide, two surviving gunshot victims. I was learning. In the past, I thought it meant triple-digit runs batted in, double-digit stolen bases, and I think in the baseball world, that's the general consensus. Or maybe it was something about baskets, assists, and rebounds in basketball. Who knew? All I knew that was in the homicide world and to Fred, it meant something completely different.

"I'm going to the hospital to interview the survivors. Hopefully, they'll still be survivin' by the time I get there. Carmen can handle it until then," he said. I wondered how Carmen was attending to anything else besides murder investigations; she was on the Passella case and now this new case? That was one busy woman. I wondered if her husband suspected her of having an affair or if he accepted more graciously than I did about Crawford that she worked her butt off. A thought occurred to me. "Hey, Fred. What does Carmen smell like?"

He didn't miss a beat. "Tacos."

"Really?"

"Yep. Woman smells like a Mexican food truck half the time. She cooks dinner for her kids before she comes to work, and I'm guessing her kitchen doesn't have good ventilation." He took off his jacket and sat beside me on the wooden bleachers. "Tacos," he muttered, shaking his head. "How's it going?"

"It's going." I was thinking about Carmen. If he could identify her smell as a taco smell that easily, he certainly wasn't mistaking it for the scent of Chanel No. 5. Tacos have a pretty distinct odor.

"Still in a funk?"

I looked at him. Instead of his usual look of disaffection, I was surprised to see that he actually looked concerned. "Nope," I said, straightening up from the slump I had been in. "Feeling great. I would like to win a game, but that's another story."

"We'll win." I wished I had his confidence. He pointed to the envelope next to me. "What's that?"

"Let's find out together, shall we? This was the last thing Paul, or should I say Vito, handed me before he ended up in my trunk last week."

Fred bristled. "And you didn't turn it over with the other evidence?"

"I didn't remember. I was a little stressed, Fred." Lame excuse, but true nonetheless.

"That's not good," he said, and I suspected that that was a massive understatement.

I dug around in my purse for the Swiss Army knife that my father had given me for my sixteenth birthday. My father was nothing if not practical; while most girls I knew were given jewelry or a nose job or some kind of token of their parents' undying affection, I was given a gift that would save my hide countless times. Try opening up a bottle of wine with diamond stud earrings. Can't be done. I slid the smallest blade under the flap and made a neat slice in the envelope, making sure I didn't ruin anything inside. I held the envelope upside down, and as I suspected, a few photographs slid out from between two thick pieces of cardboard. One was of Kevin, standing in front of his house. The other was of Crawford outside a restaurant that I had never been to and didn't know, his foot atop a fire hydrant while he talked on his phone; a woman stood beside him, glaring at him with a look of impatience that I thought was my purview alone. She was wearing a formfitting black wrap dress and high heels. I suspected that she was the one who had bathed in Chanel No. 5. She was way more attractive than I was, and a lot thinner, it should be noted. She had money and lots of it, judging from the bejeweled watch hanging from one wrist, which looked as if it cost as much as a semester at St. Thomas.

A note that fluttered out after the photos was equally cryptic: *How well do you know these two men?*

I looked at Fred, but he had taken the same class that Crawford had on neutral facial expressions. He stared at the photos on my lap for a moment before reaching into the pocket of his sport coat and pulling out a pair of rubber gloves that had seen better days; the thumb of one was stained blue, and the index finger on the other had a hole in it, but for what he needed them for, they operated just fine. He put everything back into the envelope without a word and gingerly placed the envelope on the bleacher behind him.

Fred asked the last question that would have entered my mind, given that the woman was no one I knew. "Why didn't you open these before now?"

I thought I had already clarified that, but apparently it was such a dumb move on my part that he had trouble understanding. "I had forgotten. I don't know if you noticed, but there's been a lot going on." I looked back at the envelope and asked Fred the question that hung in the air. "You know her?"

Fred continued staring at center court. "Nope."

"Could she be an undercover?" I was still thinking that the best theory about Crawford's disappearing act had something to do with his being so deep undercover that he was doing and saying things that he normally wouldn't. Maybe this woman was along for the ride.

"I guess."

"Could she be a perp?" The word sounded funny coming from me.

"We prefer to call them *suspects*," he said, even though I knew that wasn't true. It was a nonanswer any way you sliced it. "Or *persons of interest*."

"She's pretty attractive." I punctuated the observation with a casual laugh that came out a little choked and a lot forced. "If I were a man, she'd be a person of interest for me."

"Don't jump to conclusions."

Have we met? I wanted to ask him. Conclusion jumping was practically an Olympic sport where I was concerned. In my mind, I was signing my name to my second set of divorce papers, giving up on men completely, and moving to Canada, where I could make cheese with my relatives, speak French, and live with women who had far more facial hair than your average Hasid. It would be a different life, sure, but having failed at two marriages, it would be the one I deserved.

"Can I run some prints?" he asked. "I'm sure Carmen and Champy will want to see these, too."

"By all means." I tried to hold back, but couldn't. "And find out who she is." I chewed on my lip, figuring that if I bit too hard, I would have an excuse for the tears that had sprung to my eyes. "Vito Passella was shot, right?"

"Yep," Fred said, apparently deciding that we shouldn't have this conversation. "Come on. If anyone knows that, it's you." His eyes wandered around the gym, finally settling on the hoop closest to the door, anything to not look at me.

"What kind of gun was it?"

"Why?" he asked, looking back at me. "You in the market?"

I decided to tell Fred about the gun in the salad crisper, and he listened closely without saying a word. He also listened without reacting, but something behind his eyes told me that he didn't think it was normal or aboveboard to stash firearms in an old refrigerator. I told him about Crawford not being around as much and seemingly working a bunch of other cases, some of which he already knew. I asked him if Crawford had been around less and if they had been separated on purpose. He didn't really address any of that when I was done, though. All he said was "You know, we are apart more than we're together these days," and by the way he said it—sullenly with a trace of resentment—I could tell that mine was not the only relationship in trouble.

"He's still one of the good guys, right, Fred?" I asked, chuckling nervously. I was only half-kidding.

He didn't answer, choosing instead to start dribbling a basketball between his legs.

"Right, Fred?"

"They've been after him awhile," he said, still dribbling.

I walked over and grabbed the ball, flinging it behind me. "Who? The Mob?"

"No, OCCB." He picked another basketball out of the bin at center court and resumed dribbling. "I think the only reason that he stays in the squad is for me."

"Who's OCCB?"

"Organized Crime Control Bureau." He sank a three-pointer. "Guess what they do."

"Control organized crime?"

"Bingo."

"What does that have to do with Crawford?"

He dribbled around the key and hoisted up a few more shots, which, ironically, seemed to make him more talkative. I would let him keep playing his solo game of H-O-R-S-E as long as he kept talking. "Don't know. All I know is that it could possibly have a promotion attached to it."

This was the first I'd heard of this, but a bigger pension when he did finally retire wouldn't be a bad thing. "And why wouldn't he take the promotion?"

"Because of me." The ball bounced loudly off the rim, the first shot he had missed. "They don't want me."

"You're a package deal. I always knew that. OCCB should know that, too."

"Yeah," he said, looking up at the hoop and tossing the ball up, nailing a three-pointer. "Thing is that I have a reputation of not playing well with others."

"No!" I said, feigning disbelief. "How could anyone think that?"

The look on his face told me that he was in no mood to joke. "They wanted him. They didn't want me. So he always stayed."

I didn't need to ask why he went this time. That was obvious; it brought him closer to the Passella case and possibly let him keep tabs on Peter Miceli and his doings from jail. "Do you think he's already working for them and you just don't know?" Seemed to be a question that needed answering.

Fred shrugged before he threw up another three-pointer. "Hard to say. I know he did make a few trips out to Queens."

"Queens?"

"That's where they're located."

"OCCB?"

He ran a layup. "Yep."

I walked a circle around center court, my thoughts swirling. "Why wouldn't he just have told us if he was working with them?"

Fred shrugged. "Maybe because he's not?"

Which begged the question "Then who?" but that didn't need asking. Or answering. I asked Fred to pass me the ball, and instead of getting to the bottom of the mystery that had become Bobby Crawford, we played a game of one-on-one that I was winning when we heard the sound of young female voices reverberating in the hallway of the gym.

"Hey, you know what?" he asked, stripping me of the ball at the top of the key.

"What?" I asked, winded, and doing my best to cover him as he drove to the basket.

He threw up a brick, missing the rim completely. "You're not bad."

The girls came back from their run, as one, as I had suggested. I told Fred the deal that I had made with them, and although he looked disappointed at the thought of not running them into the ground, the thought of interviewing the gunshot victim was more appealing. We ended practice earlier than we should have with the Joliet game being right around the corner, but our hearts weren't in it, for different reasons.

I high-fived Kristy before she left, our new ritual. I attempted to do the same with Elaina, but she slunk off, her hair hanging in her face, looking as sad and lonely as anyone could when surrounded by a bunch of jocular, gregarious girls. I almost held her back to see if I could find out what was wrong, but before I could, her sister grabbed her arm and pulled her out of the gym.

I didn't expect Crawford to be home, and in all honesty I was hoping he wasn't. My mind was wrapped around the pictures in the envelope, and as strange as the image of Kevin standing in front of his house was for its lack of drama, the picture of Crawford engaged in a conversation while a pissed-off woman stood beside him was the real deal-breaker. Case or no case, undercover or not, some things just weren't right. And that was one of them.

I pulled up the length of the driveway and was surprised to see my wayward husband emerging from the garage.

"You're home early," he said, looking more shocked than he probably wanted to let on.

"Hello to you, too," I said. He was dressed in his work clothes, an outfit that was almost identical to Fred's, except for the basketball tie; Crawford's was your basic rep tie with gold and blue stripes. He strode over to me and wrapped me in a big hug; I could feel a bulge in his breast pocket and could only assume that it was the gun from the crisper drawer, even though I wasn't sure where his regular guns were. When he was home, one was usually in the shoulder holster, hanging from one of the kitchen chairs. That had taken some getting used to. I knew what his guns felt like under his clothes, and they didn't feel like this. "What are you doing in the garage?"

"I was thinking about clipping the hedges," he lied.

"In January?" I asked. "Hedges are fine. And it's dark," I said, taking my bag from the backseat of the car and slamming the car door with a little more force than was required. "Besides, Jane has them." I walked toward the house and let myself in through the back door. "And you really shouldn't be clipping in your work clothes," I pointed out helpfully, dropping my things on the counter.

Something flicked across his face—guilt?—but he quickly composed himself and asked me what I wanted to do for dinner.

"Why? You cooking?" I asked.

He smiled, and I had to remind myself that I was really mad and confused. "I could, but we know how that usually turns out." He leaned in and kissed me. "I'm taking you out," he said, and it felt somewhat normal again.

It was on the tip of my tongue to ask about the gun—never mind the brunette in $500 shoes—but if I didn't, everything would be back to normal, or so I had convinced myself. I looked up, but no Damoclean sword hung from the kitchen ceiling.

At some point I simply had to trust him, admittedly not my strong suit. It took everything I had, but I pushed what I was feeling beside and let things coast into the space that had brought me to be with him in the first place.

I thought back to the note, its origins unknown: *How well do you know these two men?*

I wasn't sure.

Seventeen

The weekend passed uneventfully, mostly because I threw my-self into figuring out how to coach the team while Crawford continued doing whatever it was that he was doing. He was in and out of the house the whole weekend, taking phone calls on his cell in the backyard, rummaging around in the garage, and doing God knows what most of the time. I tried to ignore that we were coexisting on separate planes, and the more work I did, the less I thought about what was going on in the house.

I texted Fred upon awakening on Monday morning: "Any-thing on pix?"

His response a few minutes later was characteristically terse and bitchy: "Leave me alone. I was sleeping. I will call you later."

That was pretty clear. I put my phone on my nightstand and studied the face of the man who I alternately loved with all my heart and felt that I didn't know at all. He was sleeping soundly next to me, on his side, his face inches from mine, seemingly untroubled by the things that troubled me.

"I hate it when you stare at me when I'm sleeping," he said without opening his eyes.

"Sorry. It's six thirty. You should get up."

"I'm going in late," he said, stretching his arms over his head. "What's your schedule?"

"I have to get up," I said, even as he was pulling me back down onto the bed and into his bare chest. Fighting was futile; I was out of my sweatpants and T-shirt in minutes and trying to bring myself back to a time when being with him was the safest place I could be.

A half hour later, I was in the shower and he was back to snoring away in our king-size bed. I snuck out and got dressed quietly in the closet, springing out when I heard my phone start vibrating. I lunged across the bed and grabbed it from the nightstand, waking Crawford and knocking his ancient clock radio to the floor.

It was a text from Fred. "Is this what your gun looked like?" he wrote, attaching a JPEG of a gun. I waited while it loaded, staring intently at the screen and trying not to think about Crawford at my back. The gun loaded onto the screen, and even with poor resolution and a minuscule area on which it could be seen, I could tell it was identical to the one I had found in the refrigerator.

I stared at the screen and tried not to look as if I were going to vomit. I don't know how Fred had gotten that information in the time since we had last seen each other, but he was crafty like that. He had probably had time to interview the gunshot victim on the other case he was investigating and enjoy a nice steam as well. He's nothing if not a multitasker.

The bond between partners can be thicker than that between a married couple, and sometimes I suspected that Crawford and Fred were closer than my husband and I would be. They had been together far longer than we had and spent more time together than we ever would. They shared everything, I presumed, even though neither was known for his communication skills. So I wondered why Fred had offered this up. Was he hurt by Crawford's imminent departure to the unit that he himself wanted to be in or was he telling me something else? Was he getting suspicious now, too?

Crawford was coming back to life just as I was deleting the text message. "A message from your boyfriend?"

I laughed nervously. "What?"

"Why else would you have deleted it so quickly?" He yawned. "Is it that hot guy in the Business Department who always makes you sweaty? Professor Tall, Dark, and Handsome?"

"His name is Fareed Muhammad and he's not that tall."

"Oh, okay. Is it him?"

I scrambled off the bed, ignoring Crawford. I rummaged through the bottom of the closet for a pair of shoes that would be appropriate for school while soothing my sore feet at the same time. While I was digging around in the airlessness of the closet, I tried to rearrange the expression on my face to one of indifference, unstudied and natural. I wasn't sure if I had succeeded. I pulled out a pair of low, black pumps with a kitten heel and slipped them on and pulled a scarf from the drawer, which I tied around my neck. With my black pencil skirt and cardigan sweater, the addition of the scarf made me look like a stewardess. I turned around, trying to breathe normally despite that all I could see was red.

Crawford apparently agreed. "Are you beginning beverage

service soon? Where's the closet exit? What do I do in the case of a water landing?"

"You start swimming." I pushed a bunch of papers aside on my dresser, trying to locate a necklace.

"You've been really distracted lately," he said, sounding a little wounded.

Me, distracted? Pot, meet kettle. I located the necklace and pulled it over my head. I walked back to the bed and lay on top of him, planting a long kiss on his lips. "Better?"

"You can't stay home? I remember a time when you would call in sick at the drop of a hat."

I pushed myself off him and started for the hallway. "When was that?"

"Back in the day when you didn't delete text messages the minute you received them."

I hesitated at the door to the bedroom. I wasn't the one who was photographed with a pissed-off-looking brunette in stilettos, but I didn't want to bring that up. I also wasn't the one hiding a gun in the garage. "It was Max. And she used a lot of curse words. I hate when she does that."

"What difference does it make? Nobody's looking at your phone."

"I'm a teacher and a basketball coach," I started before stopping myself from going further. My back was still turned to him. "And why am I explaining myself to you? I deleted the message. It's not a big deal."

That's how we left things: him rolling over to go back to sleep and me agitated over the text from Fred and Crawford's reaction to it. At least I had forgotten, momentarily, about Vito Passella.

When I was in the car, I dialed Fred's cell. "Yo," he said.

"Anything else on the photos? The note?"

"Nope. Not a print, not a postmark. Nothing. I gave them to Carmen and Champy for further review."

"And who's the woman?"

"Nobody knows."

"Who did you ask?" I asked.

"Don't worry about that. Just let it be known that nobody that I know has ever seen her before, which could mean one of two things: (a) she's an undercover or (b) she's not."

That was helpful. I started the car. "Should I be worried?"

"About what?"

About the woman! I wanted to scream, but I didn't. It was too early to start sounding as needy and paranoid as I felt, so I tamped down those feelings in favor of the ones where I feared getting whacked by the Mob. "About everything. About Crawford," I said softly.

"Leave that to me."

I didn't have a choice.

Eighteen

I was in my office later that day when there was a knock at my door. The new mailman came in and handed me another box filled with textbooks. I supposed there would come a time where I would actually have to open the boxes, review the books, and make a decision, but for now they sat in a corner of my office, unopened and not reviewed. And maybe there would come a time when getting the mail wouldn't be a fear-inducing activity that made my heart stop every time I heard the sound of the mail cart's wheels squeaking in the vast anteroom to my office.

I cracked open the anthology that I was currently using for

class; it fell open to an excerpt from *The Liars' Club*. That was appropriate. I decided that I would assign that to my Freshman Composition class; maybe I could learn something about the mind of a liar. I headed off to class, trying desperately to regain my emotional equilibrium while thinking of the unidentified woman from the picture.

Outside my classroom, I caught the eye of Luis, my janitorial Deep Throat, mopping a small patch of mosaic over and over, obviously avoiding my gaze. "Hey, Luis!" I said, sliding over to him. "Lay off the wax before someone kills themselves," I said, grabbing on to a marble column for support. "Listen, I need your help." I outlined my request; I wanted him to keep his ear to the ground about Kevin and, even though he had no reason to help me, I figured I had made it very clear that I would stop at nothing to clear Kevin's name. If anyone had access to the goings-on at school, it was this intelligent, yet invisible, maintenance man. And if I had learned one thing from my father— other than the value of carrying a good Swiss Army knife—it was that people in the service sector were often overlooked by members of white-collar society. My father had heard and seen more during his tenure as a UPS driver than one brown-shirted package carrier should have. "You have anything, anything at all, that you want to tell me?" Sure, it was a reach; why would he volunteer information? I would have liked to have been more specific, but I didn't have anything to offer.

He looked chagrined, lowering his voice as a group of students flew by. "I'm sorry I told you anything to begin with."

"Well, you did. And now you're in this thing with me, and I think you know more than you're letting on."

He laid his mop against the marble column. "I don't want to lose my job. My wife and I have two kids to put through college, and if I work here, they go to school here for free. Do you know what that's worth?" he asked, any vestige of the old "*no hablo*

English" Luis gone in a flash. "Listen, if I hear anything, I'll let you know. Right now, I got nothin'."

Once I set my mind to something, I'm pretty single-minded, but seeing his concern that his job would be at stake because I just couldn't stop snooping made me pause. "Okay," I said. "Got it. Forget that I asked." I took my hand off the column and straightened up. I was on my own, a situation with which I was not unfamiliar. "Are you coming to the game tonight?"

"If I can get out of here on time," he said pointedly, letting me know that my harassing him about some information he may or may not have had was seriously impacting his ability to finish his work.

I saluted him. "Fine. Consider me gone." I headed off down the hall toward the back staircase, which was the last public area before you hit the convent on the other side of the big dining hall. I took the stairs two at a time, hoping that I would get to class before the students had hightailed it out of the classroom. When I arrived, a few stragglers were lingering in the hallway, but the majority of my students had left.

My day ended after I had taught three more classes of completely disinterested students, thinking that if their ennui continued the next day, I would cancel classes for the rest of the week. I guess Crawford was right: my work ethic stank. I decided to head back to my office to refuel before the Concordia game. The day could not have started any worse, with my earlier conversation with Crawford taking center stage, so I prayed for a win to bring my outlook back into the positive realm. We hadn't exactly argued, but it certainly didn't embody the way we usually spoke to each other. I didn't know if I would see him at the game, but I didn't care as it related to me. I was only concerned that he show for Meaghan, who was starting to get a little high-strung about her father's job and how she saw him less than she ever had, the fact that she and her sister were shuttled back and forth between their parents for the majority of their young lives.

How well did I know him? I thought better than I knew myself. Was I wrong? Had I ever been right?

I closed my office door, kicked off my shoes, and pulled open my desk drawer, where I found a giant chocolate bar that I had stashed there at the beginning of the semester. I pulled the wrapper off and leaned back in my chair, milk-chocolate goodness dancing on my tongue as I consumed the entire candy bar, giving no thought to my waistline, the size of my thighs, or my double chin.

When I was done, I swung my chair around and stared out the bank of floor-to-ceiling windows that comprised one whole wall of my office. I had to right the ship that was my marriage, formerly a sturdy vessel that was now filled with holes and taking on water. Was I within my rights to give Crawford an ultimatum, such as "Tell me everything or it's over"? I was getting crazy just thinking about the secrecy, but more so because Fred was unnerved and had kind of sold Crawford out to me. That was concerning, but there were other things, too. There was the secret phone call. There was the gun. And the brunette. I mulled this over as I watched students walk up and down the back staircase behind the building, seemingly without a care in the world.

I reminded myself that I had married one of the good guys, and nothing could change that.

I didn't think so anyway.

How well did I know him?

I had to ask myself, when do you stop giving someone the benefit of the doubt and start looking at things for the way they really are? I had asked myself this question more than a hundred times during my first marriage, and when it became apparent that the truth of the situation overruled my never expecting anyone to renege on the trio of "love, honor, and obey," I had kicked his ass to the curb. Obviously, things weren't like that with Crawford, but I also wasn't ready to take everything he said at face value, something I had done—to disastrous results—with my late ex. To say I was gun-shy was both a bad choice of words and about as accurate as you could get.

The phone rang several times before the signal reached my consciousness. I turned around and grabbed the receiver. It was nearly four thirty and my thoughts turned to my boss, Sister Mary, who wouldn't be happy that I had canceled a class, but I had failed to let the call go to voice mail and had committed to having a conversation. I was surprised when I heard Fred's deep baritone on the other end.

"Won't be at the game," he said.

I was disappointed. I had a good feeling about our chances that night and was hoping he would be there to help me coach the girls to a win. "Too bad. I think we can win this one, Fred. Work?"

"Yep."

I never expected many details from Fred, but the one-word answer was mildly concerning. "Anything you want to tell me?"

I could practically hear the wheels turning in his brain on the other end. Finally he said, "You're going to find out eventually."

My body went hot, then cold.

"We've got a situation. It's Lou Bianco."

Nineteen

Fred was right. I would have found out eventually.

News on a small-college campus travels fast, but I had no idea how fast until minutes later Meaghan burst into my office. Considering that I had learned the news from the investigating homicide detective on the case, I was surprised that she, too, had heard the news. That was the only thing to explain her visiting my office, a room she avoided if only to make sure she never ran into Sister Perpetua, who scared the bejesus out of her. "Did you hear what happened?" she asked, her cheeks flushed with either the cold or the thought that she had a tragic, but juicy, piece of news to share. It was hard to tell.

I don't know why, but I chose to play dumb. "No. What happened?"

"Mr. Bianco was beaten. He's in a coma." She flung her backpack onto one of the guest chairs and flopped down into the other one.

"What happened?" I asked, genuinely interested; Fred hadn't given me any information to speak of, hanging up after delivering the news of Bianco's assault. I didn't know why Fred was involved if it wasn't a homicide; he said Crawford was on the scene, too, and that made me feel better if only because I knew where he was. The one thing I wondered about was why Crawford hadn't called me and Fred had, but that was a discussion for another time.

"Nobody really knows. The girls' mother came by school and told them. Tiffany told me that Elaina screamed so loud that the whole floor could hear it."

Mrs. Bianco? That reminded me—I had never seen her. "The girls have a mother?" I was still a little shaken by Fred's call and that Meaghan knew more than I did even after having spoken to one of the detectives on the case. Obviously the girls had a mother. Why had I never seen her?

Meaghan was still breathless, but not breathless enough not to respond as if my question had been the stupidest she had ever heard. "Of course they have a mother."

"I just mean . . ." I decided to go down a different path. "Do you know what happened?"

Meaghan leaned in, her elbows on her knees. She looked around anxiously. "According to Tiffany, it was a robbery." Her knees went up and down in a spastic rhythm; despite trying to play it cool, she was a wreck and who could blame her? It wasn't every day that a friend's parent was the victim of an assault so bad that they had been left comatose. The news had rattled her. "He owns a check-cashing store and someone broke in and beat him up."

I ignored the queasiness that was roiling in my stomach. I focused on the obvious question. "How did Tiffany find out?" I asked, doubting that Mrs. Bianco had allowed Elaina's roommate to stay in the room when she delivered the news.

Meaghan blushed a little deeper, betraying that the answer to this question wouldn't color Tiffany in the best light. "She was kind of listening at the door."

It didn't matter ultimately. I found out what I needed to know—that Lou Bianco had been beaten—a little sooner than I needed to know it. I consulted the folder in front of me, the one that held the numbers of all of the coaches at the various D-III teams in the area and called the coach of the Concordia team to cancel. While I was on the phone, I studied Meaghan's face, her eyes still black-and-blue, her nose still swollen, and watched as a swell of tears grew in her eyes, threatening to spill out at the slightest provocation. I gave the coach only what she needed to know and asked that she help me out and deal with whoever at the county level needed to be alerted that the game was canceled. The refs needed to be called and the game would either have to be forfeited or rescheduled; I didn't really care which. Fortunately, she was more than happy to help, which is more than I could say for some of the other coaches in the league, who would probably have told me to handle it myself while chalking up a W. I hung up and sent an urgent e-mail to the rest of the team, copying the athletic director. I turned my computer off. "Come on," I said, getting up from my desk. "We'll go to dinner. Are you hungry?"

The tears that were threatening sprang forth. I kicked the door closed with my foot and Meaghan fell into my arms, sobbing in that breathless, gasping way that is painful to witness, even more painful if you're the one crying. She was mumbling into my shoulder, but I made out one sentence: "I want my mother."

Me, too, I wanted to say, but instead, I sat her down and pulled a bunch of tissues out of the box on my desk. The one good thing about having a small office is that you can basically execute any task from a sitting position, be it filing, typing, answering the phone, or using the trash can. We sat like that for a long time, side by side, watching the lights come on next to the cemetery, illuminating the road that wound through the campus, waiting for her tears to subside. She blew her nose loudly. "I'm sorry," she said finally.

"About what?"

"I don't need my mother. I have you," she said, but in a way as if she didn't really believe it. She was trying to make me feel better, and that wasn't necessary, given the circumstances. I appreciated the sentiment and effort nonetheless.

"It's not the same," I said, and took in her relieved face. "I married your dad and you inherited me, and while I would love for you to consider me something like a mother, you have a mother. And she loves you very much. I would never do anything to suggest that our relationship was the same." Meaghan started crying again and I waited while she got it out. "Mr. Bianco's situation scares you, doesn't it?"

She nodded. "I worry about my dad."

I was honest with her. "I do, too."

"You do?" She swiped the wet wad of tissues across her nose.

"You'd better believe it." I took her hand. "But then I remind myself that he's smart, he's careful, and he does everything by the book." I wasn't so sure on that last part, but I gave it a great line reading. "And he's got Fred. Who would hurt him with that guy around? Oh, and he always gets to the bodies after they've been killed. I forgot that part."

She started laughing. "Right. What could happen with all of that?"

A lot, I thought, as I said, "Nothing." I stood again and grabbed my coat from the back of the door. "Dinner?" I asked again.

"Would it be okay if we didn't and I just went back to the dorm?" she asked, a little tentative. Unlike her sister, she went out of her way not to hurt my feelings.

"It's fine. Call me later if you need to."

She grabbed her backpack and started for the door. "Thanks."

"De rien."

"Huh?"

"Aren't you in first-year French?" I asked, pushing her out the door and into the main office area. "Sheesh. Go get dinner before the dining hall closes." That she understood. She took off across the polished hardwoods, skidding to a stop by the door to the office area, looking every bit the kid that she was. She gave me a little wave before disappearing into the stairwell.

Luis was standing on the landing above, mopping as if his life depended on it. "I guess you heard?"

He nodded solemnly, still mopping.

"Heard anything beyond the basics?" I asked. The stairwell was overheated, but it still didn't explain the flush in Luis's cheeks.

He shook his head. "The Bronx can be a violent place."

"True."

"Lots of money at a check-cashing store."

"It was a robbery, right?" I asked.

"I guess. Sounds like that was the motive."

"Okay. Let me know if you find out anything. You've got your ear to the ground, Luis, and I am counting on you."

I went back into my office to get my bag, hearing the phone ring and giving it a second's thought as to whether to pick it up. I decided to answer it and was happy to hear Kevin's voice. There was no preamble or greeting. "Did you see the news? About that guy who got beaten? It's Lou Bianco."

"Wow, bad news travels fast."

"It's all over the TV news."

"Fred called me. It's awful. Are they saying anything about what happened?"

Kevin related the same story that Meaghan had about the break-in at the check-cashing store. "It doesn't sound like they have any suspects. I caught sight of Bobby at the scene." It wasn't a homicide. Why had he been there? I wondered again. "Has he lost a lot of weight?"

I wouldn't know, I thought. I hadn't seen him in a while. "Yeah. He's doing South Beach," I lied. I changed the subject. We didn't know a lot about what had happened to Lou Bianco but would soon, I suspected, if Loose Lips Fred Wyatt had anything to say on the subject. "So, Kevin, who was the young lady who answered the phone the other day when I called?"

"A young lady answered the phone?" he asked as if that weren't even a remote possibility.

"Quit stalling. Yes. And unless your cleaning lady sounds like a perky Irish national, you have some explaining to do."

"Alison, she's my cousin. She's staying with my mother, but since my mother doesn't have a computer, she uses mine when I'm at work. It must have been Aileen."

That was far less dramatic than I was expecting. "Oh. That makes more sense than you having a girlfriend."

"Why?"

"Because you're a priest and you probably shouldn't be dating," I said, thinking that that was obvious. I didn't know what he was driving at. "Hey, do you want to have dinner?"

"Name the day."

The game was canceled and I didn't have anything to do. Crawford would be working, something he seemed to do all day, every day. "How about tonight?"

"Works for me."

"Steak House?" I asked. The Steak House was Kevin's and my favorite place when he worked here.

It was his turn to hesitate. "Somewhere a little more off the beaten path, perhaps?"

I understood. It wouldn't be good for him to be seen in the immediate vicinity of school, so we picked a place in between the East and West Bronx that would be close to both of us but that wouldn't attract too many people associated with St. Thomas. It would be just like old times, except that now Kevin didn't want to be seen by anybody remotely related to the school. I tried not to dwell on that as I cleaned off my desk and prepared to leave the campus.

I skidded into the Irish restaurant that Kevin and I had agreed on an hour later, stressed and a little late. Kevin was already at a table with his ubiquitous glass of chardonnay in front of him, making short work of the contents of the bread basket while he waited for me.

I took my seat across from him. The waitress appeared and I ordered a martini, figuring that by the time dinner was consumed, I would have my wits about me and would be able to drive home completely sober. I also planned on eating a giant steak, the news about Lou Bianco having done nothing to dampen the ardor I had for restaurant food, particularly rib eyes smothered in herbed butter, a dish that I had had at this restaurant before. While I waited for my drink, I told Kevin—chubbier than ever, if that was possible—about the events of the day, including my conversation with Meaghan. He was suitably shocked and then chagrined. "Maybe this wasn't the best night for dinner."

I put my hands up. "*Au contraire*. This is the best night for dinner."

"Does Crawford ever get a break? The mayor is constantly talking about how crime is down, but the crime rate around here seems to be skyrocketing. And murders? Don't get me started. I mean, you alone—"

"Yes, I know one of the more recently murdered victims. Do we have to go there?"

We agreed that we didn't. Dinner was pleasant enough and I had to admit that Kevin seemed a bit happier than he had previously. Was he finally getting used to this new life, the one where he was just a member of society, not beholden to the vows of his ordination? Having a pleasant dinner with him, I had to ask myself, did he even want me to get to the bottom of his situation? I grabbed the check from him when it arrived and put my credit card in the envelope, holding it out for the waitress. She swept in and took it, leaving us alone for a few more minutes.

I steered the conversation back to the team and to the horrible situation regarding the Bianco twins' father. "You probably know some of the girls on the team," I said, listing a few of them until I got to the Bianco sisters at the end. "And the Bianco sisters. Elaina and Kristy. Do you know them?"

"Sure," he said, laughing. "The school's not that big, Alison. They're twins, right?"

"Right. Big Catholics, are they?"

"No more so than the rest of the heathens at the school," he said, the smile still on his face.

"Huh," I said, signing the check when the waitress brought it back. I looked up. "Interesting, those two."

"How so?" Kevin asked, polishing off his wine.

"Well, Kristy's quite the player, but Elaina . . . well, how can I put this kindly?" I asked. "She seems a little out of sorts on the court."

"Not everyone is suited for basketball. You know my brothers. All big-time athletes, but except for boxing, I am hopeless." Kevin, a small, myopic kid, had been given boxing lessons by his mother so that he could protect himself on the mean Bronx streets.

"That's the funny thing. I have no idea why she made the team."

Kevin didn't respond, and it was in that silence that something went unspoken.

The silence went on far longer than it should have, and I looked at my watch as a diversion. "Will you look at the time? I have to run." I stood. "Kev, I'll call you."

I hurried out of the restaurant, more at loose ends than when I'd got there. Something in Kevin's eyes had suggested to me that he knew the Bianco sisters more than just in passing but he wasn't at liberty to say, a rule left over from his time as a priest. Anything anyone had told him in the confessional or just in counseling was kept in his mental vault, never to be discussed.

It had been on the tip of my tongue to ask him about Peter Miceli, but I was at that stage with everything in my life where I felt like the less I knew, the better. I thought back to the photos and the note. How well did I know these two men in my life?

I put on news radio while I was driving home, but nothing was reported on the Bianco robbery, which wasn't entirely surprising given that it was just another day, another break-in, in the Bronx. Nothing to recommend it from a sensationalistic perspective. I drove through the city streets on my way to the highway and thought about Bianco's daughters and how this would affect them. To me, he had seemed overbearing and unusually invested in their basketball careers, but when it concerned the latter, he wasn't all that different from most of the parents in the area, never mind the country. He wasn't the only parent to live vicariously through his children and their involvement in sports, and he wouldn't be the last. My casual observance of the twins led me to believe that they had a relatively good relationship with their father, Kristy maybe more than Elaina, who seemed to be getting increasingly despondent, about what I wasn't sure.

Was it the lack of playing time? Spending time in the shadow of her more talented and ego-driven sister? Something else? It was hard to tell, but she seemed to be hanging on by a thread, and with the situation surrounding her father, that thread was sure to break.

Twenty

The next morning, I was alone, or so I thought. I took the opportunity to scan the city papers to see what I could find out about Lou Bianco, but they all had the same information: check-cashing store, robbery, aggravated assault. The case seemed pretty straightforward in its series of events. Probably a holdup gone awry. Whatever had happened, the cops had few leads, but it was still early. As Crawford always told me, the first forty-eight hours were the most critical, and if they didn't have any hard leads after that time, chances were the case would go cold.

Footsteps coming up from the basement, its door right next

to the kitchen in the main hallway, made me freeze. Trixie, sensing my nervousness, got tense, the hair standing up on her neck, her throat emitting a low and menacing growl. The door swung open and Trixie lunged toward it, stopping short when she saw Crawford appear in the hallway.

He held his hands up. "Don't shoot!"

Trixie jumped on him and licked his face, which was covered with dark stubble, the bags under his eyes grayer and deeper than I had ever seen. His white dress shirt was wrinkled, sweat stains forming half-moons under his arms. I didn't know which question to ask first, so I went with the most obvious one. "What were you doing in the basement?"

He smiled. "Do we have hedge clippers?"

"Why the sudden interest in yard work?" I asked, putting my hand on the counter to steady myself. My knees weren't exactly knocking together, but the scare, coupled with some really strong coffee, was going to bring on tremors if I didn't get ahold of myself. "I gave them to Jane. Remember?"

"I have a few hours off so I thought I'd take care of those shrubs in the front."

My, you're convincing, I thought. "How could you possibly have a few hours off? You work constantly." I thought he might need to be reminded of that.

"Fred's got things under control for now."

"Any leads on the Bianco thing?"

"May be Mob-related," he said, stating the obvious as well as a theory I thought was already well established.

"Isn't everything?" At least it seemed that way to me.

"In my line of work, it's not out of the realm of possibility. Let's just say the world of check cashing isn't the cleanest around. We're looking at the money-laundering angle."

"What about Vito Passella?"

He looked confused. "What about him?"

"Are they related?" I watched his face for some sign that he was going to lie or bend the truth. "You can't say that you didn't already think of that?"

"There's nothing to lead us to believe that they're related," he said evenly. He made a gesture as if he were clipping hedges; the conversation was over. "Hedge clippers?"

"Garage."

"What?" he asked, taking in my dubious expression. "Is there a problem with that?"

I didn't answer.

"And we've got bigger problems than overgrown shrubs."

I raised an eyebrow questioningly.

"Rats," he said.

An involuntary shudder went through me. I knew exactly what he was talking about. Before my ex, Ray, had left, we had been overrun with rats in our basement, drawn as they were to the bag of dry cat food that had been left there long after our one pet, a cat named Tabby, had died. Their point of ingress had never been discovered, and the exterminator had been on monthly retainer for many years until I decided that the rats were never coming back, the offending bag of cat food having been long discarded. The traps had sat empty and the bait station untouched. "They're back?" I asked, thinking of the dirty clothes that would have to be carted to the Laundromat until every last one of those beady-eyed suckers was dismissed. I looked accusingly at Trixie. "Thanks for the heads-up," I said to her, as if she had some role in protecting me from rodents great and small.

"Yep. And they're in the garage, too. Do you still have the number of the rat guy?" he asked, knowing the whole story about Tabby's demise, her leftover food, and the band of rats who had set up shop in the basement all those years ago.

Tom, the "rat whisperer," as I had come to call him, had looked close to retirement the last time I saw him, but I told Crawford that the number was in the Rolodex in the office upstairs. "I'll call him," he said.

"Did you see one?"

The look of disgust on his face told me he had. "If there's one thing I hate, it's rats. And I see them far more often than I'd like."

I still wanted an explanation on the hedge clipping, though. Crawford was a reluctant suburban denizen, having lived his entire life in Manhattan. He had never shown any interest in yard work before, so this increased interest made me suspect.

"Didn't you work all night?" I asked.

He nodded, pulling his shirt out of his pants and stretching. "Yes. The overtime when I retire is going to make for a very nice pension."

"Enough for me to retire?" I asked, getting a cup out of the cabinet for him and pouring him some coffee. I handed the mug to him and smiled sadly. "I don't think I can do much more of this, Crawford."

He put his coffee down on the kitchen table. "Teaching's really getting to you that bad?"

"No, not teaching. This." I waved my hands around the kitchen. "You. The job. The danger." The woman, I thought to myself. The gun where a rotted head of Bibb lettuce should be, Bibb lettuce being my least favorite in the lettuce family. Your daughter, the one who worries about you day and night.

He sighed, but it wasn't a defeated sigh, it was an angry sigh. That was a new one to me. "I can't talk about this anymore." He was unbuttoning his shirt as he walked away, and by the time he started up the stairs, it was off. He paused on the second step in his undershirt and dress pants. "Do you have any idea how tired I am?"

I guessed that was a rhetorical question because he didn't wait for my response. I could see where this was going and I wasn't going there. I was tired, too. I was tired of being afraid and tired of this feeling that was tickling my spine every time I saw him. I was tired of not trusting him anymore. Instead of saying any of that, however, I just turned on my heel and walked out the back door.

Twenty-One

School was a welcome diversion from thoughts of murder, basketball, the Mob, and police work—whatever order you put such disparate topics in. I had fallen down on what I had put forth as my main goal: finding out the truth about Kevin, and I decided to devote myself to that fully. Doing so would serve two goals: first, it would help Kevin because I remained convinced of his innocence, and second, it would get my mind off how my life was just a little bit unsettled at the moment.

I thought about what I wanted to do next. Burnished sunlight flooded in through the windows of my office, and as if she were being illuminated by heaven above, Sister Mary appeared on the steps, her short, gray hair looking silver and shiny. She moved with purpose, as always, taking each uneven, broken step without looking down. Whenever I did that, I fell. Not Mary. She was like a mountain goat traversing stone steps that should have been replaced fifty years prior. I thought back to my conversation with her a few days before in which I enjoined her to help me find out what had happened to Kevin, and I waited a suitable amount of time before I pushed away from my old desk so I could make my way up two floors to her office on the administration level of the building.

Before I exited the floor, Dottie stopped me, still in a purple rage about something the details of which I was still in the dark. "Okay if Luis puts in those new lightbulbs?"

"New lightbulbs?"

"The ones that use less energy," she said, her back to me.

"I guess." I started toward her desk but stopped short. Whatever was bothering her couldn't have anything to do with me, and as a result I didn't want to get involved.

I found Mary behind her desk, pushing various pieces of religious iconography around. "God knows I think the cleaning people do an impeccable job of keeping this place spick-and-span, but I wish they wouldn't move my things around." She picked up a statue of the Virgin Mary—a new one, it appeared—blew some nonexistent dust from Our Lady's crown, and placed her gingerly next to her phone.

I wanted to ask how they could clean her desk if they didn't move the religious artifacts around, but I wisely kept my mouth shut.

It was almost as if she had read my mind. "They are in descending order of importance theologically, so it shouldn't be too hard to figure out where they are to be returned."

I nodded. Not that it mattered. She was on a tear. Now was either an incredibly good time to give her my pitch—how she could be Robin to my Batman—or a colossally bad one. It was a crapshoot. I rolled the dice. "I need your help."

She stopped fiddling with the statues and the holy water and regarded me from above the top of her glasses. "I can only imagine what you're going to drag me into. I am hoping it's school-related?"

"Sort of."

She sat up straight in her chair and regarded the figures, now all in their proper places. "Sort of," she said, the words rolling off her tongue as if they were epithets. "Sort of."

She was toying with me in an attempt to intimidate me, but it wouldn't work this time. It had worked in the past, but she wasn't dealing with the sniveling Alison Bergeron of long ago; in her place was a betrayed and knocked-about woman who had nothing to lose as well as a friend to vindicate. This Alison Bergeron had stared at the lifeless body of a Mob soldier turned mail carrier, and she would not be intimidated. I kicked the door closed with my foot and pulled a chair as close to her desk as possible, leaving just a couple of inches for my knees. "Help me find out what really happened to Kevin." I picked up a bottle of holy water and looked closely at it. It didn't look any different from the contents of the Poland Spring bottle that I had consumed in the car. "Help me find out why someone made it so that he was kicked off the campus and probably out of the priesthood."

She took the bottle from my hand and placed it back in its proper position on the desk. She threw in a glare for good measure. "And that's what you think happened? That someone framed him?"

"It's my best guess."

"How?" At least she hadn't said no outright.

"Every group has a gossip or someone with their ear to the ground. I'm sure the convent's got their version of the town crier. Who is it?"

She looked only mildly surprised that I would come up with this theory. She studied me for a few seconds and finally said, "It's Alphonse." When I gasped, she held up her hand. "I've already said too much."

"How could it be Alphonse?" I asked, a mental picture of the aged nun with her ear literally to the ground. "She's almost blind."

Mary raised an eyebrow. "Which makes her an incredibly good listener." Mary sat back in her chair and crossed her arms over her chest. "Which is how she knows you're browbeating some janitor into helping you find out more about Father McManus."

"What else does Alphonse know?"

Mary stood. "That's enough for today."

I stood, too. "So you'll help me?"

The nod of her head was barely perceptible but enough to satisfy me.

I went back to my office, content in the knowledge that I now had someone to help me attempt to get to the bottom of Kevin's woes. The thought did cross my mind that Kevin had never asked for my help, but I tossed that aside with the justification that he had probably been too proud to ask. I skidded around my desk and into my chair to give my e-mail a quick check before class. I had a lunch invitation from Fareed and Abe, which I accepted gratefully. I moved my mouse around a slip of paper that was on the St. Thomas standard-issue mouse pad. The paper fluttered to the ground and I bent to pick it up, staying under the desk when I saw the name on the paper and the words that followed it:

Elaina Bianco. Ask her about Father McManus.

Twenty-Two

Girls talk. That was the only explanation I could think of. When I saw her name and the message on the scrap of loose-leaf paper, the only thing I could think of was that loose lips sank ships, and Elaina Bianco had loose lips. Maybe she had said something to Tiffany Mayo? To Kristy, her sister? I could only imagine that Luis had left the paper on my desk, his changing the lightbulbs the perfect cover for giving me some information about Kevin and his situation.

The question was whether Elaina Bianco was Student X, as I had taken to calling Kevin's accuser, or just someone in the know.

I decided that during my next class, which thankfully was a fifty-minute period of writing for my freshman creative-writing students, I would think this over. How could I gracefully broach the subject of Kevin's situation without appearing as if I was investigating? That was the question of the day. I am not known for my subtleness, but I was working on it.

Obviously, now was not the time to talk to either Bianco sister about Kevin or anything else, not with their father languishing in a coma in a Bronx hospital. But I did call Kevin. I caught him just as he was leaving for work.

I told him about the note. "What does that mean, Kevin?"

He didn't respond immediately. When he did, I got a lesson in clerical confidentiality. "There is such a thing called internal forum, Alison. Have you heard of it?"

I hadn't but once he explained it, I realized I knew the gist of the term.

"Internal forum dictates that once someone comes to me, and that person requests a confession, whatever that person tells me is confidential until the day I die." He paused. "Until the day I die," he said slowly, as if I hadn't heard him the first time.

"What if the person dies?"

"I still must take whatever they told me to my grave."

"Why are you telling me this?"

"To get you to leave it alone." He had never sounded cross with me until this very moment. Up until now, I hadn't been as clear in expressing my desire to clear his good name. "Leave it alone. Stop looking into this. Let me live my life."

"I am letting you live your life, Kevin. It's just . . ."

But he had hung up. I was speaking to dead air. I felt a little nauseous. He was pretty deliberate in what he had told me and how he had phrased it. What would I do with that information?

I shoved the piece of paper into my messenger bag and ran up to the sixth floor to teach my class, even though "teaching" today meant sitting there and making sure none required the Heimlich maneuver while they worked on their narrative essays.

Class seemed to be over no sooner than it had started. I raced down the stairs toward the cafeteria and my lunch date with Abe and Fareed, still thinking about internal forum and what it meant in relation to Kevin and the Bianco sisters, if anything. Both Abe and Fareed had seemed interested in Kevin's plight when we had been together at the faculty meeting, and I didn't have to be subtle with them. I would hammer them for any information they had, although I wasn't optimistic that they would have anything to contribute to the conversation besides warm words for Kevin's well-being.

Marcus was behind the grill and turned when he heard me call his name from in front of the lunch line. "What'll it be?" he asked, even though he wasn't taking anyone else's orders. I could feel the collective glare from a group of professors behind me, some of them nuns, as I asked for a grilled-chicken sandwich. The rest of them waited patiently in line as Maria, Marcus's assistant, took their orders and passed them along. A few short minutes later, I was on my way to a table already occupied by Abe and Fareed, who were patiently waiting for me before beginning their meals. Fareed had a healthy-looking salad, and Abe was eating something brown-bagged and probably kosher. I took my plate from my tray and set it down on the table, looking guiltily at the extra french fries that Marcus had gifted me with my sandwich.

"Shall we pray?" Abe asked, and I wondered how he was going to pull off a grace that would please a lapsed Catholic, a practicing Muslim, and himself, a Jew, but he did, carefully inserting mentions of Yahweh, Allah, and God into a smooth melding of all three faiths. He included a mention of Lou Bianco and the girls, asking God to bless them during this difficult time. When he was done, he dug into a Tupperware container of reheated chicken matzo-ball soup, slurping noisily.

Fareed cut up his salad into tiny pieces with a plastic fork and knife. "So, Alison, the game at Manhattanville really didn't go our way," he said in his usual understated way.

I was momentarily mesmerized by his brown eyes and had to shake my head to return to the conversation. "We'll get there."

Abe leaned in, the smell of dill emanating from his breath. "I heard that President Etheridge may be very close to hiring your replacement, Alison." I was relieved that now that Kevin was gone, Abe seemed to have assumed the title of campus gossip. Kevin's gossip always had a lot of blanks that needed to be filled in, so that most of the time I hadn't a clue as to what he was talking about.

My eyes grew wide and I used this to express my delight instead of talking with my mouth full of ketchup-covered chicken.

Fareed remained unruffled at this incredible news. "Who might they find, Abe?"

Abe dropped his voice to a whisper, even though at our table by the window we were far from anyone else. "From what I gather from my sources," he said, leaving me to wonder who these "sources" might be, "it's a young woman who graduated from the University of Tennessee and played in the WNBA for one season until she sustained a career-ending injury."

"So she's a Volunteer," Fareed said quietly, spearing a chickpea and putting it in his mouth.

"Yeah, me, too," I said, already feeling this anonymous young woman's pain. "Nothing says *volunteer* around here more than being the head coach of the Blue Jays."

"No. A *Volunteer*," Fareed said. "Students who attend the University of Tennessee are called Volunteers. A *Vol*, for short."

"Oh, right," I said slowly. I thought I had exhausted all of the ways I could look like a moron, but apparently I had found a new one.

Abe cocked his head. "Volunteers?"

"It refers to the large numbers of men who volunteered to fight in a series of wars on behalf of the United States," Fareed said.

"Aren't all men and women who go to war considered 'volunteers'? Except in times of draft, that is," Abe said, truly interested in the distinction.

As is often the case when I'm around, the conversation drifted away from its original topic. Today, apparently, the topic was semantics, namely the definition of the word *volunteer*. I attempted to get us back on track before Abe asked any additional questions about the university, its mascot, or its record in basketball. "Do we know who she is?"

"I don't have a name," Abe said, cramming a matzo ball the size of my head into his mouth. Chicken soup dribbled down through his beard. "But I heard she was quite the star at Tennessee."

I put my sandwich down and stared at my plate, thinking about how I would really feel if I was replaced in the middle of the season. At first, the thought made me happy, but then after some consideration I wondered if that was it. Although my life's dream had never been to be a basketball coach, never mind the Blue Jays' coach, I now found myself having to admit that I kind of liked the role. With Crawford so deeply involved in his work and perhaps married to another woman—one could never be sure, based on photographic evidence—working as hard as I did to make sure that the Blue Jays weren't completely embarrassed during their regular-season games had become something of a welcome diversion. I was also getting closer to Meaghan, an interesting and pleasant side effect of working like a dog all in the pursuit of a winning, or not-losing-too-badly, basketball team.

Fareed caught my mood and asked me if I was okay. I plastered a big grin on my face and assured him that I was. How could I tell the two of them that after heartily complaining for the past several days, I was now unhappy about being relieved of the onerous task of coaching the Blue Jays? I shoved a french fry in my mouth and looked out the window at the river, my personal version of popping a Xanax. I immediately felt calmer.

After a brief lull, I prodded Abe for any information he had on Kevin and his situation. He shook his head sadly, a bit of matzo ball flying off his beard and landing on my sweater. I wondered how long it was appropriate to wait before brushing it off without appearing really grossed out. I waited, but I was aware of its presence as Abe prattled on, revealing that he knew exactly nothing about Kevin's situation.

Fareed watched him carefully and, when he was done, looked at me. "He doesn't seem to know anything, but I might."

"I know plenty, my friend!" Abe protested half-jokingly, banging his hand on the table and disturbing the pearlized droplet of matzo ball on my shoulder.

I reached up with my napkin and blotted my shoulder. "Okay, Fareed, spill it."

He was stalling and I couldn't figure out why. We had met under the pretense of lunch, but was the real reason we had come together to hear all that Fareed knew about Kevin? I would never know because Meaghan bounded up to our table, her face flushed and her breath coming out in chuffs. Fareed fell silent. Whatever he had to tell me was not something he was going to reveal in front of a student, my stepdaughter at that.

"Meaghan," I said, standing. "You know Dr. Muhammad and Rabbi Schneckstein, right?"

She nodded. "I can't get my father on the phone," she said, panic in her voice.

Welcome to my world, I wanted to say, but given the distress on her face, I knew that now was not the time for sarcasm. "Is everything all right?"

"It's Erin. She's missing."

Twenty-Three

My first call was to Fred.

Meaghan had all the same numbers I did, and if Crawford wasn't picking up for his daughter, he certainly wasn't going to be picking up for me.

"It keeps going to voice mail," she said, "over and over." Fareed had gone up to the food area and bought her a bottle of cold water, while Abe enjoined her to eat a piece of matzo, afraid that she was going to faint. Fareed stood at the edge of the table and Abe fussed over Meaghan on her right, while I sat on her left.

"Start at the beginning," I said. I knew I had a few minutes until Fred arrived in the cafeteria, and I wanted to hear if any details in her story would lead me to figure out, on my own, where Crawford's other daughter had gone. She and Meaghan were in contact constantly throughout the day through texts and e-mails, each keeping the other apprised of her daily activities. Erin would declare herself a dance major when the time came, and that gave Meaghan endless hours of amusement, listening to her sister complain about ripped tights and unreasonable improvisational-dance teachers. Through Meaghan's texts with Erin, I knew what else was going on outside the dance world: Erin was thinking about English as a second major to appease her father, she had a job in the school library, and she hated her noisy roommate. We discounted her complaints about her living situation, though; if there was one thing that Erin Crawford wasn't, it was easy. I certainly wouldn't want to live with her full-time.

I thought about calling the girls' mother. It was still early enough overseas, but did I really want to sound the alarm without any information? I decided to hold off before I called Christine.

Meaghan was starting to hyperventilate again, and Abe did his best to calm her down. I had to admit, the guy was a definite calm in a storm. I wasn't sure if it was because he had so many kids himself or if it was his role as a rabbi, but his presence seemed to be helping.

It seemed like hours, but in less than twenty minutes after I had called him, Fred came through the swinging doors of the cafeteria, parting the sea of students who were streaming toward the door and out into the hallway. It might have been my imagination, but a few seemed to move a little faster when they saw him, a reaction that was not uncommon when people got a glimpse of him. He looked calm but he was a man with a purpose. I saw him step on two backpacks in his quest to reach our table, his feet crushing the contents so that both bags were flat when he was through with them. He stopped at the table and regarded my fellow teachers and Meaghan, the girl now openly crying.

Through gritted teeth, I asked him where Crawford was.

"Out, I guess," he said. "Doing something else. Can't get him."

It was time for my next class, and I asked Fareed if he would go up to the sixth floor and tell the students class would be canceled for the day. He looked grateful for the diversion and assured me that he would touch base with me shortly.

Fred grabbed a chair from another table, swung it around, and sat on it backward, his knees coming up almost to the top of the chair. "So when's the last time our little cranky friend texted you?" he asked, knowing Erin about as well as I did and knowing that she wasn't called "little Miss Sunshine" for nothing around our house.

Meaghan smiled, grateful for the levity. "Yesterday."

"Yesterday in the morning or yesterday in the evening?" Fred asked, jotting some notes down on his pad.

Meaghan pulled out her cell phone and showed Fred the last text that she had received. He read it and remained impassive, but the words on the screen made my heart stop. "Going out for a run" was all it said, and the time was six in the morning. She had been missing for about a day. I wondered why Meaghan had let an entire day go without letting us know that Erin hadn't texted or called, but I decided that asking her that would be insinuating that she had had some control over her sister's whereabouts or well-being.

Fred, however, wasn't quite so delicate. "Why didn't you let us know yesterday?"

Meaghan tensed and I implored her to tell us her thought process.

"We had a fight, okay?" she said, defensive. "The 'going out for a run' was her way of telling me that the conversation was over."

"You had a fight that began before the sun came up?" I asked.

"It started the night before and she was so mad that she texted me the next morning."

Fred let me ask the questions. "What did you fight about?"

Meaghan looked at Fred. "Do I have to tell?"

He nodded. "Yes, you have to tell."

She looked at me. "She doesn't like you."

That wasn't a surprise, but it didn't hurt any less to hear it verbalized; I think Erin refers to me as "that bitch" more than by my actual name. She also hated Tim, her mother's new husband; his four children, who up until he had married Christine had been motherless, their mother having died when the oldest was five; her aunt Bea, who made her go to church when she visited; and most of the extended Crawford family. Erin was an angry, immature girl who had never quite recovered from her parents' separation, several years earlier, and their divorce, which she saw as a direct result of my relationship with Crawford. As much as he tried to tell her that his marriage had been over for many years before he met me, she never believed him, and that had made my forging a relationship with her difficult.

I tried not to let the hurt show on my face. "It's okay, Meaghan. I understand. Do you think she could have run away?"

Meaghan threw her hands up, frustrated. "Anything is possible, I guess. She's a pill and a pain in my ass," she said, spitting out the words as if she had been saving them up for a long time and couldn't wait to get rid of them. She put her head on the table and sobbed. "Do you know how hard it is to have a sister who is so . . ." She searched for the word.

"Negative?" Fred guessed. "Unhappy?"

"Miserable," Meaghan said from beneath her folded arms.

"Do we know for sure that she's missing or is she just not returning your texts?" Fred asked.

"I called her roommate and she said that she never returned from her run."

I saw a flash of anger move across Fred's face. "Did the room-mate think to call campus security?" he asked as gently as he could. He wanted to throttle someone, and my guess is that it was the roommate.

"They hate each other so I'm guessing Tammy was thrilled when she didn't come back," Meaghan said.

Abe took in Fred's anger, and that was all he needed as his cue to leave. He leaned in and breathed chicken-soup breath all over me, and this time, it was a comfort. "I'm here if you need me, Alison." He patted my shoulder. He packed up his Tupper-ware and garbage, kissing the top of Meaghan's head before he moved away from the table, in violation of every personal-space and contact rule the school had for instructors regard-ing contact with students.

"What about Fez?" I asked Meaghan.

She shrugged. "He hasn't seen her. They had a fight. That's what they do." She sniffled loudly. "They fight and then they make up."

I looked at Fred. "What do we do now?" I asked quietly.

"I'll put in a call to the New Paltz police department. I'll drive up there this afternoon. Boy Wonder can handle any of our stuff and anything else he has going on," Fred said, using his favorite nickname for my husband. He tapped Meaghan on the arm and she raised her head. "Give me your phone, sister."

Meaghan relinquished the phone and placed it in his mitt-like hand.

"What do you want to do, Meg?" I asked. "Stay here or come back to our house?"

"Stay here," she said without hesitation. "I'm going to pre-tend that everything is fine and that she'll call and we'll make up and it will be the same as always." She looked at me. "But I want my dad."

I looked at Fred. "Can we make that happen?"

"Doing my best," he said in a tone that suggested it was best to leave it at that. He stood. "Your phone charged?" he asked, looking at me. My track record on that account was spotty, at best, but today my phone was fully charged. "Is it *on*?"

"Yes, it's on," I said, digging into my pocketbook and surreptitiously turning the power on. I gave Meaghan a hug. "Let's not jump to conclusions," I said, not taking my own advice. In my mind, Erin wasn't dead, but she wasn't completely safe either. I tried to stay in a good place where Crawford's piss pot of a daughter had gotten her dander up about one thing or another and split school for a perfectly good reason. Such as a road trip with her tattooed boyfriend, Fez. Never in a million years did I ever imagine that Erin's running off with Fez would be a positive scenario, but there you have it. At least they had a nice ride if they had indeed left. As my mother used to caution, "Never say never."

"What exactly did Fez say when you talked to him?" I asked.

"Just that they had had a fight and that they hadn't spoken since then. He hasn't seen her either."

"Was he worried?"

"They were on a break, according to him," Meaghan said.

"On a break?" I asked. "They were just at your game."

Meaghan shrugged. "I'm just telling you what he said."

"I'll want to talk to him," Fred said. "Is his information in your phone?"

Meaghan nodded.

"Can I ask a question?" Fred said. We waited a minute, thinking that whatever he had thought of would be relevant to Erin's disappearance. "What kind of name is Fez?"

"The same kind of name as Charlemagne," I said, hoping that he would leave, head to New Paltz, and find Erin asleep in her bed at the dorm.

He shook his head, and the sunglasses that had been perched

atop his skull flew off. "No. Charlemagne is a real name." He reached out and, without having to get up, picked up the glasses, which were at least two feet away. He tipped back dangerously on the back two legs of his chair and I imagined the sound it would make—something akin to a sonic boom—if he went over.

"Not really."

"Yes, really," he said. "*Fez* is made up." He put his glasses back on his head.

"Well, that's his name, Fred. Maybe we'll find out that his Christian name is something boring like William or James, but for now, he's Fez."

"Does this Fez have a last name?" he asked Meaghan.

"I think he only uses one name."

"Like Cher?" Fred asked.

"Who?" Meaghan asked.

"Cher? 'The Beat Goes On'? 'Half-Breed'?" he asked, exasperated. "Who doesn't know Cher?"

Meaghan shook her head. "I don't know who that is. He's just Fez. One word. Like The Edge."

"That's two words," Fred said. "The article definitely counts."

"Okay," I said, "time to move on. Fred, go to New Paltz. Meaghan, go to your dorm room and take it easy for the afternoon. E-mail me your schedule, and I'll talk to your professors to let them know what's going on." I handed her the backpack that she had been wearing when she came in and wrapped my arms around her. She had stopped crying but I could tell that she was close to breaking down again. "Will you make it back to your dorm or do you want me to go with you?"

"I'm fine." She took a deep breath and made her way through the now empty cafeteria to the swinging doors at the front of the room.

I looked at Fred. "How bad is this?"

"I don't know."

"Should I call Christine?"

He thought about that. "Not yet. I'm hoping that we resolve this sooner rather than later."

I crossed my arms over my chest. "Can you find Crawford?"

"I don't know." The look on his face told me that he wasn't sure if he really wanted to.

Twenty-Four

By the time practice rolled around I still hadn't heard from Crawford, yet despite the rising tide of bile that was roiling in my digestive tract, I wasn't full-blown hysterical, which surprised me. There had to be a reasonable explanation for Erin's disappearance. And Crawford's. I left about fifty messages on Erin's phone, and when that didn't work, I texted her, each text message increasing in its length and fervor. I don't know how I had managed to get through the rest of the day, but I had, and I offered silent prayers to someone—be it Yahweh, Allah, or just plain God—that Fred got to New Paltz, found out that this was all a huge mistake, read Erin the riot act, and was back before dinner. I hope he had put her in time-out. I needed him at practice, but more than that, I needed him to find her.

Although I had resisted doing so, thinking that we would find Erin before a call would be necessary, I finally broke down and spoke to Christine. Time was passing and it was getting to the point where if I didn't call when I did, it would be the middle of the night. She sounded calmer than I would have, given the circumstances, chalking up this disappearance to one of Erin's flights of fancy. I promised her I would call her back as soon as we found her. Which we would, I assured her, sounding more confident than I felt. It was only the catch in her voice at the end of the call that indicated to me that she wasn't as calm as she was trying to sound.

I figured that continuing with my day, with intermittent checks on Meaghan via phone, was the best way to move forward. I taught, I graded papers, and I met with students, trying not to let on how I felt. I think I did a fair to middling job.

I went to practice, armed with a new Bradley quote that was mine alone: "Leadership is unlocking people's potential to become better." You can do better than that, Senator. It looked as if I would only be leading for a short time longer, but as Max had counseled, I had to give it everything I had. With any luck, Kristy would be back and able to play. We were playing Joliet, our former "brother" school, now coed like St. Thomas, but which was our biggest rival. Joliet is only a mile or so down the road from us, but in terms of competitiveness, it is at the top of the list. While the men's team was legendary and D-I, the women's team was not. They were only marginally better than St. Thomas, historically, but managed to kick our collective asses almost every single year. In the history of St. Thomas, we had only beaten Joliet once on the basketball court, and that was when the Fonz was still our best player and Sister Dolores Margaret was playing a position we who played basketball like to call "tall, hacking forward." A little research had revealed that Dolores Margaret—when her name was Celeste Tuscadero— had fouled out of a shocking 92 percent of the games she had played (I had done the math), many of which St. Thomas had lost, which made me realize that staying out of foul trouble might be the key to the modern-day Blue Jays' success.

I imparted this wisdom, along with my Bradley quote, to the girls. Meaghan's face, the sheen of panic still glistening on it, was tense and guarded, and she kept silent as I laid out some new strategies that we would be employing in our game against Joliet. I did my best to pretend everything was normal, but kept my cell phone in my pocket, hoping that it would vibrate with a call from Fred. The girls were down; that was obvious. I tried to rally them, telling them that they should try to practice and do well so that they would be ready to face Joliet like the winners they were. We were about halfway through practice when my prayers were answered and the phone rumbled to life, scaring the hell out of me. I threw a ball at Bridget McGee and told the girls to run some layups while I spoke to Fred.

He was uncharacteristically talkative. "Didn't find her, but found the boyfriend. I don't know what she sees in him."

"Amen, brother."

"No, I mean I don't know what she sees in him."

I heard him the first time.

"He's got his act together," he said. "He's shooting for pre-med, works in a homeless shelter, and studies when he's not working. Doesn't sound like Erin's type."

Certainly didn't. I thought he was an "artist" and "didn't play by the rules," according to Erin, and in my opinion premed certainly didn't fit in with that image. I asked the obvious question. "Does he know where she is?"

"Nope. But he thinks she dropped out, something I wish he would've told Meaghan when they talked."

Crawford was going to *plotz*, as Abe Schneckstein would say.

"Did she anything about where she was going?"

"Nope on that, too. She told him that she was sick of school, sick of living in the shadow of, and I quote, 'a perfect sister,' and wanted some space." Fred sighed. "And then she took off."

"For parts unknown." I watched as the girls made layup after layup, my heart lightened a bit by this and the news that Erin had left school of her own accord. "Anything from Crawford?"

"No. You?"

"No. You on your way back home?"

"Yep," he said. "I'm going to miss practice but I'll be there tomorrow."

I let him know that our coaching days might be coming to an end, and surprisingly, he sounded disappointed. Coaching the team had seemed to alleviate some of the stress of his job, he told me. "Well, then we need to go out with a bang," he said, and by the way he said it, I didn't think he meant that all we needed to do was win. I asked him to be more specific. "I'll call you later," he said, and hung up.

I pulled Meaghan to the side and gave her a brief update, relief etched on her face. We both agreed that we wouldn't feel better until we saw her, but that we'd hold it together until then. The team had fallen into a loose approximation of a group that was practicing for a game, so I clapped my hands together and called them all together. We reviewed the strategy for the Joliet game, which amounted to nothing more than "score more points than they do," which in my mind was beautiful in its simplicity. I had actually managed to figure out a way to keep Kristy Bianco in a place where she could shoot and score and not be fed on her weak side, so we did some drills that would hopefully accomplish that goal and that wouldn't tip her off. If I had learned anything from Senator Bradley's hallucinogenic visits, it was that we needed to focus on the positive, something I am not so great at, if I am being completely honest with myself.

Max called while the girls were running drills. "She'll turn up, you know," Max said before I could tell her that Erin had dropped out. "Remember the time I ran away?"

"Which one?" I asked, stepping into the hallway of the gym to continue the conversation.

"The first time."

"Yes, I remember." I pictured myself sitting in the Fiftieth Precinct—the same precinct where Crawford worked—with Max's distraught parents, giving the officer Max's description and a tiny photo of her from her senior year in high school. Fortunately, Max had returned within the first twenty-four, having run out of money after a night of clubbing in downtown Manhattan. Her parents were happy to see her, but not the blue hair she was now sporting, nor the small tattoo of what was supposed to look like a shark but that looked more like Charlie the Tuna that peeked out from under the strap of her tank top. "I'm trying to forget."

"She's clubbing or getting a tattoo or a new piercing."

"How could you be so sure?"

"If anyone had taken that kid, they would have returned her within fifteen minutes," she said. "Listen, are you ready for the big game?"

"I guess." Frankly, my mind was on so many other things that I couldn't wait for the Joliet game to be over. Everyone on campus was excited for the game—posters hanging everywhere announcing the game and boasting of our chances of winning—and as always, it was seen as the most important game of the year. A lot of pressure was on the team, which many on campus saw as having the best chance in years of beating the Joliet women. Additionally, their star guard had broken her leg. With Meaghan playing good ball, and their best player on the disabled list, we seemed to be golden for a win.

"It's going to be great," Max said, a little too enthusiastically, which made me suspicious.

"You're coming?"

"Of course! I wouldn't miss it!"

"What's going on? I thought you were too busy to come to our games now?" Although she had come to the first few games, she had let me know that her appearance at future games would be spotty. Max had been launching a new cable reality show—*Hooters Girls: PIs*—which was taking up much of her time. Max's network—Crime TV—was touting the show on just about every channel on the dial, so it seemed as if every time I turned on the television, I saw a big-breasted woman in booty shorts wrestling a cheating husband to the ground.

"I'm just very excited," she said, taking her enthusiasm down a notch, but it wasn't enough to convince me that she didn't have some ulterior motive. I had too much on my mind, however, and decided, unwisely, to put it aside. Being one step ahead of Max is practically my part-time job.

After another hour or so, I dismissed the team, grabbing Meaghan before she headed out the front of the gym. "Let's remember: Fez says your sister dropped out. I bet she's still hanging around New Paltz, torturing everyone in her wake."

Meaghan rolled her eyes. "That sounds about right." She took a long drink from her water bottle. "So you think she's all right?"

"Well, we don't know that for sure," I reminded her, quickly amending when I saw her crestfallen face, "but it would seem that way."

"She got us all worked up over her dropping out of school?"

I shrugged. "Looks that way."

"What did my father say?"

I looked around the gym, considering how I was going to answer that question, deciding ultimately that the truth was better than any thin lie. "I haven't heard from him." I waited a beat. "Yet." Covering for Crawford's lack of communication with us was becoming a part-time job for me.

We started for the door. I put my arm around her shoulders,

pulling her into me. "Erin will turn up and you'll do great in the Joliet game. And your dad? He'll get some time off and we'll go away together for a weekend and forget all of this stuff ever happened."

She looked down at me. "How can you be so sure about all of that?"

She had a point. I smiled and pulled her closer, realizing that there was no way to answer that question.

I was exhausted, trying to stay alert on the ride home. Although worrying about Erin had allowed me to take my attention off worrying about Crawford for the afternoon, the specter of her not being found swam around the edges of my consciousness, and although I told myself that I wasn't thinking that negatively, in all honesty I was. Knowing that she had taken off of her own accord was small comfort. I wanted her found.

I was still concerned, too, about why I hadn't heard from Crawford. He loves those girls more than life itself, and although our first five or so messages hadn't revealed our reason for calling him, after hours had passed and he hadn't called back, I had felt it necessary to let him know that we were dealing with what could potentially be an upsetting situation. Still nothing from him.

I pulled into the driveway and noticed that Crawford's car was at the curb. I hadn't seen him since we had sparred about the basement and the potential rat situation that morning, and when he had indicated that he had a few hours off, I immediately assumed that I wouldn't be seeing him anytime soon. My guess was that he would leave for work after getting some sleep and I wouldn't see him for days. I got out of the car and ran to the back door, wondering how he could be home when he should have been out scouring the tristate area for his missing daughter. And why he hadn't called me back.

I went in through the kitchen. Crawford was sitting at the table, a beer in one hand, and the *New York Times* crossword puzzle in another. He looked up, looking calm and relaxed. Before I could speak, he asked, "Five-letter word for 'strepsirrhine primate'?"

"*Lemur.*" I threw my messenger bag down and tried to get his attention.

He held up his hand to hold me off until he could jot the letters into the little squares on his puzzle. "Nice work." He stood and wrapped his arms around me, a little tighter than was necessary. He pinned my arms at my sides, a curious way to show affection, in my opinion. I tried to speak but couldn't. "Always check the premises," he whispered.

I looked up at him, immobile in his bizarre hug. "Huh?"

"Erin's here," he whispered, and rolled his eyes upward to indicate that she was on the floor above us.

Now I knew why my arms were pinned at my sides; if they hadn't been, I would have punched him in the face. "How long?" I asked through clenched teeth.

"Last half hour."

"Why didn't you call me?"

"I figured you were on your way home."

"No. Earlier. Why didn't you call me back earlier? When we first found out that she was missing?"

"I left my phone here by accident."

"You left your phone here by accident," I repeated slowly, not really believing it. I heard Erin's footsteps on the stairs. I looked at his face as he turned to greet his daughter and thought to myself, And I don't know who you are. Erin appeared in the doorway to the kitchen, greeting us with her usual disaffected snarl. "You had us worried sick," I said, approaching her after I had disengaged from Crawford's death grip. "Your sister is beside herself, not to mention everyone else who we involved in this mess."

I'm usually the one who is making peace in the family, not causing trouble, so the look on her face was priceless. Shock and awe was an apt description of what was passing across her angelic features. I've been led to believe that I can't say anything against the girls because they "already have a mother"—so sayeth the wise Erin—so I keep my mouth shut most of the time. But this time, I was incensed. Once the shock and awe wore off, the look on her face turned to a combination of surprise and petulance. "Who else did you involve?"

"What?" I asked, my anger clouding my ability to hear clearly.

"Who else did you involve?"

"The New Paltz police, Fred, and Fez."

"Wow." She came all the way into the kitchen and hopped up onto the counter. "Did you put an APB out on me?" She yawned. She stretched her arms up into the air in a gesture of utter boredom. Turns out Max was right: I caught sight of a new tattoo on her stomach, a Virgin Mary oddly enough. She had professed to be an atheist while still in Blessed Sacrament high school as a freshman and had endured four long years of daily chapel services and Masses that took place far more often than even a practicing Catholic would have liked. Served her right, the insolent little snot. I couldn't figure out why she would have a Blessed Virgin tattooed on her stomach until I saw that Christ's mother was wearing high-top sneakers.

I looked at Crawford. "You can handle this." I started upstairs toward the bedroom. "And then, you're taking me out to dinner."

"What will I eat?" Erin whined. "All you've ever got here are maraschino cherries and moldy cheese."

"Figure it out!" I called from the second-floor landing. "And don't touch my vodka!"

Trixie peered out from under my bed, her eyes letting me know that she wasn't happy that Erin had come for a visit. Erin has the same effect on Trixie as Max does, inducing a combination of fear and loathing. I coaxed Trixie out from under the bed and whistled at her to jump up beside me. She usually wasn't allowed on the bed, but that didn't stop her from resting her head on my pillow and stretching out to her full length. I stroked her belly, more to calm myself than to calm her. "I know, Trix. I can't stand her either."

"You're not supposed to say that out loud," Crawford said, appearing in the doorway to the bedroom.

Under any other circumstances I would immediately have been chastened by admitting how I felt, but after what Erin had put everybody through that day, I didn't feel any remorse. "Sorry," I said halfheartedly, "it's been a long day."

"Sounds like I missed out on a lot." Crawford pushed Trixie farther down the bed and sat beside me. "Where do you want to go to dinner?"

I got up and closed the bedroom door. "She dropped out."

"I know."

"Unacceptable."

"I agree."

"So what are you going to do?"

He looked up at the ceiling. "I'm going to calm down—"

"You seem pretty calm to me."

"Can I finish?" he asked. I nodded. "I'm going to calm down, have a long talk with her, then put her recalcitrant little ass back in my car and deposit her back at New Paltz."

I didn't know what I expected him to say, but that pretty much met my expectations. It was a good start. "We're not going anywhere until I get some answers," I said, leaning back against the door. My anger over the situation with Erin emboldened me, and I decided that now was as good a time as ever to get the answers I needed from him. He looked at me expectantly, which I took as acceptance. "Okay, first. Where were you going that first morning? You were walking into town."

"To get the paper."

"You never came back."

"I met someone who I needed to meet and they drove me to where I needed to go. It was work."

"That's pretty vague."

He shrugged. That's as much as I was going to get.

I moved on to my next question. "I found a gun in the refrigerator in the garage. Where did it come from?"

He didn't hesitate, which made me feel better; it didn't appear as if the wheels were spinning as he tried to make up a story. Unless he had already anticipated this moment and had his story ready? Whichever the case, the explanation sounded plausible. "It was for a case. I had nowhere to put it. It was only there less than a day. That's all I can tell you." He watched my face for signs of disbelief, but there were none. What I really wanted to ask him was if he had killed Vito Passella, but for some reason, I didn't. Maybe I didn't want to know the answer, which could have ranged from "Yes" to "No, but I bought the gun that did." Any way you sliced it, there was no good answer. I had to trust him, something I wasn't excelling at lately. "What else you got?"

He was either telling the truth or he had really rehearsed for his new role.

"What's your name?"

"My name?"

"Yes, your name. Here with me. And for whatever case you're working on."

"Robert Edward Crawford. Here and there. But you can call me by my Indian name, Hung Like Horse."

I burst out laughing, becoming somber when I remembered I had one last question to ask, hoping the answer was the right one. "Who's the woman?"

"The woman?"

I told him about the pictures, watching his face for any sign of what he might be thinking, but there was none.

"Where are the pictures now?"

"That's all you have to say? They're with Fred. Or Carmen. I'm not sure."

He thought about that for a minute, deciding which way to go. If they were with Fred, he could get ahold of them; that was obvious to both of us and didn't need saying. "She's part of the case."

"A good guy or a bad guy?"

He shrugged. "Hard to say."

"And what about Vito Passella?"

He sighed. "I've told you everything I know. The only thing I can tell you is that the Vito Passella case is under control."

"Meaning?"

"Meaning you're not in danger and you never were." He ran a hand over his face, trying to wipe away the fatigue and stress. It didn't help; he still looked as if he were going to collapse.

"How could you possibly know that?"

"I just do. That has to be good enough for you." He waited a second, waiting for my response, but I had none. "Dinner?" he asked, changing the subject.

I took his answer at face value; I had no reason not to. "What about that one?" I asked, pointing at the floor; presumably Erin was still in the kitchen.

"She's not invited." He got up and kicked the door closed with his foot, coming back over to the bed. He pushed me back gently covering me with his body. He kissed me. "Let's put all things related to Erin on hold until we eat, okay? I told her to take the dog for a long walk, so we have about five minutes," he said, looking at his watch. "That means I don't have time to get you liquored up."

He kissed me and I pondered the situation. I had to trust him. What other choice did I have? He was constantly reminding me that he wasn't Ray, referring to my first, and worst, husband. I knew that. Nobody could approach the level of betrayal that Ray had set as a benchmark. But still, the last few weeks had been stranger than normal. I was sort of used to his weird schedule and his unorthodox hours and work habits, but the last several weeks had raised the weirdness factor tenfold; even Fred thought so. I had an idealized version of his work life in which he and Fred had a cup of coffee together in the morning, responded to whatever homicides needed their attention, and ended the day with a handshake. I wasn't naïve enough to think that my version was correct, and I knew that they often went out on their own or with other detectives, but Fred's sullenness over whatever Crawford was doing made me uneasy. It was okay—even normal—for me to complain. But Fred? That just didn't seem right.

Crawford raised up on his elbows and asked me where I'd like to go to dinner, returning to his plan to get me liquored up.

I thought about it but couldn't come up with anything that I felt like eating. I begged off, noting the disappointment on his face, but convinced that behaving as if everything were normal was beyond even my above-average acting skills.

Twenty-Five

I wasn't going into the basement for anything save a nuclear disaster now that the rats had returned. What that meant is that I now had to get Sun's Dry Cleaning back on the payroll for laundry by the pound, which was not an insignificant outlay of cash every few days and a major inconvenience. Sun's was a green dry cleaner, and the only one I wanted to use, but they were in the next town over, five miles in the opposite direction of school. I was going to need to make time every few days for pickup and drop-off, not really sure if the rat guy had come by yet or even if Crawford had called him the next morning. I dug out the old laundry bag that I kept for emergencies like this and for when the washing machine went on the fritz—which occurred far too often—and raced around our bedroom, shoving dirty clothes into the mesh bag. Although his personal hygiene is unrivaled, Crawford is kind of a pack rat (no pun intended) and has a habit of stuffing his dirty clothes into his corner of the closet, so I got on my hands and knees and dug out what he had stored in there, making sure I had gotten everything before I backed out and tied up the bag.

I was in and out of Sun's in about thirty seconds flat, already late for school and for my first class.

Crawford had made good on his promise to get Erin back to New Paltz. Not content—or trusting—enough to put her "recalcitrant little ass" on Metro North, where she would be deposited in Poughkeepsie only to take a shuttle bus over to campus, he drove her up. Smart move. I didn't trust her as far as I could throw her, and I had extremely limited upper-body strength. I was thrilled that she was out of the house and hoped that I wouldn't see her for a long, long time. Like graduation day.

Practice that night was our last one before the Joliet game, and the girls were revved up. Elaina, of course, was the exception, as her usual droopy self. Fred was in no mood for fun and frivolity and ran the girls ragged, shades of the late Coach Kovaks coming back to haunt them. Meaghan looked exhausted, but Kristy was full of energy, running plays and imploring her teammates to rise to her level of excellence. She continued to be impressed by her own prowess and not shy about letting anyone know that she thought she was the best on the team.

So far, she had little competition. Although Meaghan was "the best under the boards," according to Fred, Kristy was our high scorer. Tiffany Mayo was second in scoring. Elaina had still not seen any playing time given her lackluster displays in practice and our need to keep our top players in each game. She didn't seem to mind, content to sit at the end of the bench during games and to shoot around and run drills during practice. She was not a good basketball player, that was for sure, but I wasn't sure if it was her lack of energy for anything related to basketball or life in general.

While they were not entirely untroubled by their father's health, it didn't seem to take them away from practice, or impact their schoolwork, something I had checked with their teachers. They were concerned when asked, but it never came up otherwise. Maybe not having him at the games and monitoring their every move on the court was liberating. It was hard to tell. As talkative as Kristy was, she mostly talked about basketball and herself. Elaina, on the other hand, was quiet to the point of being withdrawn, and no amount of prodding was going to change that, it seemed.

I still wondered why I hadn't seen their mother at the games, but I guessed that basketball was Lou's purview alone. Still, what proud mother doesn't come to see her child play, particularly if that child is the star of the team? After Kristy hit a three-point shot, I pulled her aside.

"How's your dad, Kristy?" I asked while the other girls went about the business of playing basketball.

"He's doing okay, I guess." Her face took on a childlike quality that I hadn't seen before. "He's still in a coma."

"How are you and your sister holding up? If there's anything we can do for you, you just have to let me know." I had told her this before, but I wanted to reiterate that the school, and her team, were there for them.

"We're okay." She clapped her hands together. "I just want to beat Joliet!"

Clearly, she had other things on her mind than her father's well-being. "Me, too," I said. "Will your mother be at the game?"

She smiled, looking at something behind me. "Why don't you ask her yourself? She's coming in right now."

I smelled her before I saw her, the scent of Chanel No. 5

announcing her arrival. I already knew what she was going to look like before I turned around, since the face of the woman from the photographs that I had received was etched in my mind.

For once, I was glad when Crawford didn't come home that night. I wasn't going to bring her up to him; my experience with being cheated on led me to believe that this was the best course of action when presented with certain evidence.

I slept restlessly when I did actually sleep. The rest of the time I spent in my bed either staring up at the ceiling or flipping from one side to the other, making the bed shake. Trixie, whom I had allowed to sleep with me just this once, or so I told myself, was not pleased with my fidgeting and even had the temerity to growl at me once or twice. I didn't want to upset her; if things with Crawford continued as they were going right now, Trixie would be my partner in bed for the foreseeable future and beyond.

Jacqueline Bianco had come to the gym to meet me and Fred and to let us know that in her husband's absence, she'd be attending the games. She made no excuse for not having come before, but she let us know that the girls spoke highly of us, even if her husband didn't, something that was unspoken but which both Fred and I ascertained by her omission. She thanked us for looking out for the girls during this difficult time and told us to call her anytime if we needed to. Then she left, leaving Fred and me wondering just who she was and why she had been photographed with my husband. It had to be work-related, we warily determined, desperately trying to convince ourselves that this was the truth.

I finally got up at four and wandered around the upstairs of the house, but not before checking to see if Crawford had his badge on him. Either he did or he had found a new hiding spot; it wasn't in his nightstand.

I took my laptop back to bed with me and fired it up, doing a search on Jacqueline Bianco once the outdated computer came to life. There wasn't too much on the woman except a link to her interior-design business. I mulled that over a second and looked around my bedroom. I could definitely use some interior-design help. What a coincidence that my players' mother, not to mention my husband's "friend," was in the business. I decided I would give it a day or two before I contacted her out of respect for her period of grief over her husband's hospitalization.

I also tried to look at her Facebook page, holding my breath as I scrolled through her photos, which, curiously, I didn't have to be a "friend" to view. If I saw a picture of Crawford in there, I was sure to vomit all over my bed, but thankfully, all I found were early pictures of the girls with their mother, as well as a few of her and her husband looking happy and in love. None of this jibed with the image I had of her in my head with Crawford or as the missing mother at her girls' games. Something didn't add up.

For some reason, knowing that I had a legitimate way to contact her that didn't involve St. Thomas, basketball, or her daughters gave me peace of mind, and I fell into a deep sleep, awakening to find the laptop still on top of me and the sun streaming through the windows three hours later. I mulled over the strategy for the upcoming Joliet game and wondered how we could eke out a win against such a formidable opponent.

I also thought about the note that I had received, the one that implicated Elaina in this whole mess with Kevin. I continued to ponder that all the way to school and while I prioritized the things on my desk that needed my attention. Obviously, Kevin wasn't going to tell me anything outright; he couldn't. But something behind his eyes during our dinner discussion led me to believe that he knew the Bianco sisters better than he was letting on, and that was something I needed to explore in the most discreet way possible. In my thinking, the only way the note could have found itself onto my desk was when Luis had changed my lightbulbs. Seems like my friend Luis—who I still couldn't confirm was the one who wrote the note but was pretty sure had—knew more than he was letting on. I let that marinate for a few minutes before logging on to my e-mail account to see what needed my immediate attention. I saw that I had over twenty messages since the last time I checked, all sending good wishes and encouragement for tonight's game. Within the St. Thomas hierarchy, they went all the way from President Etheridge on down to Marcus, my friend in the cafeteria.

No pressure, though.

I remembered then that prior to our discovery that Erin was missing, Fareed had said he had some information about Kevin's situation, so I called his office. The phone rang a few times before going to voice mail so I left a message asking him to call me.

Curiously, for the first time in days, Crawford had contacted me before I had contacted him, sending me a text letting me know that he was definitely going to be at the game. In the text, he let me know that he had told Meaghan the same thing. I prayed that he didn't let her—or rather, us—down. Nothing was worse than getting our hopes up only to be disappointed again by his absence. So much was riding on the game, even though I wouldn't be the St. Thomas Blue Jays' coach much longer if the rumor mill was truly working at optimum efficiency, and I needed Crawford's steady presence in the stands. I'm sure Meaghan felt the same way. I hoped he knew how important it was to both of us.

The day sped by, as it often does when I am not looking forward to what I have to do after school ends. I gathered up my schoolwork and headed over to the gym early so I could get my bearings. I was surprised to see Meaghan sitting way up in the stands, her backpack beside her and her long legs stretched out in front of her. The gym was empty otherwise. I called up to her.

"What are you doing up there?"

"Just trying to relax."

I picked my way up the stairs, wondering how I thought a tight pencil skirt and high heels were appropriate for a college professor, let alone a college basketball coach, but alas, my sartorial decisions often bit me in the ass. I was used to it. I pulled my skirt up a bit to give me some room to move and made my way up to her, plopping down beside her. "What's up?"

"Getting my head in the game," she said, taking a long drag off a bottle of Powerade.

"Did you talk to your sister?"

"I didn't think that was such a great idea right before the big game. I'll call her when things settle down a little bit." When she was sensible like that, her jaw set, she reminded me so much of her father, it was eerie. "She really dropped out, huh?"

"Not for long, if your father has anything to do with it." I looked around the gym, wondering what it would be like later on. "She needs to be put in time-out. Permanently." I don't normally say anything disparaging against Meaghan's sister, but she had put all of us through hell, particularly her twin.

Meaghan seemed to agree. She reached into her bag and pulled out a Ziploc bag. "Cookie?"

"Thanks," I said, realizing I was hungry. I took a big bite.

The two of us sat in companionable silence in the gym, which started out empty but gradually began filling up as game time got closer. I made my way back down to courtside and waited for the rest of my players and Fred, who ambled in a half hour before tip-off. We herded the girls into the locker room and discussed some plays before attempting a pep talk.

"I guess you've all been hearing the rumors," I started, looking at their faces, some scared, others disaffected, but all united in their anticipation of the game. "As far as I can tell, they are only rumors, but I think you're going to be getting a new coach."

I waited for the collective sighs of disappointment or groans of dismay, but none were forthcoming. They all stared back at me, waiting for the rest of my pearls of wisdom. "So, I want to thank you for the opportunity to coach you. You've done a great job."

"We suck," someone muttered.

"We don't suck," I said. "Let's focus on tonight's game. It means a lot to our history and to the St. Thomas community, so do your best."

I waited for some kind of sign that they were listening or were excited about the game, but all I heard was "Is that it?"

"Does someone have something they'd like to say? Something to share?" I asked, the good teacher I was.

Kristy Bianco stood and went to her left, something she hadn't been able to do all season. "I don't know about the rest of you, but I want to win."

That statement was met with a resounding hue and cry of assent. Kristy clapped her hands together and went into a tirade about our mediocre record and how detrimental it was to the school, the Athletic Department, and each of them as individuals. She even invoked the memory of Coach Kovaks, who, last time I checked, everyone still hated, despite being dead. She called each of them out, including herself, for the ways that they had failed the team and the school. Although it left Bridget McGee in tears because of Kristy's assertion that "Spazzy" couldn't hit the basket if it was lowered four feet, her speech was rousing and effective. The girls started to come to life, and the locker room buzzed with energy. Fred looked at me and shook his head sadly. I was surprised that she could muster up some emotion after everything she was going through with her father; maybe it was her way of dealing with the pent-up feelings of his beating and hospitalization? Who knew? All I knew is that she had taken but five minutes to energize the team in a way that I hadn't been able to in over a week's worth of coaching.

"This job really doesn't play to your skill set," Fred said, uttering perhaps the understatement of the year.

"You think?" I called the girls back to order. "Okay, then, let's go out there and win!" I offered a little jump in the air for effect that left me grabbing for a locker to steady myself.

Out in the gym, I could hear loud music thumping, something that I had never heard before during any game, let alone a Lady Blue Jay event. I looked at Fred. "Where is that music coming from? It sounds suspiciously like Madonna. Are people voguing out there?" I walked toward the locker room door and opened it, gazing upon a gymnasium that had transformed from the partially filled room that I had left little over a half hour ago into one that hummed with life and excitement. Nobody was voguing, thankfully, but every seat in the bleachers was filled, one side St. Thomas, the other Joliet, people displaying banners rooting for their respective teams. I walked across the gym floor and took my place on the sidelines, looking up into the stands and meeting President Etheridge's gaze before finding Crawford seated between Erin and Max. Apparently, either he hadn't taken his daughter back to school or she had come back specifically for the Joliet game; I didn't know and I didn't care, as long as she was gone from my life after the game. He looked more miserable than I had ever seen him look at his favorite sporting event. For some reason, that made me happy. Misery loves company. He gave a weak wave and shrank down between the two pint-size sirens on either side of him. I was happy that he had kept his promise and come to the game.

The lights dimmed and I made a mental note to find out who in the AV department had decided that we needed music and lighting, or even if we had an AV department, and why they had never made an appearance at a game before tonight. I looked around and noticed that Fred hadn't followed me out onto the court, and that the team was standing in the shadows to the side of one set of bleachers, not taking warm-ups as they were supposed to. I stood alone on the sidelines. All of a sudden, in the darkened auditorium, the lights came up and someone introduced the "St. Thomas Dancers." The visitors' locker room door burst open and twenty of the most curvaceous and well-endowed young women I had ever seen came out onto the court, wearing white booty shorts and sports bras that barely covered their enormous breasts. I looked around and saw that I wasn't alone in wondering where the St. Thomas Dancers—a group I had never heard of—had come from. They certainly didn't look like St. Thomas students, most of whom, myself included, had packed on the freshman fifteen and then some by this time of year. Strains of Jimi Hendrix's "Fire" blared through the speakers as the women got into something akin to a kick line and began dancing as if their lives depended on it. Flesh jiggled and hips gyrated, and lots of hair—real, fake, and everything in between—was tossed around with wild abandon. I turned around, slack-jawed, and looked at Crawford, who looked as if he had walked into a nightmare. I knew how he felt. I avoided President Etheridge's gaze and couldn't even stomach the thought of catching the eye of one of the twenty or so habited nuns in the stands. If Jimi Hendrix had only one itching desire, and it was to stand next to my fire, mine was to have the floor open up and swallow me whole.

Even though she had told us, just the day before, that she would be at every game, I saw no sign that Jacqueline Bianco was here.

A voice that sounded vaguely familiar came over the public address system and announced the Lady Blue Jays, who ran out from their place next to the bleachers and between the two lines formed by the bevy of dancers, whom I now recognized as Max's Hooters waitress acquaintances/private investigators. Kristy Bianco was so energized by the pregame festivities that before she exited the line, she did a backflip that, if not executed properly, would have broken her neck, ended her sports career, and taken away any chance the Lady Blue Jays had of ever beating the Joliet Jaguars.

The girls came over to the sidelines and stood in a circle. I motioned them to come in close. "Listen," I said. "I have no idea what's going on or even who those women are, but obviously our focus needs to be the same, and that's to win this game."

Meaghan was nodding enthusiastically. Bridget McGee was still sniffling a bit, but had composed herself a bit in the wake of Kristy's browbeating.

Fred finally appeared by my side and reviewed a few plays with the girls, his whiteboard covered with what appeared to be hieroglyphics but which the girls seemed to be able to read and understand. "Now go out there and kick some ass," he said.

Fortunately, the girls' version of ass kicking was different enough from Fred's that I felt secure in the knowledge that nobody would get hurt.

I hoped.

My head still wasn't clear after the bump and grind of the St. Thomas Dancers, a group whose very existence was confounding. I listened as the emcee—another nameless mystery employee of the school, apparently—announced the members of the Joliet team. Kristy, our captain, and the captain from the Joliet team met in center court and conferred with the referee. She came back and reported that the Joliet captain had given her the stink eye or something like that and that now Kristy was out for blood. I implored everyone to stay calm. "Just play your best," I said.

Fred led the girls in some kind of organized cheer that wasn't quite as rousing as the St. Thomas Blue Jays cheer that they usually did and sent the five starters on the court. He turned to me. "You're a regular Tony Robbins."

"Shut your freaking pie hole," I said, and judging by the look on his face, he wasn't expecting so snappy a retort. I took my place by the bench and sat down, pulling my skirt down over my knees.

"You ever think of wearing pants?" he asked, dropping his sizable bottom onto the bench beside me.

I didn't go into my whole rationale for wearing skirts over pants and my deep-seated fear of the matching pantsuit, so I kept quiet and tried to concentrate on the game, which was quickly turning into a one-sided rout despite that we were only two minutes into it. The game was rough, and the refs had a tough time keeping a lid on the barely controlled violence under the boards. The more frustrated the Blue Jays became, the sloppier they got, and the less control they had of themselves and the game. My pleas during our regulation time-outs to have them calm down fell on deaf ears, and even Meaghan—generally as mild-mannered as can be—was hot under the collar.

Every time-out that was taken, whether by us or the Joliet squad, was punctuated with Max's Hooters waitresses shaking their groove things on center court. Each time, the crowd went wild. In the back of my mind I knew who had to be responsible for this pulchritudinous display and was kind of sick to my stomach, but everyone but me seemed to think it was a fantastic idea.

Bridget, my most sensitive player by far, was as usual near tears during the last time-out we took before halftime. "Some guys are saying things about Kristy," she said, wiping her nose on the bottom of her jersey.

Kristy shot her a look. "It's *fine*," she said, but her tone indicated that it wasn't.

Bridget pointed over to the Joliet side of the gym to a group of young guys who were certainly rowdier than most of the other fans in the bleachers. I took Kristy by the shoulders. "Ignore them. You're having a good game."

Her usual steely resolve seemed to waver slightly but she nodded. That she was playing as well as she was given that her father was in the hospital was a testament to her mental fortitude.

Fred peered over the tops of the girls' heads to get a better look at the guys Bridget had pointed to. "You mean the juice-heads in the Joliet gear?"

Bridget nodded before putting her hand into the circle as we broke.

By halftime, we were down twenty-seven points, and I rifled through my basketball handbook to see if the mercy rule had been enacted and I just hadn't noticed. It hadn't. The girls had been playing exceptionally well, but they were no match for the Joliet team, who played the fastest game we had ever encountered. By comparison, the Blue Jays looked out of shape and allowed themselves to be completely dominated by the running game. I shepherded the team toward the locker room, passing by the group of rowdy Joliet students, one of whom tossed an empty box of Milk Duds at Kristy's head while making some kind of crack about the dubiousness of her gender and sexual orientation. He threw in an allusion to a primate just for good measure. But his next comment—one about sleeping with a priest—made my blood run cold. I froze in place. It didn't take me long to decide what to do, and I instructed Fred to take the girls into the locker room, despite his entreaties to just keep walking and let him handle the situation. The team stood at the bottom of the bleachers and watched as I climbed between the slats in the seats and made my way three-quarters of the way up to the location from which the box had been thrown.

The Joliet side of the gym went silent first, followed by the St. Thomas side as the spectators realized that I was in the stands. When I reached the row where I suspected the culprit was, I confronted the first Joliet-sweatshirted student I saw and leaned in close to his face. He smirked, and that's when any restraint I may have had went out the window. I also knew that I had found the guilty party. "You think this is funny?" I asked him.

"Yeah, I do," he said, and I could smell the alcohol mingling with his Milk Dud–scented breath.

"What's funny about it?" I asked calmly, although I felt anything but. The tension of the last several days was bubbling to the surface, and when I thought back to the way I handled the situation, that was my only explanation for why I had decided to take this on myself. That, and the part about the priest. And maybe the primate.

I heard Fred bellow my name and, in the distance, the sound of his giant feet pounding on the bleacher seats as he made his way up into the stands. I hoped he had security with him, but our security team is notoriously slow and incredibly old, a deadly combination in an emergency situation. "What's so funny is that dyke can't go to her left."

It wasn't enough that we were losing by twenty-seven points; now, my players had to endure derogatory comments from drunk spectators. I took a deep breath even as red swam in front of my eyes. Mercifully, when I turned around to check, I saw that Fred had gotten the team into the locker room prior to his ascent, so I was pretty sure that Kristy hadn't heard what he had said. But I also knew that classic bons mots like that had a way of making their way around campus and would probably be far more profane once they were relayed to her. And they would be relayed to her at some point; that was certain.

"You have incredibly bad manners," I said, trying to breathe normally. "And now I'd like you to leave."

The kid didn't move, although a few of his friends—the ones who had a better view of Crawford and Fred—tried to encourage him to do as I said.

I felt a hand on my arm and heard Crawford say, "Honey. Let's go."

"Yes, honey, let's go," the kid said, cracking up. His friends, obviously less impaired than he was, didn't share his enthusiasm for this encounter and started to disperse.

Crawford leaned over me and I got a quick whiff of Chanel No. 5 again as he grabbed the kid's hood, pulling him up out of his seat with one graceful motion despite the kid's being almost as tall as Crawford and outweighing him by about fifty pounds. I found out later that he was a member of the Joliet football team and holding on to his place on the team by a thread, given his less-than-stellar academic record. He clearly didn't have a lot going on between his ears, but that didn't make his disrespect any easier to take.

I watched as Crawford dragged him down the stairs, Fred appearing out of nowhere and hanging behind to catch either of them if they fell, and frog-marched him to the emergency-exit door. Once Crawford got the door open, he flung him out into the night, pulling the door shut tight. One of the septuage-narian security guards was standing at the bottom of the bleachers, his eyes wide, obviously grateful that he hadn't had to get involved.

The gym erupted in cheers, St. Thomas and Joliet fans united in their elation at the best halftime show they seemed to have ever seen, the St. Thomas Blue Jay dancers notwithstanding.

I made my way back down the stairs to the gym floor, where I was confronted by the refs. One of them—a short guy with a mustache—looked at me sadly. "I'm sorry, Dr. Bergeron, but we're going to have to ask you to leave. Going into the stands is a violation and is punishable by immediate expulsion from the gym."

I had expected as much. "Can I speak to my team before I leave?"

The other ref wasn't quite as sympathetic to my plight. "What part of *immediate* didn't you understand?"

The eyes of several hundred spectators on me, I decided that I wouldn't make an issue of it and walked slowly across the gym, my high heels sounding like gunshots in the silence of the place. I don't know who it was—although I suspected it wasn't Mark Etheridge, whose ire I undoubtedly would be subjected to the next day—but someone started clapping slowly in solo support of my incredibly stupid decision. As I reached center court, the cheers got louder until the gym was filled with the sound of thunderous clapping and cheers as I approached the exit. I wasn't sure what the rule was—did I have to leave the building or could I spend the remainder of the game at the candy counter? I decided not to ask and to just bask in the glory that was my solitary march to what was probably going to be my immediate dismissal from the team if not the school.

The cheers died down a few seconds after I had exited, and I looked around the hallway to see where I could plant myself so as to have access to the sounds of the game, if not the sights. Mary Catherine's perch at the candy counter seemed to offer the best aural vantage point, so I pulled up an errant folding chair that sat outside what had been my ex-husband's first office at St. Thomas and sat beside her.

"I heard the whole thing," she said, looking at me dolefully.

"Pretty dumb, huh?"

"You had to protect your player." She perked up as someone approached the candy table, and I was surprised to find myself looking at Fez.

"Fez!" I said.

Mary Catherine, obviously intrigued, looked at me, one eyebrow raised. "You know him?"

I nodded. It was all becoming clear—the St. Thomas Dancers, the smooth, mellifluous voice on the loudspeaker. This had all of the hallmarks of an Erin/Max collaboration. The more I thought about it, the more alike they were—little, crafty, and completely ill-advised in their actions. "Are you our new emcee?"

Beneath all of the piercings and scraggly hair, I got a glimpse of the barely-out-of-his-teens kid he probably really was deep down. He blushed deep red. "Erin made me do it."

"Of course she did," I said, coming out from behind the table and linking arms with him. "Now get back in there and keep track of what's going on. Report back when you're not doing your color commentary." Kid smelled awfully good for some-one who tried so hard to be alternative, I thought, as I detected the subtlest scent of expensive cologne. "I thought you were a premed and art major."

"I minor in communications, ma'am."

He was growing on me. "Go back in. I suspect halftime is almost over if the end of that Beyoncé song is any indication."

I returned to my place beside Mary Catherine, whose busi-ness was suffering as a result of the St. Thomas Dancers; they were keeping the fans in their seats, something that was great for the game but not so good for the concessions. "How long have you been doing this?"

She rolled her eyes. "Too long. It's a work-study."

"It's better than what I did while I was here." I helped myself to a bag of M&M's. "I worked in the Sisters' dining room."

"Blech." She got up on her tiptoes and looked through the window in the gym doors. "Game's about to start again." Her business effectively on hiatus until another break in the action, she sat back down.

Mary Catherine had always struck me as having her finger on the pulse of what went on at St. Thomas, so I decided to pick her brain. "What do you know about the Bianco sisters?"

She looked at me, surprised. Clearly, this wasn't where she expected our conversation to go. "Why do you ask?"

I stretched my legs out under the table and ate a handful of M&M's. "I don't know. It's just that that jerky Joliet guy said something about Kristy 'sleeping with a priest'? That sounded weird to me."

"It wasn't Kristy," Mary Catherine blurted out, immediately chagrined. She got up and looked into the gym again. "Game hasn't started yet," she reported unnecessarily.

"Not Kristy? In other words, it was Elaina?" She didn't an-swer. "Someone else?"

She scuttled out from behind the table. "I have to go to the bathroom. Can you sell the candy?" She ran off, remaining in the bathroom, or parts unknown, for the rest of the game. I ended up carting all of the candy out of the building at the end of the game, sticking it in my trunk for safekeeping until I could figure out what to do with it. We had lost, just as I thought we would, if I was being perfectly honest with myself. After helping myself to another bag of M&M's, I leaned against the trunk of my rental car and thought about what Mary Catherine had said.

Oh, how the mighty have fallen, I thought, after I exhausted myself with thoughts of the game and its aftermath. One day, you're a basketball coach, and the next you're selling candy.

Twenty-Six

As usual, Crawford was gone before the sun rose the next morning so we didn't have time to discuss the previous evening's festivities or Jacqueline Bianco. I had begged off, pleading exhaustion, when he offered to take all of us—Meaghan, Erin, and Fez—out to the diner for sundaes after the game. He didn't seem too upset that I didn't want to go out with them and sent me on my way with a kiss and an "I love you" that sounded hollow to me after what I had learned about the identity of the woman in the picture.

It didn't seem like the right time to pepper him with questions about Jacqueline Bianco and why he was in a photograph with her. As a matter of fact, I wondered if there would ever be a good time to discuss this new wrinkle. What could this woman possibly have to do with whatever case he was working on? The photo had been taken long before Lou Bianco had been attacked. Did something suggest that Lou was mobbed-up before he was assaulted?

All I knew for sure is that I was exhausted, but that wasn't going to keep me from making some decision about the fate of my marriage to a man who was becoming increasingly unknown to me.

The loss of the game, as well my loss of decorum or any semblance of sanity, was featured prominently in the local newspaper that everyone at St. Thomas seemingly suddenly had a subscription to, because although everyone was disheartened at our drubbing at the hands of the Joliet team, high fives were being distributed liberally as news of my hotheadedness filtered throughout the hallways of our staid institution. I didn't feel like high-fiving, though. I was embarrassed and exhausted after tossing and turning all night, wondering how I could have handled the situation better. Along with my undesired notoriety, I had also earned a whopping $1,500 fine for my indiscretion and a request for a written apology from the president of Joliet, Brother Michael Bowers, as well as their athletic director. I just wanted the whole thing forgotten, so the next morning I wrote a check to the league, as well as the apology letters. I wasn't in the mood to fight anymore, even though fighting was all I had wanted to do the night before. I decided to mount a good offense and zig before he zagged, so I went to Etheridge's office first thing to offer my contrition.

Fran, Etheridge's secretary and an old ally, let me know that he was ensconced in his luxurious office with Father Dwyer. She buzzed into the office to let Etheridge know that I wanted to see him.

Dwyer looked down at the floor when I entered; he didn't

rise or acknowledge me. He studied his shoes as if he had stepped in something distasteful that needed his immediate attention.

Etheridge, on the other hand, greeted like me as if I were a long-lost friend, which made me immediately gird my loins, so to speak. A smiling Etheridge is dangerous, I had learned. "I'm not going to stay long, President Etheridge," I said, dismissing his invitation to sit. In this instance, something about being the tallest person in the room was comforting. "I'd just like to say that I'm sorry for what happened at the game last night. It was completely inappropriate and out of character." Well, sort of. I have been known to be a bit of a loose cannon at times, but I hoped he had a short memory.

He held up a hand to silence me and I braced for the inevitable tirade. It never came. "Alison, thank you for your apology, but it's not necessary. The kind of passion you displayed was completely appropriate, given the circumstances. Pay your fine, apologize to Brother Bowers and Athletic Director Mitchell, and put this whole thing behind you."

"Okay," I said hesitantly. This wasn't exactly the reaction I was expecting, but it was welcome nonetheless. I turned and started for the door, which Fran had closed after I had entered.

Etheridge asked me to stop just as I reached it, my hand on the knob. "And, Alison, one more thing."

I turned, but left my hand on the knob, just in case a hasty getaway was warranted.

"I hear that you've been asking around about Mr. McManus's dismissal," he said, making it clear that he no longer considered Kevin a priest.

I knew his smile was a fake. I tightened my grip on the doorknob, knowing what was coming next.

Dwyer chimed in, "I gather you know what *cease and desist* means?"

I figured that for a rhetorical question and let it hang in the air. I focused on a first-edition *Moby-Dick* that sat on Etheridge's mahogany bookshelf, thinking that my eyes couldn't have landed in a better place, given the circumstances, and my company. *Call me Ishmael?* More like *call me screwed.*

"Cease," Etheridge said. "And desist." I looked at him, ensconced behind his monstrous desk, the office version of Porsche in terms of significance. "Nothing you might be able to uncover will exonerate Mr. McManus. Are we clear?"

Again, I didn't think that required a response, but I wondered why this was a priority for them right now. Suspicious. I let myself out quietly. I figured I had done enough damage to my career and the school's reputation in the last twenty-four hours and I didn't need to shoot myself in the foot, so to speak. I shot Fran a look as I walked past her desk. She kept her head bent over a stack of papers on her desk. As I got to the exit, I heard her whisper, "Keep trying. Just don't be so damned obvious about it."

I didn't think that I had been, but I was determined to take her advice. Fran thought that she had her finger on the pulse of St. Thomas and that she was connected in a way that no one else in the school was, given her position. But in truth Fran only got half of the information, and only half of that was true. People were afraid of Etheridge and what he might inadvertently hear from Fran, and for that reason people avoided her like the plague. If she had heard that I was being indiscreet, that was saying something. I hurried out of her office and into the hallway, where I bumped into Sister Alphonse, who was inching her way down the hallway, leaning heavily on her cane.

"Good morning, Sister. I'm sorry for bumping into you."

"Happens all the time. You'd think a six-foot nun would be hard to avoid, but everyone's always finding a way to take me down," she said, wavering slightly. "If I were twenty years younger . . ."

If she were twenty years younger, she'd be close to eighty, so

I wasn't sure what her point was. I grabbed her elbow to steady her. I didn't know how old the Fonz was exactly, but she had to be approaching the century mark. "Where are you headed, Sister?"

"All I want is a blasted cup of coffee. Do you think that would be too hard to find in this place?"

"You're on the fourth floor, Sister. We need to go down to the first floor."

"Whatever it takes, Dr. Bergeron." The Fonz is a genius at recognizing voices, and she and I go way back; she was one of my professors my freshman year. "I don't care if we have to go to the moon. Just get me a darn cup of java, please."

I didn't have class for another half hour, so I ushered Alphonse to the elevator and took her down to the first floor and the cafeteria, remembering Sister Mary's assertion that despite Alphonse's being legally blind, she knew everything that went on in the school. She was Fran with better connections—nuns talk; they certainly don't have anything else to do—and more of a network. No one would believe that an ancient, half-blind nun would do anything with the tidbits that she gleaned in normal conversation, but something told me that she was just waiting to uncork a bottle of gossip whoop-ass on someone. Might as well be me.

We took a seat at one of the more private tables, and I helped her sweeten her coffee with three packets of sugar. "None of that fake crap," she said. "Real sugar, please."

"That's how my friend, Kevin McManus, takes his coffee. You remember Kevin McManus, yes?" Not the smoothest segue, but I didn't have much time. The trip down in the elevator and into the cafeteria had taken a lot longer than I anticipated.

"That was about as smooth as a hair shirt, Dr. Bergeron. I may be old, but I'm not senile. Or dumb. I figured that you weren't getting me down here as part of your Christian duty. What do you want to know?"

I leaned in, my elbows on the table. "Okay, listen. I'm hearing things about Kevin and this student and they don't add up."

She snorted. "Well, for one thing, it's a female student accusing him. And if I know anything, it's that that man, despite being a celibate, is as gay as a three-dollar bill."

I wasn't sure what that meant exactly, but I got her point. The thought had definitely crossed my mind that Kevin was gay, but since he had spent most of his adult life as a celibate, did it really matter? I decided to ignore what she said. "So we agree that this is not the tightest case."

"Tight? Tight is Louise's ass. Tight is Professor Denali's knickers. This case is not tight, as you say."

Wow, the Fonz did get around. Lorraine Denali, a chemistry professor, was known for her painted-on skinny jeans and awe-inspiring backside; her classes were standing room only every semester. How Alphonse knew that was beyond me. The woman was a habit-wearing version of a *TMZ* reporter. "So we agree. What else do you know?"

"I know that President Etheridge would like nothing better than to take this school back sixty years, liturgically. I'm not sure why. I also know that that henchman of his, Dwyer, isn't as clean as the driven snow in that regard either. He's not exactly a champion of Vatican II." She took a sip of her coffee. "More sugar, please."

I was more than happy to oblige and poured two more packets into her cup.

With a couple of jolts of caffeine to her system, Sister Alphonse was more than willing to vent her spleen. "Did you hear this load of hooey about doing away with female altar servers?" She shook her head. "As if they could marginalize females any more in this Church. And if they have their way, those who don't fit into their ideal of Christian perfection will not be allowed to worship anywhere, if you know what I mean." I did but was surprised she was so connected that she knew that the

Gay and Lesbian Student Union was in jeopardy. She rested her bony hands on the table and her rheumy eyes looked off toward the river, even though I knew she couldn't see it. "I knew what I was getting myself into. I wanted to help people. And I think I did, for a time. I believed in the Church. But now? I don't know." She folded her hands in prayer and bent her head, and I got a glimpse of her vulnerability. Up until now, I had just seen her as a cranky woman in a habit. "We are all God's children."

Her sadness was palpable. I tried to imagine what it would be like to come to the final chapter of my life, knowing that the things I held dear were being compromised by a bureaucracy that I had pledged my allegiance to at an early age. I looked around the cafeteria and spied Father Dwyer coming in through the swinging doors. Our eyes met and he raised one eyebrow questioningly when he identified Alphonse as my partner. I dropped my voice to a whisper knowing that Alphonse's hearing was excellent. "Dwyer just walked in, so our time is running out. What do you know?"

"Not much. I'm trying to find out more from my sources."

I couldn't imagine who was playing the role of mole for an elderly nun, but I decided it didn't matter. Alphonse was gossip gold and I wasn't going to press her for any more information than what I needed to exonerate Kevin. Dwyer was winding his way through the maze of tables in the room so I had to be fast. "Who's the girl?"

"I don't know for sure, but I think she's on your team," she said, just as he arrived at our table.

"Sister Alphonse!" he said enthusiastically. "Dr. Bergeron," he said with far less positivity.

Sister Alphonse nodded in his direction. "Father Dwyer," she said, not brave enough to be rude to him to his face and in public.

"We were just leaving," I said, helping her up from her chair and grabbing our coffees. We left Dwyer standing by the table, the two of us making double-time out of the cafeteria. Given Alphonse's physical limitations, double-time amounted to time-and-a-little-extra, but eventually we were in the hallway, where I pointed her in the direction of the convent, reminding her that our conversation wasn't finished. I turned around to head in the other direction and came face-to-face with Dwyer.

"Friends with Sister Alphonse?"

"Oh, we go way back," I said. "I don't know if you knew this, but I am a St. Thomas alumna."

He nodded slowly. "Yes, I had heard that." He gave me one of his insincere smiles. "When would you like to get together to discuss the Holy Day of Obligation issue?"

I smiled back. "I've got a rather full plate, Father. I don't know if you heard this either, but I'm coaching the basketball team, defending my girls against belligerent fans, and trying to keep up with my normal course work. Adding another 'obligation' into my schedule may just be the end of me." The smile was beginning to make my cheeks ache, but I managed to hold it in place.

Students were beginning to flood the hallway and we moved to the side to avoid being trampled. Dwyer looked chagrined. "I know you are not enthusiastic about my appointment here, Dr. Bergeron."

That didn't even begin to scratch the surface of my lack of enthusiasm, but I let it go. "Father Dwyer, I think you and I should agree to disagree about all things pertaining to religion. Can we agree to that?"

He considered that. "On one condition."

"Shoot."

"You stop looking into Father McManus's dismissal." His eyes searched my face for some indication that I would consider that a reasonable request.

That was the last condition I thought he would have offered. "Why? What don't you want me to know?" The students continued to surge past us in the narrow hallway, which, having been constructed years earlier, wasn't equipped to handle this kind of traffic.

He pursed his lips, his demeanor sad. "I'm concerned that you'll learn things about your friend that you might not appreciate."

"Like what?" Kevin may eat too much butter and enjoy his occasional chardonnay, but he is as clean as the driven snow, to quote Alphonse, despite what the allegations against him might have suggested.

Dwyer put a hand on my shoulder, his tone patronizing. "I just don't want you to be disappointed, Alison," he said, using my first name to further assert his superiority over me.

"Oh, Kevin would never disappoint me."

"You're sure about that?" he asked, smiling sadly. When I didn't answer, he continued, "Sometimes people disappoint us and we can't anticipate when or how. But in our spiritual arsenal, to protect ourselves, we have prayer. Pray for Kevin, Alison."

I was stunned. I watched him saunter off, his hands in his pockets, whistling a hymn I recognized as "The Servant Song." I drew in a shaky breath and felt hot tears spring to my eyes; I wiped them away quickly. I wasn't sure if he had planted a seed of doubt in my mind or if I was just enraged. As I walked toward my office, I concluded that it was a little bit of both.

Twenty-Seven

Back in my office at the end of the day, I checked my messages.
I had one from Sun at the cleaners; I jotted down the number
so I could call her when I crossed one thing off my own call list:
calling Tom, the rat whisperer. There had been no sign that he
had visited the house, leading me to believe that Crawford
hadn't called him. I dug his number out of my Rolodex—I kept
his card at both home and school, that's how much rats wigged
me out—and punched it into the telephone. He picked up after
several rings, the sound of his voice immediately calming me;
he had that effect on me.

"Begley's Pest Control. Tom speaking."

"Tom, it's Alison Bergeron. Dobbs Ferry? Rat problem?" It had been a few years since we had last seen each other, but he remembered me with those two pieces of information.

"Sure! Cape Cod with the damp basement?"

"That's me," I said, wondering how my life had been reduced to the style and unfortunate characteristic of my house. "Listen, has my husband called you?"

"No. Why? Do you have a problem?"

I pushed aside my annoyance at Crawford for not having called the rat guy and told him that we needed a visit. "I'll leave a key in the planter on the front steps. I've got a dog now but she wouldn't hurt a fly."

"Or kill a rat, I gather?"

I laughed. "Or kill a rat."

"I'll get there as soon as I can tomorrow. Don't forget about the key."

My next call was to Max. She feigned ignorance when I asked her what gave her the impression that St. Thomas needed dancers. "Cut the crap, Max. This had your grubby fingerprints all over it."

She considered that for a moment and decided to go the hurt route. "I was just trying to help."

"By putting a bunch of scantily clad Hooters waitresses out on the court? The knee pads were a nice touch."

"Thanks!"

"I'm serious, Max. That is not appropriate. But I'm astounded that you were able to get twenty women to move in unison like that. That was completely impressive."

"That was Erin. She already had the routine. It was just a matter of getting the girls to learn it." She started chewing something. "Skype is amazing."

Of course it was Erin. I had suspected it all along: Erin was Max in training. Now I had proof. "Seriously, Max. We can't do

stuff like that. Especially without the administration's knowledge."

"Oh, they were totally on board."

That tidbit rendered me speechless.

"I spoke to Mark the other day and told him that we needed
to beef up the enthusiasm surrounding the basketball program."

"Mark?"

"Etheridge."

"No, I know who Mark is, I'm just wondering how you're on
a first-name basis with him."

Her snort on the other end of the line did nothing to answer
my question, but her rhetorical question did. "Do you know
how much money I give that place?"

Yes, I did. Anybody on the mailing list of the annual report
knew how much Max gave; it was a lot, to say the least, and I'm
sure that Mark Etheridge would allow Max to call him Judy, if
she wanted. He would allow her to do just about anything, including mounting a T&A floor show for all to see at the Joliet–St.
Thomas game. "So you ran this past the president of the college
and he gave you his approval," I said, trying to follow the chain
of events.

"Sort of."

"I don't want to know. All I need to know is if this is going to
be a regular part of our home games."

"I don't have that kind of time!" she said. "Do you know how
much work went into that?"

"I can only imagine."

"Listen, I've got to go. A thank-you would have been nice,"
she said before hanging up.

I sat with my head resting in the palm of my hand and stared
out the back window of my office, the floor-to-ceiling glass offering a beautiful view of dusk settling over the cemetery that
lay beyond the winding road that connected the lower campus
to the upper part. As usual, Max and I were united in a goal—

giving the St. Thomas Blue Jays more exposure—but taking two completely different paths to get there. This is just the sort of thing I would have bent Kevin's ear about, but there was no Kevin. That meant I had to suffer in silence; Crawford would let me rant but wouldn't show the requisite pique that Kevin would. Kevin and I would be on exactly the same page, with him matching my level of consternation over Max's high jinks. I missed him and wondered if our friendship would survive this. He had walled himself off from me and I wasn't sure why. Was it because he had no interest in being associated with anything remotely related to the scene of the crime? Was St. Thomas a painful place for him now? I suspected it was.

I wasn't doing a good job of coming through on my promise to help him, a promise that I'm not sure he even wanted me to keep. I owed it to him—and to myself—to follow through, though I was at a loss as to how to do that. It seemed as if some of the students had their suspicions and knew more than they were letting on, but browbeating was going to get me exactly nowhere. I turned over a variety of scenarios in my head but kept returning to one thing that Crawford had said: "Check the premises."

Check the premises.

Seemed reasonable.

Two hours later, when I was assured that the building was mostly empty, I made my way up to the chapel, located at the far end of the administration floor of the building. I was pretty confident that all of the daytime staff had left around six, as was usually the case on a weekday. I had called Fred and asked him to get practice started without me; I would be late. I didn't give him any explanation—the police frown on routine breaking and entering—but told him that he could leave once I got there if he wanted.

Earlier that day, I had called Dwyer's office and asked his secretary if I could schedule an appointment with him for exactly this time, hoping that she would say that he would be eating dinner and unavailable. She said exactly that; I felt confident that I would be able to get into his office unimpeded, but you never knew. I had to be careful.

I walked through the chapel, muttering to myself and asking God to forgive me for what I was about to do. I had probably done worse, but breaking into a priest's office was up there in terms of offenses. I convinced myself that (a) it used to be Kevin's office and that made it okay to go in, and (b) what I was doing was in the name of justice and all that was good. Whatever. I would tell myself whatever was required to assuage my guilt.

Dwyer's office—or Kevin's former office, as I liked to think of it—was located behind the altar, adjacent to the sacristy. What did I expect to find? I wasn't sure. But Crawford's words rang in my mind, and to find out what had happened to Kevin, to find out just who was setting him up for his fall from grace, I had to start where it all began. Right off the chapel, adjacent the sacristy, tucked away and somewhat hidden, you only knew it was there if you had been there yourself. If you hadn't, you'd never know that this is where the chaplain spent most of his day. His secretary wasn't even close to the office, as she shared an office with the secretaries for the deans of Academics and Housing. The office was perfectly situated for the type of work that the chaplain did; if someone needed counsel, they were afforded complete privacy. Unless you were being followed, no one would ever know that you had visited the chaplain's office, which I guess was a good thing if you had a problem that you wanted to keep yours alone. All you had to do is go in the direction of the altar and head through one of the side doors, and you were taken to a back hallway that connected each side of the chapel and ran behind the altar. I tried to make as little noise as possible as my heels clicked along the marble center aisle even though I was confident that I was alone.

I scurried past the confessionals, long unused by the student population, who, as a group, needed a good blast of reconciliation more than anyone else, and blessed myself out of habit as I crossed in front of the massive crucifix that hung over an altar more elaborate and ornate than our little school warranted. The chapel was dark but I knew my way around it by heart. Although I had been honest when I had revealed to Mary Catherine that I had worked in the Sisters' dining room, I had neglected to mention that to make extra money to pay my tuition—during a UPS strike that my father had participated in right before his death—I had also been hired to clean the chapel. It had gotten a lot more use back then, and cleaning it was no easy task, but it had been a good way to supplement my income. I knew every nook and cranny in the vast space, which, given its size, was no small feat.

Kevin never locked his office but I suspected that Dwyer wasn't quite as trusting. Since I locked myself out of my own house fairly regularly, Crawford had taught me how both to pick a lock and/or use a credit card to gain entry. I had two items in my possession: my American Express card and a bobby pin that I'd found in the deep recesses of my desk drawer, probably left over from graduation the year before when I had pinned on my mortarboard. My trusty Swiss Army knife was not going to be useful in this situation, one of the few in which it wasn't. I knew the old locks on these doors were notoriously sticky; it was hard enough to get in with a key, let alone a credit card. I reached Dwyer's office door and turned the handle; the door was locked, just as I expected, so I started with the credit card. I slid it between the door and the jamb and felt around, thinking that it would be the less reliable of the two options, but my heart leaped when I heard felt the credit card slip between the works and the handle turn in my hand.

I entered the office and closed the door behind me, careful to lock it so that if someone did decide to come in, be they one of the after-hours cleaning staff or Dwyer himself, I would buy myself a few extra moments. I hoped that wouldn't be the case, but you never knew. I knew from my days of cleaning and visiting Kevin in his office that like many of the offices in this old building that had small, strange closets and fake doors, this one had a small crawl space next to the desk in which Kevin kept his gym bag in case its contents stank to high heaven; in that little cubbyhole, the smell would be contained. We were never sure why it was there, but we called it the "sweat trap" because that was its purpose for him: to trap sweat. We had also come up with other uses for it over the years; I would complain to Kevin about students whom I would consider putting in the sweat trap, even temporarily, and sometimes we would muse about trapping Etheridge in there when he did things that enraged us. I wondered briefly what Dwyer kept in there. Probably the remains of the small children he ate for breakfast after drinking the blood of a slaughtered lamb, I thought, elevating his sinister nature in my mind to that of a warlock.

The office was in complete darkness. No lights were on, and with no daylight left to flood through the mullioned windows high on the walls, the office was a study in shadows. Dwyer's desk was neat, not a paper covering the blotter. A word-a-day calendar faced his chair, the word *surreptitious* highlighted on this day. How appropriate, I thought, as I poked around, looking at pictures of his extended family, his ordination, and a cruise he must have taken with some fellow priests, judging from the pampered look of the other men in the picture. Pasty white, they were all clean-cut and looked as if they didn't spend too much time outdoors or doing any heavy lifting. Friends from the chancery, the place where decisions concerning the lives of mainstream Catholics were made daily and affected many in an adverse way? Or fellow diocesan priests who were down in the trenches ministering to those in struggling parishes? It was hard to say, but my money was on the former. Dwyer seemed as if he ran with a pretty connected crowd.

I didn't see anything of interest on the desk or the credenza, so I opened the desk drawer, where I assumed the files were kept. I looked into the drawer, the files of which, in contrast to Dwyer's neat and tidy desktop, were in complete disarray. Papers spewed out, and the drawer was jammed with folders and hanging Pendaflex from which papers burst forth, prohibiting the drawer from opening completely. I yanked on it to free it, flying backward in the wheeled chair, hitting the back wall of Dwyer's office with a thud. I checked to make sure I hadn't cracked the plaster, but it was fine, a testament—no pun intended—to late-1800s construction.

I don't know what I hoped to find beside a file named "The Case Against Father Kevin Francis Xavier McManus," but when I started looking more closely at the drawer's contents, I realized that in addition to breaking and entering, I was impinging upon students', and possibly faculty members', right to privacy. I thought back to Kevin's diatribe about "internal forum." I wasn't a priest, but did I have a right to look for information, perhaps stumbling across a file that held secrets about a student or fellow faculty member? That wasn't acceptable to me, my ever-changing moral code notwithstanding. I sat at the desk and put my head in my hands. What was driving me to make sure that everyone knew Kevin was innocent? Was it that I wasn't sure myself and wanted hard proof? Was I really driven by devotion and loyalty to my friend? I closed the drawer and decided that on a scale of 1 to 10 on the scale of bad ideas, this was a 15.

I stood and looked around the room, spying a picture I had previously overlooked. In it, a considerably younger President Etheridge and a baby-faced Father Dwyer stood side by side on a soccer field, both sweaty, both looking triumphant. Had I not had complete disdain for both of them, I would have found the picture heartwarming. It reflected the image of two young men who were far from the bureaucrats they had both become.

I picked up the picture. It took me a minute to realize, as I stared intently at the two young men in it, that the sound I was hearing wasn't that of my heart beating but of footfalls getting closer and closer. I dropped the photo, making a minor racket, and looked around for a way out. The sweat trap wasn't large enough for a human being, and it had also housed Kevin's sweaty clothes for far too long for it to be a viable option. I had gotten a whiff of his gym bag once, and it wasn't something I wanted to remember. I looked at the door next to the desk and knew that a full bathroom was attached to the office. I opened the door and went in hastily, gingerly closing it behind me. I took off my shoes and climbed into the tub, pulling the shower curtain—a lovely striped number that I had helped Kevin pick out—as silently as I could across the metal pole.

Father Dwyer's bathroom was as messy and dirty as the rest of his office. The shower looked as if it hadn't been cleaned in weeks and the mildew around the grout was extensive, making its way up the once-white subway tile. I wondered why the office staff wasn't charged with cleaning the office; my recollection of Kevin's tenure was that the bathroom had always been relatively clean. It had been, at least, when we had hung the shower curtain. I heard the door to the office open and someone sit down heavily in the chair that my bottom had inhabited just moments earlier. I prayed fervently that Father Dwyer, who, I presumed, was the person who had entered, would do a little work and leave. I also prayed that he wouldn't have to use the bathroom, because the thought of standing behind a moldy shower curtain while someone relieved himself was just too much for me to bear.

I heard the desk drawers open and shut, sounding as if whatever the person at the desk was looking for wasn't at his or her fingertips. Not until I heard the voice did I realize it definitely was not Father Dwyer making the phone call.

"No, it's not here." There was silence for a few seconds while the caller waited for a response. "I'll keep looking, but I'm telling you, there's nothing here."

I strained, pulling the shower curtain aside slightly to see if I could hear any better. As clear as the voice was through the bathroom door, I still couldn't figure out who it was. The voice sounded vaguely familiar but not familiar enough for me to make a positive identification. The phone call was short, and a few minutes after hanging up, the person left. I waited a few minutes to make sure that the person was really gone before climbing out of the shower, my high-heeled pumps in my hands. I looked at my watch: seven thirty. I had missed the first half hour of practice and hoped that Fred wouldn't be too perturbed. I had also been gone a lot longer than I had anticipated and would have to make a pit stop back at my office to pick up my purse containing my keys and phone, which I had left there thinking that this would be a quick mission.

I tiptoed across the tiled floor and listened at the door. Just as I decided the coast was clear, I heard the door to the office open again and someone else come in. The person walked around the office before settling in at the desk; I was beginning to recognize the groan of its springs every time someone sat down. Now, instead of standing behind the shower curtain and being offered some protection from the person in the office, on the off chance that the person decided to use the bathroom, I was fully exposed, staring at myself, wide-eyed, in the bathroom mirror that hung over the sink. I tried to slow my breath, thinking that I was panting audibly, but once I inhaled, I realized I hadn't taken a breath for more than a few seconds.

The person on the other side of the door turned out to be Dwyer; I heard him leave a voice-mail message for a student confirming an appointment. After that, he opened and closed drawers. When he finished with that, he began tapping away furiously at his computer keyboard. While I listened to the sounds of someone toiling in their personal space for more than an hour, I bargained with God. If you let Father Dwyer leave without having to go to the bathroom, I will attend every Holy Day of Obligation Mass and even the ones that aren't obligatory, such as random saints' feast days. I wondered when St. Thomas's feast day was as well as those saints that I had encountered in an academic setting over the years: Catherine Labouré, Louise de Marillac, and St. Anne de Beaupré, my late mother's personal favorite. If he leaves in the next five minutes, I promise to be nicer to everyone I know, even Dottie. If he leaves in the next thirty seconds—which I hoped was the case as my own bladder was starting to protest—I will say the rosary every day, and twice on Sundays. Please, please, please just make him leave.

I've always been something of a believer in the power of prayer, even if it only puts one's positive energy into the world, but standing in that filthy bathroom, I became a true believer. Like that, I heard Dwyer rise from the chair and make his way to the door that led to the chapel. After that, his footsteps grew gradually fainter until I heard nothing. I waited another five minutes for good measure before peeking around the door and into the empty office. The coast was clear and I stepped out, noticing that the short distance between the bathroom door and the door to the chapel seemed to have grown by about twenty feet. I wasn't sure whether to take it slow or run as if my life depended on it; the hubris I had earlier exhibited when I had decided to break and enter was gone now that I had almost been caught twice. I decided that running was my best option and I sprinted for the door, running out into the chapel and making my exit alongside the long-abandoned confessionals. I looked behind me a few times to make sure that I wasn't being followed, my heels making sounds like thunderclaps on the marble floor. I made it to the heavy oak double doors and pulled one open, turning around one last time.

Luis was on the other side of the door in the antechamber of the chapel, moving his ubiquitous mop back and forth rhythmically, humming tunelessly to himself, earplugs jammed into his ears. He looked up when he sensed my presence, startled. He dropped the mop and pulled out the earplugs. "What are you doing here?"

"Praying?" I said, moving past him without offering any further explanation. "I'm late for practice," I said as an excuse for my rudeness. I was at the end of the hallway and flying down the back staircase to my office before he had a chance to ask any further questions.

The voice-mail message light was blinking furiously when I entered my office, but I didn't have time to check my messages; I was now more than an hour and a half later than I had said I would be when I asked Fred to begin practice. He was going to be pissed. He didn't like change, and he certainly didn't like being told one thing when another was going to happen. He was a little strange like that. Inflexible. Unyielding. Just a royal pain in the ass when things didn't go his way.

I grabbed my bag and headed over to the gym, running in shoes that had no business being run in. My arrival coincided with that of a black-and-white squad car—a "cruiser" as I thought of it until Crawford corrected me—and two uniforms jumped out, asking me to point them in the direction of the gym. My heart almost stopped. A radio motor-patrol car and two police officers showing up at the gym? Didn't take my incredible sleuthing skills to figure out that something bad had happened.

I followed the two cops, two baby-faced guys straight from the academy, into the building, but instead of going into the gym, I headed down the hall. My bladder was on code red and I ducked into the ladies' room quickly to take care of business, knowing that nothing was going to make sense until I was done. I washed my hands hurriedly, dismayed to find no paper towels in the holder, and ran into the gym waving my wet hands back and forth to dry them. The team stood around center court looking worried, not playing basketball. Fred was holding a ball under his arm, and next to him was Crawford, looking stricken. The uniforms were talking with the two senior detectives, so intent on the conversation that no one acknowledged my presence.

"Five foot ten, brown hair, usually wearing high heels, so that puts her close to six feet," I heard Crawford say. "I'm not sure what she was wearing today, but she usually has on a skirt and one of those sweaters that has buttons down the front," he said, looking confused and lost. One of the girls chimed in with "Cardigan," to help him out. I put my bag down on the bleachers and walked toward the group, wondering why Crawford would be giving the cops a description of someone who sounded just like me. I strode across the court, ready to take charge of whatever situation had befallen my team. Fred pointed.

"That's her."

One of the baby cops snapped his leather-bound notebook closed. "That was easy."

Crawford looked at me. "Where have you been?"

All heads turned and waited for my answer. Now I knew why the cops were here and that knowledge brought no comfort. Yes, I guess I had been missing, but it was only for a little shy of two hours. Why would the cops have been called? I had to think fast. We could play this a couple of different ways. I could say that I was in the chapel. That was true. I could say that I had been in Father Dwyer's office. That was also true if not entirely accurate. Should I reveal that I had been hiding in a shower? Probably not. I decided that instead of telling the truth, I would lie. And lie well.

"I was correcting papers." It was just nebulous enough to be the truth. "I'm way behind." I looked at the team and asked them to go into the locker room and wait while I cleared things up. "You called the cops? I was correcting papers." If I said it enough, I might actually believe that that's what I had been doing.

Fred looked at me and raised an eyebrow.

"You told Fred that you were 'going to see a guy about a thing.'" Crawford assumed a defensive posture, his arms crossed. "What does that even mean?"

The cops looked at me as if to say, "Yes, what *does* that mean?"

I walked up and gave him a quick peck on the lips. "It's a euphemism."

Fred looked at the cops, who, now that I wasn't a missing person, were totally enjoying the floor show. "I had that once. It's not pleasant."

"A *euphemism*. It's something that means something else," I said to Fred as simply as I could, given the furrow of his considerable brow. I looked back at Crawford. "Between coaching the team and carrying my usual five courses, I'm way behind."

He didn't believe me; I could tell. Good. Now we were even. I hadn't believed anything he had said in weeks. He had the good sense to let it go, though, and turned his attention back to the cops. "I'm sorry for wasting your time, guys. Seems like we had a little mix-up."

That was the understatement of the year, but it got the cops out of the gym so I could explain my side of things to Crawford, who needed to explain his side of things, even though we both knew that would take way longer. Only after it became just the three of us in the gym did I realize he had no color in his face. "What's going on?" I asked.

I think his first reaction was to say "Nothing," but after having called the cops to report me a missing person, it was clear that that wasn't going to be a reasonable answer. The thought did cross his mind; I was sure of that. "We thought you were missing."

"I got that from the two cops who raced in here. I was correcting papers."

"Why didn't you answer your phone?"

"Because I was correcting papers." I figured if I went full tilt in the indignation department, it would lend my story more credence. "I purposely don't pick up the phone when I'm working. Sheesh."

"Maybe if you say it enough, you'll believe it yourself."

So he was onto me. That didn't change that I was not copping—no pun intended—to what I had done, which turned out to be less than what I had planned to do, if that made any sense. On the ladder of moral superiority, I felt that I had climbed a rung by not going through Dwyer's files willy-nilly even if I had broken the law anyway. I looked at Fred. "Will you go tell the girls that practice is over?"

"It hasn't even started yet," he said, muttering, "thanks to you," under his breath.

"Well, then consider it a gift from me." I turned my back on him and motioned to Crawford. "A word, please?"

We walked out to the front of the gymnasium; the light over the door had burned out and we could barely see each other in the dark. It was cold and windy and I wanted to get to the bottom of this, but in a place where nobody could overhear us. I was still wearing my coat, a pink velvet number that had seemed like a great idea at the time that I had bought it but that did nothing to cut the wind that was whipping around the side of the building, bringing with it the leaves that hadn't been picked up by the maintenance staff. "What's this all about?" I asked. "Frankly, it seems like a bit of an overreaction, don't you think?"

"It's not like you to not be where you say you'll be."

I looked up at him and didn't like what I saw. Dark circles under his eyes, a thick growth of stubble, pale complexion. Something had him spooked and I wasn't sure what it was, but if it was my being gone for an hour and a half, we had a problem. That, to me, didn't warrant going into full panic mode. Why, after such a short amount of time of my being "missing," would he be so worried about me that he had called the police? The whole thing made even less sense than my breaking into a chaplain's office, even if I had helped the previous chaplain decorate the place and had proprietary feelings about it.

"What is this about, Crawford?" I asked again, softly this time. It seemed to me that if I pushed, he would cave in, and I couldn't take that. I put my hand on his chest, even though taking it out of the warmth of my coat pocket was the last thing I wanted to do. "What's got you so unhinged?" It wasn't the time to bring up Jacqueline, even though I wanted to.

Before he could answer, a group of players burst through the side door and into the cold night, one of them Meaghan. "Can we get something to eat?" she asked.

A couple of players, before moving on, expressed their relief that I had been found safe, even though none of them seemed terribly concerned that I had been "missing." Meaghan stared at both of us expectantly; she looked like a little kid. I wasn't hungry but I also wasn't interested in pursuing this conversation with Crawford, so I nodded. "Sure. The diner?"

We were seated at a booth—me on one side, Crawford and Meaghan on the other—the adults pretending that everything was just fine, but knowing that the opposite was true. I filled the potential dead air with conversation about the team and probed lightly about Elaina Bianco and her history as a player, but Meaghan didn't know too much. I had come to realize that my stepdaughter was incredibly single-minded: if it didn't have to do with her specifically, she stayed out of it. She had little to impart about the Bianco sisters and the reason that one was a star while the other was a first-year player. Meaghan was studying the menu intently and I took that opportunity to look at Crawford across the table. His mind seemed to be on anything but cheddar versus American cheese for his hamburger. He hadn't let on that he knew Mrs. Bianco during my interrogation of Meaghan, but I already knew that he wouldn't.

I gave him a tentative smile, but I was worried. It wasn't like him to go off the deep end like that, and had I known that my little stunt would involve the police department, I certainly wouldn't have gone into Dwyer's office. As with many of my attempts at sleuthing, this one had gone horribly awry. I couldn't think of anything worse than being trapped in a shower while two uniformed cops making barely $40,000 a year were dispatched to make sure you weren't dead. While thinking this through, I realized that I was starting intently at Crawford, who was, in turn, staring intently at the television hanging behind me and over my head. I decided to ask him why he hadn't called the exterminator.

He was distracted but by the time I turned my head to find out what had him so interested on the local news; the focus had turned to sports and the latest Rangers' loss. He drew his eyes slowly back to mine, still not really paying attention to me, but trying desperately to look as if he were. "Rats? They're gone."

"Gone?" I repeated as Meaghan cried out, "Rats?!" I assured her that we were taking care of it and that she wouldn't be affected by them, even if she did decide to spend the weekend at my house.

I had Crawford's full attention now. "Yeah, I called the guy the day that I saw one and he took care of it."

For some reason, I didn't want to tell him that I knew that this was a lie, so I let him keep going. He was more than happy to elaborate.

"And I plugged up a small hole I found near the foundation by the patio, so we should be in good shape now," he said, taking the lie to a whole new level.

"Really?" I asked. It was becoming apparent to me why the guy had been romanced by OCCB. He could lie with the best of them, a trait I didn't find admirable, but which they might. I wondered what else he had lied about and how often.

"Yes," he said. "We're all good."

No, we're not, I thought. Thankfully, the waitress arrived and took our order, which gave me a few seconds to digest this information. While Crawford dithered between the hamburger and the turkey club, I ran through a few scenarios in my head. In the first, there really was a rat but Crawford had forgotten to call the exterminator and didn't want me to make a scene in front of Meaghan. In the second, there was still a rat but the exterminator had been diagnosed with early-onset Alzheimer's and had forgotten that Crawford had called him or that he had even been to our house. In the third, there was no rat, and for some strange reason Crawford wanted me to think that there was. Which led me to conclude that Crawford didn't want me in the basement.

If that was the case, I knew exactly where I was going the first chance I got.

He finally picked the hamburger with grilled onions and mushrooms; I let him know that I didn't want to hear anything about indigestion later that night, nor did I want a good-night kiss.

There's nothing worse than being kissed by an odoriferous liar with stomach issues.

Twenty-Eight

I had forgotten to call Sun the dry cleaner the night before, so I waited until I was sure they were open and rang the store. Crawford had slunk out in the wee hours of the morning, as he was wont to do these days, so I stared at Trixie's beautiful face while waiting for someone at the store to pick up. It was rush hour, and I knew from past experience that many commuters dropped their things off at the dry cleaner either on their way to the train station or before they merged onto the highway on their way to the city. Sun herself picked up after a few rings, sounding rushed and out of breath.

"Hi, Sun, it's Alison Bergeron returning your call."

"Can't get blood off shirt!" she called into the phone while obviously ringing up someone else's order. "Forty-nine seventy!"

"Excuse me?"

"Blood! Shirt! It's in there for good." She rang someone else up with a much larger order that totaled almost $80. Green dry cleaning doesn't come cheap. "I have to charge you. I just wanted to let you know before you came here and made a scene."

I'm not in the business of making scenes at dry cleaners, but she had clearly had this situation before and wanted to mount a good defense to counteract whatever offense I might employ while in the store. I told her that I was happy to pay for the bloodied shirt and that I would see her later. I hung up the phone and sat down slowly, laying the phone on the kitchen table. I looked at Trixie and worked out the details in my mind, trying to recall what I had stuffed into the laundry bag before bringing it to the store, my thoughts going in myriad directions, given the events of the previous night. It was tights weather so I hadn't shaved my legs in months, eliminating the possibility that I had cut my femoral artery while attempting to defuzz my legs with a dull razor and had forgotten. Crawford used an electric razor to shave his face. I hadn't been attacked by any knife-wielding psychos of late. Then, it finally hit me: Meaghan's jersey. I looked at Trixie and sighed in relief. I must have thrown Meaghan's jersey into the bag after she had spent the night here, her bloody nose wreaking havoc on her jersey. It would take a miracle of laundry science to have gotten that stain out; it covered most of the shirt. It was so bad that I had told her to throw it out, thinking that the least St. Thomas could do was stake her to a new one, but I remembered her telling me that she had thrown it in my hamper; obviously, it had inadvertently ended up in my laundry bag.

Trixie looked relieved as well. I put her on her leash, but instead of taking her outside, I broke her heart by opening up the basement door and telling her we were "going in." The two of us stared down the long flight of rickety wooden steps, pondering our next move. Stay here and wait to see if anything moved, or dive right in? I decided to go with the latter and started down the stairs. Trixie, on the other hand, decided to stay put, putting all of her weight on her hind legs and literally digging in. I would find a deep groove in the floor later where one of her nails had gouged the wood during our standoff. I looked at her from my perch on a wobbly step about halfway down the flight. "You're not coming?" I asked her, as always expecting an answer. I turned and went back up the stairs and into the cabinet next to the refrigerator where I kept a stash of her cookies. I took a bunch in my hand and led her back to the steps to the basement, the cookies just out of her reach. She followed me obediently down the stairs and into the basement; I gave her one cookie to keep her interested in our plan.

The stairs end in between the two major areas of the basement: on the one side, you have the boiler and the furnace, and on the other, the washer/dryer combo and some storage. If you're on one side of the basement, you can't see the other, as a wall bisects the area. It is a representation of terrible architecture, but I had to assume that when the house had been built—in 1947—someone had had some kind of justification for doing so. I didn't like to think too long and hard about what that might be, movies about women trapped in basements haunting my memory every time I carried down a load of laundry. My basement was a hellhole, and I spent as little time down there as I could.

Trixie doesn't like a lot of things—barbecue-flavored kibble, for one—but she absolutely adores rodents. Big rodents, small rodents—it doesn't matter. On countless occasions a squirrel has caught her eye, and before you know it, I'm popping my arm back into its socket after she has taken off, forgetting that on the other end of her leash is my limb. She won't hurt them once she gets to them, but does like to make her presence known. I gave her another cookie and let her off the leash in the basement, giving her instructions to seek and destroy, even though experience told me that if she found a rat, it would be her new playmate. I leaned against the washing machine, long unused, and watched as she poked around behind the boxes filled with Christmas decorations, some leftover mulch in a ripped plastic bag, and some canned goods left over from the last time a hurricane threatened the area. She returned after a few minutes, bored and looking for another treat, which I stuffed in her mouth. Nothing was down here to interest her, not even a dehydrated rat turd, which she would eagerly have devoured, her love of all things scatological well known to all who had walked her in a wooded area. This place was as clean as a whistle, or so my canine detective friend had declared by her lack of interest.

I looked up at the ceiling, contemplating my next move in this weird chess match that was my marriage. I had a husband who habitually lied to me, who was jittery and nervous, and who kept odd hours. Occasionally, he got picked up in town by unidentified drivers. He smelled like another woman's perfume, hid guns in old refrigerators, and was often distracted. He had his picture taken with the mother of two of my players. My modus operandi up until this point had been to wait him out until whatever cases he was working on were over, but something was telling me that he was keeping more from me than I thought and that he was worried for my safety, both troubling scenarios.

Above me, I could hear the dog's nails clicking along on the hardwood floor and then a muffled thud as she took her position by the back door, where the sunlight streamed in and warmed her. I thought for a moment that I should join her, finishing the paper and my cup of coffee, and leaving well enough alone. I had blood-spattered laundry to pick up and a full day of teaching, followed by a home game. Did I really want to continue in this unpleasant vein?

I had just turned the corner and returned to the center of the basement when I came face-to-face with Crawford, who looked like the walking dead.

I gasped and punched him simultaneously. "What are you doing? You scared the life out of me. What are you doing here?"

"I live here," he said.

I started up the stairs after my heart stopped pounding with him on my heels. Trixie was lounging by the back door, just as I expected, not even lifting her head to acknowledge us as we entered the kitchen. "I thought you went to work."

"I had to run a few errands."

"At six in the morning."

"Yeah. At six in the morning." He went over to the coffeepot and poured himself a cup. "And before you go getting crazy, I did not call the rat guy like I told you."

I leaned on the counter, rubbing my fingers over my eyebrows to alleviate the headache that was taking the express train from every nerve ending in my head to the back of my eyes. "Why would you do something like that?" I asked, not looking at him. I can't tell when he's lying anyway, so there's no point in looking for some kind of facial tic that might give his half-truths away.

He took a long swallow of black coffee before answering. "I didn't have a chance to call him, but I didn't want Meaghan to think that we had rats. I will call him today, unless you already spoke to him."

It sounded reasonable but could I believe him? "We don't have rats. Trixie did a full search of the place and didn't see a thing."

"And you trust Trixie more than an exterminator? Someone who's paid to find vermin?"

Trixie's about the only being I trust in the whole world right now, I wanted to say, but didn't. He took my silence as tacit agreement.

"I think we should keep out of there until the situation is resolved," he said in that way he has of making it sound as if it's the law. It's not. It's whatever I say it is, and sometimes he forgets that at his own peril. Again, he took my silence as a complete buy-in and went back to drinking his coffee.

He told me that he was going to try to sleep for a few hours. That he was going to try to sleep after downing a cup of strong, black coffee was ridiculous, but I kept my mouth shut. If he wanted to feel like an elevator stuck between floors—his exhaustion going down, his caffeinated blood going up—that was his business. I grabbed my messenger bag and headed for the car and to Sun's to pick up my questionably clean laundry.

Sun's was still packed with commuters when I arrived, and she was in high dudgeon. The clothes carousel was spinning endlessly, and with the headache I had developed at home just getting stronger by the minute, I had to avert my eyes lest I throw up on Sun's immaculate tiled floor. After she sent several people off with their orders, she looked at me and grabbed the big bag of laundry from the floor behind the counter as well as a box from the shelf that contained all of the cleaned dress shirts.

"Forty-six fifty," she said without preamble.

"Sorry about the blood, Sun."

Sun was a small woman with a waterfall of shiny black hair cascading down her back. She swung a few stray pieces over her shoulder. "It's okay. Next time, let us know and we'll try pretreat."

I didn't go into an explanation of how I didn't know that the jersey had ended up in there and how I had asked Meaghan to just discard it, any chance of our getting it clean lost when we had let the blood dry. I handed over two twenties and a ten and waited for my change.

"Blood is really hard to get out of dress shirts."

"Harder than a basketball jersey?" I asked, taking the change from her and putting it into my wallet.

"I wouldn't know. We've never done a basketball jersey." She laughed. "That must be some team your kid plays on if there's blood on the jersey. But tell us beforehand. We'll pretreat."

I looked at her, the realization dawning on me slowly. I thanked her and went into the parking lot, tossing the clean laundry into the backseat and taking the box of shirts into the front. I ripped the box open and went through the shirts—six in all—undoing all of the careful folding Sun's team had done. When I got to the last shirt and unfolded it, I finally saw what Sun meant.

It must be really hard to get that much blood out of a white oxford dress shirt, especially when it is accompanied by the proverbial lipstick on the collar.

Twenty-Nine

My mind was racing by the time I got to school.

No rats plus lots of blood was just scratching the surface of what I didn't know about my husband. I deserved some answers but didn't think any would be forthcoming, so as is my usual custom when faced with an obstacle, I decided to do something incredibly stupid. I decided that I was going to follow him.

Acting sick for me has been only moderately successful in the past, but I called Sister Mary and left her a voice mail in which I gasped, fake vomited, and pretended to lose consciousness, demonstrating some amazing acting chops. I called one of the

TAs on campus who owed me a favor and asked for coverage for my ten o'clock class, hoping that everything I wanted to accomplish would be done by two, when I had to teach again. Just as I was packing up, my phone rang. Fortunately, it was Fareed, not Mary, who would surely have broken me if we had engaged in conversation.

"Hi, Alison. I'm just returning your call."

It took me a minute to figure out why I had called him, and then it dawned on me. "Fareed, thanks for calling me back. You had mentioned to me that you had some information regarding Kevin's situation and I just wanted to follow up."

A silence far longer than necessary followed.

"Fareed?"

"Yes?"

"Information?"

"I don't have any," he said quickly. "I thought you were calling about the winter dance."

"You did?"

"Yes. We're chaperoning together."

"We are?" Boy, this conversation was devolving fast. And would the fun never end? First, I was forced to be the basketball coach, and now I was being pressed into service as a chaperone at a dance I didn't even know was taking place. "Forget about that," I said, trying to gather my things as quickly as possible. When Crawford had said he was going to get a few hours of sleep, that could have meant anywhere from forty-five minutes to four hours; I had to hurry if I was going to catch him. "Listen, I don't have time right now, but I heard you correctly. You have information and you were going to tell me. I'll call you when I get back." I picked up my bag. "I'm sick," I added for good measure.

"I'm sorry to hear that, Alison, but I won't have anything to tell you when you return."

We'll see about that, I thought as I hurried out of my office and practically ran to my car, trying to look sick while speed-walking in case anyone of note saw me. Such as Sister Mary. Or Father Dwyer. Or worse—Etheridge. I made it to the car without being spotted and hightailed it off campus and onto the Saw Mill River Parkway, praying that Crawford had fallen so dead asleep, but not that dead asleep—I did have a two o'clock class—that I could find him and at least discover where he went "to work." I sighed. His being at the precinct close to campus had made getting together easy; I could buzz over anytime I found a dead body or wanted a martini—or both—and he would usually be there. Now I had no idea how he spent his time or even where he punched the clock.

I was stopped at a light on the north side of the parkway when I spied his staid Volkswagen Passat traveling in the southbound lane at quite a clip. That's the other thing about cops: besides considering what they say being the law, they speed. All the time. And they don't worry about getting pulled over because when they do, just uttering five little words—"I am on the job"—will get them out of just about everything. (Incidentally, if you're not a cop, don't try this. If you're found out, and you will be, you'll go to jail for impersonating an officer of the law. Or so I've heard.) I sank down in my seat as he approached the red light so that hopefully he wouldn't see me and I could continue with my subterfuge apace. I was in the left lane and he was in the right lane on his side, but he seemed to be concerned with a conversation that he was having using his Bluetooth. It was weird to see him talking so animatedly to someone other than me, laughing raucously at one point, grimacing at another. It's not as if I didn't think he interacted with other adults and enjoyed himself immensely, but this behavior, coupled with my recent discoveries, gave me pause.

You're not allowed to have fun if you're not with me, I thought, as the light turned green and the cars started moving. I looked around and made an illegal U-turn, praying that there was no police presence on this lovely winter morning to get in my way.

There wasn't. I kept a safe distance behind him in the right lane, a few cars obstructing my view of him and, with any luck, his view of me. He went the way he would usually go to work, merging onto the Henry Hudson Parkway, but instead of getting off on Broadway, he continued as if he were going to Manhattan. I fished around in my glove compartment for my E-ZPass, hoping I could find it before I had to pick a toll lane. I found it and threw it up into the windshield, watching him sail through, cursing him for using all of the E-ZPass special Velcro and leaving me with none to use on my car, hence the wild waving every time I traversed a major highway or tried to cross a bridge. The bar finally flew up and I craned my neck to catch sight of him again, spying him in front of a Honda Odyssey that seemed filled to the brim with Hasidim. I dropped back and let a car come between me and the minivan, hoping that I hadn't blown it.

I had no idea where we were going, but if he headed any farther south, we were going to end up in Brooklyn, and that would be a problem. I had only been to Brooklyn once and had no sense of how the borough was laid out or even the major roads in and out. We continued from the Henry Hudson to the West Side Highway, where clearly it was going to be even harder to remain unseen; the West Side Highway is a narrow road that runs along the Hudson River, and while it's beautiful, it's also windy and doesn't afford a lot of cover for wives following their wayward husbands.

I don't know how many yellow lights I went through, but it was a lot. I lost count after five. I was far enough away from Crawford's Passat and the lights changed frequently enough that I found myself flooring it far more often than I should have been. He finally pulled over into the left lane and made a left on Canal Street. Now, things were getting complicated.

Chinatown is hard enough to walk through, let alone drive through on a busy weekday. We wended our way through the packed city streets, and I was no closer to finding out where he was going. The terrorist attacks in 2001 had changed everything, and a lot of streets were still closed to traffic all these years later, but Crawford clearly had a destination in mind. As he beat a light and made a quick left, the light turned red and I was stuck. I had lost him. I attempted the same turn just a few minutes later but he was gone, no sign of his sensible station wagon amid the crush of cars on the street. I searched for a few minutes, grateful for the cars in front of me, creeping along at a snail's pace. When it was clear that I wasn't going to find him, I pulled into a spot on the side of the street that was metered, but I didn't put any money in it; I wasn't staying long.

I went with my general thinking posture: hands at ten and two and head resting on the space between them on the steering wheel. I was dismayed that I had followed him and even more dismayed that it was all for naught. I hadn't gotten any closer to finding out where he went when he left our house and what he did once he got there. I had lied to my boss and now had to pull an amazing recovery so that I could come back to school and teach my classes without anyone being the wiser. Yes, I thought, you're a dope. I knew this plan was doomed from the start, but I just couldn't help myself. I was about to leave when there was a tap at my window. Crawford. Man, he looked awful. I rolled down the window.

"Do you know how many yellow lights you blew on the way down here?"

"Seven?" I said helpfully.

"Thirteen." He was not amused. He went around to the passenger side and got into the car, slamming the door shut with more force than was required. "God, this is not funny anymore."

"Was it ever?"

I had a point and he knew it. "Why were you following me?"

"Because I don't know where you go or what you do or who you see." It was out of my mouth before I had time to think, but he got the gist of my paranoia. "And you smell like perfume all the time." At least I hadn't blurted out that I had found the other gun or that I thought that he had either given himself a home gallbladder operation or he had had some kind of extremely violent encounter that had resulted in someone's evisceration.

He put both his hands over his face, and if I didn't know him as well as I did, I might have thought I heard a small sob escape. He spoke from behind his hands. "I know I've given you no reason to trust me, but you have to."

I looked out my window, wondering how I was going to do that.

"I thought you were occupying your time trying to find out what happened to Kevin."

I looked at him. "How did you know that?"

He raised an eyebrow. He knew everything I was doing. At all times. And that, in itself, was somewhat troubling.

"I'm nowhere on that."

"There might be a reason for that."

The words hung in the air. I knew where he was going with that but I didn't like the route he was taking. "He's innocent."

"How can you be so sure?" He was weary of this conversation, and of every other conversation we had had in the past few weeks.

At that moment I realized I wasn't so sure. I had been chasing an elusive thread of innocence that I had grabbed at the beginning, but I was no closer to finding its end. Crawford knew that, yet he had let me keep going because it meant that I was leaving him alone to do God knew what. I realized I hadn't truly looked into his eyes in weeks so I turned his face so that I could. He tried to avert his gaze but I held tight.

"What do you want from me?" he asked, an opening shot that didn't have a lot of force behind it.

"I want you to tell me the truth. I want *you* back." I want to pick up your shirts and yell at you about the ketchup stains on the cuffs, not wonder why there's blood all over them and why they are stashed in the closet. I want to be angry at you because you never do yard work and you're a lazy layabout on the weekends, not to be curious as to why you spend so much time in the basement and the garage. I want to pretend I am asleep when you come home in the middle of the night after doing a double shift with only conversation and sex on your mind instead of lying awake hoping that you'll come back. I want the Crawford who really has no business loving me to love me again in that weird kind of detached way that he has and that I adore.

"I never left," he said, but without conviction. He knew the truth. He put his hand on the door handle. "I have to go. I have an appointment. Do you have a game tonight?"

I had traveled twenty miles and had gotten exactly nowhere. I had a feeling that if I checked when I got home, the gun would be gone, just like the last one. "Yeah."

"Home or away?"

"Home."

"I'll try to make it." He was nearly out of the car when he leaned back in and grabbed me, pulling me so close I couldn't breathe. He put his lips on mine for a long time, but they were cold and hard. He finally pulled away and I filled my lungs with air. "Never think I don't love you."

It wasn't an undying declaration but it would have to do. Based on the way we had been living for the past few weeks, the bar for romance had been set pretty low.

He walked away, crossing the street against the light and not at a crosswalk, making time as he approached a pizza place. Outside the store was a man who looked familiar to me but part of whose face was in shadows; I couldn't get a good look to identify him. At first, I thought Crawford would stop and talk to the man, but he avoided him even as he passed right by, going into the store. I waited a second before putting the car in drive and easing out of the spot and into traffic. As I drove past the store, I tried to get a good look at the guy, who stood, statue-like, under its red-and-green awning, but it was impossible on a busy street in lower Manhattan with the shadows providing him cover.

I looked in the rearview mirror and saw that he had left. Whether he had gone into the pizzeria was anyone's guess, but my guess was that he had. Something about the way Crawford had carried himself, the closer he got to the guy, made me think that the store was where he was headed all along. Why was another story.

I let it go as I drove north and picked up the West Side Highway again. I'm at that age where if I try to remember something, inevitably I won't. I decided that the less I thought about the man—a nondescript guy in his midforties with gray hair and a weathered face—the easier his identity would reveal itself.

I had more important things on my mind, after my conversation with Crawford. For one, why did he feel the need to profess his love for me in such an awkward way? Does that mean that Jacqueline was really part of some case, as weird a coincidence as that would be? And more important, why did he look so scared?

Thirty

I went back to school and became a walking advertisement for Cold-EEZE, telling Sister Mary that it was nothing short of a miracle. I felt so much better than I had earlier and, yes, I would be teaching my afternoon classes. She looked at me suspiciously when I ran into her in the cafeteria, eyeing my plate of spaghetti with spicy marinara, made especially for me by Marcus. It was enough to feed three people and I was going to eat the entire thing along with the half a loaf of garlic bread that Marcus snuck onto my tray. All that I needed was a nice glass of Barolo, and I was all set.

Following my lying husband had made me work up quite an appetite, and I carried my tray to a table by the window to eat my food in peace. Within thirty seconds of my sitting down, Fareed appeared, looking as if he were dodging the secret police. "I can't stay long."

"Good, because I don't like to be interrupted while I'm eating." I forked a large quantity of spaghetti into my mouth. This trait is one thing I share with Trixie: do not disturb us with a full plate—or bowl—of food in front of us.

"Look at me." The tone of his voice made me drop my fork and look up. "We cannot be seen together. We cannot talk. I will contact you when I can."

"Um, okay." I stifled a giggle. It felt good to laugh after being near tears for the entire drive back. I guess I had missed the memo written in invisible ink that told me we were engaged in some kind of cloak-and-dagger operation that would require us to be apart. We taught in different departments and didn't spend a lot of time together as it was; how much time did we need to spend apart exactly?

"I'm serious," he said, his face a mask of gravity. "I will call you." With that, he was off, disappearing into the sea of backpack-toting students, all clamoring for some kind of lunch item at the counter.

I finished my spaghetti and was happy to see that I had managed to eat and not completely destroy the front of my blouse with stray drops of sauce. A paper, left over from the breakfast service, sat on the corner of the table, the headlines screaming about a woman who was fired from her job as a stockbroker because of her revealing wardrobe. I had problems, but that, for sure, was not one of them. I flipped through the paper to see what some of these offending ensembles looked like and was surprised to find that, while tight, they were definitely more conservative than what some of the female students on campus wore, in addition to some of the professors.

Or Carmen Montoya. I saw her come through the doors of the cafeteria, her blouse hugging her curves, her jeans molded to her toned thighs and ample backside. She sat across from me. "Hey, girl. I'm hungry. What should I have?"

I tried not to appear as unnerved as I was. In the past, Carmen was an entertaining player in the theater that was Crawford's work life, but every time she appeared now, it was in an official capacity. She threw her giant pocketbook on the chair next to her and folded her hands on the table.

"I would stick with the hot food. The cold cuts are of indeterminate origin," I said.

"Good to know." She sauntered back to the counter to order lunch. Marcus glanced over at me, wondering who this self-possessed and attractive woman was, and I pointed at myself as if to say, "It's on me." He nodded and took her order. She returned to the table a few minutes later with a hot roast beef sandwich dripping coleslaw and mustard, courtesy of Marcus, along with a giant soda. She took a big bite and rolled her eyes back into her head. "Heaven."

I pulled my hands under the table so that she wouldn't see them shaking. "How did you know where I was?"

She waited until her mouth was almost empty before responding. "You weren't in your office so I figured you'd be in here. They don't call me *detective* for nothing."

"How are your kids?" I asked, in case she was here to visit me instead of interrogate me.

"Girl, please. Driving me crazy." She took a long sip of her soda and wiped her fingers on a paper napkin. "Oldest one is good. She's at Cornell. If I get number two out of high school, we'll be in good shape. The other two? I'm still molding them into my perfect image." She took another bite of her sandwich. "Hey," she said between mouthfuls of roast beef, "did you know that your husband knew Jacqueline Bianco?"

That didn't take long. I shook my head.

"When did you find out that she was the woman in the picture?"

"When she came by school to meet me."

Carmen continued to inhale her sandwich. "Maybe one of my kids could go here so I could eat here occasionally."

"You can eat here anytime you want," I said, feeling queasy.

"I have a feeling if I did, you'd never come out of your office," she said, finishing up in record time. She spent a long time wiping her hands clean. Her fingernails were painted a dark crimson, almost black, but were immaculately manicured. I wondered how she kept herself looking so hip and happening with four kids and a job that was more than full-time. "Any idea what the connection might be?"

"I thought you could tell me that."

She pursed her lips. "Nope."

We sat in silence for a few minutes, each waiting for information the other might offer. Finally, she looked at me. "I believe that he's still one of the good guys. You know that, right?"

I held a hand up. "Don't say anything else." I was dangerously close to melting down. As much as she intimidated me, I was also comforted by her presence. I thought that if she didn't work with my husband—or work at finding out about my husband—we could be friends.

"There's an explanation for this," she said, almost to convince herself. "There always is."

Something dawned on me. "Isn't your husband high up in the police department? Couldn't he tell us what's going on? What Crawford's probably working on?"

The look on her face was one that I recognized from Crawford's arsenal of facial expressions: her features rearranged into something approximating sadness, but what was really there was consternation. Seems that she had already acted on my suggestion and hadn't gotten anywhere. "He's high up all right, but that's no help to us."

"Anything on Vito Passella?"

She looked up at the ceiling. "I wish. I thought that case was open-and-shut, but . . ." She threw her hands up in the air. When it was clear that we had nothing else to share with each other, she got up, and as was her custom, she embraced me. "I'll see you around, *chica*."

The only way to make things right, in my experience, was to take matters into my own hands. I left the cafeteria and went back to my office to catch up on e-mail before heading out to talk to Fareed. My conversation with Carmen, brief as it was, had left me a little more depressed. If she didn't know what Crawford was doing at work, how could I know? She spent a lot more time with him and knew him better in a professional capacity. Why had she come to see me today? What was she hoping to find out? Frustrated, I left my office and descended the back staircase one flight. I wended my way through the rabbits' warren of offices that resided below mine, finding Fareed in his tiny, corner office. The building where we teach and have our offices is old—1800s old—and instructors are jammed into every corner and alleyway the school can find. Fareed's office was stuck behind what was once a grand ballroom and next to a hidden staircase that everyone knew led straight up to the convent. He had his back turned to me when I walked in, seemingly contemplating a picture of a seascape that hung over his filing cabinet. I closed the office door behind me, interrupting his train of thought.

"Spill it." I pulled the guest chair out and plopped down.

He turned around so quickly that he nearly spun himself off his desk chair. He righted himself by grabbing the side of his desk. "Alison!" he said in a loud whisper. "We can't do this."

"Fareed, knock it off. I'm not a Savak agent."

His face paled. "How do you know about Savak?"

I tried to concoct a good story whereby I had been beaten and tortured during my years as a spy, but that was about as believable as Crawford's self-performed gallbladder operation. "Wikipedia."

"Not funny, Alison. My uncle died at the hands of a particularly cruel Savak agent."

We were not off to a good start. "Okay, then. I'm sorry." I looked around his little office and took in the pictures of Iran that he had hung on his walls. "Listen, Fareed. You have to tell me what you know. I really want to find out what happened to Kevin. I really will not rest until I get the truth on this."

Fareed studied my face for a long time before answering, and I could feel the sweat breaking out on my neck. If I were into hunky, exotic-looking business professors—which I definitely *was not*—I would have been flattered with his attention. As it was, his staring was starting to make me uncomfortable. He ticked off his reasons for not talking about Kevin's situation. "Rumor has it that (a) he doesn't want your help, (b) he has embraced secular life wholeheartedly, and (c) we will find ourselves in what you would call a 'whole heap of trouble' if we continue to ask around."

"Who told you all of that?"

The look on his face told me that he knew it was futile to play dumb; I would just keep pressing until he cracked, despite that I hadn't studied the torture techniques of the Savak. "Father Dwyer."

"Really?"

Fareed leaned in across the desk, coming as close to me as the piece of furniture would allow. "He said that if I spent any more time with you on this matter, there would be repercussions."

My raised eyebrows said it all.

"No, I don't know what that means, but I need this job, Alison. I can't jeopardize my career at St. Thomas."

Clearly, he was more attached to his teaching career than I was.

"I really like Kevin, Alison, but I can't get involved."

I understood. Fareed was a nice guy, but like the rest of us, he had a mortgage, kids, car payments, and the like. Kevin wasn't really doing all that much to get himself out of this pickle, as far as I knew; this was my reason for being at the moment, and I am sure that was confounding to everyone. "So he threatened you?"

Fareed shrugged. "Not in so many words."

By the look on Fareed's face, I knew that he had shut down and that was going to be the end of our conversation. I got up. "Thanks, Fareed."

"For what?"

"I don't know. Your support of the team?" I chuckled. "We need all the support we can get."

He looked chagrined. "I wish I could help, Alison."

He couldn't, though. His job was on the line. What I couldn't figure out was why.

Thirty-One

I was not prepared for the game.

Neither was Fred. He looked as if he had seen a ghost, and that, more than anything else that had happened thus far that day, upset me. To this point he had been pretty guarded about his feelings about Crawford's behavior of late, besides letting his feelings of abandonment be known, but now that I had cued him in on the more sinister aspects of Crawford's action, he was at sea. He stood with his whiteboard, looking as if he would rather be anywhere but on the basketball court with a team who had come to adore him and me, his faithful companion and head coach. I attempted to wrap my arm around his waist, only making it halfway before encountering his holster and gun. He flinched slightly, not used to having someone so close to his weapon.

I gave his waist a little squeeze. "Don't worry. I'm not going to use your gun against you."

He tried to smile but couldn't.

"Hey, wave to Max. She's trying to get your attention." I pointed her out in the stands. Once again she had found a way to sit beside Fareed and his ever-loving hotness. She waved vigorously in our direction, having taken a car service from her office in Manhattan up here to the game to support her husband.

The girls were lining up for layups as the practice clock counted down. Tonight, there were no St. Thomas Dancers and no color man on the loudspeaker, Erin and Fez having been shipped back to New Paltz and told to stay there under threat of death. It was just the girls and the opposing team, all the drama put on the shelf until presumably the next Joliet game. I was grateful to go back to our simple routine of layups and our stupid chant, and a prayer to the Blessed Virgin Mary that so far had gone unanswered. That all felt familiar in a world that was becoming increasingly unfamiliar.

By the grace of God or Allah or even Yahweh, we won. It was a nail-biter, but we pulled it out. Meaghan was happier than I had seen her in days, even though her father hadn't made it to the game, as he had alluded he might. She had a good game, scoring twenty-one points and grabbing five rebounds, probably her best stats to date. She was riding high when she asked if we could go out for a celebratory ice cream sundae at the diner. I was exhausted but happy that she had asked. She didn't want the evening to end and I was more than happy to oblige. I was happy to ride this wave of good feeling right along with her.

I told her to get changed and meet me in the lobby of the gym. The building had emptied out, and it was just Max and me in the darkened hallway; Fred was putting the balls away and chasing any leftover spectators out of the building so that the maintenance crew could clean up and lock the doors; Fred is nothing if not sensitive to the plight of those who work nights, having spent years working in the dark himself. Max was tapping the toe of her boot impatiently until I reminded her that Fred was in charge of dispatching everyone and wouldn't leave until the building was empty.

"I haven't eaten," she said, and if I've learned one thing, it's that a hungry Max is an extremely unpleasant Max.

"What about the hot dog I saw you shoving into your mouth during halftime?"

"That was just a snack," she said as if I had made a ridiculous statement. No one, obviously, should consider a foot-long hot dog a meal.

"Meaghan and I are going to the diner, if you want to come."

"I'll ask Red Auerbach in there," she said, rolling her eyes toward the gym. Fred came through the doors, not looking as happy as I would expect him to after an elusive win for the Blue Jays. Although Max is obtuse about most things, she is incredibly perceptive when it comes to her husband. "What's wrong?"

He looked at me. "I do have something."

Max looked at him. "Like what? Crabs? The clap?"

He ignored her. "Right before the game, someone from IT called me."

Max waved her hands in front of his face when he hesitated. "And . . ."

"Copies of the pictures you were sent were found in Vito Passella's apartment on his computer."

I had already put two and two together in my mind. I figured if he was posing as a St. Thomas mailman, he had probably had possession of the pictures and was in charge of delivering them. He had no other reason to be on campus unless bag money from strip clubs and drug sales had suddenly dried up. Fred looked so earnest, so I bit my lip and let my snappy retort of "No shit, Sherlock" stay in my throat.

"There's more," he said.

"Well, I hope so," Max said. "Anyone with a complete set of *Murder, She Wrote* DVDs could have figured out that the guy was the one who had the pictures, if not the guy who had taken them to begin with. He was mobbed-up. They have their ways of getting in touch when they need to get in touch."

"There were pictures of both girls. Erin at New Paltz and Meaghan here. Pictures of Christine overseas. He was watching everyone."

"Does Crawford know?" I asked.

"If he doesn't already, he will soon. Carmen is filling him in."

I looked up at Fred. "Are we in danger? Is Peter Miceli involved?"

He didn't have a chance to answer because Meaghan and several of her teammates burst through the heavy metal doors to the gym. "Ready?" she asked.

I thought about changing our plans and telling her that we would go straight home, but what would that accomplish? I looked at Fred. "We're going to the diner. Do you want to come?"

Fred hates the diner, but he wanted to come along. So now I had an answer to my question. We were definitely in danger.

Thirty-Two

I wasn't hungry but I ordered a sandwich so as not to raise suspicion. Meaghan has been around me enough to know that I don't pass up a chance for a meal, particularly one cooked by someone else and served to me with a parsley garnish. When it came, I made an attempt at eating, but my appetite was gone. Max, on the other hand, devoured her triple-decker turkey club, french fries, and chocolate shake before taking half of my ham on rye onto her plate.

She had almost finished the half when my cell phone trilled in my pocketbook. Caller ID identified Erin. I didn't roll my eyes but I felt like it; if she was calling me, she must have been pretty desperate. I'm usually the last one on her list. "Hello?"

"It's Erin," she said, her voice a hoarse rasp.

"What's the matter?" I asked, concerned.

"I'm sick. Can I come to your house?"

She must have been dying if she was making that request. "Have you been to the doctor on campus?"

"Yes. I have strep. It's bad."

"Did they give you anything?" I looked across the table and took in Meaghan's worried face. I put my hand over the receiver. "She's okay; it's strep."

"They gave me penicillin."

"You're allergic to penicillin," I said a little too loudly, startling the people at the counter. A coffee cup rattled on someone's saucer. "How much have you taken?"

"Just two pills. One this morning and one this afternoon."

I couldn't understand why she would let herself be prescribed something that could send her into anaphylactic shock, but my concern over the situation trumped my wondering at her stupidity. "Listen. Call Fez and tell him to come over to your place immediately. If you start to exhibit any reactions to the penicillin, have him take you straight to the ER. I'm on my way."

I hung up and filled in the blanks for Max, Fred, and Meaghan. Fred said, "I've got this," referencing the check.

Meaghan downed her soda. "I'm coming with you."

I started to talk her out of it, but realized it was no use. If her sister was involved, she was involved. There was no way around it.

We had a two-hour trip ahead of us, so I got myself a cup of coffee and Meaghan a hot chocolate to go. Fred and Max walked us out to the parking lot. "Call me when you get there," Fred said. "On second thought, do you want me to go with you?"

The night was turning bitter cold and I could see my breath

when I answered him. "No. Go home. I'll call you every step of the way." He looked dubious. "Scout's honor. I'll call you."

Max was jumping up and down to stay warm. She looked at Meaghan. "Where did you come from? So low drama."

I often wondered that myself. They had shared a womb and DNA yet couldn't be more different. I told her to call her father, and if he didn't answer, to send him a text outlining our plan.

We sat in silence until we got onto the New York State Thruway, about a half hour. I have found that I get some of my best information and have the most revealing conversations with her when we're alone in the car. The pitch black of the winter night, coupled with the cozy confines of the car, afforded us time to explore our relationship in a nonthreatening way. I decided to prod gently.

"Kristy didn't have a good game tonight," I said.

Meaghan didn't say anything, which I took to mean that she agreed.

"Why do you think that was? Is she still upset about the Joliet game? Maybe she came back too soon after what happened with her dad?" Lou Bianco was still hospitalized.

"Maybe."

"Do you think I should talk to her?"

More silence. "Whatever you think."

I let three more exits go by before I attempted to restart the conversation. "Why do you think that idiot from Joliet said what he did?"

She let out a long breath. "Do we have to talk about this?" She was leaning against the passenger-side door, her long legs pulled up to her chest, her entire posture telling me that she knew more than she was letting on.

I decided to reveal my hand. "Listen, Meaghan. Kevin McManus is my best friend in the world beside your father and Max. I don't think he did the things they're saying he did. And I also have reason to believe what he's being accused of has something to do with the Bianco girls." Meaghan started to talk but I held a hand up. "Don't ask me how I know that, but I do. Now tell me what you know." I didn't know why it hadn't occurred to me to ask her sooner, but I suspected it had something to do with the tenuous tango that is the dance between a new wife and her new stepdaughter. Meaghan and I get along well, but it took a tremendous amount of effort—on both of our parts—to maintain that delicate balance. That I was pushing as hard as I was, was a testament to how much I wanted Kevin exonerated. I had skirted many an issue with the girls that as a mother I would never have avoided, such as the crushed-up end of a joint that I had found in Erin's coat pocket or the C– that Meaghan was destined to get in Calculus, according to her teacher and my longtime colleague. She was also a freshman and I wondered just how much she could know, but I returned to my earlier revelation that girls talk. A secret is held only so long; once it becomes social clout, it's out.

"I don't know. Maybe she's gay," she said, her voice barely a whisper.

I waited. This wasn't really a revelation, and I didn't know how that piece of information related to anything.

"She was seeing Father McManus for counseling."

On how to be gay?

"She can't handle it. Her parents would flip if they found out."

This didn't surprise me. St. Thomas is known as a conservative institution, and is becoming more so with every passing year. Now that Father Dwyer had taken the theological reins, it seemed that the school's journey to the extreme right of all social issues was nearly complete. The disbanding of the St. Thomas Gay and Lesbian Student Union was at the forefront of Father Dwyer's mission, or so it seemed, and I could understand why a young woman, barely an adult, would struggle in the face of such propaganda, thinking that her orientation was something she could somehow bury deep inside her.

It's hard to believe that such thinking exists in the twenty-first century, but in all my years at St. Thomas, it was evident that in terms of issues such as this, the Church was going backward instead of forward. I felt for the girl.

"Did Kevin help her?" Our conversation about internal forum came back to me, and I thought about how anything Kevin had been told was going with him to his grave.

"I don't know," Meaghan said, pulling her legs closer to her chest. I had a little time, if her body language was any indication, to get to the bottom of this. After that, the conversation would be over. I had enough experience with the Crawford girls, and teenagers in general, to know that this was the case. "I don't know. That's all I know."

"Is this gossip around the school or did you hear it from someone in particular?"

Meaghan looked at me. "Let's put it this way: she shouldn't trust her sister."

That explained a lot, but not all of it. It explained the note I had received but not much else. Was Elaina blabbing about her sister's personal life all over campus? If so, that information provided a link between Kristy and Kevin, but not much else. After I solved the mystery of why a medical doctor had given Erin a potentially life-threatening prescription, and why she had taken it, I would return to why Kevin had been expelled from school and the priesthood. And why my husband was acting like a complete stranger with something to hide.

Did Kristy have something to do with Kevin's situation? Given the outburst of the Joliet student at the game, there was definitely a link. Kevin counseled a lot of students—many of us thought that his real gift—so she was just one in a sea of confused and unhappy young adults. There was no way I would be able to broach the subject, though; what had gone on between her and Kevin in a counseling capacity would be confidential.

The only way I could get any information out of her would be if she volunteered it.

It was late so we made it to New Paltz in record time. I left the car in the first spot that I saw, probably illegal, and we raced to Erin's dorm, Meaghan leading the way, more in shape than I was and a vastly superior runner. I was still in heels and my feet were killing me, but I pushed through and caught up to Meaghan, holding the door of the dorm for me for far longer than she expected she would have to and anxious to get to her sister. A resident assistant was manning the front desk and asked whom we were there to see.

"Erin Crawford," I said, holding out my license for her verification of my identity. "I'm her stepmother and this is her sister."

The resident assistant smiled. "Wow, she's popular tonight."

I was signing my name in the guest book but hesitated. "What do you mean?"

"Her dad's here," she said, taking the pen back from me.

I looked at Meaghan, trying not to let on how perplexed I actually was. I thanked the RA and headed to the stairs, remembering that Erin's room was only on the second floor of the building. Meaghan took the steps two at a time and waited for me at the top.

It was late, a few kids were roaming the halls, and a few of the doors to the rooms on the floor were open, sounds of music drifting out. Rap here, a little rock here, some dance there, it all combined into a cacophony of discordant sounds. I wondered how anybody got any work done or could concentrate at all.

Erin's dorm room door was closed. I knocked lightly and called in, but there was no answer. Meaghan and I looked at each other, deciding simultaneously to open the door and let ourselves in. The room was dark, but I could make out the shape of Erin huddled on her bed, a big blanket wrapped around her. She was shaking.

I walked in. "Oh, God, Erin," I said, walking over to her bed. Her roommate's bed was neatly made and there was no sign of the elusive Tammy, who, from what Meaghan had told me, spent as much time in her boyfriend's room as possible to avoid seeing Erin. I put my hand on her forehead; it was cool. I put my hand out to turn on the light on the desk next to her bed and was about to ask her where her father was.

"Don't turn that on," a male voice said, a voice huskier and more accented in the streets of New York than Crawford's was.

My hand froze, outstretched toward the lamp. "Who's here?" I asked, the darkness of the room lending an air of the sinister to an already sinister situation. I heard the door, which had whooshed closed behind us, give a final click as the lock caught.

"Never mind." I felt a hand on my shoulder. I used my peripheral vision to make out the shape of Meaghan standing next to and a bit behind me. "Don't get any ideas. This is going to go one way and one way alone. But I need your cooperation."

"Okay. Just calm down," I said, even though I had no idea if the man in the room was as nervous as I was. Someone's chest was pounding—I could hear it—but I wasn't sure if it was mine or his. "They're just girls. Leave them alone."

"They're coming, too," he said, nudging me closer to Meaghan, my back still to him.

"Coming where?" I asked, sounding a lot calmer than I actually felt.

"Someplace safe."

Call me crazy, but I didn't believe him.

Thirty-Three

We aren't related by blood and I had not carried them for nine months, but they were still my family. I had never had what I considered a maternal instinct, but at that moment I realized that if it was a choice between them or me, I was going to lay down my life to make sure that they came out of this situation safely.

He outlined how it was going to go: we were going to walk, as a group, out of the dorm and into a waiting van. He would have his arm around Erin, and Meaghan and I would walk in front of them. I assumed he had some kind of weapon but I didn't know what it was. His next directive was for Erin. "And if you try anything, things will not go well. Just do everything I say and everybody will be fine, okay?"

I protested that Erin was too sick to leave and begged him to leave her there, ignoring the pitiful sounds that were coming out of Meaghan.

Erin's voice was small when she spoke. She was still sitting on her bed, trembling. "I'm not sick. He made me say that."

"So you didn't take penicillin?"

"No." Her voice had lost a little of its usual petulant tone. "I'm not even sick."

That was a relief. At least she didn't run the danger of going into anaphylactic shock in the midst of our being kidnapped.

The husky-voiced man spoke again. "Are we clear on how this is going to go?"

We all agreed, one by one.

"Then let's get moving."

We went out into the brightly lit hallway and proceeded toward the stairwell like a strangely affectionate family, my arm wrapped tightly around Meaghan's waist, presumably the man's arms around Erin. He was still behind me, and he if was smart, attached to Erin at the hip; of all of us, she was the most likely to run for the hills, and he sounded smart enough to have concluded that on his own. I didn't think she would put us in harm's way intentionally, but I knew from experience that she was wont to take care of herself first and foremost, the rest of us be damned. We passed several clusters of students, none of whom paid us any mind, except for one who had seen an article about Meaghan from the *Daily Blue Jay*, which Erin had taped to her door. He high-fived Meaghan, startling her, but I kept ahold of her waist and steered her toward the stairs. I hesitated at the door.

"Keep going," the man said. "And stop thinking."

Either this guy was a mind reader or he had done something

like this before because he knew that I was trying to formulate a plan. My mind was racing as we descended the stairs we had run up just minutes earlier, Meaghan stumbling slightly, her nerves getting the best of her. We hit the bottom landing and I pushed open the door to the lobby.

We moved through the lobby in unison. Meaghan wasn't openly crying, but I could hear sobs catching in her throat. Erin wasn't making a sound, and I pictured the wheels in her head turning as well as we got closer to the front door and the van that was waiting to take us someplace "safe." Safe, my foot. If I had to guess, we were heading straight for trouble or worse. At that moment, when a group of students burst through the doors, I took an enormous leap of faith and bet that he wouldn't shoot us in front of anyone. I pushed Meaghan into the crowd of students and wheeled around to grab Erin, still wrapped in her down comforter. The guy, sensing that this wasn't going to go the way he planned—and frankly, it was a bad plan from the start in my opinion and one that had no hope of success—took off down the hallway, disappearing around a corner and out of sight. All I saw before he disappeared was a flash of black as I watched the back of his head, trying to remember everything I could about his height, weight, and the clothes he was wearing if I lost him.

"Stay here," I said to the girls, taking off down the hall once the shock of what had happened began to wear off. The students who had come through the door were long gone, having dispersed into the adjoining lounge and their respective dorm rooms. The whole thing had happened so quickly that no one knew what was going on, and as we were amid college students, they were all focused on their own destinations, their own lives, their own needs. Seeing what would appear to be a close-knit family making their way out into the cold air raised no suspicions, even at this late hour. I ran down the long, narrow hallway and toward the door that I thought he had exited through, regretting that I had worn extremely unpractical shoes for catching a kidnapper. I pushed through the door at the end of the hallway and then through the one that would lead to the outdoors, just in time to see the man jump into the waiting van, which was parked behind the dorm. That left me to wonder why he had tried to drag us out through the front door, but that wasn't my concern; finding out who he was and why he had attempted to take us was. I strained in the dark to see the license-plate number, but it was predictably smeared with mud and unreadable.

I stood for a moment in the dark and tried to slow my breathing before I went back to the girls. Now was not the time to go off the rails emotionally even though that was exactly what I felt like doing. I bent over at the waist and rested my hands on my knees, trying to clear my head. When I stood again, I spotted a figure coming toward me in the dark, the size and shape unmistakable, even in the shadowy gloom.

Crawford.

He strode across the lawn behind the dorm toward me.

"Okay," I said, my breath coming out in frozen chuffs. "Okay."

He reached me and put a hand on my shoulder. "Are you hurt?"

I shook my head. "What are you doing here?"

"I got your text," he said evenly.

I punched him in one shoulder and then in the other. I kept punching him until I was out of strength and crying openly. "You're lying! You've been lying for weeks! I don't believe anything you say," I cried, punching him again. My nose was running, my breath making silvery clouds in the frigid night air. "I don't believe you," I whispered, my voice hoarse.

He took my wrists in one hand, preventing me from striking him again. "You're right. I have been lying. Come on. We'll start at the beginning."

I wish I hadn't asked. Sometimes it's better not to know.

Thirty-Four

It had only been a few days since Lou Bianco had been attacked in what was a botched robbery attempt, according to the police, so I decided to take a chance and give Jacqueline Bianco a call to see if she would provide a consultation in my neck of the woods. I thought this was a dumb plan, but everyone else involved—namely Crawford's compadres at the Fiftieth—had decided it was brilliant. What did I know? While Crawford stood and watched me, I dialed the phone and waited, thinking that on a Sunday night, I would get her machine at the offices of her interior design studio. Imagine my surprise when she picked up the phone.

"JLB Interiors. Jacqueline Bianco speaking."

We had rehearsed what I would say once I got ahold of her, but I still wasn't prepared. I stammered, finally getting out my greeting. "Hello, Mrs. Bianco. This is Alison Bergeron. The girls' basketball coach?"

It took her a minute, but she finally figured out who I was. I guess the real confusion lay in why I would be calling her on a Sunday night. "Are the girls okay?"

"They're fine," I said quickly, not wanting her to worry. "I'm actually calling you in a professional capacity."

"How can I help you?"

I went through my prepared speech about my horribly decorated living and dining rooms and asked if she could help me. "If you're working, that is. And if I'm not too far off the beaten path for you."

"Where do you live, Dr. Bergeron?"

"Alison, please." I gave her my address. "In Dobbs Ferry. About an hour from you."

"That should be fine. Let me get my calendar." Her voice was smooth as silk, not letting on any suspicions she had regarding the phone call, if she had any. I already knew she knew Crawford, but she didn't know that. We went back and forth regarding our schedules until we settled on Wednesday right between my last class and the start of practice. "Let me ask you, Alison, why JLB Interiors?"

Crawford had walked me through this as well. "I like working with people who have excellent reputations. And based on what I've learned about you and your work, your reputation is unrivaled. I'm also very fond of your daughters."

He told me that flattery would get me everywhere with her; he would know.

He was right. "Well, thank you. That's so lovely to hear. I'll see you Wednesday."

I hung up and looked at Crawford. "Good job," he said.

I had executed the phone call with relative ease, but acting my part in Wednesday's charade would be much harder. First, I would have to wear a wire, and second, my bedroom would be filled with a bunch of detectives, all of whom knew me and would be listening to my conversation with Jacqueline. The conversation would ostensibly be about window treatments but would, in reality, hopefully uncover why she had used her considerable power and influence within the Lucarelli family and New York Catholic society in general to have Kevin McManus removed from his position at St. Thomas and exiled to Throgs Neck, with Father Dwyer taking his place. I would also try to find out if she had ordered the hit on Vito Passella or if he had just been some kind of pawn in a Mob game.

The *L* in JLB interiors stood for "Lucarelli." Jacqueline Bianco had been born Guiseppina Lucarelli and was the only daughter of Salvatore "Loose Lips" Lucarelli, the former head of the family, currently serving three consecutive life terms in upstate New York. But that didn't mean that the family couldn't function without him; on the contrary, business was booming now that Jacqueline's cousin Mauricio had come over from Italy to take charge. Things had never been better.

Peter Miceli had contacted Crawford just shortly before Vito Passella had been killed, warning him that the Lucarellis were involved in Kevin's dismissal. How did he come to know this information, given his new residence in Indiana? And why did he care? As my luck would have it, Vito Passella was once a Lucarelli, and prior to his untimely passing, a Mob turncoat, coming over to the Miceli side of things. Vito had overheard a conversation between Mauricio and another soldier about Father McManus and his chaplaincy at St. Thomas; Vito didn't know why, but they weren't happy with Kevin and something he had done, and it had something to do with one of Jacqueline Bianco's daughters. Peter Miceli, on the other hand, loved Kevin and had never made any bones about that, Kevin having been a source of comfort when Peter had lost both his daughter and, later, his wife. Kevin had also, unbeknownst to me, counseled Peter during the lengthy trial that had ensued after Gianna's death and Peter's arrest and had been in regular touch with Peter while he was serving time in a maximum-security prison.

Peter, it would seem, had found Jesus. And when someone started messing with Jesus' messenger and Peter's sole source of solace these days—a.k.a. Kevin McManus—Peter forgot about religion and thought only about revenge.

An eye for an eye. A whack for a whack.

A Lucarelli soldier had killed a recently appointed Miceli soldier—Vito—leaving him in my car trunk in much the same way that Peter's daughter had been left in my car trunk, adding insult to injury. The Mob is nothing if not unoriginal and wildly vindictive.

I had always figured Peter for a moron, but that he was putting pieces of the puzzle together from his jail cell impressed me. He started with Kevin's dismissal and responded, in time, by figuring out a way to put one of his guys—a mole—in the midst of things. Vito was more than happy to gain a foothold in the Miceli family, having done something that made his standing with the Lucarellis lukewarm at best. It was common knowledge that the Bianco sisters—Kristy, at least—went to St. Thomas; after all, she was the star of the Blue Jays. Vito starts working at St. Thomas, Vito knows that the Bianco sisters are students, and things start to fall into place for him. He keeps Peter apprised the entire time and is close to the truth when he gets whacked. Peter contacts Crawford, thinking that something is afoot. Crawford contacts OCCB, which puts him to work, a unit not really concerned that their new undercover's wife thinks she's going crazy and losing the love of her life to a life of crime and possibly another woman. Crawford is told to get close to Jacqueline Bianco, to see what she knows, if anything. He does this by pretending to be a client; Jacqueline lives and works in New Jersey and has no idea that he's a cop and that the condo she will be decorating in Weehawken is a rental that the police department has leased. As all this is happening, someone in the Lucarelli family has already figured out that Vito has become a double agent at worst, a turncoat at best. Not content to leave well enough alone and put things in Crawford's hands, Peter sends me the photos as a warning to stay away from Jacqueline Lucarelli, someone I would probably never have met had I not become the basketball coach. In his ham-fisted way, however, Peter's overtures only lead me to suspect that my husband has gone to the dark side and that maybe Kevin is guilty of something; what, I don't know. When all is said and done, I end up smack-dab in the middle of a Mob turf war over accusations leveled at one of my best friends.

The questions that remained were not insignificant: Who had beaten Lou Bianco into a coma, and was it related to all of this? Was the Vito Passella hit truly a Lucarelli execution or had Peter Miceli decided that Vito had served his purpose and had him discarded? And had Crawford truly gone rogue, if just a little bit? I posed these questions to him within seconds of hanging up the phone with Jacqueline Bianco.

"I don't know. We still think it was a botched robbery attempt and that Lou tried to play hero. We also don't know who killed Vito and why," he said in response to the first two questions, then paused before answering the last one. I could see that he was a little put out that I was questioning his integrity, but after he thought for a few minutes, it seemed to become apparent to him that he hadn't given me a lot of reason to trust him in the past few weeks. I could see the wheels turning behind his placid expression, and ultimately he decided to go with hurt indignation. "You don't trust me anymore?"

I went through the litany of reasons, from the gun in the crisper to the bloodstained dress shirt, why I couldn't. He listened intently. When I was finished, he explained everything again. "I told you: the gun was for a gun buy. It was for another case." He watched my face for a sign that I didn't believe him, but when he saw that I found this explanation plausible, he stopped.

My voice was barely a whisper. "Did you kill Vito Passella?"

"If I had killed Vito Passella, why would I have put him in your trunk?" He waited while I pondered that. It wasn't really an answer. "Trust me, if I was going to kill someone, nobody would ever know. And the body would never be found."

"Okay, so that's the creepiest thing you've ever said."

"I'm sorry, but it's the truth. I've learned a few things over the years."

"Like I said, creepy." I went to the refrigerator and took out a bottle of vodka and a jar of olives. "Martini?" I knew he didn't drink them but didn't want to be rude. Especially if he planned on killing me and disposing of my still-warm body.

My mind returned to the note I had received with the photos. One thing was explained, and that was the woman. But how well did I know him? I had to return to "better than I know myself." It was the only way I was going to get through this.

"I'll take a beer," he said.

Trixie wandered into the kitchen while I was shaking a container full of vodka and ice, wrapping herself around my legs, her tail swaying back and forth. She had been asleep most of the day, as is her habit on a lazy Sunday, but something had brought her into the kitchen, and I suspected it was the slightly stressed cadence to my voice. I poured the contents of the shaker into a chilled glass and added a bunch of olives for good measure. The first sip is always the best, and I let icy-cold vodka swirl around in my mouth before swallowing it down. When I turned around, Crawford had downed almost half of his beer and was sitting at the kitchen table looking down at his hands.

"What about the bloody shirt?" I asked, leaning back against the counter and taking sips of my drink, attempting to affect a calmer countenance than I actually felt.

"A uniform took a fall at the station house and I was the first one on the scene. Hit the desk during a fight with a perp and cut his head."

"Lucky for the uniform that you were there," I said, not entirely sure I believed him. "So you weren't giving yourself a home gallbladder operation?"

He looked at me as if I had lost my mind.

"Never mind." I went through my laundry list of inconsistencies and returned to the basement. "Why don't you want me in the basement?"

"Because we have rats."

"I don't think we do."

He threw his hands up. "Then launder at your own risk. You've been warned."

"And why were you in that picture with Jacqueline Bianco?"

"I'm an undercover. It's all part of the case."

"How come Fred's not with you?"

He rubbed his hands over his face. "That's complicated."

"Hard to work with?"

"Something like that. But more like Charlie Moriarty has a rabbi so he went with me."

"Now I'm completely lost."

"Sorry. He has a hook. A captain in Midtown North who has been trying to get him out of uniform for a while. Charlie's gone with me to undercover operations."

I slapped my head. "That explains it!" Charlie was Dottie's boyfriend and, as Crawford explained, a guy with enough seniority to work steady days, no weekends, and no holidays. Going to the undercover squad had Charlie keeping late nights and working days when Dottie expected him around. I felt better knowing that it wasn't anything I did directly to make Dottie mad at me. I got back to the case. "Did you find anything out?"

He pointed to the room above us, our bedroom. "Would I be planning on sitting up there with a bunch of cops in a few days if I had found anything out?"

"So you're hoping that I'll succeed where you failed?"

He didn't like that characterization of the plan and let me know. "People tell you things." He didn't look happy. "Let's call it your 'gift.'"

"More like a curse." He looked ticked enough that I thought it wise to get off the topic. "Why were you in New Paltz?" Although we had called the local police after our attempted kidnapping, we had never really been threatened, and when all was said and done, it was concluded that we had gone of our own accord, so there was nothing to report. Hilarious, huh? By trying to keep my stepdaughters safe and doing what we were told, we were not in danger, according to the police. Therefore, no crime had been committed. They didn't really care that I didn't know whether the guy had had a gun, a knife, or even chloroform; all they cared about was that we were safe and that nobody had been harmed in this botched kidnapping. I won't go so far as to say that they didn't believe us, but, well, they didn't believe us.

Crawford hadn't answered my question in a length of time I considered acceptable, so I asked him again.

"I got Erin's text," he said. "And yours. And Meaghan's." We had each texted him at some point during the drive up.

"How did you get there so fast?"

He raised an eyebrow. That was a question that didn't need to be asked. Obviously, he had done ninety the entire way. "Are we done with the interrogation?"

"One more question."

"Shoot."

"What do I do until Wednesday?" I drained my glass and picked up the shaker, where a few ounces of leftover martini resided. I poured the remains into my glass.

"Nothing. The usual." He got up and came over to me, taking my glass from my hands and wrapping his long arms around me. He gave me a kiss that made me forget that in a few days I would have a phalanx of detectives sitting on my bed listening to me talk fake decorating. "You have a game tomorrow night, right?"

It was hard to answer with his mouth on top of mine.

"That will keep you occupied for all day tomorrow. Until then, we'll figure out some other way to keep you busy."

Thirty-Five

Not content to leave well enough alone, I called Kevin.

"When were you going to tell me that you were in touch with Peter Miceli?" I asked, swiveling around in my desk chair to look at the group of students coming down the back stairs and into the building. Call it my version of "internal forum": although I had seen the letters at Kevin's house that he had exchanged with Peter, I had kept that information to myself until I felt it was necessary to divulge it. It was early Monday morning, but I had gotten to school well before my first class so I could go over some plays for that night's home game against

Ramapo College. I knew, from Crawford, that Kevin had been questioned by the police about his correspondence with Peter Miceli, but everything was very much on the up-and-up. Peter's letters were screened by the prison before they went out, Kevin's were screened before they came in, and nothing but a mutual love of Jesus bonded these two men. It all seemed innocent and probably was. Kevin didn't seem to know anything about Peter's mission to clear his name besides what he put in the letters and would have balked at any involvement on Peter's behalf from prison.

Kevin didn't even have to think; his answer was immediate: "Never."

I knew that he couldn't tell me, but I was still mad. I thought that all were under strict orders to remove Peter Miceli from their lives, their e-mail contacts, their thoughts. Apparently, Kevin had not gotten the memo or had chosen to ignore it. "He seems to know something about your 'situation,'" I said.

"I know. He's intimated that."

Sometimes talking to Kevin is frustrating. He seems to feel that I am on a "need to know" basis regarding most matters and can be irritatingly cryptic. "So what did you tell him?"

Kevin sighed. "I told him to leave it alone, Alison. What did you think I would have told him?"

"Don't you want to clear your name?

"Not with Peter Miceli's help."

That, I understood. "Why didn't you tell me?"

"Because I couldn't. I have to keep things confidential."

"But you're not a priest anymore."

"Thanks for reminding me, Alison. I'd almost forgotten," he said, obviously hurt.

I didn't know why I was angry at him; it wasn't his fault that Peter Miceli had taken matters into his own shackled hands. It probably wouldn't be the last time he did that or tried. Kevin had been doing what he had been trained to do, and I couldn't blame him for not seeing how by just being kind, by just being himself, he had opened up a whole can of worms. If he had had no contact with Peter, would Peter have been so interested in clearing his name? Hard to tell. But this Pandora's box of Mob-related problems had to be closed again, and I wasn't so interested in being the one to do it.

"Are you done being mad at me?" he asked.

"Yes. I'm sorry, Kevin. I just thought that once Peter had gone to jail, he'd be out of my life forever."

"I think he wants to help me."

"I'm sure that's exactly what he wants to do, but his version of 'help' is a lot different than most people's. When Peter helps you, people often end up dead."

"True enough. I told him that I could handle it, so hopefully he'll respect that."

I had my doubts.

"I have to go to work. Dinner later this week?" Kevin asked, giving me the bum's rush off the phone.

"Sure," I said, hanging up. Crawford was right; I had plenty to keep me busy until my meeting with Jacqueline Bianco, but I couldn't concentrate on anything else. Crawford had assured me that tertiary members of Mob families—sons and daughters, husbands and wives—lived full and completely law-abiding lives. Was Jacqueline Bianco one of those people? Nothing suggested that she was involved in any of this—Kevin's dismissal or Vito's murder—but it was a rather strange coincidence that she was a Lucarelli and the Lucarellis may had a hand in Vito's murder. Who ordered the hit?

I don't really believe in coincidences. I'm more of a bad luck aficionado.

Teaching proved to be a welcome respite from all things Mob- and murder-related, and the day passed without incident, something that was becoming extremely rare. We had a game that night and I was glad we didn't have to make the more-than-an-hour-trek out to New Jersey to face the Ramapo Roadrun-ners. Before I packed up for the night and left my office for good, I hit the ladies' room at the end of the office area to wash my hands and see just what the day had wrought in terms of my hair and makeup. As I exited, I ran into President Etheridge, who appeared to be coming from the direction of my office. The office area was deserted, most people having left after teaching or once the clock struck five. It was close to six now and the shop had pretty much closed up for the day, so to speak.

"Oh, Alison, hello," he said, looking a little flustered.

"Were you looking for me?" It's always better to cut to the chase with Mark lest he get the upper hand.

"Uh, no. Well, yes."

I waited.

"Good luck tonight."

"Thanks." Seemed like a flimsy excuse to journey all the way to my office from the rarefied air of his.

He cleared his throat, obviously uncomfortable with what he was about to say. I steeled myself. "I just wanted to thank you for all of the hard work you've put into coaching the Lady Blue Jays. The school community, and I, appreciate all you've done to save the season."

It seemed heartfelt and it was certainly appreciated, even if I didn't believe him. Our history would dictate that he wasn't one for platitudes, but it still seemed odd to me that he had searched me out to tell me this.

"Thanks, Mark," I said, putting a hand on his arm. "It means a lot to me."

He looked around, not sure where to take the conversation, so he took off, his cordovan loafers squeaking on the polished wood floor.

I headed back to my office wondering what he was doing in this part of the building at this hour, and if there was some reason he didn't want to admit that he had been looking for me. Since I had taken over as coach of the Blue Jays, Mark had left me alone for the most part. I know he wished that we had won the Joliet game—everyone on campus had—but he kept his opinions about the team to himself, and I grudgingly admitted his lack of interference was welcome and not entirely expected. I sat back down behind my desk and started going through the papers on my desk, figuring out what I needed to take home, if anything, watching the clock in anticipation of the game.

A note was on my desk that hadn't been there prior to my trip to the bathroom, though it was hard to remember what resided under the mess of papers that cluttered the top of the desk. It was typewritten, just like the first note I had received the week before, and just as cryptic:

See Jaime Dyer.

See Jaime Dyer? Who was Jaime Dyer? Quickly I put his name into the college search engine and found out that he was a junior, he lived in the Siena dorm—conveniently located on the way to the gym—and was majoring in international business, probably the reason I hadn't seen him in one of my classes. I stuck the note in my briefcase, making a mental note to follow up on this lead, or whatever it was. Clearly it had come from Mark. But why?

As I packed up, I turned my thoughts toward the game. I hadn't spoken to Fred since the night that Meaghan and I had gone to New Paltz, but I figured that Crawford had informed him about what had gone on. I hoped that their relationship had been repaired and that Crawford had also clued him in to what he had been doing. Crawford's having been pegged by OCCB was most likely still an issue, if I had to guess; working in the unit was Fred's dream, and that Crawford had so effortlessly blended into the team had to sting. But they would get over it, I hoped. They were grown men with a lot of history, and that had to trump any feelings of jealousy or betrayal. If they didn't, well, what did you expect? That's what you get when you work in an environment where everyone considers himself an alpha, but in reality, only a few are.

I headed out of the building using the back steps and started the short walk to the gym. At two times during the day the campus is deserted: in the morning before anyone has gotten up and now, when everyone was at dinner in the dining hall. I would have been surprised to see anyone on my way over, but if I had, I would have put my money on a student.

Never would I have thought I would run into Jacqueline Bianco.

She was standing beside her car in the parking lot of the dorm where Kristy lived, which also happened to be the dorm where Jaime Dyer lived, one of only two coed dorms on campus. I'm not sure whom she was waiting for, but she didn't seem as surprised to see me as I was to see her. I was close enough to her that I couldn't pretend I hadn't seen her, and that made scurrying away impossible without seeming rude, something that I can't do. Why, in the space of a few days, was I now seeing a woman for the second time who hadn't even thought it important to come to her daughters' basketball games? Why, all of a sudden, was she turning up now? Was she going to be taking Lou's place in the stands to root for Kristy and berate me for not playing Elaina?

I sped up my pace, as if I were in a hurry to get where I was going, but she wasn't having any of it. "Dr. Bergeron! Hello!" she called from her place next to a clean and expensive Mercedes. My car always looks as if it has gone through a safari in the Serengeti; as a result, people with clean cars make me suspicious.

"Hello, Mrs. Bianco," I said, doing double-time toward the gym. "I'll see you at the game." I pulled my coat tighter and put my head down, a basketball coach on the move to an important contest of strength, skill, and, if history was any indication, fouling.

"A word, please?"

I had no choice but to stop, politeness having been my Achilles' heel more than once. We had about ten feet separating us, but even in the darkness I could see that she was agitated. Her face tense, she approached me.

"About Elaina," I started, figuring that we would be heading down the path whereby she would berate me about Elaina's lack of playing time, I would make excuses about how our games had so far been so close that I needed my first-stringers in as much as possible, she wouldn't believe me, and I would race away, shamefaced, muttering to myself how I didn't want to coach this time anyway.

She looked startled. "Elaina?"

"Yes. I know why you're here."

"You do?"

I shifted my heavy bag from one shoulder to the other. "I promise you that I'll find a way for her to legitimately play on the team."

"Legitimately?"

I thought back to Elaina's missing folder and Amy Manning's contention that Elaina had taken her spot on the team for some unknown reason. "Bad choice of words," I said, immediately chagrined.

"So you know?"

I didn't know it all but I knew enough. She was on the team, and while I didn't know why, I knew it wasn't her skill that had landed her a spot on the roster. I offered a little shrug. "I know enough."

Her face went slack, which only served to hide the hardness that I knew was underneath the façade. "You don't need an interior decorator, do you?"

"I actually do," I said, my laugh sounding false even to me. I made a show of looking at my watch. "Look at the time. I'll see you at the game. And Wednesday. I'll see you Wednesday, too.

Wednesday at my house," I said, not content to leave well enough alone. Diarrhea of the mouth is an affliction with which I am intimately acquainted. I hurried off, leaving Jacqueline standing in the parking lot.

Fred was waiting for me in the gym when I finally arrived, out of breath from running across campus. "Thanks for coming," he said.

I drew my hand across my throat. "Enough with the sarcasm." The girls were warming up at one end of the court while the Ramapo Roadrunners did the same at the other end. I watched as Elaina hurled a ball up to the basket, which missed by a mile and landed like a brick at her feet after bouncing off the top of the backboard. She giggled nervously and tossed the ball to Tiffany Mayo, who put it up and into the basket in one fluid motion. Meaghan was hitting three-pointers from all around the court, a welcome sign of how she might play later on that evening. I had spoken to her earlier in the day, and she seemed to be in good shape emotionally after our trip to New Paltz, but I still worried. She was a lot like Crawford in that she held everything in, so I never really knew how she was feeling. She always seemed the same: placid, together, and even.

Fred and I met the refs, and I was dismayed when I recognized the less sympathetic ref from our game against Joliet. He gave me the hairy eyeball and I assured him that my behavior during that game was an anomaly and that he had nothing to worry about. I looked into the stands and saw my friend from the maintenance staff, Luis; Fareed; Abe Schneckstein, with only a handful of little Schnecksteins alongside him; Jacqueline Bianco, who looked as out of place at a basketball game as I would at the front row of a fashion show; and way up in the last row, my old friend, the gray-haired guy, who sat, his hands dangling down between his legs, studying both teams as if he were a scout for the WNBA. Which he might have been. Who knew? I still had this niggling feeling that I knew him, but I couldn't place him in context. Was he the father of one of my students? Did he live in the neighborhood? I couldn't remember. For the time being, all I needed to remember was how to make sure we beat the pants off the Roadrunners while not getting myself thrown out of the game.

The Roadrunners proved to be worthy adversaries, but we pulled out a 56–54 win, with Kristy having her best game ever. She seemed to have channeled whatever stress she was under into her game, making her a scoring powerhouse. Meaghan had a good game as well, but seemed a little off to me, as if she were playing on autopilot. I worried if the events of the last several weeks—particularly concerning her often-absent father—were starting to take their toll. I grabbed her after the game and asked her if she wanted to go out for dessert, as was becoming our custom after home games. She hemmed and hawed for a few minutes, citing homework, exhaustion, and an early day following before agreeing that she could use an hour or so away from campus.

The gym cleared out pretty quickly after the game with Fred doing his usual post-game reconnaissance of the area, cleaning up the balls and putting them in the trolley at the end of the court. "No Max tonight?" I asked. I knew she hadn't planned on coming to every home game, but she had been a pretty regular attendee up until this point.

"She's in a mood" was all he said, and all he needed to say. I knew exactly what that meant.

"So I guess you'll be heading straight home?"

"Not a chance. I'm going out with a couple of guys from work," he said, pulling on his sport jacket.

"Where are you going?" I asked, just making conversation as I pulled together my belongings.

"None of your business."

"Oh, so that's how we're going to play it? Meaghan and I are going to the diner. I hope you won't be there. Last thing we need to ruin our mood is a bunch of cranky cops."

"We won't. Where is she? I'd like to get out of here." He had fortunately kept his crankiness under wraps for the game but was now in a full-blown snit. I had only witnessed him and Max fighting once, and that had ended up with her living at my house for a few weeks. I hoped whatever was going on between them was just your normal, run-of-the-mill marital strife and not something bigger and more serious.

I waved him off. "Go without us. Maintenance will lock up."

He protested only mildly before walking off, his footsteps echoing throughout the empty gym.

"Meg!" I called back toward the locker room. "Let's go!" I wondered what was taking her so long. Usually, the prospect of a sundae at the diner was all she needed to get things moving along, but tonight was different. She was still in the locker room, and by my count, most, if not all, of the team had left and were either back at their dorms or at the library to do some last-minute homework. I hoped that she hadn't picked this evening to take a shower before we headed out, something she didn't normally do, but given the intensity of the game and the amount of playing time she had seen, maybe she had decided it was necessary before going out in public. When she didn't answer, I headed back to the locker room, pushing open the door and finding that the room was pitch-black. "Meaghan?" I flicked the light switch but no lights came on. I turned around and saw that I was alone in the gym, as I expected, Fred having made double-time to get to his date with his brother detectives at whatever watering hole they had decided on. "Meg?"

A loud click sounded as the gym was plunged into complete darkness.

"I should have gone with my gut and worked with you on this."

The voice was coming from somewhere at the end of the gym, the end where the exits were and beyond which safety could be found. I waited a few seconds, hoping that my eyes would adjust to the darkness, but once the gym is dark, it's like being on the surface of the moon. I couldn't see my hand in front of my face.

"Tell me what you know," the disembodied voice, a man's, commanded.

"I don't know who you are, what you want, or what you need to know, but I can't help you," I said. "And whatever you've done with Meaghan, please let her go. She's just a kid. You don't want any part of that."

"She may know something, too."

"Trust me. She doesn't," I made my way away from the locker room and toward the emergency exit that I knew was adjacent to the bleachers.

"Don't think about it," he said. "It won't open. And even if it did, would you really want to risk leaving your stepdaughter in here, wherever she is?"

"Let her go. I'll tell you whatever it is you want to know."

"I thought you didn't know anything?"

My mind raced. "Well, you haven't asked me anything. I may know more than you think," I said, even though I didn't think I did. What did I know about anything? I was as in the dark, no pun intended, as everyone else. And since I had no idea what we were talking about, we could have been talking about any number of things. "Turn the lights on. Please."

"I can't."

"You can't or you won't?"

"Won't." He paused. "I don't want to see your face when I tell you what I came here for."

It dawned on me in one brief, clarifying moment. "Turn on the light, Luis."

Thirty-Six

Luis Paz was only a teenager when he met Father Kevin McManus at a local youth-group picnic in a city park. He had been living here his whole life. His mother was a teenager when she entered illegally from Ecuador, and had died in childbirth. He was raised by an aunt and uncle who had the good fortune to have become naturalized citizens before it had become a goal close to impossible to achieve. They raised him as their own, something that they had never expected to do, their own children grown and living on their own.

Luis wasn't as old as I thought he was—just thirty—but that

was what a life of near poverty and deprivation had wrought on his handsome face. His adoptive parents had pinned their hopes on him and done their best, proud when he graduated from community college but not so proud that by the time he hit his early twenties, he had two misdemeanor drug charges on his record stemming from a youthful enthusiasm for marijuana. They had implored him to join the parish's youth group, where a young priest named Kevin McManus brought the idea of community service and social justice to a group of at-risk youths. Before long, Kevin had gotten a well-deserved reputation as a liberal and a rebel, and he had landed here at St. Thomas as something of a punishment for angering the Church hierarchy. That was long before he had become the chubby, out-of-shape, and spiritless man who lived in a two-family house with his mother and dealt with ornery brides before and during their wedding celebrations. Kevin had kept in touch with Luis and had years later found out that he was having trouble landing gainful employment with his record. Kevin had convinced Mark Etheridge to take a chance on Luis Paz, and Kevin had vouched for his goodness.

Luis, now the married father of two, never realized that just by whispering what I had suspected all along—*"El padre es inocente"*—that I would set the wheels in motion for what turned out to be a tragic turn of events, culminating in his getting into a fight with Lou Bianco that had left Lou in a coma from head trauma. He told me all of this before he broke down in tears.

We were still in the dark but I could hear Luis crying, somewhere in the gym. "Why did you go see Lou Bianco?" I asked.

"I don't know what he did, but he got Father Kevin fired." Luis rattled off a litany in Spanish, most of which I didn't understand, but from what I gathered was directed at God.

"How do you know that?"

Luis laughed, but it wasn't a happy sound. "You probably don't realize this, but when you're a janitor, you're invisible.

People talk all around you like you don't exist. And maybe you don't."

"Don't say that," I said quietly.

"You're not like that. You've always treated me like a person, and not just when you needed something. But everyone else acts as if I'm not really there. I could tell you things that you would never believe. And all because nobody thinks I'm worth being discreet around."

I believed him. I saw the way some of the faculty, even some of the students, treated the maintenance staff, and it made me cringe. When you thought about it, they kept the school running. Maybe it was because I was the daughter of a blue-collar guy and now married to a blue-collar guy, but it wasn't in my nature to overlook the contributions of the people who did things the kids that went to our school were in school to avoid doing.

"What did you hear?" I asked gently.

"I heard that one of the Bianco girls was being counseled by Father Kevin. I don't know which one. But I do know that whatever Father Kevin counseled them to do, their parents didn't like it. And they got him fired."

That was a thin thread of logic to follow at best, but I didn't say anything. I thought back to Meaghan saying that one of them was gay, but now that I thought about it, she never said which one. I always assumed it was Kristy.

"He was out of here in no time. But you know that," he said.

I did know that. Kevin was here one day and gone the next, his apartment having been cleaned out overnight by some of Etheridge's gremlins. I asked the only logical question that could come to my mind. "I know why I'm so invested in Kevin's innocence, but what about you?"

"I have one sister and she lives in Ecuador. She is thirty-two. She has two children," he said, his voice catching. "She has breast cancer. If she doesn't get here for treatment, she will die."

When he didn't elaborate, I asked him what that had to do with Kevin.

"He was helping me figure out a way to get her here. His classmate from the seminary is the Catholic chaplain at Sloan-Kettering. They were trying to find doctors who might operate on her for free. They were trying to get her here." Luis started crying openly. "Without him, I don't know what we'll do. I don't know what will happen to her."

"Can't Kevin still help you? What about his friend?"

"No. He's lost all credibility with everyone. Nobody will talk to him anymore. He's a priest with a black mark on his record." Luis ran a shaky hand across his face. "Besides, unless we can figure out a way to get her here, his friend and his connections are no good to me. He was the one making everything happen, and now that he's not here, nothing is happening."

I searched my brain for something to say to Luis that would make him feel better or that would make him believe that we could overcome this obstacle, but there was nothing. Although I didn't know a lot about the situation, I knew enough to know that finding a way to get her here, finishing what Kevin started, would be difficult at best, impossible at worst. "We'll figure this out, Luis." I asked him one more time to put on the lights.

And just like that, light flooded the gym. When it did, I took in Luis's distraught face, his hands on the light switch. But I also saw Fred's face in the round window in the door to the gym and knew that this wasn't going to end well. Before I could get a word out, he was through the door, his gun drawn. He commanded Luis to hit the floor. Fred had heard the whole thing from Luis's sad life story to his confession. There wasn't a lot I could do except run toward Fred, begging him to listen to reason.

Luis stood, his hands linked behind his head, the look on his face alternating between bafflement and terror. He had assumed this position at other times in his life, so he knew where this would go.

"I said get down!" Fred hollered.

"Luis, get down," I said. "Fred, I don't know what you heard, but he didn't mean it."

Fred looked at me in disbelief. "He beat a guy, Alison." He looked at Luis, now prone on the dirty gym floor. "You have the right to remain silent . . ."

I stood in silence as Fred rattled off Luis's Miranda rights and slapped a pair of handcuffs on him. Fred pulled him to his feet so quickly and without regard for Luis's well-being that the arrested man's feet came off the floor. I looked at Luis and asked him if he had a lawyer.

He shook his head, afraid to say another word.

"I'll take care of it," I said. "And where's Meaghan?"

He looked at me, terrified to open his mouth.

"Tell her!" Fred bellowed.

"I told her to leave, that I needed to talk to you. She left with the Bianco sisters."

Before he dragged Luis from the gym, Fred looked back at me over his shoulder. "Don't go anywhere. I want to talk to you."

After they left and I was left alone in the gym, I called the only lawyer I knew, who was also one of the smartest people I knew. That he was also Crawford's younger brother added a layer of messiness to the situation that only I could bring.

Thirty-Seven

Crawford was less than thrilled by this turn of events.

"So Fred got the guy, a full confession, and your only thought was to call my brother?" Crawford asked, rubbing his big hands across his face. We were in my kitchen and Trixie was planted by my side, sensing that all was not well in her mistress's world.

"He can't go to jail."

"Uh, yes, he can."

Crawford had been home when I arrived, and I filled him in on the whole story. Now that the undercover cat was out of the bag with me, he seemed to be around more. He had already spoken to Fred. Before he left, Fred had visited the men's room and, upon exiting, had seen that the lights were off in the gym. Knowing that I was probably still in there—"That woman of yours takes a long time to get her shit together; there was no way she had beaten me out of the building"—he waited around, listening at the door for what turned out to be Luis's confession regarding Lou Bianco's "beatdown," as Fred put it.

"If he has violent tendencies," Crawford started, holding up a hand when I began to protest, "he might look good for the Passella murder as well."

"He didn't kill Vito Passella."

"How can you be so sure?"

"I just have a gut feeling."

"Well, I hope that gut feeling, and my brother, can keep your friend Luis out of Rikers."

Jimmy Crawford called me early the next morning to tell me that the judge had set bail. "You got eleven grand in your checking account? Because that's what your buddy Luis needs to keep him from going to Rikers and an afternoon or three of same-sex lovin'."

I didn't have eleven grand in my checking account, but I knew someone who did. I called Max. "Max? Hey. Listen, I need a favor and you can't ask any questions. And you can't tell Fred."

"Shoot." I had counted on Max's love of marital subterfuge to get what I wanted, and she didn't disappoint.

"I need you to transfer eleven thousand dollars to my checking account."

"Okay."

"Do you still have the account number?" This wasn't the first time that I had relied on Max's financial largesse to get someone out of trouble.

"I do." She dropped her voice to a whisper. "But when Fred

divorces my sorry ass after finding out about this, I'm coming to live with you. *Capiche?*"

"*Capiche.*" I thought she had hung up when I whispered into the phone, "I love you, Max," but she hadn't.

"Okay, enough with that. I'll talk to you later."

By the time I was eating lunch in the cafeteria at school later that day, Luis was out of jail. That was cold comfort because I knew that he was going to lose his job and be right back at square one, now having a longer rap sheet and having to endure a trial that would surely have him seeing some sort of jail time. I pushed my turkey sandwich away from me and looked out the window. I had left several messages for Kevin, none of which he had answered, and I was back to getting those dark and surreptitious looks from both students and faculty alike. Everyone had heard some version of the story, and being at the center of it, I was now the focus of everyone's attention.

"I thought I'd find you here," Sister Alphonse said, tottering dangerously next to the table on her sensible, thick-heeled shoes.

I stood quickly and took her elbow, guiding her to the seat across from me. "Can I get you something to eat, Sister?"

She shook her bonneted head, still one of the old-timers who wore the full black habit with head gear that made her look like an Amish woman in search of Pennsylvania Dutch country. "I had some of that slop they call beef stew up in the Sisters' dining room." She fixed her unseeing eyes on me. "I figured you needed a friend today." She reached out and placed her large, bony hand on top of mine. "You did right by that boy."

News traveled fast.

"This will work out," she said. "All of the Sisters are praying."

"Well, in that case, we're as good as gold," I said, far more sarcastically than I intended.

She gripped my hand. "Never underestimate the power of

prayer. Without it, you'd never have married that hunk of a cop of yours."

I laughed. "The Sisters were praying for me to find a husband?"

"You'd be surprised what we pray for." She smiled and I could see that she had done a good job of securing her dentures today; usually, they were slightly off center and slipping while she talked. "Now go get me a cup of coffee. That's the least you can do, don't you think?"

I got up and made her a cup of coffee at the self-serve station, adding as much sugar as I thought was necessary to get it to her liking. I grabbed a couple of extra sugar packets, just to be on the safe side. I placed it in front of her, cautioning her that it was hot.

I decided to pick her brain. "So what do you think had Mr. Bianco so incensed that he made it his mission to get Kevin fired?"

She took a dainty sip of coffee and demanded three more sugar packets. Who was I to object? She had been on the planet far longer than I had or even wanted to be; if she wanted to die of a sugar overdose, that was her business alone. "Let me put it this way, dear. There are three things that parents who send their kids to this school find highly objectionable: pregnancy, abortion, and homosexuality. And not necessarily in that order."

"Really?"

"Really?" she repeated, mimicking my voice. "Yes. I've been here since the beginning of time. Things may come and things may go and you think the world is moving along, but in some corners, things haven't changed." She took another sip of coffee. "Darn it. Burned my tongue."

I handed her a napkin from the holder by the window.

"The kids who come here think that they're cutting the apron strings, but for the most part, they're wrong."

"Where are you going with this, Sister?"

She licked her lips and decided that they didn't taste sugary enough; she added the last of the sugar packets to her coffee. "Father McManus is a good man and should not have been punished for instructing students to be true to their Christian hearts. When it comes right down it, we're all equal in the eyes of God."

I was lost, but clearly she wasn't giving me any more information. "What does that mean?"

"Did Marcus make blueberry muffins today?"

I leaned in close. "Sister, you have to tell me what you know."

She thought for a moment, collecting her thoughts. Finally she said, "Let's put it this way: Father McManus was set up. He was the fall guy. He never did what that girl said he did. She was protecting herself and her family. I know it's hard to believe that in this day and age she would need to pretend to be something she's not, but there you have it."

"Kristy Bianco?" I asked.

She fixed me with her blurry gaze again. "Not her. The other one." She smiled, the hard edge gone. "Now, if you could get me a muffin and send me on my way, I would be most grateful. It's time for my nap. My work here is done," she said with finality.

I took her elbow and steered her toward the exit, grabbing a muffin from the basket on the counter before we left. "Thank you, Sister," I said, holding open the door. She surprised me by reaching out and touching my face. "You're a good girl. A little misguided, but a good girl. You always have been."

The tears that I felt pressing at the back of my eyes also surprised me; Alphonse was normally crusty and a little ornery. The Alphonse who called me a "good girl" and touched my face tenderly was not someone with whom I had spent too much time. "Thank you, Sister."

She went through the door and I stepped out behind her,

holding it open. She got about halfway down the hall and turned and gave me a wave. "I'll be seeing you."

And with that she was gone. Only a few hours later I saw the ambulance outside the convent as I walked to my car, her lifeless body on a stretcher, a little smile playing on her lips for all eternity.

Thirty-Eight

Jaime Dyer was in Barcelona, doing a study-abroad program, so I went to my go-to girl for all things gossip-related, Mary Catherine Donnery. She appeared in my office wearing an appropriate amount of clothing for the cold weather, her skintight jeans tucked into fawn-colored UGGs. She flounced into the guest chair across from my desk. "You wanted to see me?"

"I'm just going to cut to the chase, Mary Catherine," I said, folding my hands on top of a stack of folders. "Who is Jaime Dyer and what does he have to do with Elaina Bianco?"

Mary Catherine made a show of hemming and hawing for a

few seconds before she spilled it. "He was her boyfriend all through high school and into freshman year. He's the reason she came here."

"And they broke up?"

"Mmm-hmmm."

"Why?"

"Nobody knows," she said, her eyes wide.

I did but I let her continue.

"One day they just broke up. End of story." She crossed one leg over the other, settling in for a juicy gossip session. "He was heartbroken."

"Any reason for the breakup?"

She uncrossed her legs and leaned in, whispering conspiratorially. "Okay, you got me. I know everything." That was easy. Mary Catherine was just looking for someone to spill the beans to. She had held it in for as long as she could. "I heard she's playing for the other team."

"That would certainly make things difficult. But listen. Is it really such a big deal these days to be gay? To come out?"

Mary Catherine let out a laugh. "Are you kidding? Some of these kids have parents who are still in the dark ages. Next to getting pregnant, being gay is about the worst thing you could be."

I thought back to what Sister Alphonse had said. That old girl had really had her finger on the pulse of what was going on at the school, despite her advanced age. On the one hand, I found Mary Catherine's assertion hard to believe, but on the other, having met a lot of parents during my career at St. Thomas, I didn't. The reason that a lot of the kids came to St. Thomas—or rather, the reason their parents sent them here—was for its strong Catholic tradition and its adherence to Church teachings and traditions. That's what it made it so unusual for Kevin to have been placed here. He was a liberal thinker, although what he preached hewed closely to the basic tenets of the faith. However, if a student came to him, as I suspected Elaina had, and confessed to struggling with her sexuality, he would coun-sel that student to be true to themselves and not bend to the pressures of Church teachings or their parents' feelings. He would be there to help them through a difficult time and, hopefully, be there as well to see them living a full, and open, life.

"Why didn't you tell me this at the Joliet game when I asked you?"

She wiggled around in her seat for a while. "I wasn't ready."

"And now you are?"

She bit her lip. "Listen. I haven't always been . . ."

I waited.

"What's that expression? On the *straight and arrow*?"

"*Narrow.*"

She nodded. "Right. So I'm not always on the straight and narrow, but I'm trying. I didn't think it was right to gossip," she said, lowering her eyes.

"And now you do?"

"Now I think that whatever will help Father McManus is the right thing to do. Guy's bailed my ass out a few times with my parents."

Kevin's goodwill was far-reaching. From Luis's ill sister, to Elaina Bianco, to Mary Catherine and her peccadilloes, he was a regular one-man Christianity band.

I had drifted off, alone with my thoughts, when Mary Cath-erine cleared her throat.

"Thanks, Mary Catherine. See you at the next home game." I had all that I needed from her, and I certainly didn't want to hear anything else about her motivations for giving me her opinion now.

She looked puzzled and I couldn't blame her, but she didn't press, taking the opportunity to leave while the leaving was good. I overheard her talking with Fareed, who was outside my office, about her grade in his class. Sounded as if things weren't going so well for Mary Catherine in International Business I and she was doing her darnedest to wrangle a better grade than Fareed seemed willing to give her.

When he was done debating with Mary Catherine about the merits of her last paper, he knocked lightly at my open door. "Can I come in?"

I motioned to the chair that Mary Catherine had just vacated.

"I feel bad about the way we left things the other day," he said.

"Fareed, I totally understand your position."

He looked chagrined. "I just want to tell you that Father Dwyer is not your friend."

"I already knew that."

"I fear that he is a dangerous man."

I thought that was a rather exaggerated characterization. "Dangerous?"

He quickly amended and shook his head. "Not in the way you would think. Not in a physical sense. But he craves power and will stop at nothing to get it."

"I kind of already knew that, too," I said, thinking about Dwyer's behavior. I wondered aloud if he would be officiating at Alphonse's funeral Mass; she would be rolling over in her grave if he did, no love being lost between the two of them.

Fareed looked out into the office area and, seeing a few faculty members and students in the vicinity, pushed the door closed with his foot. "Can I be completely frank?"

"Of course," I said, wondering where this was going.

"If I didn't know better, I would think that Father Dwyer has set his sights on Mark Etheridge's job."

Well, well, Fareed. You *are* more than just a pretty face. It was all falling into place, and finally the whole thing was making sense. "Fareed, I think you may be onto something."

There was a knock at the door, and through the frosted glass I could see the outline of my husband standing on the other side. "Come on in, Crawford," I called.

Fareed stood as Crawford entered.

"Fareed Muhammad, Bobby Crawford," I said as they shook hands.

"Nice to meet you, Bobby," Fareed said. "I was just leaving."

"Don't leave on my account," Crawford said, although I could tell that now that he had met Fareed, he definitely didn't want me hanging around with him, especially behind closed doors. He's got just enough of a jealous streak to be irritating.

"What were you guys talking about?" he asked.

"None of your business," I said, taking a page from Fred's conversational playbook. When I saw that Crawford wasn't amused, I added, "We were just talking about some theories regarding Father Dwyer and his motives."

Crawford perched on the edge of my desk. "Such as?"

"Such as his wanting Mark Etheridge's job so badly that he'll do just about anything."

Crawford thought about that. "Meaning what?"

"I'm not sure exactly. But it is something to think about. Lunch?"

He looked at his watch. "I don't have time."

Then why was he here?

"I just wanted to tell you to stay out of the Luis thing." He paused, looking as if he was bracing for an outburst, but I kept my cool. "I don't even want to know where a St. Thomas janitor came up with eleven thousand dollars in the space of an hour, and I certainly don't want to know how you're involved."

He already knew. I had a history with this sort of thing.

He put his hands together, beseeching me. "Please. Don't mess this up."

I figured that righteous indignation was the best tool in my emotional arsenal. "Okay! I won't get involved." Too late.

"Thank you," he said, rising. "Practice tonight?"

"Of course."

"And you know what's on the docket for tomorrow afternoon, right?"

"Yes. My appointment with Jacqueline Bianco." I stood as well. "Remind me? Why are we doing this again?"

He spoke slowly. "To find out who ordered the hit on Vito Passella. In particular, to find out if it was her. Remember?"

I slapped my head. "Oh, right. I had forgotten." My stomach grumbled, signaling that lunchtime had passed. "Any information on who tried to kidnap the three of us in New Paltz?"

He looked flustered and I wasn't sure if it was because they didn't have any further information or something else. "Nothing. The RA on duty at the desk wasn't any help, and the security camera only caught the back of the guy's head."

"What color was the guy's hair?"

He wasn't expecting that question. "Why?"

"Just tell me. What color was his hair?"

"I'm not sure we can tell. The video footage is black-and-white. Lightish?"

I took my purse from the bottom drawer of my desk. "It's just that there's been this guy at some of the games who I feel like I recognize but I can't place. I haven't had a chance to find out who he is or why he's there, but maybe it's something we should look into." Crawford told me to point him out at the next game. "Will do. Are you sure you can't stay for lunch?"

"I'm sorry. I can't."

"Supersecret undercover work?"

He smiled. "Yes. That and an out-in-the-open homicide investigation." He leaned down and gave me a kiss. "I'll see you after practice."

Before he left, I blurted out, "Sister Alphonse died."

He paused. "Who?"

"The Fonz." I found myself welling up again. "She was close

to one hundred." A tear slipped down my cheek. I had come to love the Fonz in all of her six-foot, habited glory.

"So I guess there won't be an autopsy?" he said, always detached, always the professional.

"I guess not." I looked out the window and to the cemetery beyond it, where I would be visiting Alphonse from now on. I told Crawford about Alphonse's theory as well as the information I had gotten from Mary Catherine.

"Interesting. How much stock do we put in the theories of a one-hundred-year-old nun and a young woman with rather loose morals?"

"Let's put it this way: these two women, at opposite ends of the life spectrum, both apparently had their finger on the pulse of St. Thomas society."

He kicked the door to my office closed and put his finger on the pulse that throbbed on my neck. "This one?" he asked, running his finger down the length of my neck to my collarbone. The next thing I knew, folders were falling from my desk to the floor, and the phone receiver was knocked from its holder. After a minute or two of fumbling and groping, I remembered the floor-to-ceiling windows that took up the back wall of my office. I turned, his mouth on my neck, and saw Sister Mary picking her way down the old, dilapidated steps behind the building, her eyes shaded by her progressive glasses.

I pushed Crawford off me and straightened my clothing. "Sister Mary," I said.

"More like Sister Buzz Kill. She coming this way?"

"I'm not sure, but you should go," I said, picking folders up from the floor of my office. When he didn't move, I stood and pushed him toward the door. "Go."

"Now what were you and Fareed talking about?" he asked, a smile on his lips.

"Fareed who?"

That was the right answer. He hesitated a moment at the door. "Are we okay?"

I thought so, but I didn't let on that 1 percent of me still wondered what he had gotten himself involved in that required him to keep the details of it so secret from both me and Fred, the two people closest to him in the world. I tried to look as convincing as possible when I told him that we were.

"Then why did you always believe Kevin but you doubted me?"

He was hurt and he had a right to be. It was a good question. Telling him the truth was the best I could do. "You lied to me once. A long time ago. But still, you lied."

He looked devastated, as sad as I had ever seen him look. "And that's what this is about?"

I half nodded, half shrugged.

"Will I ever get past that with you?" he asked.

I had fallen in love with him the first time I had laid eyes on him. That made it even harder when I found out that while he was legally separated for years and years, he had still technically been married to his first wife, Christine. I thought I was past it, but all of the doubts I had had over the past few weeks? They all could be traced back to the moment when I saw his wife, and the two girls, beside him. I hadn't realized it at the time, but it would take a long time for me to get past that hurt. I walked over and wrapped both arms around him. "This is the last you'll hear of it." And I meant it.

I gave him one last peck before he pulled himself together and left the office, attempting to look like a respectable member of society. I heard him give some sugar to Dottie on the way out, complimenting her on her choice of a lavender cowl-neck sweater, and listened while she cooed back. She was always a sucker for Crawford even if in her mind the jury was still out on me.

I never did get to eat a proper lunch, opting instead for a container of yogurt and a banana from the cafeteria. For most people, this would be a perfectly healthy option for the midday meal, but for me, only copious amounts of carbohydrates and a fair serving of nitrates washed down with large quantities of diet soda cut it. By the time practice rolled around, I was ravenous. I had gotten a text from Fred saying that he was doubtful for the evening's practice, so I knew that I would be on my own. When I arrived, the girls were assembled in the locker room in various stages of readiness to begin practice.

I sat on one of the benches, next to Elaina, who looked miserable and unhappy as usual. "I'm starving. Does anyone have something I could eat?"

Elaina reached into her gym bag and pulled out a Ziploc bag with a collection of granola bars, various bags of nuts, and a few pieces of fruit. I was beyond thrilled. She shrugged. "My mother is always afraid I'm not eating enough." Your mother should be afraid of how profoundly depressed you are instead, I thought.

I dug through the Ziploc and took out a few items that I got busy devouring while the team watched me. Through a mouthful of nuts and oats, I instructed them to go out to the court to start practice. "Coach Wyatt isn't coming tonight," I said, a declaration that received a smattering of applause. "Now, ladies, he means well," I said, but even I couldn't keep a straight face. He was the bane of their existence, and sometimes mine, and not having him at practice was a nice change of pace. "You can thank the good homicidal people of the Bronx for keeping him out of our way tonight."

The team headed out to the gym; Elaina and I sat, side by side, in the empty locker room. After a few minutes in which it seemed as if she wanted to talk but didn't know where to start, she finally blurted out, "Dr. Bergeron, I'm leaving the team." She saw that the granola bar that I had shoved in my mouth was preventing my replying, so she handed me a bottle of room-temperature water from her gym bag. I opened it and chugged some down, after which I asked her why.

"I'm not supposed to be on this team. You know it and so do I." She pushed a lank piece of dirty-blond hair from her face. "I have Amy Manning's place."

"Are you sure this isn't about your lack of playing time?"

She shook her head. "No. I was never supposed to be on the team. It was something my father . . ."

I waited. "Your father?"

"Never mind. Is it okay if I don't practice tonight? I'd just like this to be it for me and basketball."

"It's your decision, Elaina." I reached over and wrapped my arm around her thin shoulders. "Whatever you think the right thing to do is? That's what you should do." In hindsight, I thought that maybe I should have pressed harder, tried to convince her to stay, but at the time it was clear to me that she wanted out.

"Can Amy join the team?" she asked.

"You know, I don't even know." I leaned in and whispered conspiratorially, "I barely know how to get to the gym, let alone coach the team."

She giggled, the first time I had seen her laugh. I should have used self-deprecating humor more often, I thought.

"If I can find a way to bring her in, I will," I said, finishing off the water. I took a handful of nuts and tossed them into my mouth. "Just take off, if you want. Do the girls know?"

"Just my sister. And Meaghan. We talked about it last night."

"Your sister is okay with your quitting?"

Elaina smiled, the second time I had seen a happy look cross her face; obviously, the thought of leaving the team was a relief. "She's fine. Now she can have the spotlight all to herself. As if she didn't already," Elaina said with no trace of animosity. She was used to playing second fiddle and she seemed fine with that role.

"Thanks for being such a loyal Blue Jay," I said as we stood. I wrapped my arms around her and she let out a little sob. "Is there anything else you want to tell me, Elaina?" I asked, taking a stab that now that we were alone, and the weight of playing on a team she didn't belong on was no more, she might open up even more.

"Is Father McManus all right?" she asked, after crying softly for a few minutes.

I didn't want to let her know that in my opinion his reason for being had been erased, so I went with a noncommittal "He's okay."

"You're friends, right?"

"We're best friends. BFFs."

She broke away and zipped up her gym bag, leaving her treasure trove of healthy snacks sitting on the bench. "Then I'm really sorry for everything that happened."

Thirty-Nine

I underestimated just how important sports are to some parents. And just how devastating a gay child might be to others. In combination, a lot of lives could be damaged.

Elaina knew she was different from her sister even though they had shared a womb and DNA. She wasn't athletic, but she was a pretty decent cello player. She was dedicated to school in a way her sister wasn't, doing her all to get the best grades possible while Kristy just skated by. She was shy while her sister was gregarious. She preferred the company of other women while her sister spent so much time playing basketball that romantic entanglements weren't even an issue. Elaina struggled with the thought of coming out to her parents. She had already disappointed her father—a sports nut who would have preferred sons, whom he could shape both on and off the court, to daughters, only one of whom shared his passion for basketball—and she couldn't do it again. So when she came to them at the end of freshman year and told them that she had been seeing Father McManus and that he had counseled her that she should attempt to lead her most true and honest life, her parents—Lou in particular—had been less than pleased. In her words, he had "gone ballistic." Her mother had been less surprised and less devastated but had listened intently, thinking that he was onto something when Elaina's father had badgered her to the point where even she believed that Kevin's intentions had been less than honorable and more nefarious than in reality.

Elaina related all of this to me in the locker room, all matter-of-factly until she got to the part where she related how she'd told Mark Etheridge what her father had told her to say about exactly what Kevin had done. When she confessed to lying about Kevin's "inappropriate contact," she broke down completely. "He never touched me."

I already knew that, but wondered how anyone who knew Kevin could possibly believe that he had. I put my arms around her again, holding the door to the locker room closed with my foot when someone tried to enter. While she cried, I thought of how much pain and suffering this whole situation had wrought, from Kevin's expulsion from school and the clergy to Luis's desperate attempt to reason with Lou, to Lou's ending up in the hospital. To this broken, shattered girl, whose only crime had been listening to a misguided and misanthropic father who felt that having a gay daughter would shame his family more than anything else.

She pulled back and wiped her face on a towel that was in her gym bag. "The deal was that I told everyone that Father Mc-

Manus had done something to me"—she hid her face behind the towel as she said this—"and he went away. That wasn't enough for my father, though. He also wanted me on the basketball team until I graduated."

I started laughing. "You're kidding, right?"

"It's not funny."

"You're right. It's not. It's preposterous." When I saw that I had hurt her with my reaction, I quickly added, "It's just hard for me to believe that your father cares so much about basketball that he would go to these lengths."

"It was 'the cherry on the top,' according to him."

"Just a little added bonus?"

She nodded. Her face was red and blotchy, and her breathing ragged, after crying for as long and as hard as she had. She had been holding it in a long time, and now she was spent. She sat back down on the bench and dropped her head. "I'm so sorry."

I put a hand on her shoulder. "Are you willing to make this right?"

She was, and she told me what she planned to do. After practice, I strode across campus, my hair damp from a light, freezing rain that had begun to fall by the time I arrived inside the building that housed Mark Etheridge's office. I didn't expect to find him in his office—all I wanted to do was leave him a note requesting a meeting—and was surprised when I saw a sliver of light under the massive oak doors that led into the president's chamber. Fran, his secretary, was long gone, her desk tidied and her chair pushed in. I knocked softly on the door, entering when I heard him call out my name.

Mark was sitting at his desk with his back to the door, looking out the large windows that gave him a bird's-eye view of the eastern end of campus, the gym smack in the middle of that view. I took in the heavy crystal glass of amber-colored liquid sitting on his desk under the soft glow of his desk lamp. "I saw you coming across campus."

"The view is pretty spectacular at night," I said, walking to the edge of his desk. "Mark?"

He turned around and I could see that he had been drinking for a while, the bottle of Scotch on the windowsill nearly empty. His face was slack and his eyes unfocused. "I've known the whole time."

I figured that silence was better than conversation at this point; he seemed to want to talk, and I was going to let him. To get him rolling, the only thing I said was "The notes were from you."

He smiled, but it was a sad smile. "I'll never admit that in a court of law. Or to anyone else."

I took that as a yes.

He hands shook as he brought the drink to his lips and sipped it. "You have no idea the kind of pressure this job brings with it. It's a wonder I'm still sane."

This was going to take a while, so I perched on the edge of the wing chair in front of his desk.

"You've got parents, you've got the faculty," he said, pausing, "and you've got the Church. Everyone has a different idea of how things should be."

"I can only imagine."

"And you"—he pointed at me with his drink—"you're like some kind of crusader for justice." He chuckled. "Can't say I blame you, but you certainly don't make things any easier on me." He leaned back in his chair and held his drink close to his chest. "I figured with Kevin gone, some of the heat would be off. We'd take this place back fifty years and everyone would be happy. I just didn't take into account what kind of effect that might have on my conscience." He took his glasses off and laid them on top of the desk. "I still have one, you know."

"You wouldn't have left me those notes if you didn't."

He pointed at me. "Bingo." He stood and put his back to me, staring out at the campus. "I'll never be able to make this up to Kevin, but I'm going to try."

I didn't know how he could but I was willing to listen.

"After I resign tomorrow, I'm heading down to the chancery, where I'll tell them what I think. And what I think is that Elaina Bianco is a liar."

"Don't do anything until you talk to Elaina. She's ready to recant." I walked around the desk and touched his arm lightly. "And don't resign, Mark. If you do, Dwyer's going to make a run at this job so fast and so hard, your head will spin."

He turned around and faced me. "Don't you think I know that? That's been clear from the get-go. I've known Al Dwyer a long, long time. We were even friends once." I knew that but didn't let on. He went back to looking out at the dark and empty campus. "It's too late, Alison. I'm done here. Time to move on to greener pastures."

"You told me to cease and desist."

"I had to," he said, bent at the waist, his hands splayed out on the thick windowsill. "He's pretty connected and not just in the ways you would expect. He always has been."

I thought back to the picture on Dwyer's credenza. They'd known each other a long time. "The Mob."

Mark continued looking out the window. "You didn't hear it from me, but let's just say that Al Dwyer runs with some pretty unsavory characters. He gets to go to Bermuda in the summer and Banff in the winter, and they get absolution. Everyone wins."

I had one last question for him. "How did you know Elaina was lying?"

He looked at me, his eyes filled with tears, a man for whom things had unraveled in a way he could never have anticipated. "These days, there's not a lot I'm sure about, but there are two things that I know. One is that Kevin would never have harmed a student. And the other is that despite our long friendship, there is nothing that will stop Dwyer from getting what he wants."

Forty

It was still raining when I left the building. I had gone back to my office for a while, not sure what to make of the day's events, which had definitely not gone the way I had planned. Although I had figured out Elaina's secret before she told me, I had never thought that it could have affected Kevin in such an adverse and life-changing way. Mark Etheridge? That had been another surprise. I wouldn't have figured him for someone who would have gone to any lengths to protect Kevin and make me aware of what was going on, as clumsy and obvious as those attempts had been. He was my Deep Throat, more than Luis, and I couldn't have predicted that if I had thought about it for another ten years.

I hurried to my car, parked in my usual spot, and jumped into the driver's seat, taking a minute to get comfortable before starting the car. Before I had time to react, the passenger-side door opened and somebody, hooded and wet as well, was next to me. The cloying scent of too much Chanel No. 5 filled the car, and I resisted the urge to gag. Although I had a bottle of it on my dresser, I had had my fill of the perfume over the last few weeks. It was going out in the trash the minute I got home.

Jacqueline pulled the hood from her head; not a hair was out of place. "This was never about getting your house redecorated, was it?" she asked, turning toward me in the small space. She was smiling and it looked sincere, but that she had hunted me down and jumped into my car—still a rental—gave me pause.

I wasn't sure which way to play this so I went with the truth. "Nope. Never was." We were too close together, our quarters too tight, for me to play it any other way.

She continued smiling. "So what was it about?"

"It started out with me wondering who had killed a St. Thomas mailman and stuck him in my trunk, and it ended with finding out who was responsible for ruining my best friend's life." I watched her face for something—shock, awe, disbelief, indignation—but there was nothing. Just that same smile, empty, a shadow. Nothing behind it. "I know you had something to do with Kevin, but I don't know about the mailman."

The smile disappeared. "And why would you think I had something to do with that?" she asked, but it was a rhetorical question. "Because of my maiden name? Is that why?"

I shrugged. "If the surname fits . . ."

"I have spent years ridding myself of that reputation, Dr. Bergeron. Years. Not everyone in my 'family,'" she said, finger-quoting the word, "is in the same business. As you can see, I'm a respectable businesswoman. I run my own firm. I have nothing to do with what goes on." The funny thing was, I believed her. But she couldn't cut her losses and kept talking, going to a bad place, in my opinion. "Why don't you ask your friend Peter Miceli? I bet he knows something about what happened to that man."

I put my hands on the steering wheel and gripped it. I decided to let that pass. She was right. He probably did. At this point, however, I was content to leave it to the police. I knew what had happened to Kevin and that was all I really cared about.

She couldn't shut up, now that I had gotten her talking. "We sent our daughters here so that they'd be safe and so that they could go to school in an environment like the one we raised them in."

"Where they were taught to lie? To be so unhappy that their sadness is evident to everyone around them?" I only meant Elaina; Kristy seemed to be doing just fine.

"She's not lying. She's confused. There's a difference."

That was some twisted logic. "I spoke to Elaina earlier and she's going to tell the truth about what happened with Kevin. She's not interested in ruining someone's life."

"She's already told the truth. The truth is that Father McManus is not a man to be trusted."

I took my keys out of the ignition. We could go on forever in this vein and get nowhere. I opened my car door. "You can stay here but I don't have the time to debate you. You convinced your daughter to lie, you practically ruined a man's life as a result, yet you stuck to your story. There's nothing left to say." One leg was out, but I turned back to her. "I'm very sorry about the way this all turned out."

I started walking back toward my office, thinking that I would wait it out. She had to leave eventually. I didn't really think she was going to sit in my car all night, but then again, Jacqueline Bianco seemed hell-bent on proving her point. It was raining harder than it had been earlier, and I was soaked to the bone by the time I reached the back stairs, just in time to see the gray-haired guy who attended every Blue Jay game standing at the bottom of the staircase as if he was waiting for me. He looked up when he heard me coming, as miserable, wet, and cold as I was, and our eyes locked for one brief second. It didn't take me long to make my decision, and that decision was to run, as fast as my heel-shod feet would take me, down the service road, toward the convent, and beyond that, the river. There was too much death, lying, and Mob talk to make me think that this guy was waiting to talk to me about his course requirements for next semester. I thought about heading back to the car, but that was up a hill and I wasn't in good enough shape to make that trek and outrun him. I went with downhill instead, cursing myself for not having had the sense to look at the weather report and know that with the unseasonably warm weather we were having for the past few days, a winter rain shower was on tap when the sun went down. I only hoped that the deluge was providing as much of a challenge to run in for the guy following me as it was for me.

I ran straight down the hill, my heels having trouble gaining purchase on the slick road, and came to the sharp angle in the road that would take me around the front of the school and right past the door of the convent, where, if I was lucky, I could bang loudly enough to attract someone's attention before the guy caught up with me. I was just about at the bend and gaining ground when a car came around the corner.

Mark Etheridge had had the good sense to call a car service after his date with the Scotch bottle, and for that, the drivers in the greater Bronx area should have been pleased. It would have been nice if the car service had actually had the wherewithal to hire someone who could actually drive. Although the driver wasn't going fast—a ninety-degree turn will force you to slow down if you have any intelligence at all—he wasn't really looking where he was going and hit me, sending me up onto the roof of the car, almost in slow motion, and off again into a ditch beside the road.

It would have been nice, as I lay there thinking that I was going to die in a wet ditch on the St. Thomas campus, if Sister Alphonse had made an appearance from beyond the grave to comfort me in my time of need. Instead, before I blacked out from the pain radiating through my arm and up my shoulder, I saw the face of the guy following me, and as I slowly lost consciousness, it dawned on me where I had seen him: in the squad at the Fiftieth on the day he had retired from the job.

Forty-One

The whole school, it seemed, had turned out for Sister Alphonse's funeral. I was sitting toward the back of the beautiful chapel, waiting for the funeral to start, when Kevin slid in next to me. He pointed at my arm, held together by a few internal pins, in a soft cast and sling.

"How's that going?"

"Fine since I started mainlining Percocet," I said, moving over to give him some room. I wasn't completely mentally incapacitated, but being on painkillers certainly had its advantages. One was that I was in a good mood all the time. The other was that my memories of the last several weeks were misty, water-colored memories, just as Barbra Streisand had once sung.

I had only lain in the ditch for a few minutes before the sound of sirens filled the chilly night air. That's the good thing about being chased by a retired-cop-turned-PI: he still had a lot of connections. Mark Etheridge looked as if he were going to vomit and then faint when he saw the bend of my arm and the bone sticking out from the wrist. A compound fracture rounded out my adventures with the Mob, undercover mailmen, basketball coaching, and mistrusting my spouse. One surgery and lots of painkillers later and I was as good as new.

The meds made all of the pain go away, but along with my hallucinations about Senator Bill Bradley, I was also hallucinating about rats. Or maybe not. Tom the rat whisperer was making weekly visits to make sure our basement was free and clear.

"How's Luis?" I asked.

Kevin didn't look as hopeful as I would have liked. "He's okay. We'll get through this. Getting his sister here is our main priority." He pulled a prayer missal from in front of him in the pew, even though he could probably recite every prayer, every hymn, from memory. "I'm just glad that he was able to make bail. You don't know how that happened, do you?" he asked, narrowing his eyes.

"Not a clue." Lou Bianco was out of his coma, and his story meshed with Luis's. The best we could hope for was third-degree aggravated assault and no jail time. We didn't ponder the worst-case scenario. In the meantime, Kevin was trying to get Luis at least a steady day-laborer position, and I was working any angle I could with some of my friends to do the same, or better.

Kevin asked me about the private investigator who had been hired by Crawford. "Oh, you mean from the offices of the 'Gang That Couldn't Shoot Straight'?" I asked. The cop-turned-PI's name was Frank Thompson, and he was the guy I had seen in the stands at the games and on the street in Chinatown when I had followed Crawford. Unbeknown to me, he had also been the person who had followed me into Dwyer's office, rummaging around for what, he didn't know. He had been hired by Crawford to tail me once Peter Miceli was back in the picture and Vito Passella had been whacked. He had also been the guy who promised to take me and the girls "someplace safe" that night in New Paltz. That had been Thompson's idea alone, and once he had told Crawford what he had planned, Crawford had made haste up to New Paltz to head him off at the pass, his protestations on the subject going unheard. Thompson's plan had been to put us in his hunting cabin in upstate New York. Crawford soon realized that he had hired the dumbest private investigator known to the world of investigation, but Thompson was determined to see the job through, hence his visitation with me on the rainy night when I had gotten hit by the car. I told Crawford that maybe Thompson should find another line of work because he was an inordinately bad PI if he couldn't keep track of me or figure out that trying to kidnap three women without threatening them with a weapon was a bad idea. Crawford finally admitted that Thompson hadn't been that good a cop, but that he, Crawford, had been desperate. Thompson owed him a favor. Desperate times call for desperate measures and all of that.

And seriously flawed PIs, apparently.

Mark Etheridge was still mulling over his resignation. It seemed that our conversation had emboldened him, and his only goal now was to get rid of Father Dwyer, now making a full-bore run at Mark's job in the wake of everything that had happened. After Etheridge did that, he would turn his attention to getting Kevin reinstated as chaplain, which I wasn't sure Kevin even wanted. That was a conversation for another time. There was no telling what I might encourage him to do now that I was on a steady diet of opioids.

Peter Miceli had been thrown in solitary confinement for the infractions of having tried to contact me with the pictures and the note. His cellmate had gotten himself a sweet deal by wearing a wire and getting Peter to confess that he had ordered the hit on Passella, Vito's usefulness having expired once he contacted me. He only spent several days in the "hole" and was going to be tried for the murder. From what Crawford told me, I probably wouldn't recognize him these days. While Peter had found Jesus, he had also found exercise and was now a buff buck fifty instead of carrying an extra one hundred pounds on his five-foot-six frame.

And he couldn't have been that close to Jesus. The reason he had contacted me? He wanted to ruin my "perfect life" by casting doubt on the two people I cared for more than my own life: Crawford and Kevin. According to what he told the cellmate, I had ruined his life and he wanted to repay the debt in kind. He was so dumb that it had never occurred to him that by contacting me, he was not really helping Kevin at all. He figured that he could help get Kevin exonerated, but by that time, the damage to our relationship would be done.

Mary Catherine had been right all along: if the Mob wanted to ruin your life, they did so by taking away the things you loved. If I had believed the note and the pictures, both Kevin and Crawford would have been gone from my life.

In the chapel, the Mass started, with several pallbearers wheeling Sister Alphonse's casket down the center aisle. As I cried—Percocet was making me more emotional than usual—Kevin put his arm around my shoulder and I leaned in and wept openly. We unfortunately had to sit through a Father Dwyer memorial Mass, but I was so spaced-out that it hardly mattered. I had come for Alphonse and that was all that mattered, Dwyer's rote homily be damned.

She would be buried in the cemetery that I had full view of from my office. As soon as the ground thawed completely and my arm was out of its sling, I would head over there and pay Alphonse a proper visit. I had missed her wake and hadn't had a chance to thank her, in person so to speak, for what she had told me, but I would let her know one spring day when I could safely travel among the grave markers, both new and old.

Kevin and I walked out to the parking lot together. "Lunch?" I asked. "Crawford's going to pick me up in a little bit, and we're going to go out." I couldn't drive and had to rely on Crawford for transportation. I was out sick and Sister Mary had a temp covering my classes for the next few weeks. I was suspect enough when I wasn't high as a kite, and we all thought that this was the wisest way to handle my teaching while I was nursing myself back to health.

"I wish I could but I have—"

"A date?" I asked, joking. Although Kevin wasn't a practicing member of the clergy anymore, he was a still a priest in his mind. Mine, too.

He blushed. "Work."

I leaned in and gave him a kiss on the cheek. "Managing the bridezillas. You're just the man for the job." I put my good hand on his shoulder. "Hey, are you ever going to be a priest again?" Taking Percocet had also removed any semblance of tact I might once have had.

He closed his eyes and tilted his head up toward the falling snow. "I'm not sure, Alison." He kept his eyes closed. "I'm really not sure. What do you think I should do?"

My answer was instantaneous. "I think you should do whatever makes you happy."

He smiled, a mysterious little grin that gave no indication of what might make him happy. I had a feeling I would never see Kevin in a Roman collar again, and that was all right. He was fat—and getting fatter by the day—but happier than I had seen him in a long time. He started to walk away but turned back around. "Hey, I heard the weirdest rumor about the basketball team. Someone told me that Jamal Sanders is the new coach." He looked incredulous, and who could blame him? Jamal Sanders had been a legend in the NBA, not to mention in Joliet hoops, and now he was the coach of the Lady Blue Jays. Some things you just can't make up. "What about the lady from Tennessee?"

"Didn't work out," I said.

"And Jamal? Where did he come from?"

"Let's just say that he found himself with some time on his hands and wanted to do something good." That kind of summed it up. That, and a court-ordered stint of community service that he wouldn't be able to fulfill until he died. Seems that Jamal still loved a lady and her name was Mary Jane. She was cheap and you could buy her by the dime bag on any street corner in the city. She was potent, and apparently she made you run red lights and hit taxicabs. Mary Jane had caused Jamal to get jammed up with a DUI, his third in a year. Had he not stumbled upon the brilliant plan of becoming the Blue Jays' coach, he would be standing on the side of the New York State Thruway picking up trash alongside other lawbreakers until the next millennium rolled around. The judge, hearing the tale of woe of the Lady Blue Jays from Jamal's lawyer, who had coincidentally been contacted by none other than Max to vouch for Jamal, thought the plan sublime. Jamal would start coaching the following week, while simultaneously attending Narcotics Anonymous meetings, and the girls couldn't have been more excited.

Crawford pulled up and waited while I gave Kevin an awkward embrace with my one arm. "Hey, Kevin!" he called from the car, finally comfortable with using Kevin's first name. "Join us for lunch?"

Kevin begged off and headed toward his beat-up Honda Fit, the one that he should have been able to fit into any parking place comfortably without hitting the cars in front of and behind it. A few new dents showed that he was still having trouble with parallel parking, if not driving in general. Maybe taking a driving course was in his future, even if pastoral work wasn't.

Crawford got out of the car and opened the door for me,

pulling my seat belt across my chest, making sure I was comfortable before setting off. I thought we were going somewhere local, but when he pulled onto the Henry Hudson Parkway going south, I knew he had other plans. We took the same route as the day I followed him, but today, instead of feeling overwhelmed, scared, and suspicious, all I felt was happiness.

Might have been the Percocet.

"We should go to the *Intrepid*!" I said as we passed the historic aircraft carrier. I had never shown any interest in seeing some of New York City's landmarks, but today, everything appealed to me. "And then Ellis Island!"

"We'll get right on that, after you heal."

We headed into Chinatown, just as we had the previous week, except that this time, Crawford pulled over and pointed at the awning for a Chinese restaurant at which we had never eaten. "Get out. Go have some dumplings. No wine!" he cautioned, knowing that wine and painkillers were a combination that I would have enjoyed immensely. "I'll be back in a little while."

"You're quite the lunch date, Crawford," I said before going into the restaurant, redolent with the smells of garlic and ginger, and asked for a table for two. The waiter, a thin Asian guy who looked to be about twelve, brought me some crispy noodles and duck sauce, which I hastily ate before Crawford could come back and hog them all. A half hour passed, and then close to an hour, the kid waiter getting antsy that I was taking up a four-top during lunch hour and only ordering diet sodas. I ordered a bunch of food to appease him. Painkillers did nothing to dampen my appetite, so I ordered enough for leftovers later that evening when a yen for reheated chow fun would certainly hit. Before long I was brought several plates of food, one plate containing the dumplings that Crawford had commanded I order.

I was facing the window of the restaurant and watched as people hurried by on the busy sidewalk. Finally I spied Crawford loping across the street, jaywalking like the seasoned New

Yorker that he was. He came into the restaurant holding a large manila envelope; he tossed it onto the table so that it landed in front of me.

"Happy birthday." He slid into a chair across the table and speared a dumpling. My birthday wasn't for months, but it didn't seem to matter.

I was wondering how the new suede boots I wanted had been squished to fit in an envelope that size. He tore open the seal and pulled out a sheaf of papers.

The only word I saw was *retirement*. I looked up at Crawford, stunned.

"Happy birthday. This is the best present I could think to give you."

I looked at him, not sure how to feel.

"Happy," he said. "You're supposed to feel happy."

I took the last dumpling between my chopsticks and dropped it into his open mouth. "Your wish is my command."